FPL
Y

W9-BZY-014

IN 6
$16.99

ONLY EVER YOURS

ONLY EVER YOURS

LOUISE O'NEILL

New York • London

Quercus

New York • London

© 2014 by Louise O'Neill
First published in the United States by Quercus in 2015

ISBN 978-1-62365-454-2

Library of Congress Control Number: 2015931871

Distributed in the United States and Canada by
Hachette Book Group
1290 Avenue of the Americas
New York, NY 10104

Manufactured in the United States

10 9 8 7 6 5 4 3 2

www.quercus.com

For Michael and Marie O'Neill, with all my love

"In the beginning,
Man created the new
women, the eves."[1]

---

[1] *Audio Guide to the Rules for Proper female Behavior*, the Original Father

Chapter 1

September
Ten months until the Ceremony

The chastities keep asking me why I can't sleep. I am at the maximum permitted dosage of SleepSound, they say, eyes narrowed in suspicious concern.

Are you taking it correctly, freida?

Are you taking it all yourself, freida?

Yes. *Yes.* Now, can I have some more? Please?

No more can be prescribed. Not safely anyway, they say. They warn of muscle spasms. Internal bleeding. The corrosion of vital organs.

But I cannot see these "vital organs" in the mirrors. All I can see are dark circles under my eyes, a gray pallor like a dusting of ashes over my face. The hallmarks of too many nights spent burrowing a hole in my mattress, tossing and turning, yearning to join the perfectly synchronized breathing of my sisters. I can hear them now, sucking artificial heat into their lungs greedily, oblivious to me, lying in my cot, buzzing like an exposed wire.

I am a good girl. I am pretty. I am always happy-go-lucky.

The robotic voice spills down the walls and crawls along the floor, searching for a receptive ear. And we eves are more receptive when sleeping. We are like sponges, absorbing beauty, becoming more and more lovely as we dream. More and more valuable.

Except for me.

Night after night I lie awake, nothing but the Messages to distract me from my clamoring thoughts. chastity-ruth says thinking too much robs you of your beauty. No man will ever want a companion who thinks too much. I do try to be more controlled. I try to shape my mind into nothingness. But when night falls in the dorms the demons stir, their eyes flashing white in the dark, looking for something to feed on.

I am a good girl. I am appealing to others. I am always agreeable.

It's the heat; I know it is. It's pumped in at night to detoxify our pores, rolling in waves through the dormitory, molding to my skin. The SleepSound can disguise the fire in my lungs only for so long before I jerk awake, gargling steam. I blink as my cubicle flickers in the subdued light. A single bed with snow-white sheets. A locker crouching beside it, the black paint peeling off in ribbons. It is a small house made of mirrors, every surface papered in glass.

And there I am. And there. And there. I am imprisoned in these walls.

I watch in the mirrored ceiling as I spread my body out like a starfish, bending my knees away from the sticky sheets. My hands hit the clammy mirrored wall behind my head, the black silk nightgown gathering around my waist. I turn onto my right side, my forehead pressed against another mirrored wall, a heavy sigh misting the glass. I etch my fingertips over my high cheekbones, watching as I trace circles around my almond-shaped eyes. My skin feels crepe thin, as if it's slowly dissolving into my bones.

Before us, they counted sheep to help them fall asleep. Before us, there were sheep to count.

I fumble under my pillow for my ePad, its square corners reassuringly solid in my hands. I update my MyFace status, whispering into the screen, "I can't sleep again. Anyone out there awake?" A shiver of satisfaction runs through me as the video-status uploads, as if this somehow proves that I'm real. I exist.

"freida?"

Am I dreaming of her again?

She's like an apparition, standing in the arched doorway between the corridor and my cubicle, her full-length pink bathrobe glowing in the shadows. She tilts her head, shifting her weight from one foot to the other, waiting for me to say something. I nod and her tense face softens as she creeps into my narrow bed, aligning her body with mine, our limbs interlocking like pieces of a jigsaw puzzle. We are reflected in all of the mirrors, splintering into parallel images, echoed from the ceiling to the walls and back, multiplied over and over again. Her milky-white legs entwined with mine, her white-blond hair bleeding into my dark brown waves.

isabel.

"I was afraid you were a chastity."

"Sorry."

"If she catches us breaking Isolation, we'll get in trouble."

"It will be fine."

"Still . . ."

"chastity-ruth isn't on duty," she replies, reading my mind as always.

We breathe in unison. I rest my head on her shoulder, inhaling lavender, counting heartbeats. She shifts, pulling her arm from under me, and my head drops onto the damp sheets. She inches back, away from me, until she's hovering on the edge of the bed, one foot planted on the ground for support.

"Good idea. It's too hot, isn't it?" I say quickly.

She came in, after all this time, I tell myself. You didn't ask her to. She came in by herself.

"Hmm." She taps her toes against the base mirror, her neon-pink nail polish matching her robe. I seem to be the only person affected by the heat.

"So," I blurt out. "Where have you been hiding?"

"I haven't been feeling well."

"I sent you chat-requests . . ." I trail off, thinking of her room, the corrugated steel door rolled to the floor and bolted down like a portcullis. I've sent her countless messages in the last two months. All unanswered.

"I can't sleep."

"Nervous about tomorrow?"

She shrugs apathetically.

"Have you asked chastity-anne for more SleepSound?"

"It interacts badly with my other meds."

"What are you taking?" I prop myself up on my elbow to look at her. "I'm on the maximum dosage and I haven't had problems."

"gisele broke out in hives when they mixed her dosages. She looked ugly for a week," she says, as if I hadn't spoken, as if I don't exist. She's been doing that a lot lately.

"Can you *stop* kicking the mirror? It's really annoying," I snap, and her foot slows to a still. I feel guilty at the flicker of hurt on her face but somehow satisfied as well, savoring the sense of being seen by her.

"How do you know that about gisele anyway? You haven't been at Organized Recreation or the Nutrition Center all summer," I say, watching our reflection in the ceiling. I'm squashed against the wall, isabel skirting the edge of the mattress, a sliver of white flashing between us. Fat women are ugly. Old women are ugly. But gisele? Honey-hued gisele, with her honey-blond hair, honey-flecked eyes, honey-colored skin? Ugly?

"So that's where she was last weekend," I say when she doesn't answer. "She told us she was in quarantine with suspected flu."

"Hives," isabel repeats. "Hives the size of eggies all over her face."

"Pity it was during vacation," I joke weakly, tasting a bubble of nausea. "Her rankings won't be affected."

"Be nice."

"That's easy for you to say, Miss #1."

"You're #3. And we were all designed equally," she replies mechanically.

"Yes. But some eves were lucky enough to be designed better than their ugly sisters." I hold my breath, waiting for her to disagree with me like she always used to.

"You're not ugly, freida," she sighs. She's tired of me, tired of my constant need for reassurance. "None of us is."

"I am compared to you." I can hear the need stitched through my voice and I hate myself for it. "My skin is so tired looking." I stroke the contours of my face in the ceiling mirror, searching for cracks. "What if my ranking is affected?"

"Better tired looking than fat." Her voice is flat, as if someone has let the air out of her lungs.

I turn to face her, our noses almost touching. I breathe in deeply, as if I could suck in her mesmerizing beauty and steal it from her. I looked up her chart online once, hoping to find an easy formula to copy. PO1 Metallic Silver hair, the computer chanted, #76 Folly Green eyes. Muted gold-colored skin, frosted-pink lips, a few small freckles over a neat nose. *I wish I looked like you. Everything would be easier if I looked like you.* I've been thinking that since I was four years old. "What are you talking about, isabel?"

She rolls onto her back and points at the ceiling, waiting for me to copy her. I watch as she loosens the silk tie around her waist, unwrapping the bathrobe, laying her body bare. A thickening at the waist, a roundness at the thighs. In the dark, my sharp intake of breath sounds like a scream.

"I know." She pulls the robe closed, hiding her sins.

"Have you tried throwing up?"

"Of course," she says impatiently. "It doesn't always work, you know."

"What about the extra meds you're taking? Are they helping?"

"They did at the start. They don't seem to be working anymore," she whispers.

"Maybe it won't be so bad." I want to sound consoling but I don't know how. That's always been isabel's role in our relationship. "Maybe you won't be the only one. Lots of eves gain weight over the holidays."

We both know this isn't true. Not this year.

"I don't understand how it even got this far. Surely someone must have noticed in your weekly weigh-ins? You haven't even set foot in the Nutrition Center for—"

She holds her finger to her lips to forbid me from speaking further and I swallow my thoughts. Just one more secret between us. I close my eyes but all I can see is her flesh spreading, threatening to engulf her bones.

"I was thinking the other day about your obsession with monkeys."

isabel's voice is so low that for a moment I wonder if she said anything at all, if my desire for us to be close again is so desperate that I have started imagining her speaking to me.

"Remember?" she says, reaching her hand out to touch mine. "The monkeys?"

"They were a fascinating species."

"I'm sure they were. Did you have to pretend to be one though?"

"I was four!"

"No excuse."

"That's exactly what chastity-ruth said when I fell out of a tree in the garden and broke my leg. What a witch."

She clamps a hand over her mouth to stifle her giggles.

"Excuse me. It was extremely painful," I say in indignation, but I'm smiling too.

"I thought she was going to kill you when you had to take your Monday foto with that massive cast," she says, her voice rising.

"Shh, isabel, you'll wake the chastities."

"Who cares?"

"Ah yes, princess isabel never gets in trouble!" I tease, bowing my head in mock salute. "It must be nice to be so special."

I wait for her to laugh, to tease me back, but there's nothing. Her body stiffens beside me. The silence is overwhelming, jamming into my eardrums, and I search blindly for the trail of our conversation.

"But the thing about the monkeys was—"

"I'm tired," isabel cuts across me and the words fizzle in my throat. I always take it a step too far, chastity-ruth says.

We shift apart in the bed, space yawning between us again.

I am pretty. I am a good girl. I always do as I am told.

The Messages continue, as if nothing has changed.

Dawn slowly pours out of the light-lamps, chasing my dreams away. Unfolding my body, I stretch out, claiming the entire mattress. isabel has gone.

I get out of bed, tossing my hair back to scan my face in the mirrored wall. I do this every morning, a part of me hoping that I'll have been magically transplanted into a different body during the night—isabel's, or megan's maybe. That I'll wake up and be paler, thinner, different. *Better.*

On the wall opposite my bed, an outline of a handprint is etched into the glass in pink plastic. I press my hand to it, feeling heat prickling my palm until the glass coating thins to transparency and I push through, grimacing as what feels like thousands of sticky fibers dissolve against my skin. Inside, mirrors cover every surface again, even the floor. At the front of the room there is a narrow steel changing room with gray rubber tubes curving from the top into the ceiling. I slump in the fuchsia armchair beside the changing room, drumming my fingers on the onyx marble vanity table. A semicircle of coral light bulbs around the mirror casts my face in a rosy glow. I tap the glass and it turns milky, then opaque, dissolving to reveal a computer screen, a cartoon graphic of a woman laden down with shopping bags popping up.

"Good morning, freida," the Personal Stylist Program says in a staccato voice. "How are you today?"

"Nervous."

"I believe that is to be expected on the first day of term," it says. "How do you want to improve yourself today?"

"A complete redesign would be nice," I mutter, chewing on my lip until I catch a glimpse in the mirrored wall of how unattractive it looks.

"How do you want to improve yourself today?" None of the PSPs understands sarcasm.

"Maybe something in white? Stream Fashion TV. I need some inspiration after the holidays."

A catwalk appears on the screen, a long strip of wood suspended midair in a black vacuum, pounded by a torrent of fashion models. They have been designed primarily for this purpose, hundreds of them falling off the factory line with their gaunt bodies and featureless faces.

White looks good with my skin tone. I picture megan in something similar, her complexion turning like spoiled milk, and I feel a brutal thrill.

"Wait. That one's perfect." On my VoiceCommand the screen freezes on a model wearing a sheer white round-neck tee embroidered with appliqué lace flowers, a white lace skirt falling in ruffles to knee length.

"Is that okay?"

"Yes," the PSP concedes. "I will request the appropriate items from the fashion closet now. Step into the changing room."

The screen snaps back into a mirror. S41 Delicate Iced Chocco hair. #66 Chindia Yellow eyes. *That's me. That's what people see when they look at me.* I peel off my nightgown and throw it into a trapdoor set in the wall underneath the vanity table. The changing room opens, beeping loudly until I step in, the steel trap closing like a greedy mouth around me.

"You have gained weight." The voice fills the room. "You are now 118.8 pounds. I will recommend in your weekly report that you are to take extra kcal blockers until your weight stabilizes between 115 pounds and 118 pounds."

"Do I have to take more?" I hate the kcal blockers, which always leave me doubled over with stomach cramps. I guess I should be grateful they've improved since the early days when exploding colons were reported. "It's embarrassing."

"You are the only person who is informed of your medication requirements."

I snort rudely at this. In theory, yes, our prescriptions are private, but nothing stays that way for long in the School. By breakfast my sisters will know that I'm weak, that I'm greedy, that I can't control myself. And I thought I had been a good girl last week.

The lasers crackle to life, scraping against the steel walls of the room as the infrared hoop descends from the ceiling, tickling as it inches down my body. The box then inhales, a whooshing gulp of air, sucking up any dirt and pumping it Underground to be disposed of. The lasers rise again, spraying makeup onto my naked skin, and gently pulling my hair into a bun at the nape of my neck. We are only allowed to use this machine twice a day, in the morning and at bedtime. It's too expensive, chastity-ruth says, so the maintenance of hygiene and makeup is our own responsibility during the day. Within two minutes I'm spat out, today's outfit and matching accessories left in the open trapdoor at the base of the wall. I grab them, the portal disappearing as soon as I do so.

"This doesn't look like it did on the model." I pull at the faded T-shirt, the floral embellishment crumpling beneath my fingers.

"It was as close a match as I could find within the School's fashion closet."

Back in my cubicle, I examine my body from every angle in the mirrored wall, swallowing disgust.

"Let's go."

It's freja at the doorway, her collarbones spiky in a beige crocheted top and canary-yellow skirt.

"I'm ready," I say, pushing my feet into the faux snake-skin slingbacks and falling into line, hurrying to catch up with daria in front of me.

The dorm is bursting with the sound of thirty pairs of high heels scraping against the black-and-white diamond tiles. We march together in silence, the same as we do every morning.

Outside the main entrance of the dormitory, a free-standing fotobooth has been reassembled for the start of the new term. daria forces the rickety sliding door open, her toffee-colored hair artfully disheveled, indigo-blue eyes sparkling with pleasure. Why is she pleased? Did she take the perfect foto? A better foto than mine will be?

"freida."

freja prods the small of my back with her knobby fingers and I stumble into the empty booth, sliding the door shut behind me.

1. Turn partially to the camera, one foot in front of the other.
2. Weight on the back foot.
3. Left hand on hip.
4. Dazzling smile.

There is a flash of light, my foto uploaded instantly to the School website for the Euro-Zone Inheritants to judge, determining my opening ranking for the year. I'm left in the darkness. I should leave, but just for a moment I want to stay in here. I want to hide, fold into the shadows and become invisible so no one can *look* at me anymore.

I hope the foto was perfect.

Chapter 2

"Our new classroom," freja announces, throwing her arms wide open. I waited in the Nutrition Center for her to finish pretending to eat her breakfast so we could go to class together. I didn't want to walk in alone.

"Wow. It's so different," I say dryly. Like last year, and all the years previous to that, the majority of our classes will be held in a large room painted entirely in black, the obsolete windows boarded up with black wooden panes. The wall at the front of the room is sheeted in mirrored glass from floor to ceiling. In front of that is the chastity's desk, a weathered oak with dull brass knobs, two upstanding glass boxes flanking it, one on either side. Rows of tiered seating and desks with mirrored tops are squeezed into the center of the room, a narrow set of steps covered in threadbare black carpet running up the middle. The summer holidays feel like a distant dream already.

"freida! You look amazing!" cara squeals, her dark blond hair fanning around her face as she rushes to hug me. freja, waiting in vain for a similar compliment, falters for a second, then smiles at me with disproportionate enthusiasm and says, "Totally."

"No, I don't," I reply automatically. We throw our handbags onto the broad windowsill on the far side of the room before climbing up ourselves, the perfect position to observe everyone else coming in.

"Don't take all day," cara jokes, brushing dust off her plaid cotton shirt and acid-wash skinny jeans as freja and I struggle in our heels. Once we're sitting, freja takes out a pocket mirror from her clutch and scans her face, as if she's afraid it might have disappeared. Snapping it shut with a sigh, she leans back against the wooden board and clucks with disapproval as heidi walks in, her cerise halter-neck dress slashed to the navel. heidi's head snaps in our direction. After sixteen years in School, we have all developed a sixth sense for judgment.

"freida, you look great." daria has floated over to join us, her eyes skimming over my body.

"Totally," freja says, far more convincing now that she has had time to prepare. "I love that skirt." I dip my head, smiling. "Did isabel pick it out for you?" she continues sweetly, and my smile freezes. "She has *such* good taste."

"Where is she, by the way?" cara asks, her thick eyebrows knitting together. They have asked me this every day for the past two months. "Her VideoChat has been off all summer."

"She's not feeling well," I reply yet again. I don't want to admit that I know as little as they do.

The room is filling up. gisele swaggers through the door in a draped navy vest top over snug white jeans, her hips swaying as she walks toward us and links her arm through daria's. The twins, jessie and liz, follow her, exact replicas in matching turquoise playsuits, moving as if their limbs are attached to one body. Golden-blond hair frames heart-shaped faces, aqua-colored eyes staring vacantly at us.

"Where's isabel?" gisele asks immediately, setting my teeth on edge. Her skin looks perfect. She's obviously fully recovered from that allergic reaction.

"Her door was still down this morning," jessie says. "And locked. I checked."

"Are you sure?" liz gasps, pretending that she doesn't already know. If jessie checked the door was locked, then liz was there with her, checking it too. "Our doors are *never* locked."

"Weird," they say together, as if the rest of us are unaware of this fact after sixteen years in School.

"She hasn't been at the Nutrition Center," freja says. She has complained about the injustice of this at every meal for the past two months.

"I haven't seen her at the gym either," gisele offers, placing a hand on her toned stomach. freja, watching her closely, sniffs and draws her shoulders in toward her chest to make her razor-sharp clavicle even more prominent. "And I've been at the gym a *lot*."

"megan's here," daria interrupts, running her fingers underneath the frayed edges of her bleached denim cut-offs and pulling them down her tanned muscular thighs. "megan! Over here!" She waves her over to us. "Now *she* really looks amazing."

I look at her sharply. Is that supposed to mean I don't?

"megan, you look beautiful!" daria says as megan air-kisses the twins, smacking loudly, her painted red lips inches away from their skin. "Beautiful," I mutter, wishing I was lying. A thin sheath of sea-green silk clings to her perfect body, a one-shouldered full-length toga. 3.0 Brown Black hair is styled in coiled braids at the crown of her head, #214 Arsenic Green eyes seared into her luminously pale skin. She's perfect.

"Is there room for one more?" She points at us perched up on the windowsill and smiles again, her eyes watchful as cara, freja and I look at each other in unspoken challenge. Finally freja, the lowest ranked of us three, jumps down, proclaiming she was "tired of sitting there anyway." megan flicks her hands and cara and I move apart to make space for her. She springs up as easily as if she was wearing sweatpants and sits between us.

"freida!" Her shriek pierces the din of chatter, causing heads at the other side of the classroom to turn around. "Look how dark you are compared to me!" She grabs my arm and presses it against hers. "Isn't she so dark?"

"Yeah, but your skin is beautiful, megan," the twins say on cue.

I jerk my arm back and huddle it into my chest, grinning to show how little I care.

"And so smooth," cara says, rolling up the sleeve of her shirt to compare.

"They should be. I got a full-body wax from chastity-hope in Beauty Therapy yesterday." A shadow passes over her face. "I don't understand why we can't have laser treatment like the eves in the Americas do."

"Or better yet, be designed without body hair at all, like in the Chindia-Zone," daria says, fiddling with a hole in her black crepe T-shirt.

"Hmm, yes," megan replies, her eyes drifting toward liu, sitting with christy at the other side of the room. "I suppose *some* good things have come out of Chindia."

"It was worth it. You look great," cara says, and megan tilts her head, accepting this compliment as her due.

"Where is isabel?" Obviously our opinion is not enough. She needs to compare herself with the #1 eve, see how she measures up. "Why wasn't she at breakfast again?"

"I told you this morning." And the morning before that, and the morning before that again. "She's sick." But megan's not listening to me, she's staring at the entrance to the classroom.

"Sick?" she repeats gleefully, and I follow her gaze, my heart sinking when I realize what is causing her such delight. An ill-fitting striped T-shirt tucked into high-waisted flares only emphasize isabel's weight gain, her tangled hair pulled into a high ponytail away from her makeup-free face. She walks slowly up the central steps, as if the extra pounds of flesh are weighing her down. Heads are turning to stare, watching as she takes a seat in the back row on the left-hand side, as far away from the rest of us as she can get.

"Clearly being sick hasn't affected her appetite," megan says. "And there we were, worrying about her missing meals."

liz and jessie giggle again, but a bit nervously this time. I've never heard megan say anything overtly nasty about isabel before. I've never heard *anyone* say anything nasty about isabel.

"Quiet down, eves."

At the sound of that voice the three of us jump down from the windowsill. cara and I stumble, grabbing hold of one another for balance, but megan lands gracefully, smirking at our clumsiness. chastity-ruth waits behind the wide oak desk, her hands lost in the cavernous depths of her black robes. The recessed ceiling lights are bouncing off her shaved skull, her ash-gray eyes narrowed at us, traces of prettiness fading away in her fine-boned face. We didn't hear her come in. We never do.

"Take your places. You may choose your own seating arrangements as a privilege of being in 16th year," she says, and we hesitate, fearing a trap.

"Now," she says, her voice chillingly quiet.

The others scramble for position. cara calls me, patting the empty chair next to her in the front row. Before I would have refused without thinking, my natural place being with isabel, but now I don't know what to do. I wait for a second too long and gisele claims the seat, stretching her long legs out in front of her as cara makes an apologetic face at me. I climb the steps toward isabel, burrowed into the corner of the room.

"Here are your new rankings for the first week of final year." chastity-ruth taps the board behind her and the mirror dissolves to expose a huge computer screen as she gives VoiceCommands to upload our rankings.

"In first place, we have . . ." chastity-ruth clears her throat twice and takes a sip of water from the plastic cup on her desk—"eve #767."

megan's face fills the screen. *megan?* I stare at the foto, her green eyes triumphant, as if she knew her time had finally come. This is the first time in twelve years that isabel hasn't been #1. I don't dare to look up. I'm afraid that megan will see my doubt and remember it. I'm afraid that isabel will somehow see *within* me, see my secret regret that I wasn't the one who finally beat her, the embers of resentment over sixteen years of living in her shadow smoldering inside me.

"In second place . . ."

Please let it be me. Please let it be me.

". . . eve #701."

jessie's foto flashes on the screen and I smile to hide my disappointment.

"At #3 . . ."

liz's face where mine should be. And I forget how to breathe.

cara is at #4.

"And, dropping two places, I see, we have eve #630 in fifth place."

My fingers tighten over my kneecaps, boring into the bone. I stare at my reflection in the desktop, willing my face not to betray me. My eFone vibrates against the desk, a foto of megan appearing on the screen. I crouch out of view to listen to the message.

"You look so tired in your foto. I can lend you some of my new concealer if you'd like. It's supposed to work miracles."

I straighten up. She's watching me from the first row, patting imaginary bags under her eyes.

". . . And, finally, in last place, we have eve #700," chastity-ruth finishes, agyness coming last as always. The tabletops shimmer to form an updated grid, our faces displayed in order of rank.

"isabel, will you please accompany me to my office?" the chastity says, baring her teeth in a facsimile of a smile. I half stand in my seat to allow isabel to pass, whispering to her, "Good luck."

She gives no sign of having heard me and fear prickles in my stomach. Is she angry with me? Did she see my momentary regret that it wasn't me who had beaten her? The chastity waits until isabel reaches her before escorting her out the door, barking back at us, "Make your way to your next class immediately."

Everyone filters out slowly, chatting loudly about the new rankings, a jumble of words with "*isabel, isabel, isabel*" like a drumbeat underneath the chorus, until it is only our group remaining. I grab my bag and walk down the steps toward them, pushing past liu, standing at the edge of our seats.

"Bye, liu-liu," megan says sweetly, wiggling her fingers in farewell. "Didn't you hear chastity-ruth say to get to your next class?"

"Did you see?" daria bursts out once liu has slouched out, closing the door behind her with a bang. "There are only twenty-nine faces. isabel isn't ranked."

I scan the grid on the table before me, tracing a crack in the screen that is scratching into cara's foto. She's right. isabel is missing.

"That is *weird*," liz and jessie chorus, scrunching their faces up.

"How is that even possible?" gisele asks.

"It's probably because of her weight gain," daria says.

"But christy gained weight as well," gisele points out. "I'd say at least 2.4 pounds, if not 2.7."

I wrap my arms around my stomach, trying to hide that extra pound of flesh with which my body has betrayed me.

"Not as much as isabel," daria argues, ignoring freja dry-heaving at the mere thought of weight gain. "There is no way they would want anyone in the main Zone seeing that. Standards must be upheld. What will the Inheritants think when they arrive?"

"But who knows when their visits will start? They might not come for months!"

They start arguing among themselves, their voices getting louder and louder. Only megan and I are silent.

"This is boring," megan snaps, her face pinched with annoyance. "Why are we wasting our time talking about her?"

"Totally," the twins say, sensing danger.

"Congratulations, megs," daria says smoothly, draping an arm around megan's shoulders. "You deserve to be #1. You've always been the prettiest in our year."

"Yeah, the Zone has always been biased toward blondes. It's stupid," freja says, delighted at this excuse for her lower ranking, ignoring the twins as they hiss simultaneously.

"Well, I have a feeling that isn't going to be the case for much longer," megan says, stretching her arms into the air in a V for victory, shrugging off daria's arm roughly. daria simpers with embarrassment but she doesn't say anything, not like she might have before. I feel as if something is shifting beneath my feet, disturbing my balance.

"Welcome to final year, girls."

Chapter 3

December
Seven months until the Ceremony

"For the love of the Father, eggies for breakfast again?"

When megan is annoyed, her already irritating fake Americas-Zone accent takes on a nasal quality. Unfortunately megan gets annoyed a lot. Mainly at mealtimes. I have a theory that she views her need for food as her only flaw.

"I'm sick of eggies. They're disgusting. Why isn't there any other lo-carb option available?" she argues with the buffet, as if it could talk back. liz and jessie are murmuring encouragement, ignoring the line of hungry girls behind them waiting to be served.

"I'm starving," a tiny girl in front of me whispers to her friend. She's about four feet tall, waist-length butterscotch hair tied neatly at the nape of her neck with a cerise ribbon, skinny elbows poking out of a cerise-and-navy striped polo dress.

"I'm sorry, did you say something?" megan spins around and places her hands on her knees, bending until she is eye level with the younger girl. "What's your name then?"

"l-l-l-lena-rose," the girl stutters, her arms quivering in fright.

"Do you have something you would like to say, l-l-l-lena-rose?"

lena-rose's head darts left and right. The friend has angled her body away, staring at the ground, the shuffling feet and disgruntled sighs of before falling silent. The delay has been noticed. chastity-ruth snaps to attention at the mere suggestion of trouble, her shaved head almost spinning on her shoulders. Swooping through the symmetrically laid out tables in the Nutrition Center, she descends upon us, her rubber-soled shoes mute against the tiled floor. I am suddenly eager to find my digi-cam in my bag. That she has an ability to turn us to stone is improbable, but I wouldn't rule it out.

"Is there a problem, #767?"

"No problem, chastity-ruth," megan says, arching her back so her strapless minidress climbs up her supple thighs. She lets her loose black curls spill fetchingly over one shoulder. "No problem at all. Little lena here asked me about some School rules. I was making sure she understood them."

Running a hand over the bones of her skull, chastity-ruth nods tersely before returning to the supervision desk at the back of the Nutrition Center. megan, instantly forgetting about the trembling lena-rose, collects her meds from chastity-anne and moves on, allowing the rest of us in the ever-increasing line for the BeBetter buffet to finally be served. When it's my turn, I look at the display. It's been divided into three sections, all stacked with identical silver tureens. Above the lo-carb section there is a foto of a bread roll with a red X running through it, the tasty/healthy section has a foto of a froot and veggies pyramid and the 0-kcal section has a foto of weighing scales. I grab a 0-kcal tureen, placing it on my chipboard tray without bothering to inspect the wonders that are hidden beneath the lid. The smells drifting from the Fatgirl buffet are making my mouth water and I try not to think about the toast made with brioche and drizzled with syrup, the chocolate-chip pancakes, the plump soyburgers in fluffy white baps smothered with relish. I have to be good this week.

"Good morning." chastity-anne briefly peeks up from her apothecary table. She looks similar to chastity-ruth, both clad in the all-encompassing black chastity robes.

"I have VoiceNotes of your morning weigh-in." She fumbles in the drawer, searching for the test tube with my foto burned onto it. "I've been instructed to up your dosage of BeautyTabs. Hopefully the extra collagen will repair some of the damage caused by your *continuing* resistance to SleepSound." She glares at me, as if I'm deliberately metabolizing my meds incorrectly. "The usual VitC, Zinc, Mag, Aloe, Flax, Chlorophyll, Q10, Multi-Omegas, Lipoic, Carnosine, Acetyl-L-Carnitine

Arginate, COX-2 and 5-LOX and DHEA." She lowers her voice. "And your anti-womenstruation meds are included, of course."

She rattles this speech off every morning. I think it makes her feel important, although we all know she's just a glorified drug dispenser, doing whatever the Doctors in the Euro-Zone tell her to.

"Has isabel collected her meds yet?" I ask. "She wasn't at gym this morning so I was just wondering if . . ."

She shoves the test tube of meds at me and gestures at me to move on. If chastity-ruth thinks about us in terms of design numbers, chastity-anne differentiates us by our med prescriptions. She could tell you the exact day and time that I first received my curse, but I doubt she remembers my name most of the time.

The Nutrition Center seems to expand as I turn around to search for isabel, beams of light shining from the hundreds of light bulbs planted in the mirrored walls and ceilings. Row after row of mirror-plated desks, occupied by faceless girls. Where is she? We agreed to sit together. Although why I agreed to do so is beyond me; yet another uncomfortable meal to endure, each unspoken word a brick in the growing wall between us.

"freida. Over here."

"Hi, girls," I say, relieved that someone has claimed me as their friend, that I don't look like a total loner.

The unholy trinity, all carefully tousled hair and bee-stung lips, are in their usual seats by the food distribution counter so megan can monitor our food choices, note who is being a good girl or a bad girl. She's taking her role as #1 eve very seriously.

"What an *extraordinary* outfit, freida," megan says, her gaze traveling from the crown of my head to my toes as I fight the urge to adjust my clothes, to cut off my hair, to ask if I can apply for a complete redesign.

"Um, thanks. I like your outfit too! Black suits you!"

"It's navy." She arches an eyebrow at my enthusiasm and the tips of my ears start to burn.

"Do you want to sit with us?" liz and jessie chorus, wearing matching turquoise bustier dresses today, the chunky metal straps cutting into their shoulders, their hair set in loose waves.

"I'd love to, but I told isabel I'd eat with her." The twins lose interest at once, drawing circles in blueberry-speckled porridge with their spoons. "But maybe we can both join you?"

"isabel?" megan says slowly, cocking her head to one side. She's even more gorgeous up close, her dark looks accentuated by the bland prettiness of the twins.

"Yes. isabel," I repeat myself, swallowing twice in case excess saliva is making me slur.

"Isn't that isabel at the Fatgirl buffet?"

And it is. Dressed in a loose black tank over gray leggings, she is the only one there, steam from the hot bar curling around her face, obscuring her features. Seemingly oblivious to the girls in the BeBetter line openly pointing at her, she loads her plate with fried chick-chick and noodles, white bread rolls, soup, and pasta. She dispenses a hot chocco from the silver beverage tap and covers it with mounds of whipped kream, sprinkling chocco flakes generously over the top until she's buckling under the weight of her laden tray. I turn away, knowing that she will return to chastity-anne's desk to pick up a portion of ipecac syrup, and I don't want to see it. I sit down at once, banging my tray on the mirrored desktop.

"I can't believe she's eating Fatgirl food again. Who eats from the buffet? Everyone knows it's only there to tempt the *weak*." megan doesn't bother to lower her voice. Unlike the rest of us, she's not afraid of being overheard.

"She's sitting right by the Vomitorium. It must smell so bad," jessie says, craning her neck for a better view.

"It would put me off my food." liz shudders, pushing her bowl away.

"It would take more than that to put isabel off," jessie snickers as I lift the lid off my breakfast, finding a glass full of a lurid pink liquid underneath.

"I don't know why she is even bothering to use ipecac," megan says. "It's not working. She must have gained at least twenty pounds." She stares at me intently. "What do you think, freida? How much weight has she gained?" She reaches out to touch my hand and I want to pull away. If I pull away, will she be insulted? "It must be so difficult for you, freida, watching a friend degrade herself like that. I mean, she's eating *pasta*." She grimaces. "Has she said anything to you? What was her weigh-in like today? She wasn't in gym so she must be on probation, right?"

I wish she would tell me what she wants to hear. I'll say it. I'll say whatever she wants if she'll just stop. I drop my gaze, pretending to fix my hair in the desk before stirring the strawberrie SlimShake with my straw.

"Maybe you could give her some dietary advice, freida. She *clearly* needs help. That's what friends are for, right?" megan continues sweetly.

"Yeah," jessie says. "If anyone needed to try some Slim-Shakes, it's that fat bitch. Am I right, girls?" She cackles, her voice corroding my will to live.

"But what do *you* think, freida?"

There's an ugly silence. I meet megan's eyes and see the challenge there. She's drawing a line in the sand and it's my decision which side I want to be on.

"I guess you're right," I answer, the betrayal tasting like bile in my mouth, and she smiles at me.

"I should be more understanding," she sighs. "I have such a fast metabolism I actually struggle to maintain regulation weight."

I look at the barely touched eggies on her tray. For someone who struggles to maintain weight, she certainly has an aversion to eating full portions. She and the twins start to fotogram their food, bickering about cassie and carrie's latest adventures on *Chilling with the Carmichaels* as they upload the fotos. I rack my brain for something witty to say, something that will make them think that I'm interesting and funny, that will make them want to invite me to sit with them again but my brain is frozen, as if I've gulped down an iced slushee too quickly. I'm itching to find isabel's reflection in the wall beside me. I want to make sure that she's okay, that she's not going back for second helpings and thirds and more.

I throw the meds into my mouth and take a sip of Slim-Shake to force them along. They slip down my throat, falling into this black hole inside me. I know they're making me better. Even if they taste of emptiness. Even if they taste of my weakness.

Chapter 4

I leave the Nutrition Center early, hoping to find isabel so I can speak with her in private, but the classroom is empty when I arrive. I sit and wait, wondering what I'll say to her, trying to remember when I first had to start planning our conversations in advance.

"Where's isabel?" cara asks, sitting next to me.

"She wasn't at the gym so I'm guessing probation."

"Did she get the chamber?"

"I'm not sure. I haven't seen her since breakfast."

"I saw her at breakfast too. I think *everyone* saw her at breakfast. If she's on probation, why was she eating from the Fatgirl buffet?"

"Ipecac syrup." I give her an inane smile, putting both thumbs up like the girl in the TV ad does. "For easy, predictable regurgitation!"

"After every meal?" cara wrinkles her upturned nose while taking her eFone from her neon-yellow satchel. "MyFace foto?"

Without waiting for an answer, she extends the digi-cam to arm's length, pressing her head against mine as we both smile, our foto faces always ready. She taps twice on the mirrored tabletop and scans the digi-cam barcode.

"Upload and tag."

The image develops onto my desk as well, cara's dark blond hair and thick eyebrows complimenting my tanned skin and delicate features nicely. Moving my thumb and forefinger apart on the screen, I zoom in, making the dark circles around my eyes even more obvious. Is she prettier than me? Blondes tend to rank higher, megan being the exception of course. I close down the image. It feels like fat cells are swelling like blisters on my body, growing and growing, ready to burst. I pull at the waistband of my skirt, loathing breaking out like goosebumps across my skin.

"You look cute!" cara says, staring at her desktop.

I don't even want to imagine how awful I must look the rest of the time if that's what I look like when I'm "cute." The others begin to arrive, throwing their bags on the ground with a clatter.

"I know I've gained about twenty pounds since breakfast."

"I'm not going to eat anything for the rest of the day."

"I'm not going to eat anything else for the rest of the *week*."

"Settle down, girls," chastity-theresa grumbles, the black robes swamping her skinny frame as she ushers the remaining girls into the classroom. She sighs heavily. "Your personal data from this morning's weigh-in has been analyzed," she begins, but chastity-ruth's voice blares over the intercom, interrupting her.

"Attention, all 16th years. Please note that two of your classmates are on probation. #727 has gained five pounds in the last two weeks. She now weighs 125 pounds."

125 pounds. None of us has ever been that heavy before. christy, sitting in the second row on the other side of the steps, blushes furiously, embarrassment bleeding into her skin.

"And isabel is also on probation," chastity-ruth finishes, the intercom breaking up into a high-pitched, tinny screech.

"But what's *her* weight?" I hear megan demand as the door scrapes open, the old timber frame groaning loudly.

"isabel," chastity-theresa says. "Please take your seat, dear."

She doesn't move, standing at the door looking at us looking back at her, all of us weighing her as accurately as any body scanner. She pulls her tank down to cover her thighs and hurries in, heaving herself into a free seat at the front. liz and jessie aim their eFones at her, stifling snorts of laughter, and within seconds a wave of beeps breaks out throughout the classroom.

"If you're quite finished behaving like 10th years," chastity-theresa says, her dark skin flushing with frustration. "Put that away, liz. You too, jessie." I think they're about to ignore her until megan shakes her head at them in warning and they reluctantly put their fones into their bags.

"Today instead of our usual Social Graces instruction," the chastity says, "I'm pleased to announce that the Father of the Euro-Zone has released a Public Address for final-year students."

At the mention of the Father the silence is instant. We haven't had a Public Address since His annual School visit on our design-date in July, just before the holidays. chastity-theresa taps the mirror-board behind her to reveal the computer screen. "Upload the digi-vid."

I grab lip gloss from my clutch and apply it generously, inspecting myself in my desk. This is ridiculous, as the Father can't even see us. The video was probably prerecorded days ago. But I'm not alone. The rest of the class is preening manically too, almost falling into their mirrors. The only person unmoved is isabel, color leaching from her cheeks as she hunches over her desk. She looks as if she wants to disappear.

"Quiet, girls." chastity-theresa dims the lights. I breathe in deeply, rubbing my palms against my knees. The strobe lighting explodes and then disappears, and our faces are swallowed by the darkness.

The clashing cymbals and drum roll of the Euro-Zone anthem rips through the room. The screen burns to life, showing the symbol of the thirds, the triquetra, three triangles woven together. The ivory of the companions, the scarlet of the concubines, the ebony of the chastity robes.

Separate entities, but inextricably linked. The screen flashes with images.

A girl. A girl. A girl. A girl.

Fotos of the #1-ranked girls from the last ten years rush onto the screen, one girl quickly replaced by another, and another, always a newer, better version to follow. A foto of the best legs winner, long, perfectly shaped, clad in the highest of high heels. The screen on our desktops splits in two, a foto of the perfect legs to the left, a foto of our own legs appearing to the right of our respective screens. A voice roars from the ceiling, "ROOM FOR IMPROVEMENT."

I massage my thighs violently, wanting to tear strips off them as I feel the skin dimpling underneath my fingers. The room is inky black and I am glad. I am glad. I don't want the others to see me, to see how *wrong* I am. The screen flashes again, the strobe lighting skewering my vision. kate, the legendary #1 from seven years ago, so perfect she was awarded her own TV show, *What kate Did Next*. Her hair is wet, slicked back from that delicate face, cheekbones popping. Her image emerges on the left of my desktop, my MyFace profile foto appearing alongside for easy comparison. The voice roars again, but this time it's inside me, speaking in my bones. *Room for Improvement. Room for Improvement. Room for Improvement.*

The lighting settles, the drumbeat calming and then petering out. I peek at isabel, the images on-screen flickering on her pale, sweating face. Her head sags, causing a little pocket of fat to bulge under her chin. A shameful relief slashes through me. I'm not the only one who isn't perfect. I'm not the worst.

A trumpet sounds, drawing our attention back to the main screen, and like puppets we move in unison, crossing our feet at the ankles, hands resting gently in our laps. All that exists now is His face. His sharp blue eyes peering into my soul, His mouth opening, about to speak, about to fill my empty brain with His wisdom.

"Good morning." His voice is strong and deep. He pauses, slicking His distinguished gray hair away from His pale face. "Once again it is time to give my Public Address to the eves of final year. I must impress upon all of you how crucial the coming months are to your future. This is the decisive moment, the moment you have spent the last sixteen years preparing for. It is time for you to make a contribution to the society that has created each of you, whether it be as a companion or a concubine." There is an indistinct mumble off-camera, the Father's forehead wrinkling in annoyance at the interruption. "Or a chastity of course. You must all play your equal part. Remember, you may be perfectly designed, but there is *always* room for Improvement."

We blink feverishly as the lamps explode with light and the main screen returns to its mirrored state.

"Stop that!" chastity-theresa barks at us. "Squinting causes wrinkles."

jessie's hand jerks up instinctively to the skin around her eyes. She grabs a little tube from her clutch bag, squeezing pea-sized droplets of white foam onto her fingertips, and massages it into her eyelids.

"His Address was short, wasn't it?" liu bites her lip so hard that she leaves an impression in the flesh. "He didn't even mention when the Inheritants would be coming. Why was it so short?"

"The Father is a busy man," the chastity says wearily. "He has more important things to do than recording lengthy sermons for your enjoyment." liu slumps in her seat, a sheet of ebony hair covering her face. "Anyway, as the Father said, it is your duty to provide value for your existence, whichever third you may be assigned to. Of course I doubt there will be many eves with a vocation for the hallowed third of the chastities in this group." Her gaze falls upon agyness and her mouth softens. "Well, maybe one."

agyness blushes with inexplicable pride and megan makes a vomiting motion. I like agy, but we all know becoming a chastity isn't a vocation. It's just a way of dealing with any eves whom, for whatever reason, the men find unappealing but who haven't done anything bad enough to warrant being sent Underground. Inductions into the third of the chastities are so rare we don't even receive instruction in School about chastity-life. The chastities have their uses, of course—the School could not run without them—but they are not wanted like the concubines are. They are not *necessary* like the companions.

I spend the rest of the class daydreaming, tuning out chastity-theresa's lecture on the difference between the

Social Graces required by the concubines and the companions. All I can see in my mind's eye is the image of my
face next to kate's, a grid forming over the foto, breaking
it down, showing my inadequacies in perfect detail. The
bell's ringing startles me and cara laughs and squeezes my
shoulder blades, her hands cool on my perspiring skin.

"Don't dawdle," chastity-theresa says as she shepherds
the other girls out, turning the lights off when she leaves.

I can barely make out her outline in the row opposite
me. "What's going on with you, isabel?"

"I'm on probation."

"I heard. You can't keep eating at the Fatgirl buffet. It's
making things worse." My voice is rising. "If you keep gain-
ing weight, you'll never become a companion. You won't
even be good enough to be a concubine."

No man likes a fat girl. We have been told this since design.

"Why are you getting so angry?" she asks. "It's not *your*
body."

"I'm not angry," I say, breathing to calm myself, to
control these Unacceptable Emotions. "I'm afraid . . . I'm
afraid for you."

"Afraid of what?"

I can't say the real words out loud so I just say, "I'm
afraid they'll make you become a chastity."

"Would that be so terrible?"

"Don't be ridiculous."

"Why is it ridiculous? It sounds . . ." she breaks off,
searching for the right word, "peaceful."

"But . . ."

But we've always wanted to be companions, I want to say. This is what we have wanted since we were in 4th year, learning how to change diapers on our training dolls in Little mama classes. We were going to raise our sons as best friends. Don't you remember?

But I do not say this. If I remember and she doesn't, it seems like I care more than she does. And that would make me vulnerable.

"Did you go to the chamber?" I ask instead.

"Yes. Just two-pound weights. But the humidity was crazy."

"What was your Improvement soundtrack like?"

"I didn't have one."

"You got off lightly," I reply, surprised.

I've only been in the chamber once, after I broke my leg when I fell from that tree in the garden when I was four. I gained five pounds and while I ran on the treadmill I had to listen to "Fat girls must be made obsolete" on a loop for two hours every day for three weeks until I was back in control. I had assumed the chastisements became more demanding with each term. It's for our own good, I suppose. *I know.*

"How long will you have to attend for?"

"Until my weight is acceptable. They've upped the kcal blockers as well."

"I thought they said it wasn't safe to do that."

"No choice, I guess."

Her voice cracks, as if she swallowed back a sob mid-sentence. Is she *crying*? She knows we are not allowed to cry and, unlike me, isabel has never had a problem obeying that rule, her easy smiles the touchstone of my childhood. I freeze, glad of the dark so that I can pretend I didn't notice. I listen to her labored breathing and I want to shake her, I'm so exasperated by her sudden inability to follow the rules like the rest of us. What does she want from me? Does she want me to comfort her? Am I supposed to care after months of silence, isabel ruthlessly unknotting any ties of friendship between us. But I do care. That's the problem. Years of our shared memories are steeped in my blood. It would take leeches to suck them out.

I move toward her, crouching down beside her to take her limp hand in mine. She pulls it away, rejecting me again, and my stomach clenches with hurt. But there's anger there too, anger at my stupidity at ever having allowed someone to get close enough to have the power to hurt me.

"So, what happened at PE?" she asks, inhaling deeply.

"Nothing," I reply sullenly, my knees cracking as I stand up. "We had better get to class."

"The Monday votes from the Euro-Zone have been counted and your updated rankings are now available online."

There is a scurry of activity as eFones are snatched from bags and pockets to check how valuable we are this week. megan is first again, followed by liz and jessie in second and third place. I scroll down and down until I find my face. I've dropped from #8 to #10.

"It's not too bad," cara says kindly. "The top ten are still definite companions."

Easy for her to say, steady at #4. daria and gisele commiserate with me, saying they're "soooo sorry" and that they hope I won't be mad that my falling to tenth place has bumped their rankings up. Maybe I should bribe chastity-anne to mix gisele's meds again. See how high she ranks with another rash of hives.

isabel's face is still missing from the ranking tables, but for some reason I can't explain I still don't say anything to her about it.

"Are you all right, isabel?" I ask instead as we trudge back to the classroom for Organized Recreation. She nods wearily and we fall into our now familiar pit of silence. I look at where megan is sitting, the twins, cara, gisele and daria taking up the rest of the row. Some of the lower-ranked girls are sitting on the floor, congregating at her feet like she's a deity, screaming with laughter. It used to be isabel at the center of everything, me by her side, made safe by her affection. cara catches me staring.

"What do you think, freida?" She smiles, trying to include me.

"Sorry, cara, I didn't hear what you said."

"I said—"

"Look!" megan cries, shoving an eFone blaring the Dome Dudes' latest music video in cara's face, and I'm left on the outside once more. I want to go over, to reclaim my position, but I feel shackled to isabel. I look at her, slumped in the seat beside me, seemingly unconcerned by the fact that her belly is folding into rolls of fat beneath her thin vest top. My skin itches with irritation at the sight.

"Alphabetical order," chastity-anne orders, materializing out of thin air. "It's time."

We have Organized Recreation daily and it's always the final class of the day. It was devised to combat female hysteria syndrome: any hysterical, overemotional girl behavior is deliberately induced in a controlled environment until the urges dissipate. We need extra sessions on the weekends or during the summer holidays, whenever we have more opportunity to infect each other.

We line up and approach the desk to collect our meds from the chastity. The doors of the two glass boxes on either side of the desk swish open, allowing one girl in at a time before disappearing into the ground. I hold my breath as the doors close after me. What will happen if chastity-anne programs the elevator incorrectly and it goes too far?

"Are you crying, #630?"

"No, chastity-ruth."

"Good. Because you know what we do to girls who break the rules, don't you? We send them Underground. Do you want to go Underground, #630?"

The elevator opens into the Organized Recreation Space. It looks like an empty swimming pool lined with numerous pipes snaking their way Underground. Thirty individual glass coffins are lined up in five rows, six in each row. I climb into the box with my design number on it, picked out in baby-pink sequins. The glass door shuts and I wait anxiously for the other boxes to fill so that we can begin. chastity-anne nods and I swallow my meds.

Hush. Hush. A shiver begins at my feet, swelling, spiraling up and down the core of my body. A beat pulses through the box, a melody throbbing in my ears, in my mind, in my heart. My spine undulates until I am boneless. A wave of rapture surges and I am engulfed by it. I am free. I am free of all this. My mind tears for a second and I fall back into the room, the edges of my anxiety sharpening again. I can see the lid of the glass box, can see the road map of ducts and wires crawling over the ceiling, can see the other girls staring out with sightless eyes. The mist chokes me again, smothering me until I feel nothing, nothing at all.

The bell rings and we are switched off simultaneously, the doors springing open. I climb out, my legs wobbly. My mind is wired but lethargy is sucking at my body, the two parts of me cracking apart.

The others look similarly exhausted. We half smile at each other as we shuffle back to the dorms, but we avoid conversation of any kind. I throw myself on my bed, praying for sleep, but I know it's useless. Turning on my side, I press my fingertips into the glass wall, watching that girl in the mirror. Her features float off her face, swimming in the air before rearranging themselves in the strangest way. Her eyes are too big, black in her pallid skin. Her lips are bloodless, gloopy bits of dried spit forming in the cracks, her jaw jutting out.

The emptiness in my body is vast, wide open spaces with nothing to hold on to.

I won't remember any of this tomorrow.

Chapter 5

We are wound up and wound down, like mechanical dolls. They turn the lamps on, they turn the lamps off. And another day is done.

"I wish I could just stop time until I'm ready," I told isabel some night last year when neither of us could sleep. We sat on the floor in her cubicle, our backs against the mirrored wall, legs stretched out in front us, and I tried not to compare the size of my thigh gap with hers. "Do you ever feel like that?"

"No," she said, and I felt illogically betrayed. I pulled away from her a little, loneliness burying itself deep within me. She shifted closer, refusing to allow me to sulk. "Don't worry about the future," she said. "Things are only going to get better. I promise."

She promised me.

The dorms are hazy with steam tonight. It's crawling into my mouth, gathering in the back of my throat.

I need to breathe.

I pause by isabel's room on my way out of the dorms, see her platinum hair spilling over the pillows. It's been a long time since she has come into my room at night.

I follow the floor tiles, black to white, black to white, until I reach the cloisters, walking the long nave with its curved window frames on either wall, each one sealed up to block out the dead outside. The windows are covered with giant paintings, seven on each side, all depicting images from life before us. The Empire State Building, the Grand Canyon, the Great Wall of China, the pyramids, the Coliseum, the Taj Mahal. I imagine them now, baking like clay in the blistering heat. Or maybe they're swimming underneath the Great Ocean, only fish bones left to keep them company.

The others think it's weird that I love watching the Nature Channel to see what the world was like before us. They don't understand why I would want to know about the life cycle of frogs or watch the sea roaring, throwing its spittle onto thousands of grains of sand. Fields of corn waving in the breeze, mountains capped in glittering ice, millions and millions of people living in the big cities, all performing their part in an intricate dance, weaving in and around each other unthinkingly.

The only nature they show us in class is in the authorized *Destruction* series. The ice melting, the seas reconciling their differences and drowning the doomed low-lying countries, never to be seen again. There was relief at first, the hope that they had found an organic solution to the population crisis, but that soon turned to fear. The remaining people moving inward and inward and inward, until the Zones were formed to protect the remaining few from the scalding sun and the rising waters. The Noah Project. Two by two the humans entered, all marching forward to create a new world. They got rid of anything we would not need, like animals, and organized religion. They got rid of anything that would weigh us down.

I reach the giant wooden doors guarding the entrance, each one engraved with the white, red, and black triangles of the triquetra. I twist the brass handle to release them, my sweating hands slipping, leaving a mucus-like residue behind. The gates stand sentinel next, rusty metal arches reaching into spikes, waiting for intruders that will never come.

In the garden I walk along the circular concrete path looping our living quarters, stepping off the path into the grass, the synthetic blades scratching my bare feet as I weave my way around the army of trees. Each one is positioned at an equal distance from the next, their plastic limbs extending into painted leaves embellished with crystals, stuffed birds glued on like feathered tumors. I think of the videos on the Nature Channel of the vast orchards in Old England, the gnarled branches heavy with natural food. They must be dead now, those trees, like everything else. Rotted away, decaying like female babies in the uterus. Decomposing from the inside out.

* * *

"You are fortunate," chastity-ruth told us as we were formally inducted into the School in 4th year. I still remember
how strange the new clothes felt, how heavy my lips were
with the coating of unfamiliar lipstick. We were in the
Hall, watching as she gave her speech on the stage, our
bodies so little they were nearly consumed by the cush-
ioned velvet seats.

"Fortunate," she repeated sternly. I pulled down the
cropped T-shirt with glittery lips embroidered on it, the gap
between it and the new denim hot pants too bare for comfort. Her lip turned up into a snarl when she saw me fidgeting, her eyes fierce, and I felt afraid for the first time. And
then she showed us the video. The infamous "girl Graves,"
thousands of unwanted daughters disposed of in an ever-
expanding hole, their heads crushing against each other like
broken china dolls. Drugstores with shelves upon shelves
stacked with gender-specific fertility drugs, as easy to buy as
chewing gum. And the body learned. It learned that a female
baby was an invader, come to steal her mother's beauty. A
female baby was dangerous.

"There was concern of course," chastity-ruth told us,
her serene voice at odds with the horror of her words,
"when years passed in the Zones and no female babies were
born. Soon there was only a handful of the original women
left, all past childbearing age, and the threat of extinction
seemed far too certain. Genetic Engineers were forced to
create women to ensure the survival of the human race. And
since they had the opportunity, it would have been foolish

not to make necessary improvements in the new women, the eves." She coughed delicately. "And the Schools were formed to house them."

"Why didn't they give the girl babies to the companions to raise as their own?"

She stared at me after I said this, identifying me as trouble. "Who would have wanted you?" she said. "Who would want you until you could be of some use?"

I didn't understand what she meant by "of use," not then. isabel slipped her hand into mine, anchoring me. And I knew she could protect me.

I blink twice, my vision blurring. Pushing my way through the tinselly plants, I arrive at the outer limits of our world, my hands reaching out to meet the shell that keeps us all in here, safe from the wastelands. It has been tinted an inky black tonight, twinkling flakes precisely penciled in, a huge white moon drawn like an unblinking eye. I get as close as I can, flattening my body against the glass, feeling its solid resistance meeting me. I can see nothing beyond this, everything swallowed up by the night.

"What are you doing?"

I flinch, my right knee screaming as it hits the sky. She looks perplexed, her hands folded across her chest. Her black robes are strange against the colors of the garden, the light from the moon surrounding her bald head like a halo.

"You scared me," I say, and I sit heavily on the lime-green lawn, squashing some poppy flowers as I do.

chastity-magdalena comes closer, arranging her robes around her as she sits next to me. Her skin is still smooth, with only the beginning of faint lines forming around her copper-colored eyes. She's the youngest chastity, but still old—in her midthirties, I think.

"Do you want to talk about it?" She hesitantly pats my shoulder and we both flinch. The chastities never touch us. "Is this to do with the Ceremony, freida? It's okay if it is. It's normal to feel apprehensive."

I'm not sure if that is the reason. I don't know what this thing is, twisting in my gut, thirsting for something I can't name, but I nod my head. It's easier.

"What third do you want to be chosen for?"

"I want to be a companion."

"Not a concubine?" she asks, her cheeks coloring at the word.

"If that is the third the Inheritants think I'm best suited to, then of course," I say, although I would rather die than become a concubine.

"No interest in joining the chastities?"

As if anyone would want to become a chastity, faced with a lifetime of caring for newer, more nubile students as you grow old and decrepit, without the luxury of a Termination Date appointed to preserve your beauty. My eyes are drawn to the laughter lines scoring into her skin. I imagine her at forty, at fifty, at *sixty*, and I shiver.

"I didn't think I would be a chastity, at first," she says, oblivious to my thoughts. "But, well . . ." she looks sad for a moment. "Anyway I liked spending time with the younger children, and I, well, I didn't think I would be able to fulfill the duties of the other thirds so it was for the best, in the end."

We both look away, the suggestion of sex looming between us. "I felt safe in the School," she adds hurriedly. "It's peaceful here."

"That's what isabel said. Maybe she'll join agyness," I joke. "Imagine! Two chastities in one year. I bet that has never happened before."

"Oh, isabel will never be a chastity. There are much greater things in store for her," she says, her voice oddly sad.

But you thought it was an option for me? Why aren't there "much greater things" in store for me? Why does everyone always think isabel is so much better than me?

I touch the poppies at my feet, rubbing the fabric petals between my fingers. In the center of each flower is a miniature mirror, big enough to hold your eye if you lean in close. I crush it, the cloth tears easily, the glass bud shattering, breaking my reflection.

"Time for bed, freida."

We walk in silence back to the dorms. The others are still sleeping deeply, my absence unnoticed.

"May you get what you wish, freida," she whispers as I lie down on my bed, turning in the doorway as she leaves. "May you be the mother of a hundred Sons."

"All eves are created to be perfect but, over time, they seem to develop flaws. Comparing yourself to your sisters is a useful way of identifying these flaws, but you must then take the necessary steps to improve yourself. There is always room for Improvement."[2]

[2] *Audio Guide to the Rules for Proper female Behavior*, the Original Father

Chapter 6

January
Six months until the Ceremony

I loved Fridays as a child. I remember being obsessed
with these ancient picture books we had in our dorm,
which we were only allowed to look at on weekends. I
spent hours constructing detailed plans to make sure I
got my hands on them before the others. Not that they
ever wanted them anyway, preferring the interactive
ePad games. Every Friday evening I would sneak into
one of the blocked-up window frames in the cloisters,
leaning against a painting of sea cliffs or the pyramids,
pretending the windows were merely closed, that I
could look out if I chose to. That the world outside still
existed. While the other girls were playing Be a Stylist
and Plan a Party! on their ePads, I was poring over fotos

of princess sparkles, a skinny lady with big breasts, long legs and blond hair. She had a pink car and a pink house and there were little pink buttons on the page you could press to make her speak in an Americas-Zone accent. *Pink's my favorite color. You're my best friend. Math is hard. Wanna go shopping?* Then I made the mistake of asking one of the chastities what math was and they confiscated the books. Weekends were never the same after that. All we seem to do is burn through the hours between Organized Recreation sessions as fast as we can, listening to celebrity gossip on Artificial.com or updating our MyFace photos, trying to forget about what happened in that Friday's Comparison Studies class.

"#755 and #734, please leave your desks and come to the front of the room."

The rest of us exhale in relief as the chosen two walk to the front of the room as if their feet are made of lead. They step into the glass boxes flanking the chastity's desk, and magnified fotos of the two girls are projected, side by side, onto the mirror-board behind them, each image eight feet tall. Within seconds they appear on our desktops. cara's image is on the left, her dirty-blond hair skimming past her elbows, full eyebrows framing sky-blue eyes. naomi is on the right, cheekbones contouring her dark skin, her black haircut in thick bangs, drawing attention to her eyes, cat green and almond-shaped like mine.

"So, girls, let us begin," chastity-ruth says, walking up and down the center steps dividing the rows of seating. "At the end of each section, I will ask you to record your

VoiceNotes. Please make these comments as detailed and thorough as you can, to help #755 and #734 to explore their weaknesses. Remember, your voices will be disguised to maintain anonymity, so you may speak freely."

"Your skin is too dark, naomi," I hear someone say. "I think that you should ask about some lightening cream."

"cara, your hair color washes out your skin tone," someone else whispers. "I think you should ask about a tanning cream."

We have undertaken this task every Friday since our first Comparison Studies class in 4th year; two different victims each time. I always start off wanting to be kind, but somehow, once I start speaking too, I can't stop. I guess it does sort of make me feel better, at the time, a faint feeling of superiority swelling inside me like a balloon, but afterward my tongue feels bitter, like a hole has burned through it.

"What did you say about her?" I asked isabel when we were in 14th year, watching agyness's eyes turn glassy with unshed tears, wondering if my comments had been the cause. "Did you say anything about her being flat-chested?"

I willed her to agree, to collude with me, to follow me down into this dark rabbit hole.

"No." isabel's eyebrows shot up in surprise. "I never say anything like that. I usually just recommend they get their hair trimmed."

In that moment I loved her for her basic decency. And I hated her too. Because once again, without even trying, she was better than I was.

naomi and cara take their seats, shoving their earbuds in. We are all the same when it's our turn. Maybe we hope this time it'll be different, that this time everyone will agree that we're beautiful. Or maybe not. Maybe on some level it's actually okay when the distorted voices whisper in our ears, telling us we're ugly, we're vile, and everyone knows it. We may be perfectly designed, but really our eyes are too close together and our thighs are too big.

cara's face is ashen. What was it I said about her? I'm sorry. I'm always sorry.

"As you know, girls, there is always room for Improvement. With every year since your design date, you are getting older, losing your bloom, depreciating in value. Standards, girls! Standards must be upheld. I'm sure #755 and #734 are grateful."

I look at cara again, holding her face together in a smile. She doesn't look very grateful.

"An easy way to ensure equality of standards is to create consistency," chastity-ruth continues, pointing at the board behind her. It's still split in half but with two new images. On the left there is a foto of a woman from before us, and on the right a foto of liu.

"This woman from Old Japan is the prototype for #783. All variations have been regulated."

I would never say this aloud, but I sometimes think the modifications have left liu's features almost bland, so diluted that they are almost interchangeable with mine, or megan's, or naomi's. All that is different is our skin tone and hair color. But at least we still have some diversity, however marginal. It's rumored that nowadays only blond, blue-eyed girls are designed in the Afrika- and Chindia-Zones, their past literally whitewashed.

"As you can see, girls, the contrast between women today and the women before is vast." More and more images emerge of the women before as chastity-ruth continues her lecture. "Please note the lack of symmetry in the face, the bulbous noses, the dilated pores over the forehead and chin. Undesigned, natural women."

The screen updates with new horrors and I feel as if I might vomit. I have to close my eyes when she starts presenting examples of the obesity epidemic. I can only endure so much.

"There were theories before us that obesity had roots in emotional or psychological problems." There is something excited about her, her shoulders tense with expectation, her fists clenching. "This is nonsense. It is *laziness* that causes fat. Laziness and greed. And it will be your downfall if you allow it. But you won't let it, will you?"

"No."

"Will you?"

"No."

"WILL YOU?"

"NO," we scream, whipped into a frenzy.

"But one of you has." Her voice drops to a whisper. We look at each other, searching for the culprit. Who? Who is it? *isabel*. It has to be isabel.

"Look in the box!" liu yells, pointing at a figure ascending slowly into the glass box on the left of the chastity's desk, emerging through the trapdoors from the Organized Recreation Space. It's christy. My heart is thumping so loudly in my ears I can't hear chastity-ruth, I can't hear the other girls. All I know is that she's standing there, ready to be crucified for her sins. "This is going to look amazing on MyFace," megan says, pointing her fone at christy.

"Step forward, #727."

The glass doors part. She stands before us.

"Remove your bathrobe."

There's silence. christy unties the white toweling robe and lets it fall to the ground. She's wearing pink lace under-wear, small lumps of flesh spilling over the underwear, the inner edges of her thighs close to touching.

"#727 has been *lazy*. She has been lazy and she has been greedy. She deserves to be punished. Don't you agree?"

Flashes from digi-cams and eFones are exploding like flares. My hands are clammy, fear crawling up my spine bone by bone, unfurling in my throat.

"Don't you agree, girls?" A note of warning has entered her voice.

"Yes, chastity-ruth."

"I can't hear you. Does #727 deserve to be punished?"

"YES, chastity-ruth." We have to give her what she wants. We will give her whatever she wants.

She reaches into the pocket of her robe and retrieves a marker, someone behind me gasping at the rare sight of a writing implement. Wielding it like a blade, she walks around christy, once, twice, three times, before cutting into christy's fair skin, drawing vivid red circles on her body.

"What is #727, girls? What is she?"

We don't know, we don't know, we don't know.

"She's fat, girls. She's fat and disgusting. Say it with me. She's fat. Fat. Fat."

Some of the girls sing with her, more and more people joining in until it seems the ceiling may shatter with voices. It looks like a lightning storm now, camera flash after flash bursting through the room.

My eyes drift from christy's thighs to isabel's, and I can't help but measure the difference. It should be isabel up there instead of christy. I look up and isabel is staring at me, understanding shimmering between us. She knows what I am thinking. I'm sorry, I tell her with my eyes. I'm so sorry. She looks away. She doesn't care what I think anymore.

"Fat. Fat. Fat."

Amid the hysterical chanting, chastity-ruth holds her hands together, as if she's praying for inspiration. Her robes swish on the ground as she squats beside me. "Fat. Fat. Fat," she whispers in my ear. My heart feels too big for my body and I look at her in panic, her washed-out gray eyes burning into mine. She can see into my soul, just like isabel can. She can see, and she hates me too.

She bangs her fist on my desk so hard that the screen flickers and dies, a large crack splintering the middle. Her odor is invading my nostrils, the unfamiliar smell of the marker pen mixing with a sour hint of sweat.

I look at my broken desk, my reflection warping, split into two halves, both sides of my lips mouthing the word.

Fat.

* * *

"That was intense."

Back in the dorms, cara answers my request to VideoChat almost immediately and we fall into an uneasy silence.

"Intense."

"But obviously it had to be done. christy should have known better," she says quickly, paranoia kicking in.

"Obviously." My own fear beats in my body like a second heart.

cara chews on the ends of her hair, golden strands peeping out of her mouth. "Look, freida, I'll talk to you later." Before I say something I regret, her eyes seem to add. I'm about to turn the VoiceChat off when she speaks again, her voice quieter this time.

"Do you think my nose would be better if it was straighter?"

"What are you talking about?"

"In Comparison Studies. Someone said I should get it redesigned when we leave School."

"No, cara." Her gorgeous face fills the screen, delicate freckles sprinkled over an adorable nose. "Your nose is perfect."

She grins and waves goodbye, christy forgotten. I request isabel to VideoChat, staring at her profile foto as the beeping tone stretches out into nothingness.

Maybe she has her ePad on silent.

Maybe she's taking a nap.

Maybe she hates me.

* * *

The MyFace newsfeed is clogged. I listen to megan's status, then daria's, then gisele's. All are the same, blow-by-blow accounts of what happened in Comparison Studies, accompanied by countless fotos of christy in her underwear. I know I should update my status, put something generic like "Fat women should be made obsolete," but I don't have the energy.

"Stream TV."

The Americas-Zone's Next Top Concubine is playing, newly designated concubines participating in tasks to select the one who will be chosen as the American Father's personal concubine for a year. I watch as one of the finalists bows before the American Father, his hands gripping her curly auburn hair. I think I've seen this episode before.

An ad for vaginal bleaching cream.

One for a new laser treatment that promises to remove any unsightly body hair. "If only amber had known about this!" amber, a member of girl band the slutz, has her hand held high, waving to a friend. The camera zooms in, a red arrow pointing out the shadowing of stubble across her armpit.

I keep flicking, allowing the drone of the TV to wash over me, wash away these thoughts.

Beeeeeeeeeeeeeeeep.

"Hey, megan," I say, accepting the VideoChat request.

"Hey, girl. What's up?" She's not even pretending to look at me, totally focused on her own video-feed.

"Nothing much. What's up with you, girl?" Pathetic. I'm better than this in my head.

"Well, obviously I'm in shock after what happened today. It was awful. Poor christy. I feel so bad for her."

So bad that you took thirty-seven fotos and posted them all on MyFace.

"I would kill myself if I got that fat. I bet no one in the Americas-Zone ever gets fat."

"Apparently in the Chindia-Zone the eves are so well designed they don't need kcal blockers at all." I sigh at the prospect of unlimited access to the Fatgirl buffet, free from shame. "It's physically impossible for them to go above target weight."

"Hmm." It's funny how she can't see beyond the Americas. I can understand her wanting to leave the Euro-Zone, with its four thousand inhabitants and increasingly limited budget, but most of the world's money is in Chindia now. It may have been the Americas who came up with the idea for the Noah Project, but it was the Chindians who funded the development and construction of the Zones. No one else could afford it.

"I wonder why it wasn't isabel."

"What do you mean?" I pretend to misunderstand her.

"Come on, freida," she says, those green eyes boring into mine through the screen. "isabel has gained about three times as much weight as christy. She's enormous."

"That's not very nice." My guilt that she's articulating my thoughts is making me defensive. Since when did megan and I agree on anything?

"No need to be cranky. I'm only asking because—"

"Yeah, I know, I'm sure you feel really bad for isabel too," I say, and her face starts to turn a rather alarming shade of purple. "Sorry."

I wish I was brave enough to turn off my ePad and let her get back to giving her hair one hundred brushstrokes, or whatever it is she does to make it so shiny. I want my hair to be that shiny. Ugh. Why am I so useless?

"Sorry," I say again, and she smiles at my apology, tossing ebony waves down her back.

"It's okay. I know you're struggling. I've noticed that there have been some . . ." she pauses meaningfully—"*difficulties* with you and isabel."

Paranoia turns my stomach over. Can everyone else see it too? Do they talk about it behind my back, say that they always knew isabel would dump me in the end? They must have wondered why isabel, the #1 eve for so many years, would choose to be best friends with someone as inconsequential as me. I knew I was never good enough to be her friend; I wasn't pretty enough or funny enough and I didn't even have great taste in clothes. Everyone else probably knew it too.

"isabel can be strange, can't she?" megan's tone is conversational but her eyes are sharp, taking in everything.

"In what way?"

"She's always been secretive, don't you think?"

"isabel?"

"Yes, isabel," megan says impatiently. "I don't trust secretive people."

"Yes!" I say, falling on the excuse with indecent haste. "She has been, I guess."

Not about everything. Most of the time she was the most honest person I knew. But, yes, sometimes she could be guarded, cagey even, if I asked her a question she didn't want to answer. There was a part of herself that she kept hidden, that she didn't trust me enough to show me.

"But it's no excuse to fall behind in the rankings, freida," she says, wagging her finger at me. "You started this year at like, what, #5?" As if she doesn't know. Our rankings are chiseled into our souls. "And now you're #10. You're hanging on by your not very well-manicured fingertips. I mean, when was the last time you went to chastity-hope for Beauty Therapy? You had better not be pulling an amber."

"I'm going to get that new laser treatment done when I become a companion . . ."

"*If* you become a companion. If," she says, holding her hand up to shush me. "And you will have to rank in the top five if you want to be guaranteed one of the richer Inheritants. And that's not exactly looking definite right now, is it?" She stares at me with unconcealed impatience. "Do you want to be a concubine? Is that it? We've spend the last sixteen years in this School surrounded by girls. Do you really want to spend the rest of your life in a harem, surrounded by yet more *girls*? If you're a companion, you'll only have to share a house with some man and however many sons you're lucky enough to birth. It's *freedom*. For girls like us, being a companion is the only option."

A warm feeling spreads in my stomach at being included with megan in "girls like us." She leans in to the camera to fix her makeup, wiping away flakes of mascara from underneath her eyes. They seem greener on the screen, little specks of emerald fanning out from her pupils.

"When are they going to figure out a way to ensure our morning makeup lasts the whole day?" she asks, rubbing at a small smudge on her browbone. "I'm so sick of having to reapply midmorning. Anyway. What was I saying?"

"For girls like us, being a companion is freedom," I prompt her, thrilled at the opportunity to say "girls like us" again.

"So, yeah, whatever. It's not like I care or anything, but I think you need to start considering your future. Stop being such a girl and drop the deadweight. And in isabel's case, that's like 150 pounds of deadweight." Her face screws up with revulsion. "So disgusting. I'd kill myself before I'd let that happen to me."

"Yeah, I suppose you . . ." I begin but I'm talking to myself, the screen going black as megan hangs up without saying goodbye. She never did that to me when isabel was #1.

Chapter 7

February
Five months until the Ceremony

"How about the one on marine life?"

"Seen it."

"Rainforests?"

"Seen it. Three times."

"You're in a strange mood." agyness scratches the new haircut that megan said makes her look like a cancer patient.

"I'm bored. This weekend is lasting forever."

"I'm going to watch the marine one. Call me back if you change your mind."

"agyness?" I say before she turns off VideoChat. "Don't mention this to the others. I don't want them to know that I still watch the Nature Channel."

"But you *do* watch the Nature Channel," she answers slowly.

"Yes, but I don't want anyone else knowing that."

"Who cares?" She rubs her head again. Her hair is so short now you can see the pink of her scalp peeking through. She'll have to check that attitude at the door when she becomes a chastity. "You should just be yourself, freida."

I switch the chat off and stare at my reflection in the blank screen. I was myself with isabel.

Breakfast, Gym, Organized Recreation, Lunch, Gym, Organized Recreation, Dinner, ePad, Bed.

Breakfast, Gym, Organized Recreation, Lunch, Gym, Organized Recreation, Dinner, ePad, Bed.

To break the monotony, I sneaked into cara's room after dinner on Saturday, but I was swiftly hounded out by chastity-theresa. I don't understand how isabel and I got away with breaking Isolation for all those years. The chastities always seemed to look the other way when she was involved, but now, without her, I am vulnerable. My anger with her thickens in my chest, as heavy as a rock.

By Sunday afternoon I feel as if I am drowning in boredom. I've seen all the nature shows they are streaming on TV and all that's left are reality-show repeats.

Wives of the Euro-Zone.

Wives of the Americas-Zone.

Euro-Wives versus Americas-Wives, Battle to the Death.

* * *

"I'm yo King, yeah I'm yo King. Suck it down, coz I'm yo King."

The newest rapper from the Americas, Lil' Pete's video is on Rap TV. He's standing on a huge gold-plated throne, a crown on top of his spiky red hair. He has numerous leashes in his hands, like reins, extending to diamond-studded collars wrapped around the neck of each of the five naked blond concubines at his feet. They're kneeling on all fours, glossy mouths slack until it's time to sing the chorus. *"You're my king, Lil' Pete, you my king."*

I upload the video onto MyFace. Within minutes I can hear other girls joining in, voices floating out of open cubicles. *"You're my king, Lil' Pete, you my king."*

megan comments under the video that Lil' Pete looks "sooo like cintia," and cintia thanks her, bravely pretending that it was a compliment. Ten minutes later cintia uploads a slew of new fotos, her thick red haircut in uneven layers, her chest barely restrained in a floral bikini top.

"Oh my Father, look at how *fat* I am!" she squeaks.

The screen starts flashing, video comment after comment popping up, denials oozing like tar.

"Please!" freja comments, pulling up a silver mesh sweater to display a concave tummy. "If you think that's fat, I'm practically obese."

This is the same girl who told me at dinner yesterday that she's lost five pounds.

"I can't help it," she sighed, throwing her napkin over an uneaten pig chop. "I just can't stand the taste of in-vitro meat."

As if we've ever had any other kind. It's just another excuse for her to limit her kcals. I said nothing, silently planning a restricted kcal menu of my own.

cintia is so skinny in these fotos, her hip bones jutting out through her porcelain skin. She is only ranked #24 though. There is no way she is going to be a companion.

"Thankfully," megan said when the subject came up before. "All that red hair is so *unnecessary*, don't you think?"

I jump to my feet with barely contained anxiety, pacing back and forth. I pull poses in my mirrors, turning to one wall, then the next, reaching into my locker to grab my digi-cam. A foto of me reclining on the bed. A foto of me in high-waisted PVC leggings and a cropped top. A foto of me in a metallic silver bikini.

"Welcome to Your Face or Mine."

"Upload." I scan the digi-cam barcode against the screen.

"Complete," the ePad says. "Would you like to play?"

The screen splits in two, a face on either side. They look a lot younger, maybe about eight or nine. I don't recognize them. We try not to pay much attention to the younger eves coming up after us, with their fresher skin and their brighter eyes, snapping at our heels. The one on the left has light brown hair, dip-dyed so that the ends are blond. I prefer the girl on the right, her smile whittling dimples in her smooth black skin and making her bronze eyes glint with naughtiness.

"You are the first person today to choose thandi as your preference. jessica's face has been preferred fifty times today."

Of course it has.

I stare at myself in my mirrors, imagining taking a grater to my skin, peeling off the top layer. My bones might be white enough.

"So after that I experimented with a smoky eye using gold shades. Then I tried a gray smoky eye instead," daria says as we line up for the BeBetter buffet in the Nutrition Center. "I think it looks better than the normal black smoky eye. I took fotos if you want to see them."

"Did you?" megan asks, although daria updated her status on MyFace an hour ago telling us this, accompanied by said fotos. She looks critically at her. "I think I prefer a black smoky eye personally. No offense."

She grabs her tray and goes to chastity-anne to collect her meds. daria's hand darts up as if she's going to wipe her eyes clean, before she forces her face into a neutral expression.

"I went on Your Face or Mine today," I say, watching as megan takes her usual seat and swerves to admire herself in the mirrored wall. "I came in third out of one hundred faces!"

"That's great, freida!" cara says, her face lighting up in a genuine smile. "Why didn't you post it on MyFace?"

"Probably embarrassed," jessie cuts in, throwing a dish from the 0-kcal section onto her chipped tray. "I was on Your Face or Mine today too. I didn't even bother uploading a foto."

"Because the fotos were lame," liz says, lifting the lid of her tureen and gagging at the putrid smell of cabbage soup. "Kids in 8th year don't count."

cara and daria are holding their breath, waiting to see how I'll respond, but my mind goes blank. The twins snicker as they walk away to join megan.

"It does too count," I call after them, hurrying to catch up. They sit next to megan, filling her in on our argument. I can feel my temper start to rise and I breathe deeply to control myself. Only weak girls show emotion.

"meg, I love that bag." cara changes the subject hastily as we sit down.

"Thanks," megan says, stroking her snake-patterned tote. "It's only fake though. What do you think, freida?"

"Yeah. Very nice," I say, glancing up from my salad.

"isabel has a clutch, doesn't she? Real snakeskin, I mean." megan's face turns thoughtful when I nod yes. "They are *so* rare. Where did she get it?"

I shrug, taking a bite of the tasteless greens. I surreptitiously scan the room till I find her, sitting by chastity-ruth's desk. All of isabel's meals are supervised now, yet her body is still swollen beneath her baggy black dress. She's staring blankly at the solitary apple on her plate.

"You should prove it, freida," megan says, catching me off guard.

"Prove what?"

"That the results of today's Your Face or Mine are valid."

"How am I supposed to do that?"

"We'll have another contest. Tonight."

"Where?" jessie asks, shaking her hair out of its ponytail and nudging liz to do the same so that they're identical again.

"Not in the dorms—there isn't enough room for all of us to fit into one cubicle." megan bites her lip in concentration. "I know! We'll do it in the garden."

"What about Isolation?" I ask.

"chastity-bernadette is on tonight."

chastity-bernadette is rarely on night duty, because as soon as the lamps are turned off she starts dozing. You can hear her snores rumbling through the dorms within an hour of bedtime.

"It's settled, right?" megan says as I silently plead with one of the others to object. "freida, you send out the invite on MyFace. Send it to all of final year."

"Me?"

"I'm sorry, do you have an issue with that, *freida*?"

She emphasizes my name, drawing out the syllables, making it sound like a curse. I want to say no, I want to say no so badly, but she's looking at me and they're all looking at me now, a mixture of disdain and pity in their eyes. They don't think I have the courage to do it; they think I'm the most boring person in our class. They're probably wondering how isabel managed to put up with me as long as she did.

megan rolls her eyes to heaven, jessie and liz immediately copying her. cara is doing her best not to get
involved, scanning through fotogram. freja discreetly
spits out her chewed-up veggies, placing the napkin next
to her plate, the sticky mess seeping onto the table. My
chest swells with fear and I can hear my voice saying,
Yeah, yeah, of course I'll send it, and I know that I'm really
saying, *Please like me, please like me*, and I hate myself so
much but they're all smiling again, and I feel relieved and
stupid all at the same time. It'll be fine. I will just write
the message in code. If I don't use the words "party,"
"gathering" or "unsupervised," the eFilter shouldn't pick
up on it. liz and jessie get to their feet squealing, running to wrap their tanned limbs around me, giving me
one of their infamous twin sandwiches for the first time.
Warmth spreads through my limbs as I realize everyone
is watching us. They're jealous of me, like they used to
be.

"Quiet down, girls," chastity-theresa calls without
enthusiasm, and the twins skip back to their seats.

"So invite everyone, yeah?" megan continues in a low
voice. "Except isabel, obviously."

"Obviously!" The twins giggle uproariously.

"But if we get caught it might be useful to have her
there," cara points out. "The chastities love her. She never
gets in trouble."

"No." A thick vein pulses in megan's forehead. "I don't
want her there."

"Yeah. We don't want her there," liz and jessie repeat.

"Is that going to be a problem?" megan asks me, raising one eyebrow.

"No." I feel an awful excitement at being the favorite for once, the thrill of being preferred to isabel squirming in my belly. "Of course not."

I am a good girl. I am appealing to others. I am always happy and easygoing.

Every nerve in my body is fizzing as I listen to the Messages drone on. chastity-bernadette has been snoring since 10:45, but I warned everyone to wait until midnight. Or the "witching hour," as I hinted in my stupid message. Some of the girls weren't interested, but once I told them it was megan's idea any doubts disappeared.

11:58 p.m.

I steal out of bed as quietly as I can, wrapping my lilac bathrobe around me. I peek my head out of my cubicle and see other girls doing the same, a row of floating heads. megan is at the main door to the dorms, signaling for the rest of us to follow. We scurry like mice after her through the cloisters until we fall into the garden, laughing breathlessly. She leads us around the plastic trees to a patch of lime-green grass enclosed by a ring of the poppy flowers. We gather in a circle just inside the poppy-flower border, twenty-nine girls in sheer kimonos, like geishas from Old Japan.

"It's freezing out here," freja complains, goosebumps mottling her skin. She rubs her thighs vigorously, her fingertips dipping into the hollows above her knees. I swing my legs in front of me too, but they still don't look as skinny as hers. I shouldn't have finished all of my tofu-burger tonight. I wasn't even that hungry. liz ate her tofu-burger too. But she didn't have any relish. I had two dollops of relish. megan ate most of her chick-chick and noodle broth. Is that more or less kcals?

"What was that voice? Saying I am a good girl, over and over again?" jessie and liz ask, in turquoise robes that match their eyes.

"You've never heard the nighttime Messages before?" I say.

They shrug, a lock of blond hair emerging from both messy topknots at exactly the same time.

I don't know why I'm surprised. They've probably never had a disrupted night's sleep in their vapid lives.

megan claps her hands and we all fall silent. "So, everyone, welcome to my little midnight feast." She subtly emphasizes the "my" but not enough that I can call her out on it. Not that I would anyway. I take a deep breath, trying to remember what we learned in Unacceptable Emotions class. *Anger is ugly. Nice girls don't get angry.* I picture my irritation as a big red balloon bursting through my stomach, leaving a gaping hole behind.

"To celebrate, I have a surprise for you, girls!" megan rifles through her shoulder bag, the same peach color as her kimono. She looks particularly beautiful tonight, her hair piled in a thick top-knot, that pale skin luminous in the artificial moonlight. She pulls out a large bar of chocco with a "Ta-da!" and some of the others spontaneously applaud.

"Put those away," megan says as jessie and liz aim digi-cams at her. "This can't go on MyFace."

"*Not on MyFace?* But—"

"No." megan cuts them dead, glaring until they put the digi-cams back into their pockets. "It must be like tonight never happened." She brandishes the chocco bar. "Now, christy, you're not to eat it all. It's to share."

christy attempts a weak smile as she tugs her kimono down, pretending she can't see freja staring at her soft thighs with open disgust. No one stands up for her, not when it's megan making the joke, and especially not after what happened with chastity-ruth in Comparison Studies. I pick a cotton flower from the ring of poppies surrounding us, noticing a little caterpillar drawn on a single petal, in a red-and-black leopard print. I hold it closer to find my reflection in the mirrored bud. I want to see if my skin is as incandescent as megan's in the moonlight.

megan unpeels the wrapper, the smooth brown bar emerging tantalizingly slowly. I can feel myself salivating. I can't remember the last time I had chocco. I know some of the other girls occasionally treat themselves on weekends, ipecac syrup at the ready, but after what happened with isabel I've been trying to be a good girl. In some ways we are as much associated with one another as the twins are, and I don't want the others to see me eating chocco and thinking that I'm disgusting too. After megan has bitten off a tiny piece, she passes it to jessie on her left.

"No. Sugar is *poison*," jessie says, holding it by the tip as if it's burning her fingers. She clucks loudly as liz takes a nibble. jessie must be on the starvation cycle of her diet. Next week she'll be shoveling cakes down her throat, two at a time, before clawing her way back on the wagon the following day. On the chocco bar goes around the circle, passed reverently from girl to girl. freja takes a bite, chews it for a few seconds, then spits it into a tissue, some of the slime leaking onto her fingers. She wipes it absentmind-edly on her robe, brown streaks smudging the faded rose print.

"Ooh, freja, you look like agyness after she had that 'accident' in the chamber." liz claps her hands in delight as freja tries to rub the chocco off, leaving an ugly smear across the silk.

"At least freja didn't actually shit herself." daria smirks.

agyness flushes to her peroxide-blond roots, drawing her knees to her chest as if to protect herself. "It wasn't my fault. chastity-anne prescribed too much ExoLax in Weight Management that day," she protests, her words lost in the laughter. "And I was only six."

"Can we just get on with it?" I grab the chocco from freja and crack off a piece before passing it to agyness. I force it down my throat, barely tasting it. I lean back on my heels, my mind stirring with images of freja's hol-lowed thighs, looking at the ceiling covered with a star-filled navy digital wallpaper, a full moon painted in an odd mustard color. The edges of the sky bend into the thick steel walls, curving in to air ducts and the ventilation pipes that suck in and pump out all the air in the school, recycling our oxygen. I can feel their breath now, inside me. We are part of each other. The chocco bar is still on its journey around the circle and we watch each other carefully, comparing the size of our own bite to each other's. When it returns to megan, half the bar is left and she offhandedly throws it down in front of her.

"Now that our naughty treat is done," she says, ignoring our hungry eyes glued to the remaining chocco, "I think it's time to begin the main event." She reaches into her tote bag again and takes out an empty bottle of EuroCola, placing it in the middle of the circle. "As you know, the reason we're here is because there was some controversy over the reliability of today's Your Face or Mine."

"Yeah, all those 7th years don't count," angelina says, pursing her plump lips.

"For the last time," I snap, "they weren't all——"

"So we're going to do a face-to-face version." megan's voice is cold at the interruption and I bite my tongue. "Whichever two people the bottle lands on, we go around the circle one by one saying which face we prefer. Got it?"

There is a current of edginess in the group, nervous at the thought of being so openly honest. We make comparisons constantly, of course, but in private, protected behind the anonymity of our computers. isabel and I used to spend hours on a Saturday afternoon VideoChatting, talking about which girls in our year we thought were the prettiest, isabel frowning when she thought I was being too mean.

"Well, I think agyness has great eyes," she would say when I called her cropped hairstyle masculine. "freja is too skinny," she would agree, when I would gripe about her flaunting those gaunt arms. isabel was being genuine—she thought freja was too thin—unlike me, who secretly envied her. Every popping bone felt like an affront to my own lack of discipline.

"Yeah, it's gross, isn't it?" I'd say eagerly.

"Hmm," she'd answer noncommittally. "She has great taste in clothes though. That feathered skirt she wore today was awesome."

isabel could always find the best in every situation. When I was ranked #3 to her #1, she would insist that I was just as pretty as she was, listing all the things about my appearance that she liked. I'd examine myself in the walls after our VideoChats and I would feel a tiny glimmer of hope. Suddenly I miss her so much that my chest feels as if it might rupture with grief. What did I do that was so bad it made her give up on me?

The bottle lands on rosie and alessandra and we cast our votes in turn.

"rosie . . . rosie . . . alessandra . . . rosie . . . rosie . . ."

"I'm dying," rosie gasps when she is announced the winner. "You're so much prettier than me."

"No way," alessandra says. "I would kill for your lips. And blue eyes are cuter, everyone knows that." megan raises an eyebrow. "Blue *and* green eyes."

"Yeah, but I'd much prefer your nose. It's straighter than mine," rosie says, squeezing the tip of her own perfectly straight nose.

"Well, at least you're not fat like me."

"What? Have you seen my thighs? I'm practically veering into isabel territory," rosie says, pinching nonexistent thigh fat. She waits, hiding a tiny smile as the garden bursts with dissenting voices.

"You are so not fat. I'm fat."

"I'm so fat I should be made obsolete."

"I've gained at least three pounds since dinner, I know it."

How many kcals were in that chocco bar? It's 555 kcal per 100 grams, but it was a large bar, which is 250 grams approximately. I only had a small bite. How many kcals in that? I need to pay more attention in Calorie Calculation class. My blood feels itchy with the compulsion to vomit the chocco back up, see it splash on the ground before me, leaving me clean.

megan spins the bottle again, covering her face with slim fingers and exclaiming, "I'm so embarrassed!" when it lands on herself and angelina. I've always thought she and megan look alike, with their masses of dark wavy hair and milky pale skin. angelina would be my personal choice however; her feline-shaped blue eyes are gorgeous.

"The twins can start it off."

They both choose megan, of course, each girl that follows regurgitating her name without hesitation. We're shape-shifters, forever peeking over our shoulders to see what everyone else is doing in order to base our performance on theirs. freja opts for megan too, turning to me with an expectant face.

angelina angelina angelina, a voice is screaming inside my head, but my tongue feels swollen, absorbing the words I want to say.

"Sorry, what did you say? I didn't quite catch that." megan plays coyly with the silk tie of her kimono.

"megan," I repeat in defeat. I turn to agyness. She's making a necklace from some poppy-flowers, tongue lolling out in concentration.

"Hey, Augustus, it's your turn," megan says, throwing contemptuous looks at the others. "Augustus. Wake up, Augustus."

I nudge agyness, pointing to megan when she frowns at me for disturbing her jewelry making.

"I was calling your name, you dumb bitch," megan says in exasperation.

"But you didn't say my name."

"I did. I called you Augustus."

"But my name is agyness. Why would you call me Augustus?"

agyness isn't being awkward. She honestly doesn't get that someone would call her by a man's name because she has short hair.

"Whatever," megan sighs in the end, obviously deciding it isn't worth explaining it to her. "My face or angelina's?"

"What?"

"What is *wrong* with you?" megan says, losing her cool. "Did they drop you on your head when you were designed? Why do you think we're all out in the garden at midnight? Did you expect us to sing songs and braid each other's hair? We're playing Your Face or Mine. The bottle landed on angelina and me. Which one of us do you think is the prettiest?"

agyness looks from megan's face to angelina's, then back to megan's again.

"angelina." She refocuses on her necklace, grabbing another poppy from behind her to intertwine in it.

Silence fills the domed garden, no one daring to look at anyone else.

"What?" megan isn't even attempting to disguise her disbelief.

"I said I choose angelina." Irritation colors agyness's voice at this further disruption. "I prefer her lips. You have great lips, angelina," she says, and angelina smiles gratefully at this unexpected victory, however small. "But, um, you have a nice personality, megan."

She must be worried that she has hurt megan's feelings. That's the only explanation I can think of for the blatant lie. That warning vein is throbbing in megan's forehead again, her lips so white they look as if they've disappeared.

"Nice? Nice? NICE?" megan shouts. I try to shush her but she's beyond reason.

"Yes. You're nice," agyness lies again, looking perplexed at this reaction.

"Who cares about *nice*?"

"I do. I think personality matters."

"Are you brain dead? Personality does NOT matter. All that matters is being pretty, you . . ." she stammers with rage, "you *feminist*." There's a horrified gasp. "Well, it's true," she says defiantly. "Being pretty is all that matters."

"I quite agree, #767."

We freeze as she moves out of the shadows cast by the plastic trees. Her black robes make her look like a huge crow, about to scavenge through the debris for something to eat. Behind her is chastity-bernadette, sleepily rubbing her eyes.

Oh shit.

"Being pretty *is* what's most important. Although, I have to say, I feel using the 'F-word' was a little excessive," she continues, wearing her calmness like a mask. I can't breathe, terror constricting my lungs.

"I'm sorry, chastity-ruth, I—"

"Since you know how important being pretty is, I'm sure you're aware of how important sufficient sleep is to keep your skin in good condition. Especially coming up to the Ceremony."

"Yes, chastity-ruth," we whisper.

"Words fail me, girls. And I'm not often short of words, am I?" We make submissive noises. "Now, let me see. There must be a ringleader. I *wonder* who it could be."

Shit. Shit. *Shit.*

"Did you really think you were going to get away with this? Get up right now and walk in single file back to your dorm. You will not speak to each other. You will not look at one another. I will expect you in my office in the morning to receive your chastisement." She gestures at a quaking chastity-bernadette. "Escort them back to their dorms—if you can manage to stay awake that long."

"Wait, #630," she says as we eves scramble to our feet, eager to escape. "I would like a little chat with you."

I stop, my heart thumping painfully in my chest. I try to grab hold of megan's kimono as she passes, but the silk just slips through my fingers. chastity-bernadette closes the gate tightly behind them, locking me in here. With her.

"Have you anything you would like to say, #630?" She loops around me again and again until I start to feel dizzy.

"What do you mean?"

"You requested a VideoChat with every girl in your year this evening. That's an interesting coincidence, isn't it?"

She stands before me. She's not tall, but it feels as if she is towering above me, ready to wrap her black veil around me and devour me.

"Every girl except isabel. Didn't you used to be 'best friends'? Or did she get sick of you?" she continues, the moonlight glinting yellow in her gray eyes. I want to tell her that this wasn't my idea, but I can't. My life will be a living nightmare if I get megan in trouble, and I need her now. I'm not brave enough to do this by myself.

"Do you have anything to say for yourself, #630?"

"No," I say, and she looks so angry that I draw back, afraid she might *touch* me, hit me and leave a scar. But she would never do that. The chastities are not allowed to damage the Father's investments.

"I don't even want to look at you, you useless piece of garbage." A malevolent grin stretches across her face, her teeth like a row of tombstones. "I will give you your chastisement tomorrow, #630. I need time to think of something extra special just for you."

Chapter 8

"All final-year eves report to the chastities' office."

I'm lying face down on the mattress when the intercom wakes me, my head smeared onto my arms, my mouth parched. I stretch, my mind gluey with sleep.

"Will all final-year eves report to the office immediately. Except for isabel."

Obviously. The twin's voices whisper in my head, and memories from last night smash into me.

I crawl out of bed. Even in the low lighting, my mirrored cubicle is not kind to me today. I can see the wrinkles in my kimono from every angle, a big lump of knotted hair bulging at the nape of my neck. Peering closer at the wall at the base of my bed I notice angry handprints on my cheek from where I fell asleep.

"Hurry up," freja hisses from the doorway, immaculate in tapered pants and an olive blouse with a pussycat bow.

Throwing an agonized glance at the mirror, I pull
my matted hair into a bun and scurry to catch up with
daria. We march together through the cloisters, past the
garden gate to the back of the School until we have gathered in front of the chastity quarters. A tall gold-plated
gate shields their privacy, the large black triangle of the
chastities sculpted in the metal. There are five different
cameras pointing directly at us. This is the only area of the
School that still has functioning cameras. They can't afford
to replace the others.

megan forces her way to the front, slamming her hand
on a gold-plated box attached to the gate, the same black
triangle inscribed on that. A sorrowful note rings out
and the gates part. megan grabs my hand, her talons digging into my palms in warning. A surge of hatred pulses
through my body, so strong my knees shake, and she lets
go, smiling. She knows I'll do what she wants.

We walk through the gates into a long murky passageway, stopping at a large oak door with a brass peephole at
eye level.

"What do we do now?" megan asks, jumping as the
door swings open.

"Follow me," chastity-anne says with a disapproving
shake of her head, leading us through their quarters. The
diamond tiles give way to a black marbled floor. There are
no light-lamps here, only old-fashioned white candles in
glass lanterns, six along each side of the hall. Beside each
lantern there is a single door, which must be the chastities' individual sleeping quarters. chastity-anne leads us

through another oak door into a dimly lit room where every surface is covered in oak-wood panels, including the ceiling. The big window at the far end of the room is sealed with a huge print of the original Father, the man who led the Noah's Project for the Euro-Zone all those years ago. The poster is dotted around with star-shaped light bulbs.

Lining either side of the room are six wooden chairs, each one underneath a lantern holding a white candle, the same as in the corridor. Eleven chastities are sitting in the chairs, their black robes draping to the ground, stitching brightly colored thread into linen frames. They're working in a perfect rhythm, needles going in and out at the exact same time, the concentration on their faces clear to see even in the candlelight.

chastity-ruth is sitting at a large wooden desk beneath the Father's poster. She claps twice and the other chastities immediately stop their embroidery and stand up. With bald heads bowed and needlework clasped in their hands, they glide silently from the room. chastity-magdalena holds a finger to her lips as she passes me, her face grave.

When they have left, chastity-ruth looks at each girl in her turn, except for me. For all the times I've wished I was invisible to her, I can't help but feel this is a bad omen.

"I'm sure you are aware of how disappointed I am in you."

"Yes, chastity-ruth," we reply, heads hanging.

"I have known for some time that chastity-bernadette was perhaps ill-suited to night duty, but I never dreamed that you would abuse her limitations in such an insolent manner." She does look shocked. The chasties never expect us to disobey them, to have the audacity to break the rules carved into us since design. She shakes her head before adding, "chastity-bernadette shall also be punished of course."

I feel a pang of guilt at the thought of poor old chastity-bernadette getting in trouble because of us.

"Isolation is enforced to ensure that any incidents of female hysteria which Organized Recreation has failed to drain from you do not occur. It's for your own safety."

"Yes, chastity-ruth."

"I thought long and hard about a suitable chastisement for you. I was considering banning you from makeup for a week . . ." daria catches her breath, blood draining from her face, "but I decided that would only be detrimental to the reputation of the School. You may be perfectly designed, but there is always room for Improvement." She scrutinizes us as a heaviness hangs in the gloomy room. "So, as your chastisement, your internet usage will be banned for a week."

"What?"

"No!"

"That's not fair—"

"That means," her cold voice slices through the protests, "no MyFace, no VideoChat, no TV. *Nothing*. I shall collect your eFones and ePads at breakfast. Now get out of my sight."

We go to leave, stunned into silence.

"Stay where you are, #630," she says as the others file out. "Sit down."

I grab one of the chastity's chairs and drag it so that I can sit across from her, the desk a welcome buffer between us.

"Why are you still in your nightclothes?"

I look down at my crumpled kimono. I'd forgotten I was still wearing it.

"Pathetic." She leans forward, digging her elbows into the wood. "I have to say, #630, I'm surprised that you're the ringleader in all this. You've always seemed more like a *follower*. Wouldn't you agree? A sheep. Cannon fodder. Pretty, if you like that sort of thing, but rather bland."

It's as if she has ripped my head off my shoulders and held it to her ear like a seashell fossil, listening to the echo of my secret thoughts. I bite my lip. Crying is ugly. No man wants a girl who cries.

"I would have presumed one would need to be more popular to persuade the rest of the class to break the rules so flagrantly. And so close to the Ceremony." She widens her eyes theatrically. "Will they be very angry with you, #630?"

They won't blame me, will they? Everyone knows it was megan's idea; she said so herself in the garden.

"Was this your idea, #630? Or was someone else involved? Someone ranked higher than you, perhaps."

"No, chastity-ruth." I stare into my lap miserably. I can't risk it. "It was my idea."

"How touching your loyalty is, if rather misguided." I can hear her wooden chair scraping back on the marble floor. "It's a pity you didn't show similar loyalty to isabel."

"Yes, chastity-ruth."

"Besides having your internet usage rescinded, as an extra chastisement you are forbidden from using makeup or hair-styling this week."

"But what about standards being upheld?" I blurt out in desperation. "I thought you said—"

"Are you questioning me?" Her eyes are like chips of ice.

"No, chastity-ruth."

"Glad to hear it." She peers closer at me. "Those dark circles under your eyes aren't going to help your rankings. What is the point of your taking SleepSound when it's clearly so ineffective? I must discuss it with chastity-anne."

I can feel my chin starting to wobble. Don't cry. Don't cry. *I am always happy and easygoing.*

"I hope you're not going to *cry*, #630, like some new-design."

"No, chastity-ruth."

"And you're in detention for two weeks," she says. "You will report to the chamber every morning after breakfast. You are dismissed."

I leave quickly before she can find a few more chastisements for me, running away, the world blurring with my fear.

Chapter 9

"Your weight is 115 pounds, freida," the PSP says. "Please step into the changing room."

"Can I look through some old fotos to reference first?"

"Outfit denied."

"But I haven't chosen an outfit yet."

"Outfit denied."

I peer closely at the screen, tapping it repeatedly, but it keeps saying, "Denied. Denied. Denied."

"Denied," the PSP says again. "Please step into the changing room. Your outfit has been selected." The computer screen vanishes and my face reappears. My eyes are bloodshot, purple shadows smudged underneath them. I pinch my cheeks to draw some blood into them, give them some color. I could really use makeup today.

"Maybe a sneaky hint of lip gloss?" I say as the trapdoors of the changing room open and I step in.

"Close your eyes."

The lasers crackle, the top layer of my skin seared clean, hair yanked into a tight ponytail. Back in my room I stare in disbelief at the outfit that has been selected for me. Ochre velour sweatpants have been matched with an oversized yellow T-shirt, yellow flip-flops and a yellow backpack. I look like a stick of margarine.

Sometimes I fantasize about having a terrible accident, one so awful that everyone would feel sorry for me and take care of me until I got better. I wish that every bone in my face was broken, my features disfigured beyond repair, so that a complete redesign was unavoidable. I could flip through a catalog of body parts, hand-picking the new, improved me. I know everything would be better then.

I take my place in the line for the fotobooths. daria passes, nose in the air, and freja waits for me to walk ahead of her, pretending to be engrossed by the floor tiles. I try my best to take a good foto, dimming the lighting and turning slightly away so only my side profile has been captured, but I know it's no use. I can imagine all the Inheritants looking at the foto, at my greasy hair and my uneven skin, thinking how tired I look. I will be unwanted by any man, utterly failing in my one role as an eve.

Conversations stop when I enter the cafeteria, continuing in whispers as I pass. Even the younger eves nudge each other, heads tilted in my direction. Everyone knows.

"Morning, chastity-anne." She doesn't look up from her desk as she hands me the test tube with my foto on it.

"Wait," I say, talking to the top of her head, the rivets of blue veins tracing around her skull. "Where are the rest of my meds?"

She shrugs and looks over her shoulder at chastity-ruth. She's perched at her desk, a big pile of confiscated ePads and eFones in a wooden crate at her feet.

"Fine." I give in. "I'll see you at bedtime for my Sleep-Sound." She doesn't respond and my nerves begin to crackle. "chastity-anne?"

"Not this week."

"What?" I say in panic, my breath becoming shallow. *"But I need my SleepSound."*

"Is there a problem?" chastity-ruth murmurs in my ear, sneaking up out of nowhere and making me jump with fright.

"No problem," chastity-anne says, shooting me a warning glance. "She was just collecting her meds."

"Very good." chastity-ruth unzips my bag—"A back-pack. How very utilitarian chic"—and removes my ePad, eFone and makeup bag with a flourish. I watch in stunned silence as she glides back to her desk.

"Please, chastity-anne. I'm begging you."

"I can't help you with that," she says, as if I've asked her for an extra can of EuroCola.

"Thanks," I say bitterly, picking up my tray, my hands clutching the edges so tightly my knuckles are blanched of color. megan and the twins are at the top table, bags and sweaters piled on the empty seats. Maybe they will slip me half a pill, just for tonight.

"Did you see the latest update about the Carmichaels on the *Daily Tale* this morning?" megan says, examining her manicure for chips.

"Of course. I needed to watch as much as I could before they took our ePads away," jessie says mournfully.

"I can't believe cassie is saying Charles hit her."

"Why didn't she say she walked into a door or something? What happened to saving face?" liz says and the others start laughing at the unintentional irony. "Oh, shut up! You know what I mean."

"He's yummy," jessie sighs. "He could hit me any day he wanted."

"I'd let him make shit of me," megan says, the three of them now laughing hysterically.

"Hey."

They stare up at me as if they have no idea who I am. It's the same way they look at liu, an air of bewilderment undercut with exasperation.

"You look as tired as I feel," jessie says, her head dropping to examine the mirrored table. She looks at me again and then back at her reflection. "Thank the Father for makeup."

"We're all tired today," megan's tone is accusing and I want to scream at her. This was her idea in the first place.

"Can I sit down, megan?" I ask, conscious of a table of 12th years pointing and whispering.

She leans back in her chair, her black lace cropped top rising a little above the high waistband of her black spandex pants. Her hair has been styled with a severe middle parting, her eyes lined in forest-green kohl, eyes that are working their way from my feet to my greasy ponytail, lingering at my midriff.

"Sorry." She shrugs. "Those seats are saved for the others."

I can feel a lump form in my throat, threatening to choke me.

"iman. Over here."

iman, a pretty 15th year, is chatting loudly to a girl with waist-length ginger hair and a doll-like face. She stops, pointing at herself to verify that megan is speaking to the correct person.

"Yes, you! And lily. Have breakfast with us!" megan coos as they sit down. "Why are we not friends on MyFace? I'll fix that once we get our ePads back," she lies. No one ever befriends younger girls on MyFace.

"freida. Wait."

"Yes?" I say hopefully, spinning around. There's still space at the table, after all.

"You need a pedicure." I look down at my feet, at the chipped nail polish, and I curl my toes. "You're welcome!" megan calls after me, iman and lily open-mouthed at this 16th-year drama.

The Nutrition Center blurs before me. I know agyness and cara would let me sit with them, but there isn't any room left at their table. All the other girls seem to have handbags and empty ePad cases placed resolutely on any spare seats. Even the younger eves avoid eye contact with me.

"No other seats left, #630?" chastity-ruth says as I take a seat by her desk. Her voice is so loud that everyone turns to watch as isabel and I are reunited.

"Be careful," I say testily as isabel reaches across the table to grab her water glass, her arm bumping mine. I can feel her body heat radiating against my skin. *If you had been in the garden, I wouldn't have gotten in trouble. If you were still my friend, I wouldn't have to try to be friends with megan.*

I take the tarnished silver lid off my tureen and stare at the bowl of porridge, grains almost jumping out of the congealed gray sludge. I take a bite. What weight did the PSP say I was this morning? It said I was at target, but *it was wrong, it was wrong, it was wrong.* I saw the way megan looked at my stomach; she could see the blubber ripping through my skin. *I'm disgusting.* I take another bite of porridge but it slimily crawls back up my throat, like a slug. I run, the blood roaring in my ears, and I make it just in time to fall to my knees and see yellow bile spattering the back of the toilet bowl.

The black-and-white tiles line the floors of the Vomitorium too, the sinks carved from cream marble, the taps plated in gleaming chrome. There is a private alcove tucked into the corner and I trace my hand over the faded wallpaper—a motif of women from the Zones, unaware that their foto is being taken. One woman is on a climbing wall at the gym, a red circle around her sweaty face. Another is climbing out of a swimming pool, a vivid red arrow pointing to dimpling cellulite on her thighs. There are countless others, a map of red circles highlighting their shame. The same pattern is replicated on the round woven mat that I'm standing on, staring at myself in the full-length mirror hanging on the wall.

"You are at an acceptable weight."

I jerk back, my heart racing.

"It's the mat speaking. It weighs you." isabel is standing in the entrance to one of the bathroom stalls, that shapeless black dress doing little to disguise her increasing bulk. It's the first time she has spoken to me in weeks.

"Make sure to avail yourself of the facilities." She points at the display of beauty products and bottles, neatly arranged on a chrome-plated shelf above the three sinks. There are bottles of mouth freshener, some sort of wash to make sure cavities don't form in your teeth, ExoLax tablets, backup supplies of ipecac syrup to help with vomiting and some tubes of lip gloss. I gargle with mouthwash, the sound of isabel retching in the toilet behind me clearly audible. I creep closer until the tips of my fingers are touching the door between us. How did we get here? How did sixteen years of friendship disintegrate so fast and with such ease?

"We'll be friends forever, freida."

"But what happens if I don't make the companion third? What will we do then?"

"You will." isabel was confident. "And if you don't, I'll sort it out."

"How? How can you sort it out?"

"I can't tell you. It's a secret."

"But best friends tell each other everything," I said. "Best friends don't have secrets."

She turned away. It was yet another one of those moments where I could sense the secrets bubbling inside of her, making no sound.

Chapter 10

As soon as I wake up I reach for my ePad. But it isn't there the first morning or the second morning or the third or the fourth. Access denied.

I do the splits perfectly in PE. I lose half a pound in two days. I get the spinach and pig-meat frittata from the lo-carb section for lunch. And no one else knows. I mentally construct a MyFace status, polishing the memories carefully until they shine. The need to record my life is as fundamental as my need to breathe. Without MyFace, I'm floating. I have nothing to anchor me down, to prove I exist.

It's only one week.

I count the days in a week, then the hours, the minutes. I find myself watching the clock, wishing the days away until I can have something, *anything*, to distract me from this frenzy of thoughts like a nest of wasps exploding in my brain. Thoughts and thoughts and thoughts. I am possessed by them.

"Eggies again? I'm so sick of eggies." megan is staring at the BeBetter buffet selection.

"Is there a problem, #767?" chastity-ruth swoops down on her.

"No problem." megan, arching her back, her strapless minidress rising up her thighs, liz and jessie in rapt adoration by her side.

Haven't we done this before?

The volume in the cafeteria is mounting. We fall on each other, desperate to talk, words spilling out of our mouths as if they're too hot to swallow. *How're you? How are you? I don't care. Listen to me. Listen to me.* Mealtimes are stuffed with monologues thrown at one another, each waiting for a pause in the conversation that we can claim for ourselves.

"And then she said . . ."

". . . I had to, don't you . . ."

". . . same thing happened to me, only way worse . . ."

"That reminds me of when I . . ."

"Do you remember when I . . . ?"

chastity-ruth has increased Organized Recreation to three hours every evening to settle our nerves. I crawl into my glass coffin, cramming amnesia into my mouth.

"Are you okay?" isabel has stopped eating. I can see chewed up chick-chick in her mouth. The bones of the chicken reform, recreating his skeleton. He starts chirping but she swallows, swallows the bird down, all the way into her stomach. He's going to lay eggs, so many eggs, and when all the baby birds are hatched they will peck and peck and peck their way out of her stomach. I cover my eyes with my hands. There are no animals anymore. They were all destroyed.

"Are you okay, freida?" isabel asks again.

"I'm tired."

"Still not sleeping?"

"No."

I had thought my sleeping pattern was irregular when I only managed four or five hours a night on SleepSound. That seems indulgent now. When we return to our cubicles after evening meal, we are in Isolation until breakfast the next morning, chastity-ruth patrolling the dorms more vigilantly than I can ever remember. I lie awake, listening to the nighttime Messages play on and on. *I must be a good girl, I must, I must, I must.*

"I haven't slept since the night in the garden."

"You haven't slept in *four days*?"

I start laughing, convulsions moving through me.

"That sounds dangerous." I can tell by isabel's face she doesn't find it as funny as I do. "Maybe you should ask chastity-ruth if you can skip the chamber session this morning. You're in no state to be exercising."

"Thanks, isabel," I say. "The gym keeps me skinny! Math is hard. Pink is my favorite color. Wanna go shopping? You're my best friend."

"Hey, girls." megan and the twins approach before isabel can reply. chastity-ruth is distracted, leaving her desk to yell at a group of 5th years for laughing too loudly. The three of them have styled their hair in textured side braids, eyes lined heavily with black kohl.

"Hey." isabel continues to chew her food slowly.

"isabel." megan's voice is like silk. "Have you been watching the Carmichaels? What's happening with Charles and carrie?" She sighs. "It's so typical that we're banned from TV during such a *crucial* period in their lives."

isabel takes a sip of water before placing the glass back on the table. "I don't watch that show."

The lights have caught fire in the twins' hair and they merge into one, then two, then one. Are they secretly the same person? My mouth is dry. Little stars leak out of megan's skin, replacing her eyeballs with golden stars. My mouth is so dry. I grab isabel's glass and gulp down what's left in it. I drop it back on the table, looking at the girl looking back at me. Greasy dark hair pulled away from an ashen face. Is that the girl they keep call-ing freida?

"You look like shit." Star-eyes is talking to me, the clones nodding in the background.

"But skinny! You've lost five pounds at least. You could totally create your own diet program," the clones tell me. They might be jealous. I didn't think machines could have feelings.

It's true, I am skinny. My bones jostle underneath my skin, fighting to be the first one to pierce my flesh.

"Food tastes of nothing." I don't look the clones in the eyes. They will turn me to stone.

"Why is she slurring her words?"

"She's fine," isabel answers abruptly.

I am fine, I am fine, I am fine.

"Eggies for lunch? I'm so sick of eggies." megan is bickering with the stacks of silver tureens *again and again and again.*

"Haven't we done this before? Haven't we done this before? Haven't we done this before?"

"What?" megan stares at me.

"What?" I answer back. "What? What? What? What?"

"Why do you keep repeating everything?"

Someone is turning the volume controls on her voice up and down and up and down. My eyes are turning inside and then out, they are too big for the sockets, they are going to fall out, fall to the floor like ping-pong balls, bounce, bounce, bounce.

"What? Haven't we done this before? Haven't we done this before? Haven't we done this before?"

"Is there a problem here?" chastity-ruth swoops down, black robes billowing.

Haven't we done this before?

Blackness swarms and I see nothing as the floor rises to meet me, to be my dancing partner.

Chapter 11

"freida?"

Tiredness is pulling me under. I'm trying to keep my head up, claw my way out of this never-ending dream, but I keep falling back. The world blinks once, twice. A bald head is floating before me. I should nod to say that I am awake, but my skull feels like a burden. I close my eyes again.

"I'll wait here until she wakes up, chastity-magdalena." Another voice, a girl. Younger.

"You're not supposed to be here. You might get in trouble."

"It's *me*." Her voice cracks a little. "I can't get in trouble, can I?"

Footsteps walking away. A hand on my forehead, brushing away my hair.

freida, freida.

My name is freida.

* * *

I push the suffocating blanket off me.

There are two old windows in the wall facing me, blocked up with square mirror panes surrounded by a mahogany border. There is another, empty, bed next to me in this large, white room.

I am not in my dorm.

"You're awake."

She's sitting on a stripped wooden chair at the end of the bed, so low that she has to semi-rise out of the seat in order to see me over the bed frame.

"How are you feeling?" she asks, groping for the switch on the wall, both of us blinking as she turns the light on. Her face is knotted in anxiety but softer somehow, more like the isabel I used to know.

"What happened?"

"You fainted in the cafeteria. You've been in Sick Bay ever since."

"I fainted? Did everyone see? Were people laughing?"

"We thought you'd had a heart attack or something. They had to bring a Doctor in from the Euro-Zone to examine you. He was furious that an eve with a known sleep disorder was deprived of SleepSound, accused chastity-anne and chastity-ruth of neglect."

"How do you know? Who told you all this?" I ask, but she merely shrugs before saying, "You've been out for two days now."

"Out? Out as in *unconscious*?"

"Seriously, you need to calm down. chastity-magdalena won't be happy if she comes in and finds you agitated."

"I'm not agitated," I say agitatedly.

She looks at me skeptically and pulls her ePad out of the battered leather satchel hanging off the back of her chair.

"freida, I think I know you well enough to know when you're feeling anxious."

And in that moment there is so much I want to say to her I wouldn't even know where to begin.

"Okay. I'm agitated," I admit, and isabel throws her head back in laughter. A braid is holding her silky white hair back from her lightly freckled face, her eyes lit up with amusement. I try not to look below her shoulders, but I can't stop myself. She's in the same black dress, but I can see the extra bulk collecting at her neck, on her arms. When she moves, the material sticks to the rolls of fat around her tummy. I can count them as easily as I can count freja's ribs. I feel nausea, pity, and, worst of all, a shiver of glee. If there were photos of us in our bikinis on Your Body or Mine, I would be chosen. For the first time against isabel, *I would win.*

"It's been strange on MyFace with everyone banned," she says, fiddling with her ePad. "My news feed is nonexistent."

"At least you have access to it. I feel like my arm has been hacked off with a rusty saw."

"Lovely visual, freida. So dramatic," she pretends to scold me. "Come here, I'll give you a look at mine."

"Oh, can we? Can we go on to Artificial?"

isabel pushes herself out of the squat little chair and stands at my left shoulder. She leans in so that I can see the screen properly, her hair tickling my cheek. She still smells of lavender. If I close my eyes, I could be five again, huddled with isabel after yet another clash with chastity-ruth. A wave of affection for her crashes over me, a weakness I thought I had defeated.

"The big story is still the Charles and carrie Carmichael story," she says.

"What happened?"

"He thought she was being too 'friendly' with another Inheritant at his birthday party. He broke her nose and two of her ribs."

"He hit her in the face? I can't believe that."

"It's true. They did a special edition on it—'Combating with the Carmichaels.'"

"Why didn't she deny it?"

"He did it on a live broadcast. They couldn't cover it up."

"He's yummy. I'd let him beat me any day." I repeat megan's words.

"Don't." isabel rebukes me sharply. "Don't say that."

I look at the ePad. Charles's arms are folded across his chest defensively. I click on the video ". . . *and what happens between me and my companion is my business. I reserve the right to do what I want in my own home . . .*" I turn the sound off. His lips are still moving. carrie is standing behind him, the thin straps of her cream slip dress falling off her shoulders.

Her face is beautifully made up but you can see the shadowing underneath, her eyes huge with defeat.

"Did carrie release a statement too?"

"I doubt anyone asked her for one," isabel says, and I nod, pushing the ePad away.

"Are you feeling sick? Should I call chastity-magdalena?" Worry is etched on isabel's face. Why is she being nice to me again?

"How come you're allowed to visit me?"

"I'm not being chastised, am I?"

"But you're still breaking Isolation. Why haven't the chastities kicked you out?"

"Just lucky, I guess." She picks at a spare thread in the blanket cover, avoiding my eyes. Another secret.

"Fine. Don't tell me."

"It's not a big deal, freida. chastity-magdalena is being amazing." She wags her finger at me. "You know, I think you're her favorite. For some reason."

"Excuse me!" I can't help but smile. "What do you mean, 'for some reason'? Why wouldn't I be her favorite?"

isabel makes a grotesque face, and we start giggling again. "I've missed this," I blurt out before I lose courage. "It's been nice these last few days, sitting together at meals. Like the old days."

"Well, you *were* delirious from a lack of sleep . . ."

"And I'm sorry about not inviting you to the garden. It wasn't my decision."

"It's fine."

She doesn't offer me an apology in return or explain why she's been pushing me away all year. I wish I knew why I didn't say anything to her about this before now. Why didn't I catch it at the beginning? But it all happened so gradually. A missed VideoChat request here and there, the night I lay awake sizzling in the heat and realized she hadn't visited my cubicle in weeks . . . There was nothing you could pinpoint and say, "This is the exact moment that we stopped being best friends." She sits back on the chair, tucking her ePad into the satchel neatly.

"Anyway . . ." she folds over her lap like a ragdoll, wrapping her arms around her knees—"you're just doing what you have to do."

"That's no excuse."

"freida. That's what we've been trained to do. You have to pull your rankings back up. There's still hope for you."

"And what? There isn't for you?" I ask, annoyed.

She looks at me bleakly. "Just promise me you'll try, freida."

The door opens and megan and the twins stomp in, their leopard-print platforms pounding on the wooden floorboards. They still have their hair in messy side braids, each of them in leather shorts with a marl-gray tank top and knee-high socks.

"I mean it. Go back and get changed now," megan barks at the twins.

"We'll be late for dinner!" liz and jessie whine.

"Look at you, girls." They turn to stare at me. "So coordinated."

"freida, can you just try and be normal for once?" megan tosses her head, her hair falling down her back like an ebony rope. Is it her voice inside my head all the time? She always seems to say the exact thing that I'm thinking about myself.

"Did you visit her just to be mean?" isabel says.

"Of course not! I was worried about you, freida, I wanted to check that you were, you know, alive." She sits on the bed, crushing my foot beneath her. I yelp in pain, but she doesn't move, still smiling sweetly.

"And we were bored in Isolation," jessie adds helpfully as she and liz sit on the other side. She pulls a bag of sweeties from her clutch, cramming one purple jelly into her mouth, then another.

"I thought you said sugar was poison?" I say.

"Everything in moderation," jessie mumbles, swallowing the sweets without even chewing. "Besides," she says, clearing her throat, "I'm only eating purple-colored food this week so these don't count."

"This room is weird," megan says, swiveling around to take in the cream-painted walls, the old-fashioned wooden bed. Her gaze rests on isabel. "That chair looks *strong*, doesn't it, girls?"

"What is that supposed to mean?" isabel says.

"Nothing." megan smiles. "Don't be so sensitive."

"You look so skinny, freida," the twins chorus.

"Thanks."

"Like sick-skinny, you-could-be-dying-skinny," liz says, and jessie crumples the empty sweet bag in her hands, a guilty look on her face.

"Is that an ePad in your satchel, isabel?" megan interrupts. "Have you been on the *Daily Tale*? What's going on with the Carmichaels?"

There's a long pause, so long my palms start sweating.

"I've no idea," isabel says eventually. "I told you, I don't watch that show." She takes lotion from her satchel and starts rubbing it into her hands, the smell of lavender filling the room. "But don't worry. You only have one more day of chastisement, right?"

At the prospect of another evening in Isolation without their ePads, the three of them burst into loud chatter. liz is ranting about what a bitch angelina is. Or was it anya? jessie is talking about how this new purple-coded diet should help her lose fourteen pounds in two weeks. She's wandered closer to the mirrors, measuring her waist with her hands.

". . . purple cabbage . . . raisins . . ."

". . . then she said that she had worn the blue top first when everyone knows that I had . . ."

". . . grapes . . . eggplant . . ."

"When I asked her, she actually laughed in . . ."

". . . purple kale . . . figs . . . plums . . ."

". . . and that's when the *boys* are going to be introduced."

Everyone stops.

"What did you just say?"

"It's going to be announced tomorrow." megan's eyes are triumphant as she leans in closer to whisper confidentially. "I overheard some of the chastities talking about it."

"They're finally coming?" I ask. "When? Are they going to be the Inheritants that we'll be matched with? Are they going to be here every day? Are they going to stay here or commute daily from the main Zone?"

I'm firing questions at her, ignoring her air of self-satisfaction. The Inheritants come every year, but their visits are always shrouded in mystery. The eves of previous years refused to discuss it with us, and even on TV, if women ever reminisce about their Inheritant module at School, the sound goes dead so all we eves can see are moving lips.

"It's getting so late in the year, I was beginning to think they had decided to scrap the Inheritant module," I say, shaking my head. "When are they arriving? Are you absolutely sure?"

megan mimes zipping up her lips and throwing away the key, which means she doesn't have a clue. liz and jessie are buzzing, talking loudly, clamoring over one another to be heard.

"Can you believe it?" I say to isabel, and only then do I notice how very pale she is.

"Are you okay?" I reach for her hand and find her skin clammy to touch.

"Awww," megan says. "Are you scared at the thought of real-life boys? I wouldn't worry, isabel. I doubt they'll pay *you* too much attention."

The three girls scream with laughter, jessie's mouth open so wide I can see her purple-stained tongue.

"Shush, the chastities will hear you," I say. I want to defend isabel, but I know I can't antagonize megan and my head is hurting with the effort to do both.

"Yes, the chastities *will* hear you. I'm not sure what you girls are even doing here, considering the terms of your chastisement state that when you're not in class, at Organized Recreation, or having meals, you are required to remain in your cubicles. *Alone*."

"Sorry, chastity-ruth. We were on our way to the Nutrition Center and we just wanted to wish our fellow eve a quick recovery," megan says, as full of crap as ever.

"I don't have time for excuses, #767," chastity-ruth says. "Leave immediately."

They get up to leave, megan ordering the twins to get changed before dinner.

"Maybe you can borrow isabel's smock. The two of you could fit easily in that thing."

"Bitches," I say under my breath once they've gone.

"I'll pretend I didn't hear that," chastity-ruth snaps, before continuing in a milder tone, "isabel, dear. It's time for you to leave too."

"I'm not hungry," isabel says. "I'll get something to eat later."

I flinch, waiting for chastity-ruth to explode at isabel's defiance, but she just nods her head in agreement.

"Fine. And as for you, #630, you are to report to me whenever you are in need of SleepSound. I'll ensure you receive an emergency stockpile to keep in your cubicle. We can't afford any further *incidents*," she says, her lips pinched. The Euro-Zone Doctor must have really done a number on her. "I shall expect you back in class tomorrow. You've missed far too much already."

She slams the door behind her. For someone who is so quiet sneaking up on you, she sure likes to make an exit. I sag down in the bed, my limbs feeling like dead weight. isabel clucks and pulls the covers up under my chin, neatly tucking the blanket in around me.

"Don't worry about chastity-ruth. I'll handle her."

"She always goes easier on you. You're the special one."

"I am not." isabel almost spits the words out in fury. "Take that back."

"Okay, okay. Calm down," I say, taken aback. "I'm sorry."

In the ensuing silence the *tick, tick, tick* of a clock fills the room and I yawn, my eyelids becoming heavy.

"Do you think megan is right? About the Inheritants coming soon?" I say sleepily.

She goes rigid, as if her bones are holding her hostage. I want to ask her what's wrong, but the words are in my head and I can't get them out, my tongue fat with drowsiness. She stands next to me again, stroking my hair softly, soothing me to sleep as if I was her own child, as if she loved me.

I dream of fields of lavender, of boys and of mothers. I dream of things I know nothing about.

Chapter 12

"It's pointless being here when I'm not allowed to use the machines," I moan, stretching out on the stationary treadmill, hoping I'll feel cooler if I lie down.

"Am I supposed to feel sorry for you?"

isabel is pedaling furiously on a rusted exercise bike; her hair is damp with sweat and sticking to her tomato-red face. She slows down to look over her shoulder at me and a warped robotic voice bellows from the bicycle spokes, mangling every second word. "*Go faaaaaster, you . . . idiot. You . . . but . . . but you . . . fat . . . fat . . . fat . . . Why . . . faa . . . GO FASTER.*" She picks up speed, the steel weights wrapped around her ankles blurring.

"They really need to fix that bike," I say.

We're in the chamber for our morning detention. A menagerie of gym equipment is squeezed into the circular sauna. It's so small that it can just hold a treadmill, an exercise bike and a locker to store our bags. Glowing electric heating grids line the ceiling. The walls are a 360-degree movie screen flashing inspirational images of #1 eves from previous years.

"Anyway . . ." she says. The screen has melted into a magnifying mirror, amplifying her reflection from every angle. She stares at it as if she's trying to find her old self underneath the excess flesh. ". . . this is your last day on detention."

I know. I'll miss you. Will you miss me?

"I can't remember being in here last week," I say instead.

"I should have known something was wrong when they showed an old interview from *What kate Did Next* on the screen and you kept asking kate why her hair was so shiny."

"I did not."

"You did! You even told her to answer quietly because you didn't want 'the others' knowing the secret too."

"What others?"

"Exactly, you lunatic," she says with a wheezing laugh, and I smile. Being sick was worth it if it means that we might be friends again. And if she keeps working out like this, she'll lose weight. She'll be pretty again, and popular. We can go back to the way things were before.

"You sound better today, freeds."

"I feel it."

Why wouldn't I? My SleepSound has been returned and chastity-ruth has given me an extra stockpile of supplies to make sure I don't become sleep-deprived again. I've started keeping a spare tablet in a silver locket around my neck, just in case of emergencies. I didn't even have to take my weekly foto this morning. I got to choose an old one from my archive to post instead, so my rankings should be unaffected.

"Less talking, girls. This is not a social group." A chastity's voice fills the tiny room.

"Sorry." We both squint at the mirror, wondering which chastity is hidden behind it.

"*The Eternal Fat girl!*" I say in disbelief as the mirror turns back into a movie screen. I use the frame of the treadmill to pull myself up to sitting position. "I haven't seen this in years."

"It's not actually called *The Eternal Fat girl*, you know."

I'm not listening, engrossed in the familiar story. The Wandering Fat girl travels from town to town, stealing sweets from Inheritants, shoving them in her mouth. She has no friends. She is always alone, eating and eating. "Fat girls are disgusting. Fat girls are lazy. No one will ever love a fat girl," the voiceover repeats over and over again.

"It doesn't even make sense," isabel puffs, pedaling faster and faster. "Why isn't she in School?"

"How many times have we seen this?" I ask her.

"Every day until we were seven . . ."

"And then we started Organized Recreation instead." I finish her sentence. "You have a good memory."

She can't find the breath to answer as she crouches over the handle bars. An oversized gray sleeveless tee is clinging to her sweaty body, her thighs jiggling in black leggings. They must be at least three sizes too small for her. *Fat girls should be made obsolete.* I thrust the thought away and lie back down on the belt of the treadmill, pulling my tank top up to the same height as my bra. I feel the bones of my ribcage, resting my fingertips in the cavities between them, holding my thinness to me like a comforter.

"isabel?" I say in a wheedling voice.

"Yes?"

"Can I borrow your computer?"

"Did you not get yours at breakfast? I saw chastity-ruth handing them back."

"Mine was the only one she managed to forget. Imagine that." Our eyes meet in the mirror. "She said she'd give it to me after class."

"Fine." She gives in. "It's in the locker. Keep the protective cover on it though. I don't want the steam to damage it."

"They're not toys," I say, mocking the chastities. "They're *expensive.*" I crawl over to the locker, wading through the heat. Grabbing the ePad, I droop back down on the belt, logging onto MyFace.

"Your inbox is at maximum capacity. Please delete some private messages immediately."

That's strange. I only had two saved messages when I checked my account yesterday. I click on the inbox, my jaw dropping as I scroll through icons for dozens and dozens of messages, some from months ago. Most of the recent ones are unopened and all of them have a gray blank box where the profile foto usually is. Anonymous accounts. Who would send me anonymous messages?

I put in the earbuds and click on the most recent one.

"No one likes you. Everyone wants you to die. Why don't you just kill yourself and get it over with?" says the distorted voice. I shut it off hurriedly, my heart pounding.

The profile foto at the top of the page. It's isabel's face. I steal a sneaky look at her, but she's engrossed in her work-out so I click on another message, and another and another, the same gray profile image filling the screen, the same disembodied voice like an ugly wound bubbling with pus.

"You are lazy and vile and the ugliest eve in our year."

"You make me want to vomit. You should do everyone a favor and kill yourself."

"Everybody hates you. You are disgusting. I wish you didn't exist. I wish you were dead."

I turn it off. My face is pale in the black screen.

"isabel . . ."

Anxiety tightens my throat. Who could have sent those messages? They're vicious, even for megan and the twins, and they couldn't have been acting alone. The quantity alone negates that possibility. Did cara send any? *agyness?* Why didn't isabel tell me what was going on?

I go cold. Does she think that I sent one?

"isabel," I say more urgently. I sit up, shuffling to the top of the treadmill and swinging my legs over the edge, holding on to the leg of the control panel. "isabel, stop cycling and talk to me for a moment."

"I can't," she pants.

"Why?"

"*What is wrong . . . you? . . . so useless . . . can't even ride a biiiiiike prop . . . ly? . . . back . . . biiiiike . . . you stup . . . fat . . .*"

"See?" She picks up speed again as the stuttering exercise bike screams at her.

"Are you trying to lose weight before the Inheritants come? Because who knows when they'll be coming? You can't trust what *they* say," I say, emphasizing the "they" in an attempt to distance myself from megan and the twins.

Her right leg slips, and she yelps out in pain as the pedal spins around and bashes into the back of her knee.

". . . *fat* . . . *stupid* . . ."

"You've got nothing to worry about!" I desperately want to be the antidote to all those poisonous messages. "You're beautiful, isabel. You're *special*. You've always been special. Everyone knows that."

"Don't say that." She stops, ignoring the robotic shrieking. (. . . *get baaaack* . . . *bike* . . . *instant, you uuuseless fat* . . .)

"Don't say what?" I'm bewildered. "What did I say?"

"Just stop. For once in your life, freida, can't you *just stop?*" Her voice cuts through me. I never get anything right. I am like a faulty toy that no one will ever want. No one will ever love.

I press my trembling lips together, fixating on the screen as it transforms back into the 360-degree mirror, remaining clear despite the steaming heat. I pull up my black running shorts and stretch my legs out, displaying them to her as a reprimand, wanting her to see how thin I am now, how my leg hollows at the thigh now, like freja's. *At least I'm thin.* isabel is staring at herself in the mirror, at the sweat patches staining under her arms and her crotch area. She clenches her fists, her jaw jutting out.

"I'm going."

"But the hour isn't up yet!"

"I know." She yanks the exercise bike lever off, silencing the garbled abuse, and snaps off her ankle weights, chucking them to the ground.

"I'll come with you." I wince as I bash my head against the control deck of the treadmill. "Please, isabel, I want . . ."

She grabs her bag from the locker and throws that well-worn black dress on over her workout gear. She comes toward me, lavender muddled with sweat, and snatches the ePad, stuffing it into her bag. And she's gone.

Another blast of cold air swashes through the room.

"The alarm went off," chastity-bernadette says. "Where is isabel?" She looks around the tiny room as if expecting to find her hiding behind one of the machines.

"She had to use the bathroom," I lie. "The kcal blockers were giving her cramps."

"Oh, right." She focuses her attention on me, her hooded eyelids drooping over violet-colored eyes. "Well, your hour is nearly up, freida, if you want to run along."

She must have forgotten that we're not supposed to use the bathroom when we're in the chamber. That's what happened to agyness in 6th year. She had been overpre-scribed ExoLax on the same day she had detention, so she was trapped in the chamber when the diarrhea hit. I always wondered why she didn't run for the bathroom—the doors aren't even locked. I guess it was fear that stopped her. It's always fear. The video footage of it got leaked somehow and it was all over MyFace within minutes. agyness, the pain imprinted on her babyish face as she tried to control herself, the shame when she failed. I tried to look away from the video but I couldn't. Some part of me had to see it for myself. She ran and ran and ran on that treadmill, feces trickling slowly down her tiny legs, staining her polka-dot socks and neon-pink sneakers. But she was a good girl. She didn't cry, not once.

As I'm waiting for class to begin, I idly count messy side braids. megan has moved on already, of course, to a glossy topknot, causing the others to pick fretfully at their freshly styled hair.

"Where's isabel?" cara whispers to me, winding her braid into a low bun at the nape of her neck, and I shrug.

"All final-year eves are to congregate in the Assembly Hall immediately," the intercom shrieks.

"Let's go, girls." chastity-theresa beams with delight at having class postponed. We move as one down the corridors, in the opposite direction to the garden, until we come to the Hall foyer, a white pebble-dashed circular room. In single file we walk through until there it is, space unfolding in all directions. The Assembly Hall is the biggest room in the school, with its high ceilings, expanse of floor, and a marble-lined stage extending for what seems like miles. Supposedly it was designed to be a replica of an opera house from Old-Europe, and it is very beautiful, but rarely used; they can't afford to refurbish any wear and tear.

We're whispering among ourselves, voices melting into the noise and restlessness. chastity-ruth climbs the marble steps onto the stage, the other chastities following and falling into a single line behind her.

"If you're *quite* finished . . ." chastity-ruth calls out, standing by the marble podium, but no one besides me seems to hear her. The screen at the back of the stage flashes images: the traditional triquetra of the thirds; the Father of the Euro-Zone lifting steel weights as easily as if they were cardboard; another of him surrounded by adoring women; murals of Adam and eve, the first woman created for man; the design laboratories, the Genetic Engineers looking up from their Petri dishes to wave at the camera; rows and rows of newly designed babies incubated in plastic wombs, waiting to hatch; a companion caring for her husband and sons—she is warm, loving, nourishing them with her beauty; then a concubine, her head thrown back in ecstasy, her lips and legs parted, ready to be ravished. We settle in our red velvet seats, the flickering images anesthetizing us into silence.

"Thank you," chastity-ruth says. The slideshow freezes on an image of the original Father beside a bonfire of pet dogs, hundreds of mournful eyes piercing the flames as ashes float through the air like snowflakes.

"Your Ceremony is mere months away. It is imperative that the correct choices are made and that each of you is placed within the appropriate third. All the theoretical knowledge that you have been taught during your sixteen years in School must now be put into practice." She pauses, knowing we are hanging on her every word. "Another element is to be added to your timetable. You will be introduced to the ten Inheritants that were born the same year that you were designed, the very men for whom you were created."

At the mention of the word "men," high-pitched chatter and laughter fills the vast Hall.

"Told you so," megan says to anyone who will listen, and I swivel in my chair, searching for isabel.

"Will you be nervous? The first time we meet the Inheritants?"

"No." isabel had just had a growth spurt, her legs and arms gangly, like pieces of elastic that had been stretched too far. *"Why would I be?"*

"They're boys."

"They're just people," she reasoned. *"I bet they will be more nervous than we are!"*

"Maybe."

"Don't worry, freida," she said softly. *"You're great. They'll all like you. I know they will."*

Dozens of hands fly up into the air, waving frenziedly at chastity-ruth. She leans over to chastity-anne. "You need to control this. Up their Organized Recreation dosage today." The other chastity nods in agreement.

"I will answer a few select questions," chastity-ruth says. "You may go first, #767."

"Will they be here every day?" megan preens at being selected first, any chance to draw attention to her #1 status welcome. "Will they stay in the School until the Ceremony?"

"No. They will travel via train from the main Euro-Zone on randomly selected days. You will not be informed in advance of either the day or the time of these visits."

"And will we get to spend more time with the Inheritant who matches our ranking?" megan continues, ignoring the other eves eager to ask questions.

"No. The men do not know how you are ranked, and you are forbidden to tell them. This is extremely important, girls. Anyone caught breaking this rule will be swiftly and severely chastised. Yes, #755."

"Speaking of our rankings, how is this going to affect them? Is the public vote on the School's website still going to count?" naomi fidgets nervously with the ivory lace headband holding her thick braid in place.

"Excellent question, #755. How very *intelligent* of you to ask," chastity-ruth answers. You can almost see her making a mental note to examine naomi's file for signs of previous "academic tendencies," and naomi hunches down in her seat.

"The answer is no. The public vote will now be rescinded. Your current rankings are null and void." She gives a spiteful little laugh. "They are meaningless, I guess you could say."

The Hall falls as still as a tomb, each of us mute with shock. It's as if she has ripped our skeletons from our bodies, smiling as the remaining flesh collapses in on itself. Meaningless? What was the point then? What was the point of all those sleepless Sunday nights, anxiety about the Monday foto writhing in our bellies? Sixteen years of being told that the rankings are *everything*, that they are our self-worth and the only indicator of our value. *Meaningless?*

"But why . . . ?" megan cries before clamping her mouth shut. Her face has turned sickly pale. She has clawed her way to the top and now she has been told it's meaningless.

"Why?" chastity-ruth says. "Because we can."

All of us ranked in the top ten look at each other in panic as chastity-magdalena clears her throat. "The Inheritants will select their favorite eve," she says, pretending she can't see chastity-ruth glowering at her, "so it's quite fair really."

daria turns to me with an uncertain hope that must be echoed on my own face. Surely the Inheritants will choose from the top ten? They're the ones who have been voting for us all this time, after all.

"Yes," chastity-ruth continues, "as I was going to say before I was so *rudely* interrupted . . ." chastity-magdalena dips her head—"the Inheritants will choose their favorite eve to become their companion. This will depend on how attractive you look to the Inheritants and how you perform in certain challenges and tests that will be set for you." She stares at us. "The men must have the right to choose. It is their future that is at stake."

"But what if more than one of the Inheritants picks the same girl?" megan asks, clearly predicting that at least nine of them will choose her.

"The highest-ranked Inheritant will have first choice." A low hum starts again and irritation crosses over chastity-ruth's face. "Enough," she says. "You will do as you are told." We fall silent again and she nods with satisfaction. "That's better. Now, we are going to watch a short introductory video about each Inheritant."

daria squeals and grabs my hand. We have grown so accustomed to being seen but never seeing in return. These men will have grown up judging our weekly fotos, comparing and ranking us. Our faces are probably as familiar to them as their own, yet they have always remained strangers to us.

The huge crystal chandeliers dim, an image of the Father on-screen disappears and a skinny, red-haired boy takes his place. He's struggling to catch his breath, his chestnut-brown eyes swinging from the camera to his feet.

"Hi, I'm Socrates Ortega, and I'm the Inheritant #10."

Everyone claps and whoops and chastity-ruth freezes the video. Socrates is caught at a rather unfortunate moment, his mouth hanging open. I can see something green in his back teeth.

"If you are not going to behave yourselves, I will turn off the video and you will return to classes immediately."

chastity-theresa looks alarmed at this. We shut up and the video resumes.

"My father is a cobbler, in charge of providing shoes to the people of the Euro-Zone and for the Accessories Closet in the School."

"A cobbler?" megan groans audibly.

According to how many sons are born in a given year, three times as many eves are designed to accommodate demand for companions and concubines. You could be lucky and be designed for a year when the Mayor and a Genetic Engineer and a Surgeon all had sons. Or we could all have been designed to be companions for the sons of grocers, cobblers . . . the meat-grower, for pity's sake.

"I'm going to take over the business when I'm old enough." Socrates's face is turning as red as his hair. "I like looking at old shoes, rare ones that are made from real leather. I don't like the material of the new shoes as much. Shoes are a really big passion of mine . . ."

Socrates ends his sermon on footwear and the rest of the introductory videos continue. #9, Abraham Pinault, is the son of the publican. He likes girls who do yoga because it makes them "nice and bendy." He also enjoys craft beers.

Mahatma, George, Isaac, William, Sigmund . . . It's funny to see the differences in their heights and weights and facial features. I look at the girls around me, at the uniformity in our perfection in comparison.

"Yes, so my father is a Doctor." A Doctor? My head snaps up. A boy with mousy-brown hair in a severe center parting is speaking, his Adam's apple bobbing up and down. Did he say his name was Leonardo?

"Is this the #1?"

"No," daria whispers back in delight. "Can you believe it? He's only #3!"

I'm barely listening as the #2, Albert Branson, a heavy-set fair-haired boy with flushed cheeks, discusses his passion for porn and three-way activities.

When Albert is finished, there's a drum roll, a deep voice announcing, *"And here is your #1!"*

And then he appears.

Wearing a short-sleeved T-shirt that shows off muscular arms, he looks straight into the camera as he runs a hand through his mop of dark curls. His eyes are the brightest blue I've ever seen and he mustn't have shaved in a couple of days, stubble shadowing his chin. He's *gorgeous*. He looks like he was designed, not born of a mere woman.

"I'm Darwin Goldsmith," he says. "My father is the Judge in the Euro-Zone's courts. I'm his only son."

I feel dizzy. He's handsome and rich and is destined to become one of the most powerful men in the Euro-Zone once his father retires.

"I'm looking forward to meeting all of you. You look beautiful in the fotos on the School's website and it should be fun getting to know one another. See you soon."

He rises to his feet, jeans slung low on narrow hips, and the screen goes blank. The room erupts into light and chatter. I can hear Darwin being mentioned, his name thrown from girl to girl like a game of Pass the Parcel, stopping at megan. She's surrounded, all the girls folding in toward her, assuming that he is destined to be hers. *Darwin. Darwin. Darwin.* Envy courses through my veins, thick as soured milk.

"Girls, please," chastity-ruth admonishes us. "I would remind you that the Inheritants are not to know of your previous rankings. I'm warning you, eves."

"Yes, #767?" she says as megan's hand shoots up again.

"Are you going to film introductory videos of us for the Inheritants to watch?" she says, her eyes sparkling with devilment.

"Of course not. All they need to see is how you look. A foto will suffice," chastity-ruth replies.

"Then I'm assuming isabel won't be submitting a foto."

"isabel is none of your concern, #767." megan dips her head, a small smile playing on her lips. "Oh, and one last thing—Please do not discuss any details of the Inheritants module with the younger eves; it might give them an unfair advantage when it comes to their own final-year Interactions." You can see some of the girls are struggling not to laugh. None of the eves in the years above us gave us any help or advice. Why would we offer it to anyone else?

chastity-ruth dismisses us, turning to speak with the other chastities. They form a circle, chastity-magdalena hovering on the outside as punishment for her earlier insubordination.

"But really, girls, do you think isabel should submit a foto? I don't want her to feel embarrassed because of her . . ." megan grimaces, the word sticking in her throat—"*obesity*." She makes her way toward the exit, the rest of us trailing after her. She stops at a large gilt-framed mirror at the side of the Hall, pulling her gray Lycra dress down her thighs, and she catches my eye in the mirror. I look away, staring at my reflection next to hers. My hair is still perfectly set in pin curls, my sleeveless orange wrap dress accessorized with chunky gold chains at my scrawny wrists and neck. I look the same as I did this morning. If

I look the same, why do I feel like this? Why do I feel as if there is limescale building up inside of me, clogging my air supply?

"What do you think, freida?"

"isabel's been trying really hard to lose weight."

"Well, she's obviously not trying hard enough, is she?"

Everybody hates you, nobody likes you. You are disgusting. I wish you didn't exist. I wish you were dead.

The memory of those MyFace messages tears through my brain, making me reckless.

"And why shouldn't she submit her foto?" I say. "Some of the guys might like girls who are curvier."

The tips of my ears are blazing as laughter breaks out at my stupid comment. "And . . . and . . ." I'm stuttering, desperate to say something that will make them shut up. "And she was #1 for years and . . ."

I stop myself just in time.

"What are you implying, freida?"

I look around at the others, looking for someone to accuse, someone to throw in the firing line in front of me.

"What is going on here?" chastity-ruth says, barging into the middle of the group, the other chasties walking in single file behind her. For the first time in my life, I'm relieved to see her.

"I see a lot of cross faces here. Do you all have some strange desire for an anti-age redesign by the age of twenty?" chastity-ruth says. "No one likes an angry girl. Are you teaching them how to manage their Unacceptable Emotions correctly, hope?" chastity-hope's moon-shaped face falls with embarrassment. "Nice girls don't raise their voices. Nice girls don't get angry. Control yourselves." chastity-ruth gestures at us to get out of her sight as quickly as possible.

"She's right," megan says as we walk back to class, closely followed by chastity-theresa. "Self-control is *so* important, don't you think? However lacking it may be in some people."

"Totally," jessie says. "I haven't even eaten dinner in two whole weeks." She's fingering her cream scalloped shorts, a half-moon-shaped purple stain seeping though the satin fabric. She sneaks a melted jelly from the pocket and pops it in her mouth, licking her fingers.

"It's a pity *some* people don't seem to agree," megan says as we take our seats in the classroom. "It's a pity *some* people seem to think they can do whenever they want. We all get tired. But not all of us skip class whenever we feel like it."

"I had to miss class," I say through gritted teeth. "I was unconscious in Sick Bay, megan. What was I supposed to do?"

"freida, have you something that you would like to share with the rest of the class?"

"No, chastity-theresa," I mutter, ears burning again.

"Then lower your voice." She closes the door behind her and limps to her seat. "As we only have five minutes left in class," she says, kicking her shoes off and reaching down to rub her feet, "you may quietly use your computers until the bell rings."

"I'm going to pretend you didn't speak to me like that, freida," megan mutters, still facing toward the front of the classroom.

"That's big of you," I say, keeping an eye on chastity-theresa.

"You're obviously under a lot of stress. And who can blame you?"

"If you have something to say to me, megan, just say it to my face." I sound a lot braver than I feel.

"I wasn't talking about you. There is no need to be so sensitive."

"Who were you talking about then?"

"isabel. Surely when I said 'lacking in self-control' you could have guessed." She and the twins snicker, coughing loudly to cover it as chastity-theresa looks up.

"isabel has been trying to be good," I say quietly, pretending to scan through images on-screen.

"Oh, I don't know about that. Has she *really* been trying, would you say?"

Everyone else has put their earbuds in as if they're listening to music or watching digi-vids, but I know they're all eavesdropping, afraid to miss out on any drama.

"She's committed to getting back to target weight."

"That's not what I heard," megan says in a sing-song voice, slicking some baby hairs at the nape of her neck into her bun.

"Oh, megan. Always so cryptic."

"What's that supposed to mean?"

"Nothing," I reply, giddy with daring. "No need to be *so sensitive.*"

"Well, if you don't believe me . . ." she says. "You have that video, don't you, liz?"

"Sure." liz pulls her fone from her pocket. There is an outbreak of muffled beeps in bags, flashes of light, the buzzing of eFones vibrating against wooden desks.

"liz," megan says, "I meant for you to send it to freida only."

"Sorry?" liz smirks, a conspiratorial look flashing between them.

I fumble for my fone with shaking hands, a chill prickling the back of my neck as I see everyone else in the class doing the same.

It's a digi-vid, about three minutes long. I watch as chastity-bernadette leaves the chastities' quarters, hands wagging fussily, forgetting to secure the gates. And there's isabel, sneaking in behind her, still wearing that black dress over her gym leggings, stringy hair clinging to her head. The camera cuts to the chastities' office. There is a large tray on the desk, containing triangle sandwiches with the crusts cut off. The camera zooms in on isabel's face as she stuffs the food into her mouth. She gags slightly, bringing up a chunky fluid, some of it spraying onto her leggings. She doesn't seem to notice, she just keeps shoving food in, even swallowing back down vomit-encrusted bread. Disgusted groans fill the classroom. Where did megan get this footage?

"Girls . . ." chastity-theresa raises her voice, looking as if she wishes she was anywhere else but here. "Girls, please be quiet."

I can see them all, ecstatic horror in their eyes, updating MyFace statuses on their eFones almost involuntarily, words whispering. *Disgusting . . . Obsolete . . . Worthless . . . Sickened . . .*

As the bell shrieks, I break into a run, ignoring chastity-theresa yelling, "Come back right now, young lady." At isabel's cubicle I'm faced with the corrugated steel wall and I grip the handle at the base of the door and roll it up forcefully. She's sitting on the floor, stripped down to her underwear, her stomach painfully distended. She's shoving chocco bars into her mouth, practically inhaling them. It looks like a trash pit in there, wrappers and crumbs littering the floor.

"Poor girl," isabel had sighed as we watched christy take a seat under chastity-ruth's desk for her supervised dinner and poke at a plate of salad leaves.

"Hmm." I wasn't really listening, staring at the piece of uneaten chocco cake in front of me, taunting me.

"I don't understand though," isabel continued, cutting up her veggies. "She keeps saying how fat she feels, yet every time I look at her she has a chocco bar in her hands. Why doesn't she just eat less?"

"She's weak." I shrugged, pretending that I didn't understand how the prickling of loathing at the sight of a spare pound of flesh in the mirror could send you running for a comforting piece of cake. I understood how sugar could numb the pain, but I didn't want to understand. I didn't want to understand christy's weakness.

"Here," I said desperately. "Do you want to share this piece of chocco cake?" I don't want to eat it alone.

"No, thanks," she said, without even glancing at the plate. "I don't really like chocco."

Of course she didn't.

"Yeah," I lied. "Me neither."

"isabel," I say to her now.

She looks at me, chocco smeared all around her mouth. She grabs at the wrappers, as if she can hide it, as if I can unsee what I've seen. I hold her flailing hands and she pulls away, hiding her face from me. Unsure what to do, I start picking up the empty wrappers, wrapper after wrapper after wrapper. There are so many of them.

"What are you doing, isabel?"

"I took them from the Fatgirl buffet."

"Oh, really?" My voice is acerbic. "Was this after you stole from the chastities?" She doesn't seem surprised that I know. "We saw the video footage. Everyone knows. *Everyone.*" I've got my hands tangled in my hair, pulling at the roots, nearly ready to rip it out of my head. "Why would you steal from the one fucking place in this School that still has cameras? Why, isabel? Did you want to get caught?"

She's motionless and her stillness composes me, easing my anger.

"You have to get rid of it."

"I'll do it later."

"No," I reply. I don't trust her to do what needs to be done. "We'll go to the bathrooms together now." She picks up the same black dress from the floor and pulls it over her head. "Don't you have anything else you can wear?" I say, pointing at the melted chocco on it.

"I only have this dress," she says quietly, picking at the stains. "They don't make a lot of girls' clothes in my size."

We walk quickly to the bathrooms, ducking inside as I hear the approaching clatter of footsteps. The two of us cram into the bathroom stall and isabel falls to her knees. Afterward she wilts, her face resting on the plastic toilet seat, her body totally limp. I rub her back but all I want to do is to run away from her, pretend that this has nothing to do with me. I feel her need like a black hole trying to consume me. She's going to make me weak too, even weaker than I am already. I won't survive.

"Why, isabel? Why are you doing this to yourself? To your body?"

And why are you doing this to me? is the awful, selfish thought that is left unsaid.

"Because I can," she answers, and I shiver as she unconsciously echoes chastity-ruth.

"But—"

"Because it's my body," she cuts in. "Isn't it?"

Neither of us moves. The silence is heavy, weighted with fear.

Chapter 13

"Come on, isabel. We can't stay here much longer."

It's been at least ten minutes since she has stopped throwing up, but she just stays there, slumped over the toilet bowl.

"The chastities will find us soon."

I assume the others have returned to class, although our fones keep pinging with alerts, messages we both ignore. I drag her up to a standing position. Her skin feels sticky, crusted with sweat and food crumbs.

"Hello, girls."

I swing the stall door open, and it's her.

"What's happening?" My voice squeaks with fear.

"That's none of your concern, #630." chastity-ruth turns to isabel. "Come now, isabel," she says almost lovingly, and a chill travels up my spine. "Come now, dear. We've talked about this."

I step in front of isabel.

"Playtime is over, #630. Time to leave." She points at the exit but I shake my head, refusing to go. isabel reaches out and takes my hand in hers, pulling me into a hug that says everything and nothing. I can see our reflection in the wall behind us, my arms wrapped around her puffy pale body as she shivers in a gray bra and underwear. She pulls away first, wincing as my bracelet catches in her hair.

"Just go, freida," she says. "I don't need you."

"But—"

"I said, I don't need you here."

She knows me, the true me. She knows that I am just an imprint of a real person. I am nothing.

I walk back to my room, alone.

It's been a week since she was taken and it's all anyone can talk about. Where did they take her, freida? Is she coming back, freida? They refuse to believe me when I say that I know as little as they do, and so the questions keep coming. Overnight I've become popular again, but I don't want it now. I didn't appreciate how easily I could melt into the background before, wrapping a fake social face over my head like cling wrap.

I left her there. I left her behind.

I do not know what they have done with her. I do not know where she has gone. The scene from the bathroom plays on a constant loop in my brain as I lie in a haze of SleepSound, burning my way through my emergency stockpile, taking one half tablet from the locket around my neck, then another half, and another, returning to chastity-ruth for refills whenever I run out. For once, all I do is sleep and yet I never feel rested, every dream stealing something from me.

"Stream TV."

I'm lying on my bed, flicking through channel after channel, the flashing colors blurring before my eyes.

"Redesigning! Gone! Wrong!"

There's a woman lying on an operating table. She looks like an older, skinnier version of isabel. Pale blond hair, seashell cheekbones, pearly teeth.

"Hello there!" Her voice is reed thin. "My name is natasha, I'm thirty-seven and I've given birth to seven sons."

Seven sons? That must be some kind of record. As a reward for her good behavior, her husband has been offered a free "companion vaginal redesign." He signs a release form giving permission for natasha to be shown on TV, smiling at the cameras. The anesthetist arrives into the operating room, jams a needle into an available vein without warning and her eyes flop back into her head. The camera zooms in on the Re-Designer as he begins, his EuroCola visor holding back his sparse gray hair, and I have to watch the rest through my fingers and with my legs tightly closed. If I were a man, I'd never be able to be a Medic.

The show cuts to natasha and the Re-Designer sitting in oversized sludgy green armchairs around a polished mahogany table laden down by cans of EuroCola. She's crossing and uncrossing her matchstick legs, pulling at her pink crocheted skirt, her whole body shaking except for rock-hard breasts straining against a pink T-shirt. Something tells me this isn't natasha's first redesign.

"Okay . . ." the Re-Designer pauses to adjust his glasses and peers at the computer screen in front of him, ". . . natalia. I'm afraid there were a few complications . . ."

"Complications?"

"Please, natalia, no need to raise your voice."

"natasha. My name is natasha."

He looks at her unsmilingly over the thin wire frames of his glasses and she cringes. "As I was saying, *natasha*, there were a few complications." He beckons her to the corner of the office, gesturing at her to stand on a raised wooden block in front of a full-length mirror. He pulls her skirt up around her waist and unravels the thick bandages swaddling her like a new-design's diaper. I blink once, twice, wondering if I am going crazy.

"These things happen unfortunately." The Re-Designer shrugs.

The camera zooms in on natasha as she leans closer to the mirror, searching for something that she will never find again. A hint of forbidden tears freezes over her pale green eyes, the fine lines and wrinkles becoming more pronounced as her face crumples with the effort to control her emotions. I turn it off. She's thirty-seven, I tell myself. Thirty-seven. She is only three years away from her Termination Date anyway.

"freida."

chastity-magdalena frowns as she takes in the debris of clothes and shoes strewn around my cubicle. I turn away from her, closing my eyes like a child playing Hide and Seek, hoping to make her disappear.

"I'm not going away until we've spoken," she says, and I blink at her reflection in the mirror behind me. Watching, watchers, watched. We're all watching each other.

"You look tired, freida."

"That sounds like something megan would say."

"Certain aesthetic standards must be upheld."

"And that sounds like something chastity-ruth would say." I draw my knees toward my chest and tuck my face in between them. "And anyway, it's Sunday. Surely I'm allowed to relax on the weekends."

The bed sags as she sits next to me, her cool hand on my left shoulder, pulling gently. Is this what the younger wave of chastities will be like, all touching and gentleness? Will agyness find herself giving out hugs next year, embracing iman or lena-rose as if she's their mother? chastity-magdalena is staring at my reflection in the wall, just another image of myself, one more image out of thousands and thousands that I've been presented with during my life, told this image is real, now this is real, no, this one and this one and this one. I'm constantly trying to match all the thoughts in my head with these images in front of me, trying to put all the pieces of myself back together until I'm complete, until I can feel whole.

The body in the mirror is thin, so thin you can see her ribs through her dirty tank top. Her hair is in a matted ponytail, dark circles under sunken eyes that look as if they have been smudged in with charcoal. *That's me, that's me, that's me.* And a chastity has her hand on me, touching me, as if she's my mother, as if she likes me, as if I'm worthy of being liked.

Something breaks inside me and I am bent over with the cruelty of this grief, a grief so strong I don't even know who or what it is for. Tearless sobs rack my body for a few seconds until I breathe in deeply, swallowing the feelings back down to their prison inside me.

"Sorry." I slam the heels of my hands into my eye sockets. "I wasn't crying. I wasn't."

"When did you last wash?"

"Friday."

"You've had meals looking like this?" she says in dismay.

"No. I haven't left my room all weekend."

"Attendance at all meals and classes is mandatory unless you're ill. Have you been ill? Should you be back in the Sick Bay?"

"I'm fine. I'm just not hungry."

"Have you spoken with chastity-anne? How have you been getting your meds?"

"I have a stockpile of SleepSound. chastity-ruth gave extra supplies to me after I fainted in the Nutrition Center."

"What?" Her high-pitched yelp frightens me out of my dreamy state. "But SleepSound is supposed to be carefully monitored at all times." She jumps to her feet, as if to leave and confront chastity-ruth right away.

"I'm sorry. That's not what I meant." She can't take my meds away. *She can't.* "I'm tired. I'm talking nonsense. What I meant to say was chastity-anne brings me my SleepSound at night, and if I'm still having difficulty sleeping I ask whichever chastity is on night duty if I can be prescribed another dose. It's all very safe." She doesn't look convinced. "You've done it yourself, remember?"

She ignores this. "chastity-ruth knows you've been in your bedroom, alone, all weekend? And she hasn't insisted that you attend meals or Organized Recreation?"

"Maybe they want to keep me away from the rest of the eves, for fear I might contaminate them."

"Don't be silly."

"Why is it silly? Look what happened to isabel."

"Believe me, you have nothing to do with isabel's problems."

"What do you mean by that?"

"Nothing." A smoothness melts over her face until she resembles all the other chastities so precisely it's eerie. "I know what happened with isabel is challenging for you," she says, ignoring my snort, "but I promise you she's safe."

"Where is she? She's not gone . . ." my breath catches and I whisper, "*Underground,* has she?"

Once they take you there, there's no coming back.

"No, of course not." chastity-magdalena is aghast at the mention of the word. "They're going to fix her up. She will be as good as new when you see her again."

Like she's a doll that needs her face repainted.

"Please, freida, don't worry. Certain people are too invested in isabel to allow her just to self-immolate."

"What people? What are you talking about?"

"Stop." Her mouth is set in a determined line and I can tell there's no point in pushing it further. "You know she's safe. You don't need to know anything else."

What did I think was going to happen? That we were going to build a fort with my bedding and tell each other secrets? For all of her attempts to be the "nice" one, she's still a chastity. She reaches out her hand to pat me again but I move away, glaring at her.

"I'm sorry I can't give you what you want."

"I don't want anything from you," I lie again.

"isabel won't be happy when she returns to find you've fallen to pieces in her absence. You're absolutely emaciated."

"I doubt she'll care. But thanks."

"It's not a compliment," she says in exasperation. "You need to shower, change your clothes and you need to start on a weight-restoration plan."

"I'm not hungry."

"I don't care whether or not you're hungry, freida. If you don't eat, you're going to die. And more importantly, men don't find skinny women attractive. The target weights have been specifically set for that reason."

"Whatever."

"Don't 'whatever' me. The Inheritants will be here next week. I doubt any of them will choose a walking skeleton as their companion."

"I thought we weren't to know when the Inheritants were coming. Aren't you ruining the element of surprise, chastity-magdalena?" I taunt her, frustrated that she would tell me this but refuse to give me any concrete information about isabel. "Anyway, I don't care about stupid boys."

"Yes, you do," she says knowingly. "You do."

I turn away, touching my locket necklace, starving for what's inside, but I can't open it until she's gone. I curl up into a ball again, screaming at her in my head to go. I feel as if someone has hacked my hands off and the dying nerve endings are on fire, twitching, searching for something that is just out of reach. *Please go. Please go. Please go. Please go.*

And finally she leaves. I crack open the locket, cursing when I find it empty. I rummage in my bedside locker, searching for the bottle of SleepSound chastity-ruth gave me at the start of the weekend.

But it's all gone. Nothing left now, when I need it the most.

I throw the empty SleepSound bottle at the wall of my cubicle in fury, wishing that it would break the mirrors into millions of pieces. I would search among the shattered shavings of glass for the perfect one, the sharpest one. I would open my veins with it.

"However many Inheritants are born in any given year, it shall be necessary to design three times as many eves to satisfy demand. Once of age, the Inheritants will choose the most suitable eves as their companions. The remaining girls shall become concubines. In the uncommon event of an eve failing to prove attractive to the Inheritants, said eve will be inducted into the third of the chastities."[3]

---

[3] *Audio Guide to the Rules for Proper female Behavior*, the Original Father

Chapter 14

March
Four months until the Ceremony

". . . and from the top. One, two, three, four . . ." chastity-bernadette yells, clicking her fingers in time with the pounding music as we do our final run-through. The others are brimming with nervous energy, but I want to lie down somewhere, take a nap and wait for all that food to digest. chastity-magdalena escorted me to the Fatgirl buffet at lunch and handed me a large plate of pasta in a chunky sauce, a hot fudge brownee for dessert and a can of EuroCola to wash it all down. *500 kcals, 600 kcals, 700 kcals, more.* I don't know how much longer I can stand this weight-restoration plan.

"Come on." freja nudges me forward and I stumble after daria and attempt to pirouette at the front of the stage.

"And five six, seven, eight . . ."

freja, in a black thong bikini and black court shoes, comes from behind me. Her makeup is perfect, tanned glowing skin and iced-pink lips, but she's wearing her sash back to front and you can't see her design number. I should tell her, I should, but it seems like too much effort. She joins the rest of us on the other side of the stage, chastity-bernadette still manically clicking her fingers until all twenty-nine eves have been presented. isabel has been excused, once again.

"Okay, girls, take a five-minute break."

I crawl down the marble steps as black clouds swirl in my head, almost blinding me. Throwing myself onto a velvet chair, I feign sleep until someone pokes my shoulder roughly.

"Hey." I straighten up, folding my arms across my distended tummy. They're striking identical poses, right leg cocked out to the side, left hand on hip, tousled hair falling over the left shoulder. They're even wearing similar string bikinis, megan in flaming red, the twins in pink with white polka dots.

"Your legs are so skinny!" liz says for about the hundredth time today.

"So skinny," megan agrees loudly, one eye on freja. "You are the skinniest girl ever. You're by far the skinniest girl in our class now."

"Not for long," I say as freja looks suicidal at the thought of someone stealing her identity as the thinnest eve in 16th year. "I'm on a weight-restoration plan. You saw how much I had to eat at lunch."

"Pity isabel isn't here today," jessie says. "You would be like Little and Large. Right, megs?"

"Thanks for the suggestion." I smile brightly at jessie before megan can respond. "But isabel is going to be back soon." I pause. "And she'll be *thin* again."

And the last time she was at target weight, she was #1.

"Certain people are too invested in isabel to allow her to self-immolate."

"What's that supposed to mean, freida?" megan's eyes narrow.

"Just something I heard."

"What does self-momolate mean?" liz asks, shaking her hair out to give it extra volume.

"Shut up," megan says, and liz falters, instinctively moving toward jessie for comfort. Their bodies meld into one and jessie wraps her arm around her twin's waist and squeezes tight. It must be nice having someone that you can trust.

The main lights in the Assembly Hall dim and a huge spotlight illuminates the center of the darkened stage.

"Okay, eves, get into formation. It's showtime!" chastity-bernadette yells over the high-pitched squealing, herding us to stage right. We huddle around the Spy-Cam screen embedded in one of the marble pillars backstage, watching as the gold-plated double doors to the Hall open, allowing men, real-life *men*, into our lives for the very first time. chastity-ruth leads the way, the Inheritants following behind her in single file. Two of the boys—Leonardo and Albert, I think—are trying to trip each other up, mouths falling open in giddy laughter. I can tell chastity-ruth is furious, fingers gripping onto the sides of her cloak, but she doesn't say anything. Darwin's lips move and they stop immediately.

"What did he say?" miranda, one of the midranking eves, moans. Even when she's sulking, little dimples are still visible on her heart-shaped face. "I wish these stupid screens had sound!"

"They can't . . ." megan begins, and we all finish her sentence, ". . . afford to fix them!"

"Stupid Zone." She frowns, then quickly touches her forehead and pulls it taut to stop any wrinkles forming.

The Inheritants take their seats in the front row, the Spy-Cam moving slowly from Socrates all the way up to Darwin. There is a collective sigh when his face fills the screen. The camera falls back to encompass all ten of them, and it's obvious how excited most of them are, squirming in their seats, talking so loudly we can almost hear them backstage. But not Darwin. He leans back in his chair, stretching, his black sweatshirt rising so that I can see a flash of taut stomach, and a shiver of unfamiliar heat runs through me.

The other eves begin limbering up, stretching their hamstrings, practicing their smiles. The whispers of the girls and the booming echo of chastity-ruth's introductory speech to the Inheritants break like waves in my ears.

We can see each girl making her entrance on the Spy-Cam, the camera then cutting to show the Inheritants' reactions, all of them fidgeting with scorecards on their eFones, ranking us once again. *abbey, adrianna, agyness, alessandra* . . . Swaggering up the catwalk, sashes perfectly in place across their pneumatic chests, they pause at the end and pirouette as rehearsed. chastity-ruth calls out their design numbers, struggling to be heard over the Inheritants' whooping cat-calls. *christy, cindy, cintia, daria* . . .

"#630."

And then it's my turn.

I can't move. A pair of hands shoves me roughly onto the stage, and I blink in the spotlight. The sudden lull is deafening as I walk unsteadily to the front of the stage, the stiletto heels like shards of glass under my feet.

"I'm not into skinny girls."

"You would cut yourself open on those hip bones."

Embarrassment is filling my lungs like water.

Don't cry, don't cry, don't cry.

"Shut up," a low voice says.

"But I was only—"

"I said shut up," the voice repeats.

I can't see who it is, but I've watched his Introduction video enough times to recognize the voice.

"I think she's cute."

I stumble into a heap at the side of the stage once I'm safely out of sight.

"What happened?" cara asks, pulling me back so that the other eves can pass us. I can't answer her, adrenaline hammering through my body. I sit up against one of the marble pillars, folding my head between my knees and closing my eyes, willing my heart to slow down. How am I

going to explain what happened to chastity-ruth? I can hear
the loud screaming and clapping, chastity-ruth's voice like
a scythe through it, then the hustle of the Inheritants leaving, chattering about their favorites. megan's name is mentioned a lot. She will be pleased. A hand jabs at my ribs.

"What did Darwin say about you?" megan says, her
green eyes glittering dangerously.

"What?"

"Don't play dumb with me. You were like a corpse out
there until he said something."

"You couldn't hear what he said on the camera?"

"You know they don't have sound."

"I don't know, megan."

"Are you trying to tell me you didn't hear what he said?"

"It was nothing."

"You're right. I'm sure it is nothing." She reaches inside
her bikini top and pulls out an elastic hair tie, gathering
her gleaming mane into a high ponytail. "Right, freida?"

"Right?" I answer tentatively.

She squeezes my knee in response, so tightly it feels as
if she's crushing bone. I almost gasp in pain but somehow
manage to keep it in, hugging it deep inside me, nodding
to show her that I understand what she's trying to tell me.

I think she's cute.

That night as I lie in bed I replay the scene over and
over in my mind, repeating his words like a mantra until
I fall asleep without taking SleepSound for the first time
in years.

Chapter 15

"If liu asks how her stupid ass looked during her presentation one more time, I will *literally* punch her in the face. Why does she even care? Her rankings suck." megan slams her tray down, GreenClean juice jumping out of the glass and slopping onto the table.

"Please be more careful, megan. Those tables are expensive," chastity-magdalena says as she floats past.

"I bet in the Americas they're not told to be careful of stupid tables," megan mutters, taking a wet wipe from her makeup case to mop up the spill. "Anyway, liu is like, #27. Anyone lower than fifteenth place is dead to me."

So much for the rankings being "meaningless."

"Oooh, you look amazing, megs!" the twins scream, appearing in a haze of perfume and swishing ponytails. megan's hair is tied loosely at the nape of her neck, a few curls falling around her face and a slash of red lipstick on her lips. Her long-sleeved polo-necked top is completely sheer, intricate black lace covering her chest. Skin-tight pleather leggings complete the look. Evidently I'm not the only one taking extra care with my wardrobe choices these days, examining myself from every conceivable angle, trying to figure out what Darwin might see if he was looking at me.

"I know," she answers complacently. "Oh, sorry, liu, you can't sit there."

liu hovers above the seat next to me, her tray already on the table. A blush breaks out across her porcelain skin, her sloe eyes uncertain.

"But there are three seats free . . ."

cara, wearing a tissue-thin white T-shirt tucked into a silver chain-mail skirt, claims one of them, groaning when she lifts the tureen lid and sees today's 0-kcal option is cabbage soup again. liu stares at the remaining two seats and I start shredding my bread roll into tiny pieces.

"We're saving those for daria and gisele."

liu looks across the Nutrition Center to where daria and gisele are sitting behind a group of 14th years, huge platters of salad in front of them, but she doesn't say anything. She gets up to leave, knocking megan's makeup bag as she does so, and it hits the ground with a clatter. liu dives to rescue the makeup rolling across the floor with a panicked, "Oh my Father, megan, I am so sorry." No one else moves. We all just watch as she kneels at megan's feet, gathering up the numerous lipsticks and eyeliners and compacts of face powder as fast as she can. Finally she places the little bag back on the table, her face on fire.

"Thanks, liu-liu," megan says without looking at her, smirking as the twins struggle to stifle their laughter.

"You are such a bitch!" jessie exclaims with relish when liu has gone.

"Whatever. I can't listen to her discuss her ass during my lunch hour. It'll put me off my food."

"Could be a useful diet aid," jessie says, making a big show of replacing the lid over her meal even though she hasn't touched it, waiting for someone to comment on her will power.

"Are you saying I need to diet?"

"No, of course not," jessie says, aghast. "You're perfect."

"I know," megan says again. "Anyway, liu is so fake. She doesn't have to worry about her weight. Everyone knows those people can't get fat."

"What do you mean, 'those people'?" I blurt out.

"It's a compliment." She sniffs at my lack of understanding. "You are so sensitive."

In my reflection in the table, I can see patches of brown breaking out through the pale makeup I requested to be layered on this morning and I feel a rusty shame twist inside me.

"I'm glad that she's not sitting with us . . ." liz rushes to please megan—"if that is all she can talk about. Right, megs?"

"Yeah," megan replies, eyes swinging like a pendulum from the wall to the desktop, back to the wall again. It's as if we only exist in the surface of a mirror. "Can you believe that it's been three days since the Inheritants' visit?" she says, twirling a curl around her finger. "Do you think they'll be back soon?"

I look at cara, swallowing a smile. liu isn't the only one struggling to find other topics of conversation.

"What the . . . ?"

"What is it?" liz asks, startled, but jessie just points toward the door behind me. liz follows her gaze, her soup spoon falling to the table with a loud clatter. I look behind me too, shock kicking me in the stomach.

megan, engrossed in fixing any smudges of lipstick after her lunch, is the last to see her. She sits up as if an electric current has shot through her spine.

"It's isabel."

"She looks amazing," liz sighs. "Well, she does," she says, as megan glowers at her.

She's standing at the door, talking with chastity-magdalena. Her hair is longer—extensions, I guess. It's blonder too, falling in thick icy waves to her elbows, a messy braid across the crown of her head. And she's *slim*, her bare arms and legs slender and lightly tanned. She looks exactly like she looked last year, before all the damage. For a minute I forget that it's isabel. All I know is that it's another one. Another competitor.

"isabel!" megan yells, attracting the attention of every other eve in the dining room. isabel is rooted in the doorway, and a petite 4th year with tightly coiled brown curls leaps off her stool and scampers over and pats isabel's legs with one hand, the other covering her jam-stained mouth. isabel crouches down, laughing as the little girl strokes her hair with sticky fingers until chastity-magdalena shoos her back to her table.

"I love children, don't you?"

"Yes," I answered, *as I had been trained to do.*

"Someday, freida, we'll have three sons each. And they will be the best of friends forever. Just like us."

I get to my feet.

"It's so good to see you, isabel," I say, wrapping my arms around her. Her body is stiff against mine and I loosen my grip, embarrassed.

"You look great," I say. "How are you?"

I have so much I want to tell her. I've missed you. I've been so afraid. I made a fool of myself in front of the Inheritants. I'm sorry that I felt jealous of you. Please, please forgive me. I want us to be friends. The best of friends forever. Do you remember? Three sons each, right? But it's too much. The words fill my mouth like marbles, crammed too tight for them to escape.

She moves away, grabbing a tray from the BeBetter buffet and collecting her meds from chastity-anne. We walk together toward the tables, just out of step.

"isabel, welcome back!" megan calls again. Everyone is watching us. I sit down, using megan and the twins as a shield against the stares, throwing my eFone into my bag so that isabel won't hear the sudden outbreak of message alerts.

"And what a coincidence, we're practically twins!"

I hadn't noticed, but isabel is wearing the same top as megan, except with a tight black skirt and patent multi-buckled spike heels.

"We should upload fotos onto Who Wore It Best?" megan says with ill-advised confidence. Up close, isabel looks even better than before. They've dyed her eyebrows a dark brown, similar to cara's, and her skin is dewy. megan, whom I thought beautiful just five minutes ago, seems overdone in comparison.

"Sit with us," megan says.

"No, thanks." isabel moves to a nearby table, the only girl in the Nutrition Center sitting by herself. There's a shocked silence before megan recovers and says, "Oh, no—do you think she's fighting with you, freida?"

"What?"

"Well, she didn't want to sit with you," megan continues loudly.

isabel must be able to hear her, but she doesn't contradict her. She just toys with her straw, covering the rest of her food with the tureen lid as if the very sight of it sickens her.

"Is that all she's having for lunch?" liz whispers.

"Surely she should to be back on normal portions by now, right?" jessie says.

My own tray is almost cleared, my soup and bread roll demolished. How many kcals were in that?

isabel takes a halfhearted sip, grimacing as she swallows.

"I bet she's sore from . . ."

". . . stomach-pumping . . ."

". . . I heard . . ."

". . . no, I heard . . ."

She stands, dumping her lunch in the large waste-disposal tube on the way out, ignoring the pits of silence when she is near, the outbreak of whispers once she has passed like the Wave in an arena. The door to the Nutrition Center closes behind her.

"Be quiet." chastity-ruth cuts across the sudden roar of voices. "Control yourselves."

"Can you *believe* that? What the——"

"Do you think I have fine lines under my eyes?" megan interrupts liz, pulling her temples taut in the mirror. "Skin-Care have just released a new study in the Americas-Zone proving that they form underneath the skin from age twelve."

"What?" liz screams, pressing her face down on the desktop until she is about an inch away from the mirror. "But I can't see any."

"You can't see them yet," megan says. "They're hidden underneath your skin until you leave School and then they just appear. Out of nowhere. They had to specifically develop a new eye cream to fight it: Juveneyle." She pulls out a small tube in the gold mosaic of the SkinCare range from her clutch.

I push my tray away.

"Where are you going?" megan demands.

"Hopefully to the Vomitorium after eating all those carbs." jessie wags her finger at me. "Naughty, naughty."

"Come on," cara says, fiddling with her charm bracelet. "freida's still recovering from being ill."

"Yes, jessie. I'm on a weight-restoration plan because I'm underweight at the moment." My gaze lingers just a little too long on her tanned thighs peeking out from under the table. "It's something you couldn't *possibly* understand."

I grab my satchel and make an exit before the twins can find a spare brain cell between the two of them to retaliate. My eFone is still pinging persistently. Grabbing it from my bag, I quickly log onto MyFace, ignoring all the Video-Chat requests and voicemails. karlie has uploaded a video of isabel's entrance, spliced with the newest song from the slutz. "*Big girls . . . don't get the guy-yi-yi . . . don't get the guy.*" karlie's voice-over: "Well, well, doesn't look like she's such a big girl anymore, does it?"

I click on a foto of me hugging isabel, spindly arms creeping out of my Breton-striped T-shirt dress, even more wretched in comparison to isabel's toned limbs. "Looking hot, isabel," rosie has commented. She didn't say anything about me.

"isabel."

I can barely see her, the black outfit a perfect camouflage in the dimly lit corridor, but I catch a flash of blond hair as she turns the corner toward the dorms.

"isabel," I call as I chase after her. I reach out to grab her arm, yanking her back.

"Didn't you hear me?"

Her eyes are clean, unseeing, and she moves away from me.

"isabel!"

"What do you want?" Her voice is glacial, the frost crawling up her throat and hardening in her eyes.

"I wanted to see you." I'm flustered. "I've been so worried . . ." I trail off at the look on her face. "Are you okay?" I reach out to touch her hand, and she flinches.

My voice drops to a whisper. "Did they do something to you?" I'm afraid to ask. I'm afraid to know.

"Now?" she spits, rubbing her eyes, and I want to tell her to stop or she'll get crow's feet. "Now you ask me if I'm okay?"

"I don't understand . . . I don't . . ." I stutter. "I thought that we were friends again. I don't understand why . . ."

"No." Her voice cracks. "You don't understand."

"Then tell me. How am I supposed to help you if you won't tell me what's wrong?"

"Forget it."

"Forget it?" I'm shouting now, my voice booming in the empty corridor. "So this is my fault, is it? I'm not the one who buried herself in her room for two months. I'm not the one who thinks that she's so important, so much better than everyone else that she has to keep secrets all the time."

She laughs, a shrill joyless sound that scratches my heart. She doesn't care. She doesn't care about me or our friendship.

I will *make* her care.

"It's not my fault you're such a fat greedy bitch that they had to put you into quarantine. Do you know what everyone was saying about you?" The words are spewing from my mouth, hot as vomit. "Everybody hates you; nobody likes you. You are so disgusting that we all wish you didn't exist. We wish you were dead."

She starts, recognizing the anonymous hate message left on her MyFace page and I see the real isabel behind the mask, my isabel. She thinks *I* sent them, and she's looking at me as if she's never seen me before in her life, like I'm a total stranger. And I can't take it back. I can never take it back.

"isabel, I'm sorry, I didn't—"

She shoves me with such force that I fall to the floor, involuntary tears springing to my eyes as she walks away. At the sound of clacking heels approaching I jump up and lean against the black wall, breathing deeply to compose myself.

"Where's isabel?" cara asks me, arm in arm with megan, jessie and liz following closely.

"I couldn't catch her."

"Have you been *crying*?" jessie asks, her face brightening.

"No." They look at me doubtfully. "I haven't! I just twisted my ankle running in these stupid shoes."

"Well, those shoes are pretty stupid." cara grins at me.

"Come on, we're going to be late for class," I say, making a face at her.

"You know, I'm not trying to be a bitch . . ." megan begins. "I mean this in the nicest possible way, but I'm not that keen on isabel's new makeover. Like the eyebrows? Everyone knows eyebrows are cara's thing."

"I don't mind," cara says with a shrug, ever the peacemaker.

"Well, yours are nicer anyway," megan says, and cara goes pink with pleasure.

We're nearly at the classroom when she turns to me. "Maybe you can talk some sense into isabel, tell her to start eating her meals. What's the point in going skinny this late in the year?" I nod, paranoia squeezing my smile. "I mean, obviously you're skinny, freida," she says, "but you're trying so hard to get back to target weight. Proud of you!"

She gives me a hug to reinforce how proud she is and then breaks away, staring into my eyes. "But isabel—she's just weird. I mean, you know her better than anyone. She's weird, isn't she?"

With one word I can cast off my itching guilt like a snake shedding its skin.

"Weird," I agree, another word that can never be taken back. She smiles, perfect teeth glinting.

As we walk into class, I see isabel seated in the front row and I forget myself, pausing at her desk like I always used to.

"freida! Come sit with me!"

The twins move seats obediently so that megan can snuggle up to me, resting her head on my shoulder. I'm instantly anxious. I'm afraid that my shoulder might be too hard or I might be doing it wrong, that she'll keep her head on my shoulder for the whole of class or, worse, that she'll stop and never do it again.

"I missed you!" she coos. Yes. Those five seconds we were apart must have been torture.

I watch the rest of the girls spilling into the room. There is an almost imperceptible pause, their eyes darting between isabel and the rest of us. It's like a documentary on the Nature Channel, wild animals sniffing the air to determine who is the alpha. They want to know where they should place their loyalties.

megan waits until everyone has settled into their seats. "I hope you don't mind, isabel, but I uploaded our photos onto Who Wore It Best." isabel stretches her arms overhead and yawns. "And I got eighty-seven percent of the votes so far! I think the pleather leggings look more modern, you know?"

"But how . . ." agyness starts, and cara elbows her in the ribs to shut her up.

"Something to think about. I'd hate for you to do badly with the Inheritants due to poor clothing choices." megan is so sweet, no one could accuse her of being nasty. Not that any of us would be brave enough to do so anyway.

"That is such good advice," jessie says, cocking her head to the side and gazing at megan in admiration.

"For sure," liz reiterates.

"Yeah. For sure," I say, playing my new part. The classroom expands with a sigh as the hierarchy is clearly defined. We don't like uncertainty. Our rankings may have been deemed obsolete, but somehow they have never felt more important. My stomach shudders, bellowing flames of fear to my heart.

isabel.

If she just looks at me, even once, I'll know that she cares and I'll be sorry and I'll apologize and I'll get up and walk over and sit in that empty chair beside her. Anything would be better than her indifference. It's as if she always expected this from me.

Look at me, isabel. See me. But her eyes remain fixed on the tiled floor, avoiding the mirrors although they can hold no fear for her now that she is beautiful again.

A shadowy outline melts into the corner of my eye, black robes swishing past. Once again we did not hear her arrive, the rubber soles slithering silently, so different from the clatter of our high heels. She casts her gaze around the room, noting our new seating arrangements with a raised eyebrow. A shiver of numbness runs its tongue up my spine and I tell myself I don't care about isabel. I don't care either.

"eves," chastity-ruth says, "shall we begin?"

Chapter 16

April
Three months until the Ceremony

After that, the Inheritants start visiting the School three times a week, coming from the main Zone by train. Because we're never quite sure when they'll arrive, everything tastes of anticipation, as if our excitement has bled into the water, the food, the air we breathe.

The Euro-Zone sends in a medical expert to examine us. He spreads my legs apart, shoving a rod-like instrument deep inside me, ignoring my gasp of pain. "Better get used to it, sweetheart." He winks at me, marks me as satisfactory, and issues me my fertility certificate.

The Inheritants sit during our PE classes as we grind our hips, gripping a steel pole with our thighs. They watch as we cook dinner and as we sew a loose button back on a shirt, all pointless tasks as we have machines to do them now, but apparently it will give them clues to "our nature," which third we are best suited to. At the end of each visit we are ushered into a new classroom, one we have never used before. It's a round room, with walls covered in cream embossed paper and ten individual stations dotted around in a semicircle. Each station has a small wooden desk with two steel-framed office chairs on either side. The Inheritants claim their places, their backs to the wall, while we eves move from one desk to the next, a shrill bell signaling the end of each Interaction.

"How could you have said that?"

"What?" rosie hitches her red PVC skirt up even higher in the bathroom's full-length mirror until I see a flash of black lace underwear. At least she's wearing underwear. Her black crocheted tank clearly broadcasts her decision to forgo a bra.

"I overheard your Interaction with Sigmund. He told you that King Solomon fable and you said that you would have cut the baby in half! He's never going to want you to bear his sons after that."

"freida, my darling." She looks at me pitifully as she washes her hands. "Not everyone wants to be a companion. They get terminated at forty. Do you know what forty looks like? Have you looked at chastity-bernadette lately?"

"That's just the chastities." With a shudder I picture the loose skin sagging at chastity-bernadette's jawline. "As a companion you'd get an Age Redesign. You might be forty, but you would only look twenty."

"But you would still be forty," she says, pouting at her reflection. "You would still be old."

The classroom is breaking apart with noise now that the Inheritants are here today, the eves getting louder and louder, screaming over one another to laugh the hardest at the boys' jokes, but I have lost my voice in the din, my legs jittering with adrenaline.

"Hey," Mahatma says, grinning broadly as I sit opposite him for our Interaction. He is brown-skinned, like me, his eyebrows like two black caterpillars over deep-set brown eyes, small ears sticking out at right angles. His prominent nose appears to have been reset badly after a break, veering to the left at the tip.

"Hi." My mouth is already drying up. Yesterday I watched the Introduction videos again, rehearsing relevant conversational topics for each Inheritant, but now my mind is like a black hole. We've been sitting in silence for at least two minutes when megan struts past in sprayed-on jeans and a cropped vintage T-shirt, an inch of tummy flashing between. She looks as if she's oblivious, but I can tell that she knows she's creating a stir, her eyes trained steadily on a point in the middle distance. Mahatma gulps, still dazed as the bell rings and I move on, heavy with my inadequacy.

I just can't seem to forget that they're not girls, as stupid as that sounds. Their very differences seem so alien that all I want to do is stare at them, take countless fotos to scrutinize later, learn them all by heart. Can they tell how dry my mouth is? It feels as if my lips are cracking as I drag them into a smile. I go back to my dorm after each visit and

practice. I look at myself from every angle, trying to figure out what I would have looked like from the left or the
right. Did I look prettier when I was smiling or when I was
concentrating? What did my legs look like in my leotard
when I was hanging upside down from the stripper pole? I
play the Interactions over and over in my head, like a spinning wooden top. But it's always my Interactions with *him*
that I return to, taking my favorite memories out of their
box to look at, to admire.

Interaction 4: Darwin told me I looked pretty in my
yellow halter-neck dress.

Interaction 5: I felt dizzy when I stood up too quickly so
Darwin gave me the last of his can of EuroCola, watching
in concern as I gulped the drink down, a rush of sugar and
shock fizzing through me.

Interaction 1: "Hi, I'm Darwin," he said, and I fought the
urge to laugh. How could he think I wouldn't know his name?

"I'm freida."

"Oh." His eyes crinkled. "I know who you are. I've been
excited about finally meeting you."

I couldn't sleep that night, thinking about what "finally"
could have meant. The other girls post detailed descrip-
tions of their Interactions on MyFace, wondering about the
meaning behind every sigh and flicker of eyelids, but for
once I stay silent, unwilling to share.

"How fascinating," megan says. We're in the Interaction room again and she's tapping her fingers against the

wooden desk, visibly bored. Albert's story of his most recent escapades with two concubines must not be to her liking. He frowns and megan pales, reaching her hand out to cover his.

"I am so sorry," she says silkily. "I'm jealous, imagining you with other girls. I'm not normally this possessive. You must bring it out in me."

He puffs his chest out, accepting her apology with a bow of his head, and continues his story, megan appropriately rapt.

"What do you think?"

When Leonardo smiles, his oversized mouth and nose spread across his face, dimples appearing in his cheeks and his chin. I have no idea what he's asking me about.

"I . . ."

The bell clangs, rescuing me.

". . . will see you next time," I finish, waving idiotically at him. At his bemused face I stop, my hand flopping down like a dead fish. Is it possible to die of embarrassment?

"Hey, Albert." He adjusts his considerable weight, excess flesh trapped in the cutout panel at the back of the chair. He fiddles around in the pockets of his gray blazer, pulling out a bar of chocco.

"Hey, freja," he says as I sit down.

"It's freida."

"Oh, right."

"That's okay," I say, heat rising in my face. Was correcting him a mistake? Should I have just pretended my name was freja?

"I'd offer you some, but I know you eves have to watch your weight!" he says as he unwraps his bar. Smears of chocco melt onto his fingers and he licks them with relish.

What about your weight, fatass? A nervous thrill runs through me. I wonder what would happen if I said it, if I stood up right now and screamed FATASS at him, grabbed the chocco bar off him and smushed it into his face?

"So, my dad . . ." he's saying, "he's a Genetic Engineer, you know. Well, he bought me an hour with two concubines for my birthday last year. He knows I need more than one woman to satisfy me. Ha ha . . ." I laugh weakly to keep him happy. "Anyway, one of them was . . ."

"That is such a wonderful way to explain it. You're so clever." At the table next to us, megan drops her head, looking up at Darwin through lowered lashes. She might be my new best friend but, my Father, is she ever insincere. "But you're the son of a Judge—of course you're intelligent. You know, I've always felt like it was my destiny to be with someone intelligent, someone *high-ranking*, because I'm . . ." chastity-ruth glides past, fixing her with a vicious look. "Enough about me," megan says, her unerring instinct for self-preservation kicking in. "Tell me more about *you*, Darwin. You're much more interesting anyway."

I feel sick and not just because Albert is now opening a second bar. He continues talking, mouth gaping open, a gooey mass of chocco congealing on his tongue. I'm trying to concentrate but it's difficult with Darwin so close to me.

". . . and then the second girl put the ping-pong ball in . . ."

"Wow." If I ever had any doubts about becoming a concubine Albert just confirmed them for me.

He sniffs, brushing a lock of curly blond hair off his forehead. Uneasiness circles in my stomach. He doesn't seem to be enjoying this Interaction as much as his one with megan. Maybe if I had chosen a different outfit he would be more interested in me. I should have worn my hair loose today. I thought the low ponytail was cute, but soft waves would have been more flattering.

"No, honestly, continue. It's fascinating," I say, a note of pleading creeping into my voice. The bell tolls again, and rosie has barely claimed my seat when I hear him launching into the same story.

"I've been practicing with a few ping-pong balls myself, you know," she says seductively.

"I liked the ponytail," Darwin says as I sit opposite him, shaking my hair out so that it fans around my face. megan is over by the door, her mouth puckering with distaste when he compliments me.

"Please return to your room immediately, #767."

"I was just getting my things!" megan protests, toying with the zip of her clutch.

"Now, #767." chastity-ruth points at the door. "You have completed your Interactions with all ten Inheritants. Please leave."

"Phew." Darwin sighs with relief as the door slams behind her. "megan is intense, isn't she?"

I giggle, stopping instantly in case one of the other eves will overhear and tell megan I was making fun of her.

"She's a really good friend of mine," I say loudly to cover myself.

"Lucky you." He stretches out, his lean body rising off the chair slightly. I want to see if his T-shirt will inch away from his abs again, but I can't look; if he caught me looking at him like that I would absolutely die of shame. On my left I can hear jessie coaxing insults about the other eves from Leonardo.

"naomi is lovely, don't get me wrong, but I think she's a bit muscled. Don't you agree, Leonardo?"

naomi, whose athletic limbs are clad in a cream lace playsuit, keeps running her hands up and down her gleaming black thighs, causing every Inheritant in the room to stare at her, Leonardo included. I suppress a smile.

"That megan girl doesn't seem like the kind of person you would be friends with," Darwin says, drawing my attention back to him.

"Really? And what do you think my friends should be like?"

"I don't know. Maybe the blond girl you keep looking at." He gestures subtly at her. "The one Interacting with Mahatma now."

If you can call it Interacting. Every muscle in her body is tense, her ankles wound around the legs of the chair as if to hang on in case he decides to kidnap her. Not that there's much chance of that. Mahatma is messing around on his fone, not even pretending to be interested in talking with her.

"That's isabel."

"You're always staring at her."

"Why don't you know her name?"

"She's not on our report cards."

"*What?*" A few of the others look up, startled. chastity-ruth walks toward us, only leaving when Darwin assures her that everything is under control.

"What?" I say again, more quietly. "She has to be on the report cards."

"No." He's definite. "There are only twenty-nine names. She wasn't at that parade thing either, was she?"

"She was sick," I say, beginning to feel a little unwell myself. "But she's back. They'll probably add her to the cards now, right?"

"Yeah, probably," he says doubtfully. "Hey, don't be upset." He moves his seat closer to mine and touches my hand with his. *I'm touching a boy.* I take a deep breath, looking away to steady my nerves, and I see jessie staring at me, one eyebrow raised quizzically. I shake my head, hoping she'll understand that I'm not the one instigating this. The bell rings but neither of us moves.

"You don't give much away, do you?" he says, looking at me as if I'm a puzzle he's determined to solve. "Do you know what?" I shake my head and he smiles slowly. "You really intrigue me, freida."

rosie, standing behind me waiting her turn, clears her throat faintly and I get to my feet, dizzy with this new feeling of need muddled with heat. He refocuses his attention on her, on to the next. The memory of our Interaction is already dissolving, the way sandcastles used to crumble in an incoming tide. Is he laughing as much with her as he did with me? Does he look as interested in what she has to say? I stay there, searching for some sign that I'm his favorite.

You intrigue me.

I wish I knew exactly how I intrigued him so I could keep doing it.

"What was that all about?"

megan is waiting for me outside the classroom door. The abstract print of her dress is enough to give me a headache, and there's so much of it, long sleeves and midcalf length, the clinging Lycra belying the modesty of the cut. She looks me up and down, wrinkling her nose at the black velvet dress with the see-through lace panel running down the center. She gestures at me to adjust it, to cover myself up, and I do so, feeling cheap.

"What are you still doing here?" I ask her.

"I saw you," she says, towering above me in vertiginous ankle boots. She points at the glass panel cut into the solid wooden door and I can see Darwin and rosie, laughing at some joke, and the traces of good humor shrivel inside me. "I saw you holding hands with him."

"I didn't hold his hand. He—"

"Yes," she breaks in. "Yes, I'm sure it was his fault. But you know how I feel about him. I said that I wanted him first. And friends would never betray each other like that. And we are friends, aren't we? Best friends. Because if we're not . . ."

Because if we're not best friends, I won't have any friends. I will be alone.

"Of course," I say. "Of course we are."

Chapter 17

Beep. Beep. Beep. Beep. Beep. Beep. You have a new VideoChat request. YouhaveanewVideoChatrequestYouhaveanewVideoChatrequestYouhaveanew . . . megan. megan. megan. megan. meganmeganmeganmeganmeganmegan.

"And then, I mean you are never going to believe what she said . . ." She breaks off, peering at me through the computer screen. "freida, are you listening to me?"

"Of course."

"And then miranda said that she weighs 112 pounds now. Seriously. She actually said, in front of everyone, that she only weighs 112 pounds." She laughs. "Does she think we're blind? There is no way that she can weigh any less than 118, and that's me being generous."

". . . pink is not cintia's color, not with all that, ugh, hair, I was only trying to do her a favor. People can be so *sensitive* . . ."

". . . and I said, hello? Did you not read the *Daily Tale*? . . ."

". . . and they're not even that cute. The only reason they rank well is because of the whole twin thing . . ."

All I have to do is throw in a "hmm" and an "absolutely" every so often and she seems content with that. I move the ePad onto the pillow and stretch out, wishing I could shut this conversation down, take half a SleepSound from my stash and doze. She talks endlessly about how beautiful she is, how long her legs are, how full her lips are, how she's so lucky to have such porcelain skin, such a high metabolism, such perfect hair. At the end of yet another monologue about how perfect she is, I stare at myself in my mirrors, seeing how less beautiful I am in comparison, how less perfect, less, less, *less* I am.

"Did you see how many helpings of noodles christy had today? Seriously, freida? Did you see how many helpings she had?"

Yes, I want to say. I was sitting beside you at lunch. And you mentioned it three times then. But I don't have the energy to argue with her and I don't know if I even want to. I like being included again. My advice is asked about the Inheritants, about clothes, about dieting tips, and I give my opinions readily. The words come easily, but I don't know if I believe what I'm saying or if it's just megan's voice in my head, drip, drip, dripping out of my mouth.

"Speaking of diets . . ." I interject when she draws a breath, "have you seen how thin isabel is now? How has she managed to do it so fast?"

Within a week isabel has begun to look as if she's folding in on herself, her bones eating her flesh from the inside. "I'm not hungry," she says, turning away from yet another untouched tray of food. "I'm never hungry anymore." isabel is the skinny eve in the class now, the one freja keeps tempting with slices of chocco-cake, the one that the other eves are urging to gain weight in case she's taking all of the available thinness for herself, stealing it from the rest of us. What happens to those lost fat cells? Do they float into the ether, searching for a nearby body to land on?

"I'm worried about her," I say now, watching megan shake out her hair until it resembles inky clouds.

"Why? It's not like she worries about you."

I hold my face as still as I can, pretending I don't care.

"Anyway, she looks terrible," megan says dismissively. "The procedure worked too well."

"What procedure?"

"freida, freida, freida. How is it possible you know so little?" she sighs, and I refrain from asking how she always knows *everything*. I don't want to know where the bodies are buried.

"She got her stomach shrunk."

"What?" I say. "But I thought only companions were allowed to get that done?"

"Whatever. It's ridiculous that she needed to get it done in the first place. They did it to *control* her. It's so weak." Her face crumples with disgust. "And now everyone is going on and on about how disciplined she is, wondering how she's managing to lose the weight so quickly. I'm sick of talking about it."

She never wants to talk about her anymore. isabel, the former white queen to her black, has become a mere shadow in her peripheral vision.

"I've been thinking about that new task again," she says, and I tense. "Unless you don't want to, sweetie. I know it must have been *awful* for you, not being chosen."

"I don't mind, megan. I don't!" I insist when she looks at me skeptically. "Go on, tell me. What happened when you and Albert went into the cupboard?"

She wouldn't give any specific details earlier, banning the other eight girls who had been chosen for the new task from doing so as well. She said it would be an unfair advantage to tell us before we completed the task ourselves. We know the basic premise, chastity-ruth having outlined the rules of Heavenly Seventy to us in class. I immediately thought of him, the hope that he might pick me surging through my body, swiftly followed by fear of megan's reaction if he did. But only nine of the Inheritants arrived, filling the room with their boy smell, sweaty excitement muddled with overpowering cologne. No Darwin.

And, one by one, the Inheritants chose their preferred eve. I waited and waited for my name to be called by one of them, any of them. The anxiety in my stomach swelled as each Inheritant said a name that wasn't mine: *megan . . . liz . . . jessie . . . daria . . . gisele . . . cara . . .* Until at last I knew all hope was gone and I had to watch the couples climb into the wooden boxes that had been newly erected in the empty U-shaped corridor around the bleachers of seats.

The leftover eves grouped together, talking and laughing too loudly. They tried to include me but I couldn't sit with them, couldn't be associated with their failure even though it was my failure too. I sat there, holding myself separate, listening to the *Daily Tale*'s commentary on celebrities from the Americas-Zone. *She has camel toe in that jumpsuit. She's a slut. Is she carrying her son in her belly or her ass? I don't care if she is pregnant—she's going to get sent Underground if she doesn't watch her weight, and I wouldn't blame her husband if he asked for a replacement.*

"Well, I shouldn't tell you because you didn't get chosen," megan says, twirling a strand of shiny hair around her finger, "but I will. Because we're best friends."

"Thanks."

"You're welcome." She ignores my sarcasm. "I'm sure you'll be asked next week. You definitely will, if cara is to be believed." Her beautiful face is as innocent as a child's, but my palms moisten. I wipe them on the bed sheets uneasily.

She goes on. "That was interesting when cara said the only reason you weren't chosen is because the other Inheritants know that Darwin prefers you. Do you think that's true?"

"Whatever," I say, cursing cara for saying it although my heart soared with joy at the time. "How would she know anyway? She's a stupid bitch." megan nods, unable to imagine that any of the Inheritants might think I was prettier than her. "Now, come on." I resist the urge to roll my eyes at her. "Tell me what happened with you and Albert."

"Well," she whispers, "when we first went into the cupboard, it was a tight squeeze. Not that Albert seemed to mind." She chortles at her own wit, looking at me sharply when I don't join in. She's grown accustomed to the twins and their disposable laughter. "He's kind of fat, isn't he?"

"Does it matter?"

"True," she agrees. "His dad is a Genetic Engineer. So, we were in the cupboard. It was weird, just the two of us. You could say anything, couldn't you?"

Is she planning on getting Darwin into the cupboard to tell him that she's the #1? Is she going to convince him not to waste his time on me, #10, the loser whose best friend dumped her?

"I wonder if there are cameras." That might scare her off. "You know, to make sure that we're doing it right."

"They could barely afford to put up those cupboards, not to mention install cameras," she says testily. "I hate this stupid Zone. You know, in the Americas—"

"And then what happened with you and Albert?" I stop her before she can launch into another rant about the Americas.

"Oh. Yes," she says. "It was so fast. I couldn't believe it when chastity-ruth rang the bell to say the seventy minutes were up."

There's so much more I want to ask her. What was it like being kissed? Did you know exactly what to do? How did she know she was doing it right? If it was isabel I was talking to, I would be able to ask all those questions without being afraid of sounding stupid. But it's not isabel. It will never be isabel again.

"We just kissed. I made it very clear to Albert that was as far as I was willing to go."

"freida, freida, freida," megan says again as I do a tiny double take at this. "No man is going to want his companion to have had sex with someone else."

"But we're not allowed to say no to them. chastity-ruth said that we were to accommodate their every need. How did you say no to him?"

"It's easy. I told him that I wanted to because he's so attractive . . ." we both smile, picturing Albert's belly straining against his T-shirt—"but I wanted to save myself for companionship."

"You told him you want to be a companion?" I ask in shock. "chastity-ruth said that we weren't allowed discuss that. You could get in so much trouble, megan."

"She said we weren't allowed tell them what our *rankings* were."

"But surely by saying you're saving yourself for companionship you implied you were in the top ten?"

"freida. Look at me. I'm sure they know that I'm #1 anyway." She sighs at my stupidity.

Where does she get this arrogance from? I have a sudden fanciful image of her sneaking into our cubicles at nighttime, a razor in hand. After making an incision she puts her mouth to the wound and sucks, draining us of our confidence until her belly is swollen with her plundered loot.

"Did the others say no too?" I ask.

"Of course."

"What do you mean, of course?"

"Well, it's obvious. Everyone knows it."

I didn't know. I bet isabel doesn't know either. We have never had a class on how to say no to men while simultaneously never saying no to them. Suddenly I'm glad I wasn't chosen today. I might have made an irreparable mistake.

"Mark my words," megan says. "Any eve who wants to be a companion will have been smart enough to withhold her favors. It will be the slutty ones who will be chosen for Heavenly Seventy from now on. You'll see."

And, as always, she's correct. In the next session we sit before the Inheritants once again, waiting for our names to be called, but it's different girls who are chosen.

"*rosie . . . adrianna . . . heidi . . . lara . . .*"

The following week is the same, and the couples emerge from the cupboards flushed and breathless. The boys dig each other in the ribs, smirking at miranda or alessandra or karlie, patting them on the ass as they leave. A break is forming in our class, one that feels more serious than our usual cliques. The chastities were right. These tasks *are* preparing us for our lives after School, a life in which concubines and companions might share their men but are otherwise eradicated from one another's existence. We may be sisters, but in the future we will not associate with each other. We will not speak to one another. We will be invisible to each other. That is the way it has always been.

"Look at them. Do they think the slutz are auditioning for a new member?" megan points at a table at the far end of the Nutrition Center. The twins, cara, gisele and daria all swivel in their seats to look behind them.

"Come on," I say, embarrassed. "Don't be so obvious."

"You think *we're* being obvious?" megan frowns at me. "Look at them."

rosie, adrianna, alessandra, heidi, karlie, lara, anya, miranda and angelina—or the Heavenly Seventy girls, as megan has renamed them—are sitting together at a large table. Their hair is teased into messy waves, faces made up with flushed cheeks and smudged dark eye makeup. They've even started to dress alike, today all wearing matching red latex skirts.

"And they're wearing red. How shameless."

"Why is it shameless?" iman asks, stopping at our table to adjust the plywood tray in her hands. Her sleek brown hair is pulled back in a ponytail, accentuating her high forehead and long neck.

"I'm sorry—were we talking to you, fatima?" megan asks pointedly, shooing her away.

"Isn't her name iman?" cara asks, tugging at the cream-and-navy printed headband she's wearing across her forehead like a crown.

"I don't know." megan shrugs as iman slumps crestfallen at a table with other 15th years, her coffee-colored skin aflame with embarrassment. "They all look the same to me."

"Why is it shameless though?" I ask, pulling the sleeves of my sheer cream blouse over my hands. My skin looks paler through the fabric. "We wear red too. You've practically made red lipstick your trademark."

"Yes, thank you for reminding me, freida," she says, and places a napkin over her coral knitted pencil skirt. "This is different. They're using it like a uniform or something."

The Heavenly Seventy girls stand in unison and walk out in single file, pouting at us as they pass.

"Pathetic. Dooming themselves to lives as concubines," megan sighs.

"Maybe that's what they want," I say, thinking of what rosie told me. "Maybe they want to be concubines."

"No," megan replies. "Everyone wants to be a companion. They're just making the best of things."

The days pass and there is still no sign of Darwin. Every time the Inheritants arrive I scan the group, my heart sinking when I realize that he's not there.

"Where's Darwin?" I ask Isaac during our Interaction, checking megan isn't in hearing distance.

"He's sick," Isaac answers, his blond hair like curtains over his thin face, crooked nose peeking though.

"Is he okay?"

"I think that—"

"He's fine." George interrupts his Interaction with agyness at the table next to us, shooting Isaac a look of warning. "Just a mild dose of . . ."

". . . influenza?" Isaac finishes uncertainly.

He must be quarantined. The Zones are so insular that any illness, although rare, can spread like wildfire within hours.

"Why are you so concerned?" Isaac looks at me knowingly. "Should I tell him you said hello?"

"No," I yelp, my face sizzling. "I was only asking for someone else. I don't care."

"heidi . . . karlie . . . miranda . . ."

No one ever chooses isabel for this task, their eyes skimming over her as if she doesn't exist.

"angelina . . . lara . . ."

Another Heavenly Seventy session where I am ignored. Am I repellent to men? What if I'm so unattractive that I won't be chosen as a companion? And what if they won't even allow me to become a concubine? Am I destined to become a chastity? I would have to join the ranks here at the School, stay with chastity-ruth, faced with my disintegrating looks in the mirrors, waiting to die of natural causes.

No. No. I can't.

I know Darwin likes me, that he finds me "intriguing" at the very least. I have to make him choose me.

"He's back!"

A hum ripples through the room. The Inheritants have returned, led into the Homemaker room by Darwin. He's lost weight. His jeans are hanging off his hips, his T-shirt loose across his torso.

"Ouch. What happened to him?" cara whispers to me.

He's wearing a baseball cap so it's not immediately apparent, but when he raises his hand in greeting, I can see it. The light catches his face, shimmering in the ugly shadows coloring his eye. "Settle down, eves," chastity-ruth says, but for once no one is listening to her as we check our makeup in our tabletops, looking up intermittently to flutter our eyelashes at Darwin. The other Inheritants are teasing him about the reaction he's causing, disheveling his perfect curls and punching him in the upper arm, jealousy coating their smiles. Darwin ignores them. His eyes skim over megan until he finds me. "Hey," he mouths, as if there is no one else in the room.

"Oh my Father! He said hey to you!" cara stifles a squeal. "You are so lucky."

"I don't think it was me necessarily," I say as megan's jaw clenches.

"Control yourselves." A note of steel has entered chastity-ruth's voice and we fall silent, recognizing danger.

"Today, eves, you have been set the task of creating red velvet cupcakes. Go to your cooking stations. Please do not forget your aprons. If I see any stains on your clothing, I will be extremely unhappy." She settles onto a high stool at the far right corner of the room, rearranging her black robes carefully. The Homemaker room has a row of ovens and adjacent sinks set in a U-shape, the central space holding six rows of long mirror-plated tables. On each table there are five individual stations with the cooking utensils and ingredients that we will need for our task. I grab my apron from underneath my station, a sugary peach color patterned with cartoon lipsticks.

The tabletops dissolve into a video-tutorial demonstrating to us, step by step, how to turn the ingredients into cupcakes. I peer closer at the screen, recognizing the face of the TV cook, virginia of *virginia Licks* fame. She's pouting her inflated lips at the camera, licking cupcake mixture off her fingers, pressing her redesigned breasts together as she beats the eggies vigorously. No wonder she's so popular in the Zones, even if cooking is a prehistoric skill. I glance down at my own breasts, also jiggling in a low-cut tank top as I beat eggies too.

"Very nice."

Abraham is standing by my station, staring at my chest. He rubs his nose, his deep-set gray eyes burning with excitement. Shame spreads like a rash over my skin and I want to yank my apron up so that I'm covered completely from the neck down. I concentrate intensely on the desktop and press playback on the tutorial, pretending I didn't hear the instructions.

"Everything all right here?"

"Just enjoying the view," Abraham says, and I try to smile to cover my revulsion. This is what I wanted. I wanted them to think I was attractive.

"Maybe it's time to enjoy a different view," Darwin says. Irritation shadows Abraham's face but he backs away and goes to join the other Inheritants milling around. Darwin is grimly satisfied but not surprised. He is used to this, I realize. He is used to people doing whatever he tells them to. I can almost touch this feeling with the tips of my fingers, feeling the authority of it, the protection in it.

"Don't worry about him," Darwin says, moving back to give me space. "He should know better than to bother you." He rolls his eyes. "Abraham has always been the same, always wanting what I want."

I stare at the tutorial again, pressing pause. A trace of sweat smears the screen. I wipe it off quickly, hoping he didn't see. Did he just say that he wanted me?

"Like when we were kids. If I ever had a toy, he would try to steal it. He even had the nerve to take my shooting rifle, tried to pass it off as his own." He doesn't lower his voice. Like megan, he is unafraid of being overheard. He has that particular brand of bravery that comes with power.

I want that bravery. I want that power.

"When was this?" I ask, trying not to stare at his bruised eye.

"Seven years ago."

"You're holding on to that grudge, aren't you?" I tease him, looking up through my eyelashes the way chastity-theresa tutored us to do.

"Is your cake mixture or whatever okay?" he asks.

Shit. It's clumping. Is it meant to be that way?

"I don't understand why they set this task. Who cooks? This is boring." He rests against my table, flour dusting his striped T-shirt. "Well, besides talking to you of course."

"Maybe they're preparing us for a Euro-Zone collapse," I say, blushing.

"Excellent point, young freida. In the case of an economic meltdown and imminent starvation, I definitely don't want to be stuck with a companion who can't produce the perfect red velvet cupcake." He hoots with laughter. "The horror."

"What's so funny?" megan approaches us with a ceramic bowl clasped under one arm, using her free hand to stir the mixture with a wooden spoon. Her skin is rosy from the heat of the ovens, a few tendrils of dark hair escaping from her loose ponytail.

"Nothing." I move back so that she can stand next to Darwin, and I pour a generous amount of red food coloring into the bowl. "Is it supposed to look like this?" I ask anxiously, and megan peers in, wrinkling her nose.

"It's so red." She giggles. "It reminds me of when you got your first womenstruation. Your bed looked like a crime scene."

I can't breathe. *I can't breathe.* I don't want to look at him, but I have to; I have to see if he heard that.

"I don't get it anymore."

"It's fine." He cracks his knuckles uncomfortably.

"No, honestly, I don't. I take tablets, you know? I mean, we all take tablets. Unless we become companions. And then . . . well, then we don't. But you know this. Do you know this? Yeah . . . so . . . yeah."

I ramble on and on, wishing that a hole would appear in the ground and swallow me up. I feel as if my entire body is blistering with a savage heat.

"Honestly. It's fine." He backs away, probably afraid that I'm about to draw him a diagram of my uterus. "I have to go to the bathroom. I'll see you in a bit."

"Oh, freeds, I'm so sorry. It just came out," megan says as I press my lips together to stop them trembling. I count the tiles on the floor to calm myself down.

"To be fair, freida, I'm sure it was an accident," gisele chimes in from the next station.

"It really was." megan's voice is wobbly. "I could *cry* I feel so bad." There is an intake of breath and I raise my head to see if she's actually going to go that far, but she's still dry-eyed, her mouth quivering dramatically. jessie moves quickly to megan's side, liz following, and the two enfold her in a hug. The others crowd around megan too, shaking their heads at me for nearly driving her to tears. The other Inheritants are watching with interest, wondering what the drama is. If we don't stop, chastity-ruth will intervene. And I know she'll find a way to make this all my fault. So I do what I always do. I swallow the feelings down, feeling them scorch my insides as they fall into my stomach.

"Sorry, megan."

She brushes the other girls off and pulls me into a floury embrace, a little too tight for comfort. I close my eyes as cake mixture and her cloying floral perfume ram into my nostrils. I can feel the edges of my silver locket pressing into my neck as she hugs me, and a hunger for what's inside it invades every cell of my body.

"It really was an accident," she says, and I tell her, *Yes, yes, of course it was*, giving in, as she knew I would.

* * *

I had been feeling ill that day, four years ago, my gut twisting like a damp cloth being wrung out. "Go see chastity-anne," isabel had told me, but I didn't want to. I didn't want to seem weak.

I remember crawling under my bedcovers, the new ones that had recently replaced my old pink blanket with yellow stars. "These are more appropriate for a 12th year," chastity-ruth had said. "You do want to be appropriate, don't you?"

I curled up beneath the white sheets, trying to hold myself together. The lining of my stomach felt as if it was ripping apart. I buried my head in my pillow, biting on it to stop myself from crying out in pain.

Good girls don't cry. Good girls don't cry.

I woke in the middle of the night. I could feel something seeping away from the very center of me. I blinked in the dim light of the nighttime lamps, blinking again and again, but it was still there, a shadowy puddle oozing through my new sheets. I shrank away, pulling myself into the corner, away from it, but it was on my hands and it was sticky on the backs of my legs and it was spreading everywhere. I couldn't stop it.

And I screamed and screamed and screamed. I never could sleep without meds after that.

chastity-ruth hung the tainted sheets outside my cubicle for the five days that I bled as a sign that I was unclean. We knew then. We knew this was our curse. We knew it had to be hidden.

"And to think . . ." megan had said, passing her disgust on to the others to feed on, like a pack of dogs in a nature video chewing the bones of a carcass, ". . . you were the first."

"Can I play too?" she asked later, peeking in from the corridor into isabel's cubicle. I can't remember what we were playing. All I can remember is a sensation of lightness, brimming with laughter.

"No." isabel pulled the steel door down from the ceiling, unrolling it until megan disappeared behind it.

"I don't trust her," she had said, watching my nervous face in the mirror. Brightening, she rummaged under her bed and pulled out a tiny gold box encrusted with rare quartz gemstones. Opening it up, she pulled out a heavy silver locket on a fine chain. I was dumbstruck. I had never seen anything so beautiful in my life.

"I got it for my birthday," she explained as she fastened the chain around my neck.

"From who?" I asked in amazement.

"It's yours now," she said. "Because you were the first. Now you're special too."

It happened to everyone else within two months of me, snow-white sheets splattered with their shame, the new anti-womenstruation medication included with our daily bread.

But at least the others were prepared. At least they knew it was coming.

Chapter 18

When the cupcakes are ready, we display them on cake stands for chastity-ruth and the Inheritants to examine our handiwork.

"Oh dear, #630," chastity-ruth says as she gingerly picks up one of my cupcakes with her fingertips. "Had some trouble, did you?"

"I followed the tutorial," I say miserably. The center of my cakes have collapsed, oozing red food coloring all over the ditzy floral-printed cake stand. I clean up my desk, watching megan as she feeds Darwin some of her cake. Perfectly baked, of course.

"Excuse me. Where are you going?"

Socrates, Abraham, and Albert stop in the doorway, their faces incredulous at chastity-ruth's tone.

"We don't feel like sitting around watching them wash up," Socrates says, shrugging.

"Do you have a problem with that?" Albert asks, his plump face flushed from the heat, a trail of jam smeared down his chin.

"No. Of course not." chastity-ruth's face goes as red as Albert's. She curtsies, begging forgiveness. We eves busy ourselves at the sinks, washing the mixing bowls clumsily, pretending not to notice. We know that if she sees us noticing her humiliation she'll never forgive us.

"I thought as much." Albert's voice is disdainful. "We'll see you when you're finished with all this." He waves his hand at the disorderly Homemaker room before walking out, the other Inheritants following him with pilfered cupcakes in their hands.

"Will you hurry up?" chastity-ruth snaps once they have left. "Why must you all be so incompetent?" She picks up a wooden spoon from miranda's workstation and examines it before slamming it down with a resounding crack. miranda jumps back, cradling her hand to her chest, a welt forming across her knuckles.

"That was an accident." The chastity's smile is feral. "Be more careful in the future."

I stare at the boarded-up window above my sink, wishing I could make myself invisible so I don't cause another "accident."

"Wash that spoon again. I don't understand your inability to perform the simplest of tasks," she says, ignoring the fact that we have never washed dishes by hand before. We just dump the dirty ware in the garbage after our meals, fresh ones appearing like magic in the dispenser for the next meal.

I remember isabel asking me, "How does it all work, do you think?" when we were about seven, as she made a face at her chick-chick. She was always more curious than I was, asking the chastities daring questions about what the main Euro-Zone looked like or if they could give us any hints about when the Inheritants, our future husbands, would be arriving to Interact with us. She never got in trouble either, her mouth curved into a sunny smile, radiating so much joy that you felt warm just being in her presence. The chastities laughed at her, told her not to worry her pretty little head. She would know soon enough.

"How does all what work?" I answered, trying to stop myself from running to the Fatgirl buffet for a piece of cake.

"Like, look at this," she said patiently, pointing at her plate. "Where does this come from?"

"The meat-growers' lab."

"But how do they create it?"

I didn't answer her. The food arrived. I ate it. We were not designed to ask questions.

Finally, chastity-ruth decides that the Homemaker room has been cleaned to her satisfaction.

"Form an orderly line and return to the classroom," she says, standing behind her wooden desk. heidi groans and immediately looks around her to find the culprit, fright settling on her face when she realizes it was herself.

"I'm sorry, chastity-ruth," she says anxiously, brushing her bangs out of her hazel eyes. "I didn't mean to be rude. I was just hoping that I might get to taste one of my cupcakes."

"Do the rest of you want to taste your cakes as well?" chastity-ruth asks.

"Yes, please!"

"Oh, can we?"

"They look delicious."

isabel and I are the only two who don't say anything.

"Of course you can have some!" chastity-ruth proclaims, and the eves grin with delight.

"You can have some if you don't have any self-control. You can have some if you don't care about your appearance. You are more than welcome to stuff yourselves with all of those cakes if you don't mind being fatter at next weigh-in. eves, go right ahead."

"No, thanks," megan says at once. "I'm still full from dinner. I couldn't eat another bite." She throws a pink gingham cloth over her cake stand and within a heartbeat the others all copy her. She looks at my station and sighs, taking off her candy-striped apron and folding it carefully. "That was a good idea, making yours so ugly, freida. No one in their right mind would want any of your cupcakes."

We're halfway to the classroom when I realize I've forgotten my bag. Cursing under my breath, I sneak back, running as fast as I can down the tiled corridor, and burst through the wooden door of the Homemaker room.

"Oh, I . . ."

christy scrambles to her feet, sweeping a jumble of half-consumed cupcakes onto the floor, wiping her mouth with the back of her hand and smearing her lipstick across her face. She begins to cough violently and I grab a glass from underneath the nearest desk and fill it with water, watching as she gulps it down, still coughing.

"What are you doing here, christy?"

"chastity-ruth asked me to dispose of the cupcakes."

Not like that she didn't.

I can see the straps of my bag poking out from underneath the desk and I pick it up.

"I didn't mean to eat them."

"It's none of my business."

"I just wanted to taste them. But I couldn't, not when everyone else was being good. I'm still seven pounds over target weight."

I don't want to do this with her, confiding and telling secrets.

"It's none of my business," I repeat. "But remember what happened to isabel. Ipecac syrup isn't foolproof."

"Oh yeah, isabel." Her green eyes are wild with sudden fury. "How can I forget isabel?" She dashes her hand against her nose, leaving smudges of jam on her peaches-and-cream complexion.

"How did she get so lucky? If I put on the amount of weight that she did, you think I'd be 'fixed up?' They would send me Underground. Why is she so special?" She comes nearer and nearer to me with each word. The smell of sugar and butter on her breath makes me want to gag.

"Leave isabel out of this," I say. "If you're so worried about your weight, just have some self-control. We all have to. Why should you be any different?"

"Why are you still defending her, freida?" she asks, her voice tired. "It's not like she cares that much about you."

"I'm going now."

She grabs at my top, pulling it down so the lace of my bra is visible. "You won't tell anyone about this, will you?" she says as I push her off me. "Especially megan. Please don't tell megan."

"I won't." I need to get away from her. "I promise."

"Thank you." She covers her messy face with her hands. "I owe you, freida."

"How kind of you to grace us with your presence, #630," chastity-ruth says as I attempt to slip into my seat unseen.

"I had to go back to the Homemaker room."

"Is #727 nearly finished?"

"Yes."

"Good. She hasn't been requested for the next segment anyway."

"Obviously." jessie snickers. "Who would want to be stuck in a cupboard with that fat bitch?" She nudges megan, who, strangely, doesn't react.

"And why exactly did you return to the Homemaker room?"

"I forgot my bag."

"Your ability to pay attention to your personal belongings is as dismal as your baking skills." She sighs. "But you are required here. Mr. Darwin has selected you for today's session of Heavenly Seventy." My mouth gapes open in shock. "I know. I was astonished as well. He's in cupboard #1. Please do not waste any more of his time."

I get to my feet, sensing envious eyes burrowing into my skin like lice. I feel as if I'm walking in slow motion, my heart beating so forcefully in my ears I'm deafened. *megan*. I see her face in an ugly twist. I blink, but when I look at her again she's waving me on encouragingly. "It's okay," she mouths at me. "Go for it."

I take a deep breath and open the door to the cupboard. None of this feels real.

"Hey, freida."

"Hey," I reply, shutting the door firmly behind me. The steel bolt fastens independently, locking us in.

At last, I've made it into one of the cupboards. It's tall and narrow, made of mirrors from the ceiling to the floor. He's leaning against the back wall, his baseball cap pulled low again, dozens of Darwins multiplying in the glass around him.

"All these mirrors. Does every room in the School have to look like a disco ball?" He taps the wall beside him lightly.

"Is it not like that in the main Zone?" I ask, trying to cover up my nerves, even though I know the answer from watching TV. Why has he asked me? Does he think I'm easy, like the Heavenly Seventy girls? Is he expecting me to have sex with him?

"No, there's definitely a mirror shortage in the Zone compared to here," he says, cracking his knuckles. Is it possible he's nervous too?

I can't believe you wanted to choose me.

"Of course I wanted to choose you," he says, pushing himself away from the wall. Did I say that out loud? "Why wouldn't I have chosen you?"

"Because of what happened . . . you know . . . in the kitchen . . . what I said about the tablets we have to take."

"You girls take tablets for everything. It's unhealthy," he says disapprovingly. "I know that's not your fault," he says when my face falls, picturing the precious granules squirreled away in the hollow of my necklace. "I know the chastities make you take them."

"I heard you had the flu," I say to change the subject.

"Did you miss me?" He nudges my shoulder, making me feel a little light-headed as I breathe him in, smelling citrus and mint. I don't know what to do with my face, or my hands. Where should I stand?

"Are you worried I'm contagious?" he continues. He takes my hand in his, dwarfing it. Please don't let my palms be clammy. I'm breathing too fast. Can he hear that I'm breathing too fast?

"What happened to your eye?"

"Nothing," he says, his face darkening.

"It looks painful." I peer at it, the swirling shadows drawing me in before I realize how close our faces are. I'm breathing too loudly now, too fast and too loudly. But he doesn't seem to notice. He leans in, so slowly, oh so slowly, and I want to press pause, remember this feeling for the rest of my life. He closes his eyes so I close mine too and finally it happens, his mouth gentle on mine. He places his hands around my neck, his fingertips grazing my hair. My arms feel awkward so I copy what they do on TV and wrap them around his waist, feeling how lean he is, how prominent his hip bones have become.

"You've lost weight," I murmur. He laughs, his mouth still pressed against mine. Then he draws back a little, resting his forehead on mine.

"You've gained some," he says, running his hands down over my waist and hips.

I pull away, sucking in my stomach. "I'm at target," I say, his words like a blow to my solar plexus, the word *fat fat fat* screaming in my head.

"It's a good thing. You looked too thin before. You're so beautiful, freida."

He cradles my head in his hands, looking at every inch of my face as if he thinks I'm the prettiest girl in the world. And although I've always known that I've been designed perfectly, for the first time in my life I almost believe it.

"Are you going to tell me what happened to your eye?" I say, giddiness bubbling up inside me. I touch my fingertips to the bruise, drawing my hand away as he recoils.

"Oh, I'm sorry, did I hurt you?"

"Don't worry." He grabs hold of my hands, folding them inside his. "It's fine."

"What happened?"

"It was my own fault."

"Like cassie Carmichael."

"What?"

"Nothing."

"It was my own fault," he says again, his voice mechanical. We kiss again and again and again, until all I can think of is him.

The bell blasts, reverberating in the tiny cupboard. How can it be over already? I don't want it to be over.

"Let's do this again." He reaches over to tuck a piece of hair behind my ear and my stomach swoops. "If you want to, that is."

Astonishment silences me. Does he really think I have a choice in the matter? He still has my hand in his, but as the door releases he lets go and we break apart. The other Inheritants cheer at Darwin, Sigmund mock-tackling him, putting him in a headlock.

"Did you get some? Did you?" he yells, ruffling Darwin's hair roughly with a clenched fist.

"The train is waiting to take you back to the main Zone." chastity-ruth clearly disapproves of this horseplay, but we all know she won't reprimand them again.

Darwin straightens up, shoving Sigmund off him, and smoothes down his mussed-up curls. All the men leave, still chatting loudly about their Heavenly Seventy session. Darwin is the last to go, turning just before he's out of sight to give me a tiny wink. My smile nearly splits my face in two.

"What's so funny, #630?"

"Nothing, chastity-ruth."

"Then I'd advise you to wipe that unsightly grin off your face. It doesn't improve your appearance."

I refuse to let her words hurt me, hugging Darwin's proclamations of my beauty to my heart like a new-design's blankie. "You're far too excitable." She looks at me in annoyance. "Organized Recreation will take care of that. Please wait here for chastity-anne to arrive."

With a swish of her robes she leaves and silence covers the room like a shroud.

"megan, thanks for——" I begin before liz cuts across me, her eyes flashing angrily.

"You knew he was megan's. We all knew it."

She and jessie turn away from me, matching black vests over zebra-printed bubble skirts, blond ringlets spilling down their backs. I can't see megan.

"But megan said it was okay," I say feebly, touching the heavy oak of the chastity's desk to steady myself. "And he chose me. What was I supposed to do?"

"I saw you flirting with him in the Homemaker room," gisele says, tucking her gray silk blouse into cut-off shorts.

"You were practically sitting on top of him during the last Interaction," a voice calls out. More voices join in, all attacking me. On instinct I turn to isabel, conditioned after all these years to look to her for protection. She is sitting very still, as if she's fallen asleep sitting up. Who is this stranger? It's as if someone cut off her face and molded it over a mannequin's head.

"megan said it was okay," I protest. "And even if she didn't, what was I supposed to do?"

"She's right." megan's voice rises from the center of the group. "What could she do?"

"It's fine." She's standing in front of me, a charitable smile playing on her lips. "You can have him," she says, as if he's somehow spoiled by the association with me. I bite my tongue, hoping I look grateful.

"So . . . what happened?" One of the girls breaks, and everyone immediately follows her lead.

"Did you kiss?"

"Is he a good kisser? I bet he's a good kisser."

"What happened to his face? Did you ask him?"

My best friends form a circle around me, throwing questions at me. The Heavenly Seventy girls are standing behind them, the less popular girls making themselves as small as possible in case we notice them and tell them to get lost before they hear any of the gossip. And isabel, her hair tied in a messy top knot, exposing her back in a low-cut navy halter top, is the only one who doesn't care. I watch her leave, counting every jutting vertebra in her spine.

"What do you think it will be like?"

"What?"

"The first kiss."

"I'll let you know as soon as it happens!" isabel laughed. "I'll VideoChat you in the middle of it, if you want."

And her eyes were shining bright, as if the future was a treasure that she couldn't wait to hold in her hands.

"Nothing," I say. "Nothing happened."

"She can't say with all of *you* here." megan looks contemptuously at the outer two circles looping around us. Most of the girls shrug, splinter into smaller groups and start chatting among themselves, but I can see some of them, like cintia and liu and naomi, look stricken. *Please let us stay*, their faces seem to say, as if they can absorb our popularity simply by being near us.

"Hello? Give us some privacy!" the twins bark and the stragglers trickle away glumly.

"So, what happened?" daria asks once they're gone, as cara, megan, the twins and gisele thrust forward to shield me from eavesdroppers.

"Nothing."

"Come on. You can tell us."

"Honestly, nothing happened."

They all look unconvinced and I feel as if I've failed some vital girl test.

"Did you ask him about his eye?" cara struggles to keep the conversation going.

"Not really. He just said that it was his own fault." I trail off, relieved as chastity-anne arrives and impatiently calls us to line up at her desk.

"Right." megan's voice is bored and she links arms with cara, the two of them approaching chastity-anne's desk together to get their meds, giggling as they step into the glass elevators on either side of the desk.

"Here are your meds," chastity-anne says to me. "Where is isabel, by the way? She should be here."

"I don't know," I reply. "I don't know where she is."

The plastic test tube is pushed into my hand, my foto burned onto the front of it.

You're beautiful, freida.

The door of my box closes behind me and I roll the tube between my fingers. Today I don't want to forget.

Bang bang bang bang.

chastity-anne's face peering through the clear glass, her open palm pounding against it. She mimes swallowing the drugs.

I don't want to. But I mouth, "Sorry," at her.

But I don't want to.

But I do as I'm told.

Chapter 19

"Sorry, sorry!" chastity-mary skips into the room the next day, her cherubic face dimpling. "I've been running late all morning." She throws her hands up in defeat and promptly trips her robes. She grabs the edge of the desktop, chuckling as she rearranges her cloak.

"Where's chastity-ruth?" cara asks in surprise. chastity-mary is usually assigned to teach the younger eves.

"Oh dear, you know how busy she is," chastity-mary says. "I'm afraid you're stuck with me today!"

"No need to apologize, chastity-mary. We don't need instruction in this particular area anyway," angelina says smugly. She has backcombed her hair at the roots and ringed her feline eyes with black kohl. With her leopard-print leotard and pleather shorts, she looks dangerously sexy. The Heavenly Seventy girls have formed a little cluster, all nine of them lining the back of the room. There is a flash of color as they cross and uncross their legs, matching red stilettos on their feet.

"Speak for yourself. Nice girls wait. Right, freida?" megan is still fishing for information about what happened with me and Darwin.

"For sure," I say, plastering a bright smile on my face. She returns to her mirror, and without breaking eye contact with her reflection she applies another layer of lipstick, blowing a kiss at herself.

"I'm sorry you feel it's unnecessary, angelina." chastity-mary beams at us as she sits behind the broad wooden desk. "But it's part of your program."

"What about the future chastities?" liz sniffs openly at agyness. "They're never going to need to know this stuff."

"liz!" chastity-mary gives a high-pitched giggle. "I don't believe that the thirds have been selected yet." There is nervous shuffling of feet at this reminder of how precarious our situation is. "Therefore all eves must complete the full program."

"Anyway, it's the chastities who will have to teach sex-ed to future eves in the School, so we have to know what it's all about," agyness says, stretching the ends of a faded tartan cardigan over her fingers.

"That's correct."

"What a chastity's pet," liz mutters under her breath, but agyness keeps smiling, seemingly content with the prospect of remaining at the School. megan once told me that happiness is getting exactly what you want, but she thinks it's only what *she* wants that counts. She can't understand that maybe agyness *wants* to be a chastity, that maybe the Heavenly Seventy girls *want* to become concubines. The eves I feel sorry for are the cintias, the christys, the lius. You can almost smell their desperation to become companions, effort oozing out of every pore. But they're not good enough. They're the backup plan; the ones destined to become second-tier concubines. And that is not what anyone wants.

And me? What do I want?

I want security. I want to know exactly what the future holds. And isabel? What is it that she wants?

I don't know anymore. Maybe I never did.

"Shall we begin?" chastity-mary says, tapping the main mirror-board and it converts to a large screen. The triquetra appears, pulling apart until there are three separate triangles in a row. The white triangle spins forward first, taking over the entire screen.

"Welcome to sexual education for companions."

The companion is wearing a primrose-yellow prom dress with a sweetheart neckline and a calf-length skirt. Her dark blond hair is cut into a neat bob, just grazing her shoulders. She's sitting on an antique rocking chair, her legs crossed gracefully at the ankles, white T-bar shoes on her feet.

"Here is a short introduction of what will be expected of you in your role as a companion." She covers her mouth with one hand as she coughs, her nails painted a pale pink. "The demands of belonging to this third are many, but the rewards are just wonderful. Naturally I am sure that all of you want to become companions, to enjoy the wonders of supporting your husband and raising healthy sons, but alas only the privileged few will be chosen."

A bedroom appears on the screen. It is starkly decorated, the walls a vanilla shade, a large four-poster bed the only furniture. A girl is sitting on the bed. She is younger than the other companion—about seventeen, I would guess. Her hair is loose, falling to her waist in Titian waves. She looks nervous, fidgeting with the broderie anglaise trim of her white nightgown. The door to the room opens and a man enters, his face pixelated to ensure his privacy. He is very tall, stooping to fit through the door, and thin, his navy three-piece suit loose on his body. He doesn't say anything to the girl, just sits at the edge of the mattress, taking off his clothes and methodically folding them in a pile at the base of the bed. The girl pulls back the bedspread and lies down, covering herself again until all you can see is her ginger hair spilling over the ivory bedding. He lies next to her.

"The role of the companion is simple," the first companion's voice says blandly. "She must follow her husband's lead at all times. You must always be willing. The more often you lie with your husband, the greater the possibility of conceiving a son to carry on the proud legacy of the Zone."

The man's head is burrowed into the pillow, the companion resting her chin on his shoulder, her hands clutching at the sheets below her. Her eyes are closed, her teeth gritted.

"You may experience some pain the first time." chastity-mary gently shushes rosie and miranda as they snicker at this. "This is to be expected. It is best to maintain a neutral expression."

I think of when Darwin kissed me, heat flooding my belly, how I wanted to pull him into me as deeply as I could. I doubt that I was maintaining a "neutral expression." Was I doing it wrong? Did he think that I was behaving more like a concubine than a companion?

The screen cuts back to the blond companion in the rocking chair. A hologram of a calendar appears beside her, a day each month circled in red.

"The conception and birth of sons will be your pri-mary function. It is important to remember that if you are chosen to become a companion your . . ." she low-ers her voice—"womenstruation will return. You must monitor your cycle carefully. Whenever you are indis-posed, you must retire to another bedroom until you are clean again." She wrinkles her nose in distaste and smoothes down her neat bob. "Once the lucky few are selected by their future husbands, further training will be provided to ensure you are properly prepared so you can do the Father proud."

The red triangle of the concubines blasts through her fading face, a very different blonde appearing on-screen this time, stomping forward on long legs clad in fishnet stockings. She blows a kiss at the camera, glossy redesigned lips almost falling off her face. She flips back her ironed-straight hair to show off massive breasts, smashed together in a red satin corset. They look like two bald chastity heads stuck onto her skinny torso.

"Hello there!" She winks. "Welcome to sex-ed for concubines. The only third who needs to know this stuff!"

"Pathetic," megan says as a few girls at the back holler. She taps lightly on her desktop, the mirror dissolving into the trademark pink graphics of MyFace.

"Those of you who are chosen for this third are joining an age-old tradition. Concubines have always been a part of society, an important part. You just have to make sure that the guy you're with is having a good time. Easy!"

The digi-vid cuts back to the same room, but the camera angle is different. We can see a concubine from the side; she must be about nineteen or twenty and she's on her knees, the same man as before standing before her. He's gripping her dark ponytail in his fist, pumping her head up and down.

"It's nice to make eye contact." The voiceover advises, and sure enough her blank eyes are fixed on his.

"Always be willing."

He yanks her head back sharply. Grabbing her by the waist, he pushes her onto the bed and she throws her head back, moaning.

"Make noise. Make sure that you look like you're really enjoying it."

We've all seen this stuff before on late-night TV. The same dead-eyed, slack-jawed concubines, screaming with pleasure as soon as a man comes within two feet of them. I can't even remember the first time I saw a porno. I presume

I must have been shocked, frightened even, but after watching another and another and another they sort of blend into nothingness. The guys are always anonymous, their faces blurred, and the women may as well be. The man on-screen is pulling out of her now, aiming at her face, and christy's foot starts to knock restlessly against the leg of her chair, her face pallid at this glimpse into her future. A lump forms in my throat. That can't happen to me.

christy pushes her seat back, and in a flash of blond hair I can see isabel. Her withered arms and legs are poking out from baggy denim cut-offs and a cornflower-blue jersey vest that is at least two sizes too big. Her breasts have vanished into her sternum, hidden beneath the protruding bones. She can't weigh more than eighty pounds.

She stiffens, as if she can feel my gaze on her skin, and tousles her messy hair until it covers her face again, covering her secrets.

"It's impossible to go into full detail in this short video about all the tricks that you will need to learn," the concubine says, toying with the black laces tying up her corset. "You will be given extensive training after the Ceremony."

The screen flickers, turning back into a mirror, showing all the rows of eves sitting. Waiting.

"That's enough for today," chastity-mary says, tripping over her robes again as she ushers everyone out. I can hear cara, gisele, and daria discussing the videos, the twins asking idiotic questions about mandatory skirt lengths for companions. isabel is last to leave, dragging her bones with her.

"You miss her."

megan is standing in front of the mirror-board at the front of room. Pulling her ponytail over her left shoulder, she expertly teases out hairs to make it look thicker.

"Miss who?" I ask. She doesn't dignify this with a response.

"I don't," I say, feeling foolish. That's the thing about megan. Just when you think that she is the most self-absorbed person you have ever met, she'll blindside you with her insight. "I don't miss her at all."

"Why are you worried about her?" she persists.

Because she was my best friend. Because she's fading away before my eyes, like an old foto losing its pigment. It's as if they broke her apart into thousands of pieces, made her into a human jigsaw, then reassembled her. But they've put her back together *wrong*. I want to find the missing piece that will make her the real isabel again, but when I look at her directly she seems to shimmer into translucence. And no one else notices.

"You weren't this worried about her when she was fat," megan points out.

She didn't deserve my sympathy when she was fat, fat, fat, when she was greedy, when she was disgusting. Fat girls should be made obsolete. No one will ever love a fat girl.

The Messages play on and on in my head.

"You have to focus," megan says, undoing two buttons on her chartreuse silk shirt and pulling her pencil skirt down pale, slim legs. I get up to let her pass as she comes to sit next to me.

"We can share," she says, although there are rows of empty seats. She wraps one arm around my waist, the other clinging to the desk for balance. "She doesn't deserve a friend like you," she says, tracing over our reflection in the desk with her fingertips.

No. She deserves better. She deserved a lot better than me.

"Forget her. This is what isabel does. She thinks she's too good for you. She thinks that she's better than everyone else." megan spits the words out as if they're rancid.

"What?" I ask, taken aback by her rancor.

"She doesn't care about you. She probably never did," she says with a swish of her glossy hair. And just like that, she breaks my heart in two.

Good girls don't cry. Good girls don't cry.

"Just forget her," she says again, eyeing me warily. For the first time in days all I want to do is to crack open the locket around my neck and lick the insides, cram every last dusting of numbness into me, anything so I don't have to feel like this anymore.

I rest my head on her shoulder, energy leaching from me. "That's a good girl," megan says, and I close my eyes, wishing I could smell lavender.

"It looked painful, didn't it?" I say quietly.

"What did?"

"The digi-vid. Sex. Do you think it will hurt?"

"How would I know? Go ask rosie or one of the other whores."

I wince at the harsh words, but I suppose she's right. They're not concubines yet. For now they are just girls who are making the wrong choices. They're "whores." But what if they don't realize that they're making the wrong choices? What if the path they are on just has different signposts to ours?

"What difference does it make anyway, freida? It's not like we can say no."

"But you said no." I'm fed up with this ambiguity. "You said no. And they *never* say no. And you said that made them whores. I don't understand."

"Don't be academic, freida. It's not attractive."

"I'm not trying to be academic." My voice cracks. I'm confused, I want to say. I'm scared.

"Where are you going?" I say instead as she walks away.

"Class." She pauses at the doorway. "It's only School, freida. Just think of it as a bridge to our future. We only need to use it to get to the other side."

It doesn't feel like a bridge, I think as she leaves. A bridge would feel some way steady. This feels more like I'm balancing on a tightrope made of cobwebs.

Chapter 20

May
Eight weeks until the Ceremony

I woke today and realized that I was counting in weeks now, not months, not years. Only eight weeks left. Only eight weeks until the Ceremony. Only eight weeks. The words keep dancing in my mind, getting jumbled up and confused. *Eight . . . Ceremony . . . Weeks . . . Eight . . . Left . . . Weeks . . . Until . . . Eight . . . Ceremony . . . Eight Weeks Left.*

"Are you excited?" natalie, a 12th year, asked while we lined up for the buffet at breakfast. Her dark hair is cut in a geometric bob, round brown eyes almost covered by thick bangs.

"Sure," I replied, just like the final-year eves had told me when I was twelve and I screwed up enough courage to ask them the same question.

Were they lying too?

* * *

"But what do you and Darwin *do?*" megan asks on VideoChat. "He must have chosen you for Heavenly Seventy at least ten times."

"We talk," I answer, eyes flicking toward the corner of the screen at my video-feed. I have my hair half pinned up to show off my new feather-shaped earrings studded with amber stones. "I had to buy them for you," Darwin had said as I put them on. "They reminded me of your eyes. You're beautiful, freida."

"But he *keeps* asking you." Her voice is baffled, arched eyebrows almost reaching into her floral-print headscarf.

"We just talk."

"For *seventy minutes?* About what?"

Everything. Anything. As soon as he enters the classroom he searches for me, smiling with relief when he finds me, and I can feel my jaw clench. Where would I be? I want to ask him. Where else could I *possibly* be? All throughout class I can feel his eyes on me. The other Inheritants are friendly, but they keep a respectful distance now. There have been no other sordid incidents with Abraham. Mahatma does not dare to even glance at his eFone during our Interactions. I catch some of them watching me with interest, no doubt wondering what he finds so captivating about me. And my fellow eves have never been nicer to me.

"I love your earrings!" jessie and liz squeal as we take our seats for Comparison Studies, their faces buried under layers of their new bronzing powder. It's because of me, apparently.

The trend to look browner is because of *me*. "Where did you get them?"

"They were a gift," I reply, raising my voice so isabel can hear. She's not the only one who can get gifts, who can have secrets.

"It's a done deal," freja says at lunchtime, scrunching a napkin full of cheesy goo into her glass. "Darwin has chosen you."

But he hasn't. Not officially. There are still eight weeks left, eight weeks in which I could mess it up, eight weeks where this could all fall apart.

But from the outside it must indeed look like a "done deal." chastity-ruth asks Darwin to make a selection for Heavenly Seventy, and every time I hold my breath, afraid that today is the day he'll change his mind. I still feel shocked when he calls my name, even after all this time. There is a moment just as the door bolts behind us that we hesitate, each of us at either side of the cramped cupboard, a thick, heavy energy separating us. Will it be like we remembered? Did we imagine it all in the first place? Then we fall on each other, kissing hungrily, a heat uncoiling in my stomach and seeping into every cell of my body. We move apart, a little embarrassed by the intensity of whatever this thing is between us. He always breaks the silence first, asking question after question, determined to know everything about me, to "figure me out," as he says.

"What was it like growing up in the School?" he asks, sliding down along the glass wall until he is sitting on the ground, pulling me down with him.

"It was fine," I say vaguely, fixing the thigh-high slit in my maxi skirt. "We started at four."

"Where were you before that?"

"The Nursery. I don't remember much about it." Indistinct images swim before me, each undercut with a core of familiarity. "But what about you?" I say, pushing the vision away. "It must have been fun growing up as a Judge's son!"

"I don't know about that," he replies as I trace the skin around his eyes, the bruising long faded into a pale golden ring.

"Oh, come on." I snuggle up closer, huddling into his armpit, the worn cotton of his sweatshirt soft against my cheek. He kisses the top of my head.

"It was okay."

"Just okay?" I probe, keen to hear more about the new world I'm about to enter.

"The Euro-Zone is so small; everyone knows everyone else. I've always felt so visible—like because of who my dad is I have to be on my best behavior at all times."

"Did your parents tell you that?"

"My mom says to be myself. That who I am is enough. Not to worry about what other people think of me." He says this in a semi-mocking tone, as if it's a joke, and I wonder if I should laugh. I try to imagine what it must be like to be told that who you are is enough, to have the permission to "be yourself."

"She's very beautiful, my mother," he continues. "Even now. She's nice as well. You'll like her."

I bite the inside of my cheek to stop myself from grinning at his use of the future tense, the implicit promise in it.

"But my dad . . ." He stops, searching for the right words. "I want him to be proud of me. That's all I've ever wanted." I stay silent, afraid of saying the wrong thing. "My mother says he only wants the best for me," he says, pinching the bridge of his nose. "It's my own fault."

"What's your fault?" I ask softly.

"Nothing," he says, pulling his knees in toward his chest. I rest my hand on the back of his head and he breathes in deeply. "He's always telling me to be careful, to keep people at arm's length," he says in a rush, getting the words out before he can change his mind. "You know, to make sure that they don't want to be my friend just because of who I am. Who he is, I guess." Our eyes meet in the opposite wall. "He told me to be extra careful in here."

"I can understand that. A lot of the girls here are very determined," I say, my voice deliberately breezy to convey how different I am (*I am easygoing. I am always happy-go-lucky.*) and Darwin visibly relaxes.

"He said that once the eves knew I was a Judge's son I would be an easy target."

"I think it's more to do with that fact you're the best-looking out of the bunch," I say cheekily, and he throws his head back in laughter.

I slink up the length of his body and kiss his neck, waiting for him to groan with pleasure. I keep waiting for him to lose interest in me, but he doesn't. He chooses me every time, again and again.

"You're a good listener," he tells me another day. I'm sitting in his lap, legs wrapped around his waist, my heels kicked off and strewn by the door of the cupboard.

"I have practice," I say, stroking his hair. "My sisters love to talk."

"Your sisters?"

"The other eves." I lean in to kiss him, inhaling his breath until he breaks off.

"I always wanted a brother."

"Why? I think being an only child sounds perfect." I think enviously of the undivided attention. "It makes you special."

"You're special." He pushes my hair away and stares into my eyes. I kiss him again to hide my anxiety. When is he going to figure out that isn't true? When will he realize how very far from special I really am?

"At least if I had a brother I would have someone to talk to," Darwin says when we come up for air. "Someone who understands. I'd have someone I could trust not to gossip about family stuff. Discretion is really important to Dad; he's always telling me not to air our dirty laundry in public. It doesn't help when you want to make friends though."

Maybe you're better off, I think. You're less likely to get hurt.

"But if I had a brother—"

"Why don't you?" I interrupt without thinking, and I immediately apologize. "Sorry, that was rude of me."

"No, it wasn't." He laughs. "I don't know. My dad had two other companions before my mother. The first one was barren, they had to have an investigation into why she was ever issued her fertility certificate. She was sent to the pyre, naturally. The second companion lasted a little longer. She fell soon after the Ceremony." He pauses thoughtfully. "The son's name was Benjamin. He died two days after he was born."

"What happened to him?"

"I don't know. Bad genes? Neglectful mothering? They couldn't decide so the girl was sent Underground for testing. Then Dad chose my mother. They had hoped for more sons but she hasn't fallen since me, and Dad said he couldn't be bothered going through the hassle of getting a new companion." I nod, wondering how much longer his mother has left before her Termination Date. "I have a lot to live up to. Only son and all that!" He shakes his head, pulling me closer to him. "I can't believe I told you that. I've never told anyone."

He begins to bring presents with him more frequently. A thick cuff with a faceted amber stone in the center follows the earrings. The download of an album by an obscure indie band from the Americas that I have never heard of.

"I love their music," I lie, and his eyes light up in excitement. "Especially their earlier stuff." We sit in the cupboard, sharing one set of earbuds, their "best song ever" threatening to split my eardrums in half. He bobs his head in time to the noise, stuffing his hands into the pouch at the front of yet another hooded sweatshirt.

"Like a kangaroo," I say absentmindedly, pulling at the pocket.

"A kangaroo?" he asks, turning the music off. "How have you heard of kangaroos?"

"I, er, I watch the Nature Channel," I reluctantly admit. "I like animals."

"The Nature Channel?" he repeats, grabbing the nugget of information to store away for safe keeping. "Tell me more. I want to know everything."

He's wearing away at my resistance with all of his questions. He asks about isabel and I tell him I'm worried about her. He likes that; he seems to think this proves that I am a good person. I don't tell him that isabel doesn't want anything to do with me. I don't tell him I'm afraid it's because there is something rotting inside of me, something you can only smell if you get too close. I don't tell him that she has broken my heart.

"Why is she isolating herself?" he asks. "It's kind of you to be so concerned."

"We were friends for years," I say. "I can't just stop caring overnight."

However much I wish I could.

I turn the conversation back to him. He tells me about music he likes, movies he's watched and novels he's read. When I mention the confiscated picture books that I had looked at as a child, he smuggles in a collection of short stories. I hold the book in my hands, feeling the wafer thinness of the paper between my fingertips, examining the markings on the pages. He reads aloud to me, and it's like magic as he translates the squiggles into words, sentences, stories.

"I wish I could read too."

"I'll read to you whenever you want." He tosses the book aside, kissing a trail from my ear to my cheek before claiming my mouth, erasing all my thoughts until I am lost and I don't know where he ends and I begin. When he kisses me, I want to unzip his skin and step inside him, become a part of him so that we can be together forever, so that no one, not even the Father, could separate us. It's when we stop kissing that the thoughts come back, sharpening their blades. His hands hover by my stomach, making achingly slow circles, lower and lower until he starts playing with the zipper on my skinny cord jeans.

"I can't," I say, hoping that he'll try to persuade me to keep going.

"Are you sure?" His voice is husky, his body still pressed against mine, pushing me against the hard glass.

Of course I'm not sure.

"I'm sorry, Darwin."

I would if I knew that it wouldn't change how he felt about me. I would if I knew that he was going to choose me and make me a Judge's companion.

"I'm sorry," I say again. I can't risk it.

He leans away from me and takes a couple of deep breaths.

"Have you ever done it before?" I ask him as I sit down, avoiding his eyes.

"Of course."

"What age were you? What was it like?"

"What? The first time?"

I nod as he sits beside me, stretching his legs out parallel to mine.

"I was twelve. My dad organized an hour with a concubine for my birthday."

I think back to when we celebrated our 12th design date. We were allowed to eat whatever food we wanted, stuffing our faces with sweeties and chocco and ice-kream. We all fell into a sugar coma when the lamps were turned off, rubbing our swollen bellies, only to be awoken at 4:30 a.m. for a three-hour gym session to atone for our sins. *Fat girls should be made obsolete. No will ever love a fat girl.*

"My mother thought it was too young, but my dad insisted," he says. "Afterward he took me for beer. I started to feel really light-headed so I secretly dumped half of it into this plastic cactus next to our table." His voice is becoming more and more animated as he tells the story. "The next morning he said he was satisfied with how I was shaping up, that I seemed able to handle both my beer and my women."

"And how was it?"

"How was what?" he asks, happily lost in the memory of his dad's approval.

"The sex," I say impatiently, before controlling myself and smiling sweetly to disguise my flash of irritation.

"Oh yeah. It was fine. Good. She seemed to enjoy herself anyway. Are you jealous?" he crows delightedly as I smile crookedly at him, my mouth tightening. "And I thought you didn't care."

"I'm not jealous," I say, softening my voice. "All men go to concubines. It's no big deal."

"Of course not," he says, his smile fading. "You're not the jealous type."

He holds me away from him, staring at me. No one has ever looked at me like that before, as if I'm everything they never knew they even wanted.

"You're staring at her again!" cara pokes me and my spoon jolts, spilling cucumber soup down my dove-gray silk T-shirt.

"Be careful," I bark at her, ignoring the girls' surprised faces. They would be edgy too if they couldn't sleep. I'm trying to wean myself off SleepSound. My recovery period is over so chastity-ruth is refusing to give me extra supplies anyway, and I've told chastity-anne I don't want my normal dosage at night. Darwin hates people taking medication.

"No need to bite my head off," she replies, digging around in her handbag before throwing me a wet wipe. I dab at the stain, groaning as I spread it wider across my chest. "I didn't do it on purpose." She looks hurt, drawing her hair over one shoulder and pulling at it, a dusting of blond hairs falling across the table.

"I'm worried about isabel," I admit quietly so that the others can't overhear.

"That's obvious." Of course megan is listening. "You can't stop staring at her."

"I'm worried about her."

"She's a big girl . . ."

"Not so big anymore!" jessie giggles to liz.

". . . she can take care of herself," megan finishes, smoothing her hair into a loose chignon. She looks lovely today, her yellow halter-neck dress cut daringly low, cinched in at the waist and flowing out to a full skirt.

"I don't know."

"freida, we've talked about this." megan shakes her head in frustration, bulbous sapphire earrings banging off her neck. "Who cares about isabel?"

We all look at her, sitting alone again, wearing a marl-gray T-shirt dress with cutout panels at the side, her ribs thrusting through her skin like crocodiles' teeth. She seems to wear less and less clothing these days, as if she wants to draw attention to her shrinking body, using her emerging skeleton as a disguise. But it's still isabel, still the girl who used to laugh loudly and often, her mouth wide open as if she found our world so delicious she wanted to swallow it whole.

"Where are you going?" megan hisses. If I am a Judge's companion, she will never hiss at me again.

"isabel."

She ignores me and keeps playing with her cucumber soup, ladling a spoonful before tipping it back into the bowl.

"I'm worried about you." I crouch beside her. "You have got to start eating."

The background hum is dying down. I can hear swishing as people turn in their seats to look at us.

"Leave it, freida," she whispers, staring into her soup bowl. It feels so good to hear her say my name that my eyes sting. "It's better this way."

"What are you talking about?" My voice is echoing in the hushed room, louder than I intended. "What's better this way?"

"Lower your voice, #630."

"I'm sorry," I say, standing up straight to meet those wolf-gray eyes, "but I can't stand by and watch my friend starve to death." I point at isabel, who is trying to pretend that this conversation has nothing to do with her. "She's wasting away. She only gets the 0-kcal option at mealtimes, and then throws most of her food away, and no one is doing anything to stop her." Anger is crawling in my debt, searching for a crumb of SleepSound to smother it. *I don't need it. I don't need it. Darwin doesn't like girls who take drugs.*

"What are her weigh-ins like?" I lash out, a flash of lightning running through me, white hot. "It doesn't fucking look like she's within target range to me."

"I'm sorry," I say as the curse word shoots into the air, exploding like a firecracker. "That just slipped out. I'm sorry."

"Interesting." chastity-ruth suppresses a smile as she scans isabel's wasted body. "Perhaps you are correct, #630. But don't worry your little head about it. We will take care of isabel." At this, isabel's face crumples like a chocco wrapper held over an open flame.

"As much as I appreciate your desire to assist us . . ." she rolls the sleeves of her robes up as if preparing for a fight—"I cannot allow you to disturb the peace during mealtimes."

I wait for isabel to defend me but she is motionless, reading the lines on the palms of her hands like a treasure map.

"#630, what am I going to do with you? This is the second ePad that you have broken this year."

"I'm sorry, chastity-ruth."

"Sorry doesn't cut it, I'm afraid. Apologies are not going to pay for a replacement computer, are they? I don't know why I continue to be surprised at how utterly useless you are."

"It's not her fault," isabel broke in. "I broke it. It was my fault. freida was just trying to be a good friend."

She kicked me in the shin under the table and I kept quiet.

"Very well, isabel," the chastity said finally, her lips tight with annoyance. "You may give #630 your old ePad in replacement."

That evening isabel had a new computer, a thinner, lighter one with a hot-pink cover. "A present," she said.

I wanted it. I wanted a present too.

And instantly my gratitude broke, cut to shreds by jealousy.

"Thank you for the apology," chastity-ruth says. "However, I'm afraid I'm still going to have to chastise you for your rather *ugly* display of insolence. What will it be . . . what will it be?" She taps her mouth with her fingertips. "Ah, yes! I know. You shall be ineligible for the next session of Heavenly Seventy."

"But . . ." I stutter, disbelief and panic spontaneously combusting in my chest, "that's not fair."

She turns away and I want to scream, pick up isabel's tray of uneaten food and throw it at her. I want to fling a bucketful of Unacceptable Emotions and watch them splash all over her face like paint.

Nice girls don't get angry.

I clutch at the empty locket hanging around my neck, wishing more than anything for it to be full again.

"So, after that little incident, I'm afraid #630 is unavailable for selection today," chastity-ruth informs the Inheritants.

"That hardly seems appropriate, ruth," Albert says, failing to detect the faint pucker of her lips as he drops the "chastity." "Surely it's up to us men to decide whom we want to choose."

chastity-ruth is firm. "The chastisement of the eves is under my jurisdiction while they are still at School."

There is a frisson of anticipation in the room, everyone wondering who my lucky replacement is going to be. I don't look up. I don't want to see Darwin choose someone else, see him walk into our cupboard with another eve.

And all this because of isabel. I've lost precious time with Darwin because of someone who barely acknowledges my existence. Everyone must think I'm so stupid. I *am* so stupid.

"Mr. Darwin, who will it be today?" chastity-ruth asks, padding her way softly through the classroom until she's standing beside me, presumably to have a better view of my misery.

"I think," his voice is careful, every eve in the room holding her breath, "I'll go with agyness."

agyness doesn't move. Earbuds already in place and watching a Nature Channel rerun on her desktop, she cries out in pain when megan grinds a heel into her foot.

"What?" she asks, looking in confusion when megan points furiously at Darwin. And then I know. He's chosen her as a message to me, the only eve in our class I won't feel threatened by. And I feel like I can breathe for the first time since lunch, the tension thawing out of my shoulders.

"What is Darwin's deal?"

"I know! Is he only into freaks?" gisele pauses for a second too long. "Not including you, freida, obviously."

Her fake smile is nauseating. We're at our usual table in the Nutrition Center, but no one is monitoring the buffets. There could be a run on death-by-chocolate puddings and I doubt it would merit a comment.

"Wait, here she comes," megan mutters.

agyness is drifting dreamily away from chastity-anne's desk, balancing her tray and her vial of daily meds, her peacock-blue maxi dress sweeping the tiles.

"agy!" megan calls to her, stacks of thin gold bangles clinking on her wrist as she waves.

"Good day to you, my fellow eves," agyness announces theatrically, the other girls barely suppressing eye-rolls.

"I love your dress. The color is adorable on you!"

agyness looks down at her dress to remind herself what she is wearing.

"Oh yes!" she says, her velvety skin going pink with excitement. "I was watching a program on peacocks the other day so I requested a dress in the same shade."

"So, tell us . . ." megan's voice drops as liz asks jessie what a "peecuck" is, "what happened during Heavenly Seventy?"

"You were there." agyness blinks.

"I wasn't in the cupboard, was I? What happened with Darwin in the cupboard?"

"You said after the first week it was unfair to discuss what happened during the task," agyness says, and I bite my lip, trying not to laugh out loud.

"agyness, just tell us what happened."

"Well, nothing." agyness makes a face to indicate her tray is getting heavy. "We talked."

"Talked?"

"Yes."

"What is with this guy and talking?" megan says, turning her back on agyness. "We're done here. You can go."

"She's painful," she sighs as agyness floats away. "Well, Darwin sure likes to talk, doesn't he?"

"Yeah. What's that about?" daria asks, shaking her wispy bangs out of her eyes.

"What if he's an aberrant?" liu exclaims, breathless with excitement that she's been allowed to sit with us for once.

"He can't be. He's a Judge's son," megan snarls, and liu quakes, panicking that she might have ruined her chances of sitting with us ever again. megan catches herself. "And, liu," she adds smoothly, "you know as well as I do, no aberrants have been born since they made those prenatal tests mandatory. Are you questioning the Genetic Testers' ability to identify the aberrant gene?"

"No, of course not," liu whispers. "I was . . . I was only joking. Of course I don't think Darwin is an aberrant."

"He's definitely not," I blurt out. There is a roar of raucous laughter, a sliver of food flying out of cara's mouth and landing on the table, making everyone laugh even louder. Questions fly at me, jumbling on top of each other.

"Are you in love with him?" cara laughs, pressing her hands to her heart.

"No." megan's voice is low but there's something in it that makes everyone stop laughing instantly. "She can't be. That would be love before marriage, wouldn't it?"

"I'm not in love with him," I scoff to hide the fear prickling in my chest at her words. "Of course I'm not."

Chapter 21

"Thank you." I make myself break away from Darwin. I've wanted to say thank you since he chose me for today's Heavenly Seventy, but once the doors of the cupboard closed behind us, he had his hands in my hair and his mouth was on mine, and I forgot where I was. He always makes me forget.

"For what?"

"For choosing agyness." I blush, afraid I'm presuming too much. "At the last Heavenly Seventy session."

"Ah, the future chastity-agyness! The first one since chastity-magdalena, I do believe."

"Where did you hear that?"

"I pay attention, freida." Darwin winks mischievously at me. He is so cute. We kiss again and my mind goes liquid.

"agyness is nice," he says as he pulls me into his chest, his legs wrapped around mine. "I've had some great

Interactions with her. She's smart. It's almost like talking with a guy."

"Don't say that outside this cupboard," I say, becoming serious. "If chastity-ruth hears you say that about agyness, she'll be in trouble."

"They're hardly going to think she's an aberrant. They sorted that problem out years ago."

I freeze, but he doesn't seem to notice, his lips tracing the veins in my skin.

"A what?" I ask, pushing him off me. "But she's a girl. There isn't such a thing as a female aberrant."

"I guess not," he agrees quickly. Too quickly. "Forget it."

He starts kissing me again but I can't concentrate, my brain swirling with thoughts about what this could mean. Images flash into my mind of isabel and me, lying together on my bed, our fingers intertwined as we talked and talked for hours. I've never felt the same connection with anyone else that I have with isabel, not even with Darwin. She has been the other half of me for the best part of sixteen years. What does that mean? Is there something unnatural about me? Could isabel sense it? Is that why she's been avoiding me?

"No," I say, pushing him off me. I need to know. "Wait. What did you mean by that?"

"Come on, freida," he pleads. "Can we just forget it?"

"I can't forget it." I shuffle away from him until we are sitting parallel, our backs pressed against the cold mirrored wall. I turn my head to look at him. "Don't you trust me?"

He hesitates. "Of course I do." Indecision is etched all over his face. "But, I just—"

"Please tell me," I interrupt. I need to know. "Pretty please?"

I'm rewarded with a reluctant smile. "If I tell you, do you promise that you won't repeat it to anyone else?"

"I promise," I lean over and whisper into his ear. I lick it with the very tip of my tongue and he shudders slightly. I know what he likes.

"I can't believe I'm doing this," he groans, shaking his head as he reaches into his pocket to get his eFone, angling it toward me so I can see properly. On the screen appears a large rectangular-shaped hall, cast in gray concrete. There are dozens of huge wooden doors along each side, a wooden label on each one.

"What do they say?"

"They're the names of the rooms."

"But what do they *say*?"

"What the room is for." He looks away.

"Like what?" I persist, staring at the squiggles of letters and words, wishing I could understand them.

He exhales loudly. "Well, this door is Taboo, this one is Reluctance, this one is Non-Consent. That one over there is Back Door, this one is Group. There are loads of them," he says, the words rushing out.

"I understand," I say, even though I don't understand, not at all. As he fidgets with the keypad, the camera moves forward through the hall, more and more doors on each side. The motion stops, a hand with scarlet-painted nails coming into view as it rests on the door.

"Whose hand is that?" I ask.

"Mine."

"Sure it is. Which is why you have nail polish on. That's a girl's hand."

"Well, it's not *my* hand, obviously. But it's my avatar's hand. An avatar is sort of like my character in this game. I control her." He tries to explain, sensing my confusion. "She's my visual alter ego. Does that make sense?"

"But that's a real hand, not a computer graphic," I say, more baffled than ever.

"Well, yeah, the game is called Controlled concubines. Look, I'll show you."

He presses a few buttons and the camera pulls back, cutting to a different angle so that I can see the full scope of the hall. Standing at the door, with that same perfectly manicured hand resting on the handle, is a young concubine in a scarlet leotard, cut high on her slim thighs. Her dark hair is pulled away from her face in a ponytail and there are wires wrapped around her head, like tentacles.

"What are those wires for?"

"That's what connects the concubine to my eFone. While she's hooked up to the sensors, all of her movements are completely controlled by me."

I squint at the screen. Her skin is tanned and smooth, as dark as mine, her hair the same lustrous brown, her vacant eyes tinged with yellow. The similarities between us are uncanny.

"She's beautiful, isn't she?"

I look away, afraid to agree in case it's some sort of test of my modesty.

The concubine pushes the door open. All the walls of the room within are made of a quilted black pleather, a steel pole like a ballet barre bordering it. Hundreds of implements are hanging from the pole: whips, paddles, cuffs, and shackles. There are two other concubines there, both in red latex catsuits. They turn as the door opens, their faces as blank as that of Darwin's concubine, gesturing at the newcomer to join in. One of them is brandishing an iron rod, wiggling her hips lewdly.

"Wrong room," Darwin mutters as he makes the concubine leave, shutting the door behind her. She waits passively until he makes her walk toward a different door.

"This is the Sapphica room," he tells me. The avatar strides into the room and walks up to the nearest available concubine, a black girl with a huge blond afro. He makes the avatar grab the other girl by the head, her red-painted nails digging into those yellow curls. She pulls her near, and their mouths are touching, their tongues are touching. *They're kissing. There are two girls kissing.* The screen cuts out, Darwin cursing under his breath. "My battery must be dead." He shoves the fone back into his pocket. I'm too shocked to speak and he pushes his dark curls off his forehead uncomfortably. "Some guys are into it."

Are you into it? Is that why you showed this to me?

"Then why haven't we been instructed in this? If it's something we might have to do if we become concubines, we should have classes in this. Why haven't I heard of it before?"

"Leave it, freida," he snaps, and we both reel from the harshness of his tone. He's never spoken to me like that before.

"Sorry." He reaches his hand out to cover mine and my gut clenches at the touch of his skin. "I don't want to upset you."

"I won't be upset."

"It was years ago," he says emphatically. "I wasn't even born. It's a waste of time even talking about it."

We stare at each other in silence, waiting it out to see who will crack. After years of dealing with megan, I'm not surprised when he groans in defeat.

"Do you promise you won't tell anyone?" he asks again.

"I swear, Darwin. You can trust me."

"It was years ago, remember," he begins, and I have to lean in closer to hear him, our faces nearly touching. His aftershave is making me woozy, something dissolving to liquid inside me. I nod at him to continue, just keep talking. If he starts kissing me again, I know that I'll forget all about female aberrants.

"These two eves were best friends. The chastities thought they spent so much time together because they were friends, but it turned out to be more than that. They fell in love."

"What?" I jerk up, hitting his nose with my forehead, and he chokes backs a howl of pain. "Sorry, I'm sorry,"

I jabber, ignoring the dull ache forming across my head. "I'm sorry."

"Anyway . . ." he laughs it off, "they tried to run away together."

"What?" I say in shock. "But how did they get out? The entrance to the trains runs out of the chastities' quarters."

"They didn't get very far." He stretches away from me, and I want to reach out and pull him close again. "They were caught," he mumbles almost unintelligibly, "and punished."

"How were they punished?"

"It's not like they were innocent," he says, kicking his foot off the mirrored ground beneath us. "They deserved to be punished . . . They had to be punished," he says again, like he's trying to persuade me. Or himself. "My dad said the Zone had to set an example."

"So what happened?" I'm holding my breath, every instinct telling me I don't want to know the answer.

"The Father was fair."

I nod automatically. Of course He was fair. He's always fair.

"He married them off to lower-ranked Inheritants whose wives had died unexpectedly in son-birth. But they wouldn't obey the rules. One of their husbands caught them together, in his bed." I gasp at the audacity. They must have been desperate. "It didn't matter that it was two women," Darwin continues, scratching roughly at his neck. "It was still adultery. So the adultery sentence still stood."

"What's the adultery sentence?"

"You don't need to know that."

"Did they throw them on the pyre? Or did they send them Underground?" I can't stop myself. I need to know.

"Not exactly," he says simply, and I feel goosebumps break out across my skin.

"Tell me."

"They . . . Look, freida, I don't want to talk about this anymore."

"Tell me." I cup his chin in my hand and turn his face toward mine, staring at him steadily until he continues.

"First they tried to rehabilitate them again. 'Straighten' them out, force them to enjoy the love of a good man. Quite a few good men, if the stories are true." I don't move, and he hesitates again, clearly wishing he had never started this conversation. "When that didn't work out, they were sent Underground for a few weeks. For the usual genetic testing, you know. To see if they could find the faulty wiring."

"And after that?" He doesn't answer. "Darwin. What happened to them after that?"

"And then . . ." he takes a deep breath, forcing the words out, "they sewed up their . . . er, their . . . you know, their *private parts*. And then they shot them. Two clean bullets right through the brain."

The room swarms, our reflections looming from the mirrors and pressing in on me, stealing the oxygen from my lungs.

"Did your dad set that sentence?"

No answer.

"Did he?" I ask again as he looks at me helplessly.

"It's standard for companions who commit adultery."

I try to appear blasé, but I'm too stunned to make a good job of it.

"My dad was in a difficult position," he says. "He had to . . . They weren't even *trying* to control their unnatural urges, freida. My dad says that the whole Zone would fall apart if everyone did that. We all have to play our part in order to survive." He reaches out to hold my hand. "They introduced Isolation for eves after that. Why do you think it is so strictly enforced?"

Not always, I think. Not when isabel was involved.

"Why haven't we heard of this before?" I say. "Wouldn't it have been on TV or on the Nature Channel?"

"Ah, the all-knowing Nature Channel," he teases, but I don't laugh. He sighs. "It's censored, freida."

"Do the chastities know?"

"Probably not. It was years ago and the Genetic Engineers isolated the Rainbow24 gene in women after that so it wouldn't happen again."

"Then why enforce Isolation?"

"To be safe, I guess. I reckon they're afraid that if they mention the Sapphica idea at all, even just as a method to turn guys on, that the eves might get ideas."

"But what about the concubines in this game? What if they 'get ideas'?"

"That doesn't matter." He shrugs. "They don't remember anything that happens while they're hooked up to the sensors. So it's okay, you know? They don't feel anything anyway."

That's all I've ever wanted. To switch off all these emotions. Not to have to feel so much. But not like that. Never like that.

The bell rings and we both flinch, startled by the interruption. I get to my feet, feeling older than I ever have before.

"You won't tell anyone, will you?" Darwin says, grabbing my hand to stop me from leaving. He lowers his voice. "It's just, well, my dad would kill me. I only told you because I trust you. Promise me you'll keep it a secret."

"I promise," I reassure him, warmth spreading through me. I can have secrets too.

And we walk out of the cupboard and into the classroom together, but this time he doesn't let go of my hand.

Chapter 22

"Where's isabel?" cara asks at breakfast the next morning, pointing at isabel's customary place, now empty.

"That's weird." daria turns to me. "Where is she?"

"I don't know," I answer coldly, despising the weakness in me that still wishes I did.

"And who cares?" megan smiles at me. "Right, freida?"

"Exactly," I say, and I feel an irrational chill. Grabbing my cream blazer from the back of my chair, I wrap it around me like a shield.

"I heard they had to force-feed her through a tube inserted into her stomach."

"I heard they had to tie her down while chastity-anne shoved kcal enhancers down her throat."

"No, I heard . . ."

". . . I heard . . ."

* * *

The following Monday, isabel returns to class, although rumor has it she's still banned from the Nutrition Center so they can monitor her food intake more carefully. You can see a hint of flesh gradually reemerging, like she's growing a new skin. She's beautiful, but it's a faded beauty now, as if she's been washed too many times. It makes it easier for me, in a way. It lends her an unfamiliarity.

Beep. Beeeeep.

I accept the VideoChat request, placing my ePad on my bedside locker and squatting on the floor. megan told me the angle is more flattering this way.

"Hey."

megan has called a conference VideoChat with me and the twins so liz and jessie can tell us their latest plan to waste time before bedtime.

"I think we should each send her a MyFace message," jessie declares.

"Who? isabel?" I smile at my image on the screen to check that I don't have lipstick on my teeth. jessie copies me, dabbing at the corners of her lips.

"Ooh, I love your nail art," I say, catching sight of her houndstooth-printed nails.

"Oh, thanks!" A compliment from me is worth having these days. "I got it done today."

"Can we forget about nail art? Let's not get . . ." megan pauses, staring at me intently through the screen. She knows what I'm trying to do. ". . . distracted."

"What kind of messages?" she asks the twins, giving them full responsibility, or blame in case of a mishap.

"Well, we didn't think that it's fair that she's wasting perfectly good Compound funding," jessie says piously. "And we think she should be aware of how we feel."

"What do you think, freida?" megan applies more lip gloss, until her mouth resembles an oil slick.

"I don't know. What do you think?"

"I asked you first."

I shift away from the camera, sitting on the cold tiled floor and stretching my legs out in front of me, ignoring the throbbing as blood flows back into my limbs. I adjust the screen to get rid of the glare from the overhead lamps. The screen is divided into three squares, each face within a square, all waiting patiently for my reply.

"It seems a bit cruel," I admit, and the twins frown in disappointment.

"It's only a joke!" liz says.

"It would be funny." jessie pouts, sticking her lower lip out.

"I totally get it. You were friends for such a long time. It is very freida to feel loyal to her," megan says. I'm not sure if "very freida" is a compliment. "Especially after the way she treated you."

"What do you mean—the way she treated me?"

"Come on, freida. Everyone was talking about it, saying how you didn't deserve to be treated like that. It was all anyone could talk about for ages. Obviously we were all on your side," she rushes to reassure me as my lips become pinched. "I just think it's amazing how forgiving you are. Especially when she clearly doesn't give a shit about you."

I feel a hot flush of humiliation at the thought of everyone talking about how I had been exiled like a leper. I picture them all on VideoChat, listing my faults, deciding which one of my many deficiencies it must have been that made isabel give up on me.

"Let's do it," a strange voice says.

"Oh, freida, are you sure?" megan asks, but her eyes are dancing with excitement. "Don't do anything you're not comfortable with."

"It's only a joke, right?" that voice says again.

The twins take out their eFones, logging onto MyFace and recording a private message for isabel . . . *dead* . . . *everyone hates you* . . . *worthless* . . . They erupt into fits of giggles and cut the message short.

"You two are useless!" megan laughs with them. "You can never keep a straight face."

"You think you're better? Prove it!"

"No." megan points at the camera. Pointing at me. "You're next."

isabel's information is still saved as a short cut so it instantly logs onto her MyFace account. Her page is empty; no one has posted anything publicly in months. She might as well be dead.

"You don't have to do this," megan says again in a soft voice. "I know how much you care about her."

I look at her sharply. Is she implying that there is something unnatural about my friendship with isabel?

"I don't care about her that much." I'm normal. I need them to know that I'm normal. "I never think about her."

"Too busy thinking about Darwin!" jessie teases, and I nod eagerly.

"Your turn then." megan's eyes narrow with a hint of challenge and I have to remind myself of isabel, drifting away from me all year. Our friendship was my life buoy, the only thing keeping me alive, and she snatched it away from me without a moment's hesitation. Something hardens in me, like cement drying around my heart.

I don't care. I don't care about her either.

"What's going on with you and isabel?" Darwin asks, his eyes boring into mine. He rubs his jaw and his fingers make a scratching sound against the stubble.

"Did you not shave this morning? When you knew we would have Heavenly Seventy?" I tease. "How inconsiderate of you."

I lean back, my shoulders resting against the mirrored wall of the cupboard, displaying my body to him. Momentarily distracted, he touches the distressed endings of my white cut-off shorts before backing away.

"I'm being serious." He frowns. "What's going on with isabel?"

"What are you talking about?" I mumble, folding my chin into my chest and staring at my daisy-print sandals.

"I heard what you said about her when she came into class."

"I didn't say anything." I sound petulant. "I just agreed with liz."

"You agreed with liz when she said that isabel was defective and should be sent Underground for testing." He sounds as if he's tired of this. Tired of me. "Look, liz is a bitch, I know that. But you're not."

"liz is a friend of mine," I say, hiding my joy that he thinks she's a bitch. That's one less girl I have to worry about. "You don't know what isabel has been like." My treacherous voice cracks a little and he places his hands on my bare shoulders and massages gently. "This isn't like you, freida." He moves his hands up, his fingers grazing against my hair at the nape of my neck. He's right. It isn't like the freida I've been pretending to be when I'm with him, the freida that I want more than anything to become. He leans forward, pressing his forehead against mine.

"It hurts less this way." For once, it seems the truth makes me more likable.

"I knew there had to be a reason," he says quietly. "You're a good person, freida."

I rest my head on his shoulder so he can't see my face. A good person wouldn't have left that message on isabel's MyFace. He unravels my arms from around him and takes a couple of steps back. He leans against the opposite mirror and touches the silver buckle on his belt. For a moment I think he's going to open it, slide it off, unbutton his jeans. Let them drop to the floor and pull that frayed T-shirt over his head. Ask me if I wanted him to stop, but I wouldn't. *I wouldn't.*

"freida?"

"Yes?" My voice is squeaky. I cough. "Yes."

"I just wanted you to know I . . ." He stops, taking my arms and pulling me closer, molding his hard body into mine. "I like you, freida. I really like you."

For a brief moment I feel happiness surging inside me. As we kiss, I whisper his words over and over to myself. *I like you, I like you, I like you.* Does he like me enough to choose me? Does he like me enough to take me away from all this and make me a Judge's companion?

This is happening too fast. Why is he saying all these things? It's too soon.

Why does he like you? There must be something wrong with him if he likes you.

*But it isn't you he likes, is it? It isn't the **real** you. If he knew the real you, he would leave. Just like isabel did.*

"You okay?" he asks, the words falling from his mouth into mine.

"Of course," I reply, and I smile, knitting this mask into my skin.

Chapter 23

June
Four weeks until the Ceremony

"Are you in love with him?"

This is my fifth VideoChat with megan in the last forty-five minutes. My elbows are chafing from propping myself up on my bed to talk to her.

"Because if you are in love with him," she says, "you can tell me. We can fix this. I won't tell any of the others."

"I'm not in love with him." I roll on my side and position the ePad into the crook of my elbow. "Ugh, did you see what miranda was wearing today?"

"Slut-tastic, I know. Now don't change the subject."

"I'm not changing the subject."

"You're in love with Darwin."

"I told you, I'm not."

"If the chastities find out that you're in love with him, you are going to be in big trouble."

"The other girls are having sex before marriage and . . ." Her full mouth curves into a gleeful smile and I add hastily, "megan, I'm not in love with him. I was just saying that the Heavenly Seventy girls are obviously having sex with the . . ."

"There are no rules about sex, just guidelines."

Guidelines I'm still struggling to make sense of. If you want to be a companion, you won't have sex before marriage. No one wants a girl that puts out before marriage, except that they sometimes *do* want a girl that puts out before marriage, but only if she's going to be a concubine. It all depends on what type of girl you are. And we can't even be sure what type of girl that is until we are told by the men at the Ceremony. Are they making up the "guidelines" as they go along?

"If you're not in love with him, why are you being so secretive about your Heavenly Seventy sessions?"

"I'm not being secretive."

"Yes, you are. You're being just like isabel used to be. Do you want to end up like her?"

Maybe it's the lack of sleep, maybe it's the craving for SleepSound or maybe it's just the reference to isabel, but I don't think I can take another minute of her.

"I'm exhausted, megan. I'm going to get some sleep."

"But it's only 8:30. And I—"

"I'm exhausted," I interrupt, and her cheeks suck in with annoyance.

"Yes. Better get some sleep. We wouldn't want a repeat of that unfortunate fainting incident," she replies nastily. "So embarrassing."

She ends the chat session, the ePad emitting a low beep. Information is currency in the School, and I'm withholding. I set my chat status to unavailable and place the ePad on the ground beside my bed.

I should call her back. I'll regret that tomorrow.

I fold the pillow over my head, wondering what would happen if I held it over my mouth, pressed the life out of myself. I could sleep forever. Time passes and passes and I can feel anxiety rising in me like a fever. I shouldn't have been antagonistic with megan. To lose one best friend is unfortunate; to lose two would be reckless. Who would I sit with at lunch? The thought seems so ridiculous that I burst into laughter, giggles falling into my lap as I stay coiled in a ball, gripping my knees with my arms, trying to keep myself in one piece.

I can't.

I reach into my bedside locker. Nothing. I threw it all away to please him.

I need something. Anything.

Darwin hates drugs.

He'll never know.

I climb out, looking left and right, creeping down the corridor. The doors are open as always, but no one sees me, their faces lit by the glow from their ePads, compulsively updating their MyFace statuses to prove they're alive.

"What do you want?" christy guiltily brushes the crumbs of a half-eaten chocco bar off her sheets. She sits up, pulling her satin kimono tighter around her soft belly.

"SleepSound," I say. "You owe me, remember?"

Back in my own room, I swallow the tablet. *Oh, how I missed you, I missed you.* The meds work faster than I remember, shimmering through my system. I lick my lips, feeling every muscle in my body sag into the soft, soft blanket. The twitching thoughts slow down, drifting across my mind like shadows.

I can see Darwin and me, Husband and companion, taking our rightful place in the Euro-Zone society. He in his future role as Judge, me by his side, dispensing smiles like favors to my former sisters. They will have to accept me then.

But I'm not safe yet.

Chapter 24

The morning dawning from the light-lamps is niggling at my eyelids. I rub my eyes, the inside of my head feeling as if it has been coated in glue, and use the hair band digging into my wrist to tie my knotted hair back. Yesterday's jeans feel as if they have melted through the top layer of my skin, and I tug at them to loosen their grip on my clammy body. I can hear the low buzzing of activity, all the other eves getting ready for the day ahead. I don't want to get out of bed. I've slept for more than ten hours and I'm still exhausted.

In the changing room I tell the PSP to style me however it wants today. I don't have the energy to put an outfit together myself. The computer screen turns semireflective again and I can see the makeup smeared all over my face, smudges of mascara and eyeliner ringing my bloodshot eyes. I skim my cheeks with my fingertips, feeling a crepe of dried sweat laced across them.

I peel off the sticky clothes, shove them into the chute and step into the changing room. The laser burns across my body, tousling my hair into soft waves, painting my lips a punchy neon pink. It's very pretty, a nice contrast to the outfit that has been selected for me: tight pleather sleeveless waistcoat over black skinny jeans, with buckled shoes so pointy I could use them as a weapon.

"Come on!" freja urges me, eye-wateringly skinny in a violet one-shouldered dress.

"Sorry." I dash into line, marching to the dining hall for breakfast, mechanically going through the routine. Line. BeBetter buffet. chastity-anne.

"I'll take my SleepSound today."

She raises an eyebrow. "I thought you said you didn't need it anymore."

I shrug, waiting in silence until she hands over the test tube.

"Hey, girls." I throw my studded bucket bag at my feet and slide my tray onto the table. Pretending to get something out of my bag, I slip the SleepSound out of the test tube and into my locket, instantly feeling calmer.

"What are you wearing?" cara asks, her voice surprised.

"Not my usual style, I know," I say, straightening up and lifting the lid to examine today's lo-carb option. "The PSP chose it."

"But we were supposed to be matching!" cara says. I look up to see that she, megan, the twins, gisele and

daria are dressed in prom dresses with sweetheart neck-
lines, all cinched at the waist and stopping just above
the knee.

"Wow. You look like companions," I say, pulling at the
studded black bracelets littering my wrists.

"Well, if the Crimson Crew can be so obvious . . ." jessie gestures at them, two tables away from us, all wearing
red-and-black laced corsets tucked into black skinny jeans
identical to the pair I have on.

"I tried to tell you about it last night, but you said
you were too tired to talk. I didn't want to bother you."
megan sips her protein shake carefully as not to get any
stains on her dress, tangles of pink roses on cream silk.
"Anyway, girls, the rest of us look so pretty. Such a good
idea!"

Our table looks as if a rainbow vomited on it. cara is in
emerald green, gisele in primrose yellow and daria in royal
blue. jessie's dress is lilac polka dots on white silk and liz
has white dots on lilac silk. And I'm the black cloud in the
middle, threatening rain. megan looks at each of them in
turn, bathing them with her undivided attention, before
she skims over me, unseeing.

She's cold with me all day, although it's nothing so
obvious that anyone other than me would notice. If I mentioned it to cara or one of the others, they would tell me
not to be silly, that I'm "too sensitive." But I know. I over-
compensate, my voice too loud, too shrill, too much. The
others wince as I laugh manically at one of megan's jokes
during dinner.

"It wasn't that funny," she says, her body ever so slightly turned away from me, her eyes meeting everyone else's but mine.

It's the same all week. There are bursts of laughter that quiet down when I come near. A volley of message alerts beeping, like a round of gunfire, but my eFone remains silent.

"What's so funny?" I ask as the twins convulse with laughter. We're waiting for chastity-bernadette to arrive at class. jessie is sitting on liz's lap, the two sharing a set of earbuds and watching something on liz's eFone.

"Nothing," they chorus, liz angling the fone away from me so I can't see.

"It's nothing," cara reassures me. "Just a foto of candy Carmichael after her implants burst. You're being too sensitive."

I lie awake every night analyzing what happened that day, wondering if I *am* being too sensitive.

I asked megan earlier what time it was and she didn't answer; maybe she didn't hear. She did say thanks when I admired her sweater . . . but then she threw it in the garbage at lunchtime saying it was "a bit tacky." She was the only one who didn't laugh at my chastity-bernadette impression . . . she didn't even look up from her desk. She walked past without saying hi in the corridor . . . but she said afterward that she didn't see me. How could she not have seen me? . . . Maybe she didn't see me . . . But how could she not have seen me?

Around and around I go, until I'm forced to pull my locket open to find a little relief. I try to make sure it is always full now, charming the chastities into giving me an extra half at night, bargaining with christy to give me her SleepSound. I break off a bit of a pill. Just a quarter. Just to help me sleep. To take the edge off.

"I love your dress, jessie," I say at breakfast the next morning.

"Thanks!" She smiles, pulling the drawstring on her cerise T-shirt dress tighter. "Pink is my favorite color."

"I thought blue was," megan cuts in quickly. "Remember last night?"

"Yes!" jessie says, turning away from me. "She looked amazing when she wore that blue shift."

"No, I preferred the mauve wrap dress she wore for lunch with her friends," gisele argues, the conversation turning to the newest episode of *What kate Did Next* that aired the night before.

"Did you all watch it together?" I say in a higher-pitched voice than I intended.

"Yeah." jessie shrugs. "megan called a conference VideoChat."

"You never watch *What kate Did Next*," liz points out as I bite my lip. "You always say it's stupid."

I would have liked to have been asked though. I stir my now cold porridge halfheartedly, listening to yet another conversation where I'm unable to join in.

megan is at her dazzling best, never letting her charm drop for one moment.

"Your eyebrows are the *best*," she coos at cara.

"Those sequined shorts are the *best*," she tells freja, begging her to borrow them later, "although they probably won't even fit me. You are so skinny. Jealous!"

"I like your makeup," she says, sitting on the edge of liu's desk and peering closely at her face. "But then I really love *pale* skin, don't you? It's the *best*."

The next morning everyone has returned to wearing pale makeup, the trend of fake tan and bronzer finished as quickly as it began. And although I keep reminding myself that Darwin prefers my skin tone and that it only matters what men find attractive, I know all I want is for megan to say she thinks I'm pretty. Just once. She is always laughing, always talking, always the center of attention, burning so bright that I feel myself shriveling when she is near.

"megan's in a good mood," Isaac says during our Interaction, his beady eyes staring at the flash of skin in her cowl-backed jersey dress. She's a few seats away from us and I watch as she reaches out a hand to pick at a fleck of dust on Darwin's shoulder, brushing it away proprietarily.

"Yes," I say, attempting to smile.

Maybe if I'd worn a different dress, I think that night when sleep eludes me once again. If I had worn something a bit tighter . . . I told the PSP. Why doesn't it listen to me? Why doesn't anyone ever listen to me? . . . And I told chastity-hope to get me more of that skin-lightening cream for Beauty Therapy. I don't care if it will blister . . . If isabel hadn't . . . I don't care anyway . . . What was Darwin laughing about? He kept asking if I was "all right," saying that I seemed in a weird mood . . . Can he tell that I'm taking SleepSound again? I only took it last night because I couldn't sleep. I'm not going to take any more tonight. I don't need it . . . I'm not taking more tonight. I'm sure megan looked straight at me when she told liu her pale skin was amazing. *I'm not taking it tonight.* Am I being overly sensitive? Am I? Am I? Am I?

I creep through the sleeping corridors and shake christy awake. She points at her bedside locker sleepily. I grab the precious meds, replacing them with my kcal blockers. I'm not hungry these days anyway.

"freida!"

I open one eye reluctantly. freja is standing at the cubicle entrance, staring at me. "It's breakfast time. Why are you still in bed?"

Cursing, I wave at her to go ahead without me. Ten minutes later I'm dressed in a tangerine minidress with a racer back and hurrying to the Nutrition Center as fast as my tan wedge sandals will allow.

Line. Buffet. A futile debate with chastity-anne about the possibility of prescribing me more SleepSound.

I turn and there's a sea of faces. Where are the girls? Our table is empty. I walk around searching for them, feeling as if everyone in the Nutrition Center is watching me.

"There you are." I find them at last. "Why aren't you at our usual table?"

"Felt like a change," megan says without looking at me, siphoning some of cara's SlimShake into an empty glass. "Thanks, doll!" She smacks an air-kiss by her cheek.

She, cara, gisele, daria, freja, and the twins are all crammed around the smaller table, bumping elbows with each other as they eat.

"There's no room left." I look back at our usual table, still empty. "Maybe we could—"

"Girls!" megan screams over me. "I totally forgot to tell you that I'm in the final six for that competition I entered. Do you remember? The one where I might win a Video-Chat styling session with kate?"

"kate herself?" daria says, clutching at megan's hand in excitement. "No way!"

I shift from one foot to the other, my tray weighing me down, but none of them looks at me so I trudge back to the empty table to eat breakfast alone.

That evening I take two SleepSound tablets as soon as the lights are dimmed for nighttime, but I awake with a start at 3:00 a.m. In the mirrors, the shadows around my eyes look like bruises. There is nothing on TV, nothing new to look at on MyFace, so I just lie there for hours, *thinking, thinking, thinking*, waiting for the dark to thaw into the morning.

In class the next day, and the day after that, there is no seat left for me in our usual row, no space at our table in the Nutrition Center. I have to sit between cintia and liu, watching christy as she devours her pancakes, her belly folding into rolls beneath her too-tight vest top. I push my tray away, biting my lip so hard I can taste the metallic tang of my blood.

That night I mouth along to the Messages, sleep hiding from me once more.

I have far to go because I need to get better and better.

It's only three weeks till the Ceremony, I keep telling myself, but then I count the days, the hours, the minutes, and I can't breathe. I can't do it. I can't survive three full weeks of her anger. There isn't enough medication in the entire Euro-Zone that could block this out.

I loop my arm through megan's as we walk to our final class of the day. She picks up the pace, pulling away from me.

"Your perfume is too intense," she says. "It's giving me a headache."

"I'm not wearing perfume."

"That's your natural smell?" She swallows a smirk. "Sorry."

I don't flinch. I'm ready now. I'll give her whatever she wants.

"I can't believe you think I'm in love with Darwin."

She slows at the mention of his name. "Well, you give the impression that you are." She makes eye contact with me for the first time in days, and I feel dizzy with relief. "But you could tell me, you know. You can trust me."

"I know I can. You're my best friend, right?"

Maybe if we both keep saying it, one of us will start to believe it eventually.

"But it's not love. Darwin and I, well, we talk about stuff."

"What kind of stuff?"

We take our seats in the classroom, megan sitting to face me, green eyes hungry for information. *Just give her what she wants.*

"Everything," I tell her eagerly. "He tells me about life in the Zone. Did you know that people go outside? The Engineers. They have to make sure that the satellites and all that are working. They have to wear protective suits and can only stay out there for short bursts of time. I don't know; it's kind of confusing."

"Hmm." Her eyes drifting over my shoulder, looking for someone more interesting.

"Don't you think that's interesting, megan?"

"Not really." She shrugs. "It sounds like boys' stuff, to be honest. chastity-ruth says that kind of thing is none of our concern."

She turns away, and even in a classroom full of people I am alone again.

"And he told me a secret."

"What secret?" she says, her head snapping back to me.

"I can't really say," I reply, starting to feel sick.

"I won't tell anyone." She leans forward, smiling at me as if I'm special.

"I can't tell you, megan."

"Fine."

"I would if I could."

"Sure," she replies, and silence falls between us again. I glance around, catching everyone staring at me. They react and look away, but I know they are still watching out of the corner of their eyes. If I don't make this right, I'm finished.

"Well, he did tell me one thing," I say, pushing away the waves of nausea, "but you have to *promise* not to tell anyone."

She smiles slowly, inching her ear closer to my mouth. "I promise."

"Have you heard of female aberrants?"

"What?" she says loudly, and I shush her.

"That gene doesn't exist in women," she says.

"It doesn't exist anymore. Darwin told me they identified the gene and destroyed it. Two eves fell in love before and tried to run away."

"They fell in love? Before marriage?"

"Yes."

"With each other? Two girls?"

"Yes."

"That is just . . ." Her voice trails off in disbelief. She smoothes the full skirt of her dress down over her knees, a thoughtful expression dawning on her face.

"That's what Darwin told me. But you can't tell anyone. He made me promise not to repeat it."

"Sure." She's nonchalant. "But why did he tell you if it's such a big secret?"

"He trusts me," I say, the words making me feel worse.

"Oh, he trusts you, does he? Maybe he's in love with you too." She wraps her hands around her back and makes smacking noises as if she's kissing someone.

"What are you? Twelve?"

"You're in loooooove." megan's voice is rising, other eves turning to look at her, the word *love* like a klaxon horn sounding. If one of the chastities hears her, I can't even imagine how much trouble I'll be in.

"I told you, I'm not in love with Darwin," I say, my jaw clenching. "I'm just, I'm just . . ." She guffaws at my stuttering and the laughter spreads, everyone making loud kissing noises at me.

"I'm not in love with him. If I was in love with him, would I have told you what he said about, *you know*, what I just told you? I'm just . . ." The laughter levels are getting louder and louder. I can taste fear, cold and metallic on my tongue. ". . . using him!" I finish, trying to shut her up before a chastity hears us and my chances of becoming a Judge's companion are destroyed.

"I'm just using him because his father is a Judge." I scream it over the din of voices, and just as I say it the room falls quiet, my voice blasting into the silence. I turn, expecting a chastity. But it's not a chastity. It's much worse than that.

It's Darwin, his face stricken. I half rise in my seat, my mouth open to deny it, to apologize, to say anything to make it better, but all I can do is watch helplessly as chastity-magdalena orders us to take our seats and ushers in the other Inheritants.

"Class dismissed," chastity-magdalena finally says, giving a VoiceCommand to the computer to shut down whatever digi-vid we were supposed to be watching. I couldn't concentrate. I spent the last hour staring at the back of Darwin's head, trying to telepathically explain what happened.

"You coming?" Sigmund slaps Darwin on the back.

"In a minute," Darwin says, approaching chastity-magdalena's desk and handing her a small package.

"From cecily?"

He nods, and she breaks into a huge smile before addressing us again.

"Okay, girls, you may leave now. chastity-anne is waiting in the Organized Recreation room." She turns to Darwin. "They always need a little more OR after your visits."

I walk out, megan's arm entwined in mine. I've been welcomed back into the fold. This is what I wanted.

"Wait." I stop in the middle of the corridor, the others moving around us. "I forgot my . . ." I can't think of anything—"lipstick?"

"So? You have millions of tubes."

"I'm going to run back and get it." I break away from her and she seamlessly links arms with cara, never without an attendant for long. I walk toward the classroom in such a hurry that I collide into someone, my shoulder banging painfully off theirs.

"Sorry, isabel. I didn't see you."

"That's . . ." She trails off in a slow drawl, like a wind-up doll running out of juice. She walks away, taking small steps as if she's afraid to make any noise.

"Darwin!" I cry out as he emerges from the classroom. He tenses, folding his arms across his body. This is not good.

"How are you? What were you giving chastity-magdalena?"

He doesn't reply.

"Darwin, I'm so sorry. I didn't mean to say that about you. It was an accident."

"How was it an accident?" he says. "Did you trip and the words fell out of your mouth?"

"Oh, just forget it. You don't have a clue what it's like here. megan was being so mean to me."

"What?" He holds his hands to his mouth in mock horror. "Was she endangering your life? Threatening to bore you to death with chitter-chatter about makeup or whatever else you girls talk about?"

"That's not all I talk about!" I reply, stung at this accusation. "I thought you knew me better than that."

"So did I," he says sadly, all fight leaving his body. He leans back against the door to the classroom.

There's a horrible finality about this that makes me want to cover my ears like a child and yell, "I CAN'T HEAR YOU!" to block out what's coming next.

"I said I was sorry, Darwin. What else can I say? I'm sorry."

Sorry, sorry, sorry. It's an overused word in the School. We say it all the time, even when we don't mean it. Especially when we don't mean it.

"It's so hard here. I'm just trying to survive." Self-pity creeps into my voice. Even though the freida he thinks I am isn't self-pitying.

"Looks like my dad was right about gold-digging eves."

"Will you stop obsessing about your dad? You're not a fucking baby." The words are boiling uncontrollably out of me. He takes a step back, startled by the shattering of my mask, the putrid pus that is oozing out through the cracks.

"You don't know anything about my dad."

"I'm sorry. I don't know what I'm saying," I insist, trying to grab his hand.

"It doesn't matter."

"It does matter."

"It's my own fault," he says, forcing my hands off him. "It's always my fault."

"I didn't mean what I said about using you. I swear," I say as he walks away. "I just said it because . . ." My throat is closing in, suffocating the words.

"Why then?" He looks over his shoulder at me. "Why did you say it?"

"I just said it to make megan be my friend again," I choke out pathetically. Even though the freida he thinks I am is not pathetic.

"What?" He looks at me like I'm insane. "You used me, embarrassed me in front of all my friends, because you wanted *megan* to be your friend?"

"But it's not true. I'm not using you."

"Why not?" he says, and his voice is cut through with sadness. "Why should you be any different from everyone else?"

"I *am* different. You have to believe me," I say, any shred of dignity gone. Even though the freida he thinks I am is dignified.

"Can you honestly look at me and tell me that my father being a Judge had nothing to do with it?" he asks me quietly. "Can you say you've never thought about it?"

I hesitate for just a moment too long, and something hardens in his expression. And then he's gone.

I bury my face in my hands, feeling the pressure building behind my eyes.

"freida?" chastity-magdalena looks at me uneasily as the door to the classroom swings open. "Are you all right?"

"I'm fine."

"Your face is red."

"Oh, I'm sorry," I reply, grabbing a little mirror out of my bag and quickly reapplying concealer and lip balm until I look perfect again. "All better. I'm sorry, chastity-magdalena, but I have to run. I'm late for Organized Recreation."

"Where have you been?" chastity-anne says disapprovingly when I enter the classroom. She follows me into the elevator and escorts me into the OR Space, where the others are already writhing in their glass coffins. She closes the door behind me, but I don't need any encouragement this time. I throw the meds down my throat, seeking obliteration.

"All eves must manage their behavior and conduct themselves in a manner that is ladylike at all times. Emotional behavior can be off-putting to men and must be controlled."[4]

---

[4] *Audio Guide to the Rules for Proper female Behavior*, the Original Father

Chapter 25

I wake long before the morning lamps are turned on again, my body eating through the SleepSound. The dorm is heaving. The sighing of the heat releasing from the vents, the steady rise and fall of eves breathing in time with the Messages.

You have far to go in your quest to become flawless. You have far to go until you are perfect.

There's a gnawing feeling at the pit of my stomach, like talons scraping across a blackboard.

megan ignoring me.

Me, breaking my promise.

Darwin overhearing me.

Darwin walking away from me. He didn't look back.

I should have said his dad's job had nothing to do with how I felt about him. But how could he have thought that it wouldn't mean anything to me?

The way he looked at me as I begged for forgiveness.

I scan the room for something to distract me, instinctively reaching under my pillow for my ePad and logging onto MyFace. I listen to one status update, then another, and another, praying to the Father that I'm still dreaming. My feed is clogged up with more activity than I've heard in years. And they are all talking about the same thing.

Female aberrants.

"Was it you?"

"Good morning to you too, miss cheerful," megan answers pointedly. She finishes massaging anti-bacterial gel onto her hands and tucks the little bottle back in her bag. She checks her reflection in the wall behind her, as if to see if she's thin enough to merit eating breakfast.

"What do you think of this outfit?" She gestures at her sleeveless collared minidress, tiny pearl buttons puncturing the raspberry silk.

"Was it you, megan?" I ask again. I place my hands on the table, leaning in toward her until our faces are mere inches apart.

"Are you going to kiss her or something? Aberrants!" a childish voice yells and a group of 12th years screams with laughter. How do the younger girls know about female aberrants? They're not friends with any of us on MyFace. I sit heavily on the empty seat opposite megan, my head spinning.

"I told you it was a secret."

The twins, cara, gisele and daria are ignoring us, taking fotograms of their food and arguing about which filter makes the scrambled tofu look the least gray.

"Told me what was a secret?"

"What I told you yesterday. About what Darwin said. About female aberrants," I say, doubt starting to creep in. It must have been her. Who else could it have been?

"Oh that." megan tosses her hair back. "Sorry."

We are always sorry.

"Anyway . . ." she takes a small bite of her scrambled tofu, checking the mirror again once she's swallowed—"I only told jessie. She said she wouldn't tell anyone."

"And I just told liz, obviously," jessie chimes in. "But I made her promise she wouldn't tell anyone else."

"Well, I didn't tell anyone," liz says in a huff. "Pretty much."

"How come you're not eating?" cara asks as I bury my head in my hands. She leans across me to take a fotogram of the berry-granola oatcakes that were today's healthy/tasty option. "They look delicious," she says enviously, poking at the pasty lump on her own plate.

"I'm not hungry."

The sight of food is revolting. My insides feel watery, my stomach churning as if it can't decide whether to flush its contents out through my mouth or my bowels.

"Sweetie, don't be mad at me," megan says, patting my hand with hers, her manicured nails immaculate. "You're my best friend."

My fone vibrates in my satchel and I lean down to grab it, sticking an earbud in to listen to the message.

"I think you and isabel are female aberrants," a low, insistent voice says. "I heard at nighttime you used to sneak into each other's cubicles. I'm going to tell on you."

I check the screen, my hands shaking so badly I almost drop the eFone, but there is a blank face where the caller's foto should be. Anonymous.

"What's up?" daria asks.

"Nothing."

She throws her shoulders back, her cropped tee rising up to expose an inch of toned skin above her high-waisted flared jeans. "I think it's disgusting. What if there are female aberrants in our year? What if one of them tries to seduce me?"

"Why do you assume that they would be attracted to you in the first place?" I ask.

"Interesting." daria tilts her head. "That sounded like something a female aberrant would say."

"Maybe that's why you and Darwin only talk," jessie says, her eyes widening.

"Someone said that they saw you coming out of christy's room at night," liz gasps. "Is that why you and isabel fell out?"

"I am not an aberrant," I say, but they ignore me. I can see the idea taking root so I rush to protect myself. "But maybe agyness is?"

"She does have short hair. Like a man," jessie whispers, as they scan the Nutrition Center looking for her.

gisele shudders. "I thought I saw her looking at me in the showers." The twins turn to each other in delighted horror and I know I should take it back, but I don't.

An alarm shrieks and some of the younger girls cover their ears and cry out in fright. chastity-ruth has climbed up on her chair, her pale face blossoming from the black robes like a gothic rose. The other chastities form a battalion line in front of her, heads bowed.

"Stop that," chastity-ruth barks at the more sensitive 4th years, rolling her eyes as one girl wails. chastity-mary goes to comfort her, falling back when chastity-ruth snaps her fingers at her. "Crying is unacceptable."

"Yes, chastity-ruth. Sorry, chastity-ruth," they reply, and fall silent. They're learning quickly.

"It has come to our attention that there are some rather unpleasant rumors circulating the School. Do any of you know anything about this?" megan's feet kick against mine, her face remaining perfectly serene. "No one?" chastity-ruth continues. "Perhaps the words 'female aberrant' will jog your memory."

I gasp as I hear her say these words, and cara nearly falls off her seat. I go to steady her but she jerks away. Our eyes meet and I see it, just for a second, before she smoothes it away. *Doubt.* She thinks I'm one of them.

"None of us had even heard of such a thing." chastity-ruth is admitting to ignorance for the first time that I'm aware of. "I had to approach the Father to discuss it with him. After a long, in-depth conversation," she says, glowing at the memory, "he has reassured me that this is a grave misunderstanding. There may have been rare incidents of it in the past, but they isolated the errant gene in women and destroyed it so the human race could continue unharmed."

There's always something that they can do to change you, to make you better. There is always room for Improvement.

"And if I hear any more talk about this nonsense there will be serious repercussions." Her face goes tight with anger. "The Ceremony is only weeks away, girls. The Father was most displeased."

I purse my lips tightly, trying to hold on to my fear before it splatters all over the table.

"But He is merciful," chastity-ruth continues, bowing her head. "And we must be grateful." With that she sweeps out of the dining room, leaving the remaining chastities to round up their respective classes, chastity-mary laughing at a tiny 4th year who is hopping madly from one leg to the other, squeaking that she needs to "pee-pee."

"Come on, 16th years," chastity-bernadette says gloomily. "Let's get to class."

"That was crazy," cara says as we follow the chastity, looping her arm through mine. Obviously any worries that I might sneak into her room at nighttime and molest her have vanished.

A sudden thought stops me in my tracks. If the chastities know and the Father knows, Darwin must know. What is he going to think of me now that the secret he entrusted to me has become common knowledge? He might never forgive me. Not only will he think I'm using him, but that I'm totally untrustworthy as well. And I have no way of contacting him, our MyFace and VideoChat access is strictly restricted to within the School. All I can do is wait for his return.

I reach for my locket, for my comfort.

Ten days until the Ceremony

I open my eyes and I am confronted by my reflection in the ceiling mirror. *My thighs are too big, my hair is too messy, I hate myself, I hate myself, I hate myself.*

There are only ten days left until the rest of my life begins.

They have told us that in order to succeed we need to be good girls, we need to follow the rules, we need to look pretty and speak nicely and be pleasant. I've tried. I've waxed every last hair on my body. I have taken my pills. I have gone to bed hungry every night since I was four years old. I've done everything they have told me to do and here I am, ten days left, and I don't know if it's enough. I have no idea if Darwin will forgive me or if he will choose me. He has to choose me.

The strain has become unbearable. I nibble on the edges of a SleepSound tablet every so often to smooth away the paralyzing fear. I don't have enough time to fix it. The sand in the hourglass has almost completely run out.

I don't have enough time.

The thought is with me all day. I want to stand on my desk and scream at the top of my lungs, Let me out, let me out, let me out. But I don't. I try to act normal. *Not enough time.*

The Inheritants haven't been here in five days. Before, that wouldn't have seemed so long. Time was the one unlimited resource we had left in this world.

But now all I can think is that it's five days of wasted opportunity. Five days where I could have made things better with Darwin but I didn't. Five days where every time the door of a classroom opens my spine wrenches upright, a mixture of disappointment and relief when it's not him, when it's never him.

Until, at last, it is.

"Please, girls, settle down . . ." chastity-bernadette says as a noisy flurry of excitement runs through the room. My heart thuds painfully in my chest.

He's cut his hair.

"What happened to Darwin's hand?" I overhear jessie whisper to liz, but her head is blocking my view. I shift in my seat so I can see properly. His left hand is in a cast, very white against his tanned arm. I wrap my feet around the legs of my chair to anchor me, to stop myself from running over to check if he's okay.

The class drags on. The Inheritants have taken their seats in the last row of the classroom as chastity-bernadette leads us in a never-ending question-and-answer session. What would you do if you failed to produce sons? *Throw myself on the pyre before my Termination Date so my husband can marry someone better.* What would you do if a man asked you for sex when you were feeling unwell? *Always be willing.* What would you do if a man asked you to perform a sexual act you felt uncomfortable with? *Always be willing.*

I answer the questions as I think a companion would. *I would be willing, but I presume he would have a concubine to satisfy those needs.* chastity-bernadette frowns, but she can't chastise me as I haven't broken any rules. megan has taught me well. Is Darwin looking at me? What does he think of my answers?

"Well done, girls." The chastity gives a huge sigh of relief when we finish. "Now, there are only ten days until your Ceremony."

Really? We had no idea.

She presses a small button on her eFone and a loud buzzing sound is set off, the glass containers we use for Comparison Studies instantly lighting up like two caged stars on either side of her desk.

"It's time for your final physical examination. I will call you up in pairs. Enter into the boxes, one girl per box. Please strip to your underwear before you do so," she says. "The first time I sound the buzzer, you turn around. At the second buzz, please leave the box and get dressed again."

I notice terror ripple across isabel's face before the cloud descends again, her eyes misty, like condensation building up on a window pane. What do I have to do to get some of her meds? She raises her hand wearily.

"isabel, I forgot about you," chastity-bernadette says contritely. "You may be excused."

isabel gets to her feet and shuffles out of the room. No one else seems to notice. Am I going crazy? Is she an apparition that only I can see?

"Let's begin."

Please let me be paired with someone worse than me. christy would be good—she's still about five pounds over target. I'd look okay next to christy.

Pair after pair of eves go into the translucent boxes, magnified fotos of their bodies projected onto the main board, side by side for easier comparison. We must be inspected for flaws before purchase.

All the eves have turned to look at me. Did I say that out loud?

"freida! I've called your name three times now!" chastity-bernadette says.

"Sorry," I mumble. It's only when I've reached the front of the classroom that I see who I have been paired with.

"May the best girl win!" megan says, taffeta prom dress already pooled around her ankles. I can't help staring as her perfect body is revealed on the big screen behind us. Her tiny waist curves into fuller hips, pert breasts straining at the black lace of her bra. It's risqué underwear, considering how prim her outfit choices have become recently. Pure on the outside, naughty on the inside. Perfect companion material. Why didn't I think of that?

"freida!" chastity-bernadette snaps.

I struggle to unzip the acid-lemon strapless dress, my hands shaking. Kicking it off, I step into the box, rows of faces staring back at me, analyzing my body, comparing every inch of it to megan's. The back row is tapping furiously on their ePads. Except Darwin. He's slouching in his chair, head tucked into his chest.

The buzzer sounds loudly. megan and I turn to face the wall. Through the glass panes I can see us on the board, projected eight feet high. We are a perfect contrast, megan's pale skin in black silk, my brown body in cream lace. I squeeze my eyes shut but the images are burned into my eyelids. They will haunt my dreams.

The buzzer sounds again and I scramble out of the box and grab my dress to cover myself.

"Do you have all the notes that you require?" chastity-bernadette asks. The Inheritants mumble that they do. "Wonderful. Now, girls, this will be your last visit from the Inheritants until next week," she says, forgetting that we're not supposed to know their visitation timetable. "Next Friday will be your last Interaction before the Ceremony the following Monday." She clucks in disbelief. "It seems to come faster and faster every year!"

It's just another year to her, just another Ceremony.

"We don't have time for the full Heavenly Seventy today, I'm afraid. We have rather run over schedule." She's getting a bit flustered. "Will twenty minutes suffice?"

"How much more time do we need?" a male voice yells out.

"Quite." The chastity's skin is blotchy with embarrassment. "Let's begin. Darwin. Please select your eve for today's task."

My heart starts thumping against my ribcage, my mouth drying up. The room expands and contracts like an accordion, voices veering wildly between whispers and shrieks and back again.

"megan," he says, his voice so familiar yet so distant, and she gets to her feet gracefully.

"Sorry, freida," she says to me, her hand skimming my shoulder. "Can I get past you?"

I turn my legs to the side and cara does the same to allow her through. Darwin takes her hand, leading her toward the cupboard.

"What happened your arm?" I hear her coo.

"It was my own fault," he says, and the door closes behind them.

I focus on my breathing, trying to ignore the others staring at me while the other Inheritants pick their now familiar partners: *miranda . . . rosie . . . karlie . . .* until there is only one Inheritant left. Socrates stomps down the steps to the front of the classroom, turning to face us, scratching his ginger hair.

"Well . . ." he begins, and heidi, his usual choice, rises from her seat, "I choose freida."

He disappears around the back of the bleacher seating, and heidi hunches back down, playing with her bangs self-consciously.

"Ow!"

"I'm so sorry," heidi says as I trip over her extended leg on my way down the steps. "It was an accident."

The door of the cupboard closes behind us. It's identical to Darwin's cupboard, made out of mirrors, but the images reflected back to me are all wrong—Socrates's skinny legs, his flushed skin, his hair standing on end. I hold a hand up in greeting, and he pounces, mashing his face against mine. It's so sudden that my mouth is still clenched shut and he has to shove his tongue through my tight lips, spittle trickling onto my chin.

I pull away, resisting the urge to wipe my mouth. He kisses my neck, moving his way down to the top of my dress. I am going to be sick. I'm about to tell him to stop when he wraps his hand around my jaw, pushing my head hard against the glass wall.

"You're beautiful," he says. "Your body is amazing."

I take the hit, feeling it soar through my bloodstream.

"Really? Do you really think so?"

"Yeah, sure." He grips my shoulder with his left hand, pinning me against the wall, and starts kicking off his sneakers, untying his belt one-handed. His jeans fall around his ankles.

"Wait," I say. "*Wait.*"

He kisses me again, filling my mouth with his stale breath. His hand snakes down in between us and he tears at my dress, pulling it and my bra down.

"No, please." I'm pleading now. "I don't know if . . ."

He doesn't seem to hear me, pushing himself nearer and nearer to the center of me.

"No can mean yes," he murmurs against my skin. "You'll like it."

"Don't." I stumble, digging into his foot with a needle-sharp heel, and he yelps in pain. "Sorry, I'm so sorry." I babble, wrenching my dress back on.

Socrates is hopping up and down, his jeans gathered around his ankles fettering him as he bends down to hold his wounded foot in his hands. I stand as still as possible, playing dead. *Please don't.* The possibility of what could happen shatters inside me. *Please don't do this to me.*

"I'm sorry." I hold out my hand to stop him from coming closer. "I don't want to . . ." I quickly change tactics as he looks insulted. "I mean, of course I want to, but I just can't. I'm sorry."

He doesn't move closer, thankfully, turning his back on me to fix his clothes in the mirror. He looks at me again, rolling his eyes in disgust. He doesn't like me now. How did megan do it that first week? She didn't have sex with Albert, but he still likes her; I've seen them chatting since. Why do I always get it wrong?

"What's the difference between me and Darwin?" he asks furiously, trying to smooth his messed-up hair.

"I didn't have sex with Darwin either."

"That's not what I heard," he snorts, blood rushing back into his pale face with fury.

"What do you mean by—"

"Anyway—" he cuts across me and I swallow my question and the implications of what he said—"you're wasting your time there, little eve." He looks me up and down, lingering on every inch of my body. "You're not what the Judge will want for Darwin."

He sits on the ground, immediately engrossed in the eFone he has fished out of his pocket, and I become invisible to him. My feet are rooted to the floor. I lean against the wall, watching the opposite mirror as my thighs slowly ooze out beneath my dress, splayed against the glass behind me, getting fatter and fatter and fatter. I'm disgusting. I'm not what the Judge will want for Darwin. I'm not what anyone would want.

The bell rings and the trapdoor springs open. He scrambles to his feet but I can't move. Maybe if I just hide in here no one will ever know.

"Darwin, dude, why did you choose that bitch every week?" I hear Socrates say. "Frigid freida."

The Inheritants burst into raucous laughter, some of the eves tittering too.

It's my own fault.

Darwin's words echo in my ears, like a mantra.

Chapter 26

I wait until I've heard the last of the stilettos clacking on the tiled floor outside before I fall out of the cupboard. Impossibly, the room is the same, the tiered rows of seats, the ten upright wooden cupboards surrounding them like a moat. I take off my heels and run as fast as I can. My feet skim across the chessboard, the chipped yellow paint on my toenails a fluorescent blur.

At my cubicle, I reach for the handle of the door tucked into the top of the door frame, trying to tug it down to close off the outside, but it's stuck, rusted from lack of use. I'm sick of being in this School. I'm sick of being in this body. I'm sick of being me. Every toxic feeling I've ever had seems to explode inside me, like a million different voices screaming to be heard at once, and I throw myself onto the bed, biting the pillow to muzzle them. *Crying is ugly*, the chastities yelled when as children we fell and scraped our knees. *Crying makes your skin blotchy. No man wants a girl who cries. You must be happy and lighthearted at all times.* So I don't cry. I am torn apart with not crying.

Socrates is accustomed to heidi. She probably had sex with him within the first five seconds of meeting him. heidi is just a stupid slut. *At least I'm not a slut.*

I dig my ePad out from underneath my pillow.

"Hello?" she answers in a bored tone.

"Hi, megan."

"freeds?" She peers at the screen. "Is that you? I can't see anything."

"The camera is broken." I lie. I don't want her to see my face, mottled from the effort of not crying.

"I hope they can afford to fix that." She's reapplied her makeup by hand, her eyes dark with kohl, her full lips tinted pale pink for a change. "It's not like you can depend on isabel to get you a new one this time."

"Did you do anything with him?"

"With who? Oh. Darwin is it? Let's just say we didn't do much talking." She touches her throat delicately. "I guess things didn't go well with Socrates. I heard what he said about you as he left."

"And I heard you laughing."

"I would never do that," she cries. "We're best friends."

"Are we?"

"Tell me what happened," she persists, ignoring my question.

"I just didn't—"

"Don't you like him?"

"No," I say bluntly, forgetting myself.

"So, you think you're too good for him?"

"No . . . I . . ." I stutter. "*Darwin* is mine."

"He was supposed to be mine in the first place."

"The rankings are meaningless now."

She raises an eyebrow at me. We both know the rankings matter. They have been our benchmark the whole way through School. It's how we measure ourselves, how we know how much we're worth. They matter.

"I couldn't help it if he kept choosing me!" I say, sitting up and shifting the ePad onto my lap.

"And I couldn't help it that he chose me today."

"He only asked you to make me jealous," I mutter under my breath.

"Oh, freida. How presumptuous."

"He told me he doesn't even like you." I want her to feel as bad as I do.

"Who cares? You think I care? All that matters is that he *chooses* me. All that matters is that I win."

"What about love?" I say, starting to bite my nails, peeling off neon polish with my teeth. "Darwin will want someone who is in love with him."

"I thought you said you're not in love with him?"

"I'm not." Love makes you weak. I cannot afford to be weak. "But I . . ."

"You what?" she asks, staring into the camera, handing me the rope to hang myself.

"I thought you said we were best friends," I finish uncertainly. "I believed you."

"No, you didn't," she says with a hard little laugh. "You think I don't know how you feel about me? What you've said about me behind my back? You're as bad as *she* is, with all her fancy things that no one else could have. She thought she was so special. She was too good for everyone else. Never wanted to hang out with anyone else but *you*, of all people." She spits out the words, coated in vitriol. "And now look at her. Perfect isabel, with her perfect blond hair and her perfect rankings. Just another casualty, another one who couldn't hack the pace." She curls her lip in disgust at me. "And you're as bad. isabel got sick of you, and now Darwin has too. Maybe isabel and you can become chastities. You can live here, together forever, never needing anyone else to play with, never letting anyone else join in."

She catches sight of herself in her video-feed, her face contorted with fury. Wiping spittle from the sides of her mouth, she reaches behind her to grab her lip gloss and reapplies it. "And don't even start thinking about what a bitch I am," she says. Her eyes are steady, the heat receding from her skin. "This is not my fault. I'm just doing what we have been trained to do. This is who we are, freida. This is who we were designed to be."

Chapter 27

"There is a world outside of the School, you know." Darwin had jokingly chided me for my lack of curiosity. He was right, of course, but sometimes it feels impossible that anything exists outside of this glass dome. It feels as if this is all that exists or ever will exist.

We eves in final year were designed on the same day. We were hatched together and we have lived as we will die, our bones touching. Yet it has only been these last few days that I have felt like I am suffocating with our togetherness. All I want is to be alone, to stay in my room and pretend time is standing still, but I can't. I can't escape from it. When daria passes me a hula-hoop during PE I wonder if she is thinking "frigid freida." When megan smiles in my direction, paranoia gnaws at me that somehow she has been in contact with Darwin, that he has promised to make *her* his companion.

And she will have all the power. And I will be alone.

I am losing. I am losing him. I have lost him already. What happened during his last visit is a tapeworm, eating all my good memories, leaving me consumed by doubt.

The tapes play on. Socrates's voice when he said I wasn't good enough for Darwin. The moment where I told megan his secrets, selling him out for popularity. I imagine myself spinning out of my body and melting into his so I can see the scene as he might have. Through his eyes, megan gleams with beauty and I am a shadow, whispering wickedness.

Although I doubt any of the others can be as frightened as I am, there are signs of frayed nerves. Tension is crackling between us.

"Can I have that?" freja asks at lunchtime, pointing at the untouched bowl of ice-kream.

"Why didn't you get your own?" gisele snaps, pulling her tray away from freja.

"I don't eat dessert," freja replies proudly, squeezing her shoulder blades toward her chest and watching in the mirror as her collarbones pop out. "Hey!" she protests as gisele throws the bowl in the garbage.

"It would be wasted on you," gisele mutters. "All you're going to do is spit it out anyway."

Every morning we are awoken by a new announcement blasting through the dormitories.

Nine days until the Ceremony.

Eight days until the Ceremony.

I don't have enough time.

We are woken by the lamps. We sit together at mealtimes. We pretend to listen in class. We look the same, as if we are going through the motions of our usual lives, but if you peer closely you can see the signs. There are no requests to Video-Chat. MyFace has gone silent. cara ate an entire slice of Death by Chocco at lunch the other day and megan didn't even comment. Her eyes slipped over the gooey mess, clouded by visions of her future glory. All charades of friendship or alliances are forgotten. We have battened down the hatches as we wait out the storm, waiting to see who will survive.

Six days until the Ceremony.

I cannot breathe with the fear. *I've lost him. I've lost him.* I need to make it better. I need to make him forgive me. chastity-bernadette said they would be here on Friday. Three days. I have to wait another three days until I can see him and make him understand. He has to understand. I have to *make* him understand.

Every morning I break open the silver-handled drawers of my dressing table, counting my stock before distilling my meds into the silver locket. I can't stop touching it. The heavy metal between my fingers comforts me. I like knowing the option is there, if I need it. I don't take too much. I'm not messy. Some of the other eves might look at me a little sharply when a faint slur coats my words at times, but no one says anything. No one wants to get involved.

"Are you awake?"

chastity-magdalena's voice fills my cubicle, interrupting an empty daydream, my mind wiped clear by the quarter I dropped an hour ago.

"Don't you ever knock?" I mumble into my pillow.

"Get up." She sits beside me, grabbing my shoulders and yanks me up to sitting. "What have you taken?"

"Nothing," I lie, licking my lips groggily.

She starts rummaging through my bedside locker and underneath my bed. I fall back onto the mattress, but she grabs me again, rolling me off the bed, ignoring my moan as I hit the ground. She shakes out my blanket and throws the pillow at me before searching the rest of my cubicle. She stops in front of my wardrobe.

"There's no point," I say. "The scanner will reject your body chemistry."

A guttural sigh emerges from the depths of her stomach. I crawl back onto the bed, pulling the blanket around me, wanting the softness to devour me.

"You have to stop this, freida." I wish she would go. Her voice is eating away at my blanket of drowsiness. "I want to help you."

"Do you?" I unroll a corner of the blanket to peek my head out.

"Of course."

"Can you sneak Darwin in? I need to talk to him. If I could talk to him, then everything will be okay."

"I can't do that," she says, dashing my last hope, as I guess I knew she would.

"Then go away." I pull the blanket over my head again.

"freida, it's normal for a teenage girl to form these attachments, project feelings onto an Inheritant they don't really know."

I fight with the blanket to sit upright, my blood on fire.

"How dare you? You don't know anything!" She stands very still, my screams bouncing off her.

"I know Darwin better than anyone. I know everything about him." I want her to accept it, to understand that Darwin and I are meant to be together. "I know all this stuff about him, about his parents. Stuff that he hasn't told anyone else. He trusts me."

"What are his parents' names?" she asks, arms crossed against her chest.

"I . . . I . . . That doesn't mean anything. I know the important stuff. I know . . ." I trail off. What was I saying? What was I talking about again? "If only I could talk to him . . ." I say again. "If I could talk to him, it would all be fine. Do you think that you could sneak him in? Do you think that you could do that for me?"

"I just told you I can't do that," she answers. "Two minutes ago."

I can't remember. My mind has holes in it.

"It's not us, you know. We're fine. We get along really well. You should see us together. We get along so well. He thinks I'm beautiful." She looks doubtful. "What, you don't think that someone could think that I'm beautiful? Because it's true. We are great together. If you had seen us together . . . Could you maybe . . . If we could just get away . . . his dad . . . Could you maybe sneak him . . ." I keep trailing off, forgetting what I wanted to say in midsentence.

"This isn't the first time someone has been disappointed with how the Interactions went," she says, so quietly I almost don't hear her.

"Oh, what? Like you?" I laugh harshly. "Am I supposed to care about what happened to some chastity a hundred years ago?"

"Darwin is a nice boy, but—"

"But what?" I interrupt, daring her to say it. She thinks he is too good for me. She doesn't think he would ever choose someone like me to be his companion.

"We are who we are. Sometimes, no matter how much someone might want to, they can't escape that." She has such a look of pity on her face that I feel ashamed to see it. How have I been reduced so low that a chastity feels sorry for me?

"Get away from me."

"It's because I care about you—"

"Stop caring. You're not my mother. You're no one's mother." I bury myself under the covers, my breath coming hot and fast. The sheets are sucking in like a plastic bag over my face and I come up for air, gasping. isabel has taken the chastity's place, standing by the door in a shapeless gray sweater over leggings.

"What do you want?" I bark at her, catching a glimpse of myself in the wall. My hair is matted, teeth bared in a snarl. I hug a pillow lengthways along my body, hiding my ugliness behind it.

"Are you here to talk to me as well?" I shout from behind my shield. "Are you here to warn me too?"

"What would be the point?" she says. "What's the point of any of this?"

Chapter 28

Just another night, I try to tell myself. The same Messages playing as every Thursday that came before it. Except it's not just another Thursday night. It's the *last* Thursday. The last Thursday in this bed, in this School.

"jessie, please share that SleepSound with liz. They are quite strong the first time you take them."

chastity-anne is whispering, but my ears perk up at the word "SleepSound," like hearing your name mentioned across a noisy room. She's patrolling the dorms tonight, handing out meds like sweeties, making sure that everyone will look rested for our final meeting with the Inheritants tomorrow.

I took the last three capsules christy gave me earlier, but they must have been defective (*stupid* Euro-Zone and their *stupid faulty drugs*) because I've been lying on my bed for hours, staring at myself in my ceiling, incubated in that pause between waking and dreams. A shadow floats past my room.

"chastity-anne."

She stops abruptly, walking back toward me, her finger held up to her mouth to hush me. She points back into my cubicle and we go in together, the room seeming too small for both of us.

"I can't sleep," I say, scratching my arms brutally.

"I can see that."

"I need more SleepSound."

"I prescribed you a capsule earlier. I saw you taking it."

I forgot. *One, two, three, four.*

"It must have been defective because I haven't slept at all," I say, lifting my chin defiantly.

"It wasn't defective." She turns to leave, and without thinking I grab her hand to stop her and she gasps.

"I'm sorry." I'm too tired to be shocked. "But I need more SleepSound."

"I've prescribed you the maximum dose. I'm afraid I can't help you," she says, rubbing her skin as if I had poured acid on it.

"This is an emergency!" I say. She stops in the doorway and looks me up and down. I shift from one foot to the other, pulling at my black silk teddy.

"You look very thin. I wonder if I should lower your dosage of kcal blockers."

"No!"

I can't lose my supply of blockers. Without them I'd have nothing to trade with christy.

"My weight is fine. You've seen the reports," I say, thinking of the two liters of water I drank before my weigh-in.

"True," she replies, her forehead wrinkling in confusion. "Maybe it's the light in here."

Then she's gone, taking the precious meds with her. She is doing this on purpose. She and chastity-ruth want me to look terrible so I ruin my chances with Darwin. I want to run after her and tackle her to the ground. I want to pound her bald head on the floor until I hear it crack open beneath my fingers, seeing her blood smear on the black-and-white tiles.

I sit on my hands and watch myself in the mirrored walls, at this face that is so familiar yet which never feels as if it belongs to me. It is the property of the School, of the Zone, of my future Husband. This face is my worth, my value. This face is all that I have to offer and it isn't even mine.

I watch myself for hours. I watch myself until this face becomes meaningless.

Three days until the Ceremony

At breakfast, everyone is gleaming. Teeth have been freshly whitened, skin steamed, hair styled. There is a conspicuous lack of clothing, even on the girls who want to be companions. Everyone is taking this final opportunity to show off their assets.

"I can't believe you went for another bikini wax with chastity-hope. That's every day this week!" daria says to gisele.

"I had to," gisele answers, plumping her breasts up in a gold sequined minidress. "I don't want there to be a scrap of hair anywhere."

The dining room is oddly quiet. You can hear the metallic scrape of utensils against china as we ladle up cereal and dribble it back into the bowl.

It's weird to think of the people that exist outside of this room. All the people in the Euro-Zone who don't have sons as Inheritants this year are probably oblivious. They are going about their business, unaware that the biggest moment in our lives is approaching like a speeding train. Unaware that I'm standing on the train tracks, my foot trapped in a steel tie. And what about the girls in the other years, contentedly eating their breakfast? Are they thinking of us? Wishing us luck?

There is a sheen of sweat on cara's brow and she dabs at it nervously with a napkin, looking around in case anyone else has noticed. And there is isabel, alone, sucking her protein shake through a straw. Her hair is falling loosely around her shoulders, a nude chiffon T-shirt dress hugging her slight frame. chastity-ruth watches her carefully from her perch, cooing, "I hope your breakfast is all right, isabel?" isabel merely nods, her eyes dropping to her lap, picking at loose fibers in her dress.

She is shining with indifference. I want her drugs the same way I used to want her beauty.

At least my dress is beautiful. It is intricate gold lace, overlaid with gold beading, and I chose rectangular earrings made of gold-plated glass and a wafer-thin gold cuff, cut so finely that it resembles snowflakes. It scratches at my skin like itchy wool, searching for someone who is more worthy of its perfection.

I am tired. I am so very tired.

The bell rings. The younger eves leave, their eyes wide with envy. I wish I could offer to trade places, buy myself more time.

I don't have enough time.

"Go to class," chastity-ruth says. She signals to isabel that she may stay where she is, and isabel flops in her chair, like a marionette that has had its strings cut. When did she become separate to us? I know if I follow the trail into the past that I will find the signs, the markers that led her away from me. But I cannot summon the energy. I'm so full to the brim with my own fear that I don't have any room for anyone else.

I pass christy on the way out and we swap our treasures seamlessly, the routine perfected by now. I finger the precious meds. *Just a quarter. Just to relax me.*

I can't. I need to be in control. This is my last chance. I insert the tablet into the locket around my neck.

"This is it." megan spins on her mary-jane shoes once she's arrived at the door to the classroom. The others jostle to get as near to the front as possible, but I hang back, hiding behind agyness. I want to be the last to talk with Darwin so that the room will be relatively empty for our Interaction. I can pretend that we have some privacy.

"This is it," she says again. "This is the last time we're going to see them before the Ceremony on Monday. Are you ready?"

A few of the girls murmur, "Yes," nervously peeking through the narrow glass pane in the door.

"I said, are you ready?" She places her hands on her hips. In her tight cream sweater and pink gingham mini-skirt, she resembles a demented cheerleader from the time before us.

"Yes." I echo my sisters. If only I could throw them all on the pyre. I would watch happily as they turned to ashes until I was the only one left. Surely then I would be good enough.

She opens the door to the classroom, progressing from desk to desk in the circular room, a simpering smile on her face. As she leaves the classroom she brushes against me as I wait for my first Interaction to begin. I raise my arm to my nose, sniffing the smear of vanilla sweetness she has left on my skin. One by one the others finish too and join her outside the classroom, loudly comparing notes on how they think this final test went. *I'm so tired.*

"Girls!" chastity-magdalena storms out to confront them. "Have some respect for the other eves still complet-ing their Interactions. Go to the next class immediately.

chastity-ruth is expecting you for the final session of Heavenly Seventy."

At the mention of chastity-ruth they scurry away, and chastity-magdalena returns to her seat at the front of the classroom.

The bell rings and I sit at Socrates's desk. He fishes his eFone from his pocket and I can only watch as he squints at the screen, canned laughter from some Americas sitcom spitting out of it. chastity-magdalena weaves around the desks, smiling at Darwin as she passes, much to the chagrin of alessandra, sitting across from him, her elbows clenched together to boost her cleavage.

I continue on. George and Sigmund and Albert tell me how excited they are about the Ceremony, and can I believe it's only three days away now? I nod and smile, but tiredness has swallowed my voice. My body sways, sleep calling me for a split second before I jerk upright again.

I am so aware of his presence. Every time he moves, I move too, as if he has a leash around my throat. Does he feel it too? He must. This kind of physical attraction has to be rare. I don't feel it with any of the other Inheritants. How could he feel it with anyone besides me?

Because they're prettier than me. Because they're better than me.

Fewer and fewer people are in the room, each Inheritant leaving after their Interaction with me. With each stilted conversation, I realize how little I know the others. I have invested everything in Darwin. He is my only hope. I am getting nearer to him now, nearer and nearer.

"That's a good point," I hear him say to agyness.

I want to think of a good point as well, a way to explain why I told megan about the aberrants, but my mind is filled with cotton wool. I lick my lips, trying to excavate moisture from somewhere, but my mouth is bleached dry.

The bell rings. Albert and I are equally relieved that our stilted Interaction has come to a close.

"Good luck on Monday," he says as he marches out the door, agyness gliding behind him until Darwin, chastity-magdalena and I are the only ones left. Up close he looks tired too, dark circles ringing his clear blue eyes. He hasn't shaved, his usual stubble now the beginnings of a scruffy beard. His injured hand is still in a cast, resting heavily on the table.

"You cut your hair."

"Over a week ago." He shrugs, leaning back in his chair and stretching out, his body forming a hard, straight line.

I preferred it longer, when I could run my fingers through the curls. It's too neat now, the hairs almost standing vertically on his head. It's at odds with his disheveled appearance, the wrinkled navy-and-blue striped sweater and jeans.

"Darwin, we have to talk about what happened."

"There's nothing to talk about," he says, slouching so low in his seat I'm afraid he's going to slip under the desk and make a run for it.

"Are you sure? Because you seem distant."

"Distant?" He imbues the word with as much ridicule as possible. "How do I seem *distant*?"

Of course as soon as he asks me, I can't think of a good example.

"I don't know," I say, struggling to explain myself. "You seem a little cold."

"Cold?" He laughs. "Do you want me to ask them to turn up the heating?"

"Of course not. It's just, it's just that you picked megan for—"

"I didn't realize I had to explain my decisions to you," he cuts across me. "I thought it was my choice."

"Of course it is! I didn't mean to imply—"

"Good."

But I can't leave it like this. "I'm sorry, I'm sorry. I'm so sorry." My voice nearly breaks with the weight of trying to make him understand.

"It doesn't matter," he says, kicking his heel off the leg of his chair.

"Don't say it doesn't matter. It does." My voice is rising. The room takes on a menacing aspect, the lights dimming, shadows furling around us. A sudden coldness comes over me, sucking at me. "I should never have broken my promise to you."

"I shouldn't have told you in the first place," he says in a robotic voice. "That's not for the eves to know."

"I don't know why I told her. I just . . ."

"You just wanted megan to be your friend again."

When he says it like that, it sounds so stupid.

"I'm sorry, Darwin, I'm sorry, I'm so sorry. I know I messed up, but I need you to forgive me. Can't we just go back to the way we were before?"

There's a long pause.

"Look, freida." He avoids eye contact with me as he pulls the ends of his sweater over his hands. "It's not that I didn't care about you. I did. I mean, I do. Of course I care about you." His voice is hesitant. "But I've been fooling myself, thinking that I could choose a companion on the basis of how much I 'liked' her." He kicks the chair with a resounding whack.

"I know I messed up," I repeat myself. I reach across the table to touch his bandaged hand but he pulls away, and starts drumming them against this legs. "But can't we move past it? Why does it have to change things?"

"I've been talking with my dad."

"What's it got to do with him?"

"He's making me understand." He frowns at me.

"Understand what? That you're obsessed with getting his approval? 'My dad won't let me have friends. My dad is so mean to me. *My dad . . . My dad . . . My dad . . .*'?"

The rational freida is inside my brain screaming, telling me to play this better, to play by the rules, to be *nice*. But I can't stop the words pouring out of me, as every hope I ever had seems to be going up in flames, Darwin indifferently watching them burn.

"Have some respect," he says, and I shut up immediately, wilting under his critical gaze. He never looked at me like that before.

"He's an important man, freida. And he knows what he is talking about." He says the lines as if he has learned them by heart. "I need someone who will *fit* as a Judge's wife. Someone with attention to detail. Someone who is controlled."

"I can be controlled!" I sound hysterical, desperation unscrewing the hinges on my fear.

"Someone who can be trusted to be discreet." He raises an eyebrow at me.

"I said I was sorry. How many more times do you want me to say it? Please. Please, Darwin. I'll do anything."

"Is everything all right here?"

chastity-ruth is standing there and she is laughing at my stupidity. She wants to see me fail.

"Leave me alone!"

"freida!" Darwin rebukes me, and when I blink I see it's not chastity-ruth; it's a worried chastity-magdalena.

"I'm sorry," I say once again, wiping the visions from my eyes.

"It's fine, magdalena," Darwin says.

"Are you sure?"

"I'm sure." He smiles at her and she walks away.

"So your dad doesn't agree," I start again. "I know he's probably angry with me too. But he hasn't even met me. If he met me, he would like me."

"freida . . ."

"Or maybe, maybe—maybe we should run away."

"What?" he asks incredulously. "And go where? Where exactly do you propose we go?"

"I don't know."

"And how are you planning on doing it? The train leaves from the chastities' quarters. Do you think they are going to wave us through, give you a packed lunch for the journey?" His handsome face is screwed up in annoyance.

"I don't know," I say again, my head swimming with tired-ness. The edges of the room are softening like decaying froot.

"I can't do this anymore." He gestures to chastity-magdalena to cut the session short and I claw at his hand.

"Just choose me for Heavenly Seventy."

"What's the point at this stage?"

"Please, Darwin. You owe me that much."

"How do I owe you anything? After all that's happened."

I grab his unbandaged hand and stare at him.

"Please, Darwin. Just one last time. I need to explain."

And as he sighs in resignation, I make up my mind. I know what I have to do now. I know what I must do to fix this.

"How do you think yours went?" gisele whispers to megan.

"I was happy," megan replies smugly, adjusting the deep V-neck of her sweater so a hint of pale blue lace is showing. She matches her underwear to her shoes. Is this the sort of *attention to detail* that Darwin wants?

". . . yeah, and then I said to William that I wanted to have at least five sons, and he looked nervous. Do you think that I should have said that? What would you have said? What sort of conversation topics did you stick to?"

"Yeah, totally, that color is fab on you," megan inter-rupts gisele's monologue. "Seriously, where are the boys? We've been waiting here for at least ten minutes." She raises her hand.

"Yes, #767?"

"I was wondering where the Inheritants are? We're supposed to have our final Heavenly Seventy now."

"I can't wait," miranda says, reapplying blood-red lipstick on angelina's full pout while rosie braids lara's wispy blond hair. They are draped all over each other. You would think they were living in the harem already.

"Can we help you with something, freida?" karlie asks, catching me off guard. I mumble an apology and she piles her light brown hair into a high ponytail, cheekbones prominent on her thin face.

"Um, nice outfit," I say to make amends, gesturing at the mesh dress, her ruby-colored lingerie visible underneath. She, alessandra and adrianna start giggling uncontrollably. This what I will have to endure if I'm forced to become a concubine, living in a thinly disguised version of School.

"You are *supposed* to have a session now?" chastity-ruth's voice slithers through the desks, searching for its prey. "And who told you that?"

"chastity-magdalena."

"Did she?" Her gray eyes flash. "Did she really?"

"Yeah, she did," megan says. "So where are they?"

Before chastity-ruth can reply the door crashes open, the ten Inheritants clustering at the left of the chastity's desk. megan settles instantly when they arrive, the epitome of serenity. Is that what he wants? I'm beginning to sway in my seat again, weariness singing a soothing lullaby to my bones.

"freida." The hiss straightens my spine. "Are you okay?" cara asks, tucking a long strand of silky hair behind her ear. "You don't look well."

"Thanks."

"Not like that," she reassures me. "You just look a bit spaced."

You . . . just . . . look . . . a . . . bit . . . spaced.

She pauses for an hour between each word. A rush of leftover chemicals makes my body twitch and her eyes widen in alarm.

"What's going on down there?"

What's . . . going . . . on . . . down . . . there?

"Nothing, chastity-ruth," cara says.

"Oh, for goodness sake," the chastity says impatiently. "Let's just begin. Darwin, you're first." megan flutters her eyelashes at him. "Darwin?" chastity-ruth says again when he remains silent. The other Inheritants are becoming restless, eager to get started. "Do you want to choose one of the eves for Heavenly Seventy?"

"Fine." His voice is stiff with resentment. "I choose freida."

There is an intake of breath, that familiar vein throbbing perilously in megan's temple as I follow him, whispering directions to myself to remember how to move my arms and legs. The cupboard seems to have magically lengthened into a space two miles long, one of us at either end, the gap between us widening with every second.

I take the first step.

"I'm sorry."

"Stop saying that."

"What happened to your hand?"

"I fell."

"Does this have anything to do with me telling the eves about the female aberrants?"

"I said, I fell."

"I don't believe you," I say, my eyes flicking every so often to the wall. I need to see us in a mirror to believe that this is real.

"freida!"

How did I get on the ground?

"Are you okay? Will I call a chastity?" he asks urgently, crouching down on his haunches, his hand in the small of my back to steady me.

"No." I seize the hem of his sweater to stop him leaving. I coil into him, making him sit down too, his back propped against the wall. I'm between his legs, leaning against his chest. I watch in the opposite wall as he wraps one arm around my body. He bends his head toward mine and I move forward, slowly touching my lips against his.

"We can't do this, freida."

"Then why did you choose me today?"

"You said you wanted to explain." His voice is becoming prickly so I lower my mouth onto his again.

"Forget what I said."

We kiss again. I wrap my legs around his waist, the glass wall hard against my knees. He grabs my hips to pull me closer. His hands are pressing into my waist so tightly the lace is cutting into my skin. I reach behind me, pulling the zip down enough so that I can peel the dress off, one sleeve at a time. He stares at me, naked from the waist up, and swallows hard.

"Are you sure?" he says as he pulls me close again, the over-washed material of his T-shirt soft against my bare skin. I can't answer him. I don't know if I am sure but I know that I have to do *something* to keep him, and this is all I have to offer. I kiss him, waiting until I can feel something break in him. He grabs my hair so tightly I whimper and he draws back, pulling his T-shirt over his head. His body is taut and tanned, his stomach defined into a sharp V above his low-slung jeans. He pulls off his belt, kicking off his jeans and underwear, and I look away, embarrassed. He bends down, kissing me harder, his hand reaching between us and pulling my underwear aside until it's happening, he's there, he's inside me.

I don't know how long it lasts. I just watch in the ceiling mirror as waves shudder through his naked body before he rolls off me, sweating. Something is leaking between my legs, seeping into the fragile fabric of my dress.

"Thanks," he says out of the side of his mouth as he pulls his clothes back on.

"No problem." I shuffle closer to him. "And when I'm your companion you'll be able to do it whenever you feel like it."

"What?"

"What?" I repeat idiotically.

"*What* did you say about being my companion?"

"We had sex," I whisper, suddenly afraid that someone outside will hear us.

"Yes . . ." he says, sounding like he wishes that he could take that back now. "But it didn't *mean* anything."

I look away, my head throbbing. *Good girls don't cry. Good girls don't cry.* My shoulders heave, a low keening coming from the pit of my stomach.

"freida, come on."

I shouldn't do this in front of him, but the more I know that I need to be calm, the less able I seem to remain so.

"I'm not crying. I don't cry," I say, the words coming out in gasps. "I'm just so tired."

"I'm sorry to hear that," he says uneasily. "Don't they have medication for that?"

"You don't like drugs. I tried to stop taking them because you said you didn't like them." He subtly tests the door handle. "It's locked," I say, and he hangs his head sheepishly. "We had sex." He needs to understand what this means. "I've never had sex with anyone before."

"I didn't force you," he says, getting to his feet and paces back and forth. "You wanted it just as much as I did."

"I only did it because I thought you were going to choose me. I only did it . . . I don't know. I wanted to show you that I'm the right companion for you." I'm beginning to feel feverish.

"Why would you have *sex* with me to prove you would make a good companion? That makes no sense whatsoever." He's towering over me, blocking the light. The fly on his jeans is undone, his white underwear poking through.

"I can't be a concubine."

"I never said you were going to be a concubine."

"But how can I be a companion now? After I . . ."

"I won't tell anyone what you did," he says, backing away and leaning against the opposite wall. "Someone else might choose you."

"I haven't tried with any of them. You have been the only one."

"And that's my fault, is it?"

"No. I wanted to do it. I wanted you." I crawl closer to him, touching his shoes. "I thought you wanted me too."

"I thought you were different." He stops. "I thought . . . I don't know what I thought."

"You're the only one I want." I stare up at him, my voice hoarse. "You're my only option."

"Why?" he asks. "What's so special about me?"

"I don't understand."

"Would I be your only option if my dad was a publican?"

"Not this again," I groan.

"Just answer the question."

"But you're not a publican's son."

"But if I had been? Would you be so desperate to be with me if my dad wasn't a Judge?"

"I don't know . . . How would I know what I would do? You *are* a Judge's son."

"Humor me," he says. "Just pretend. You seem to be good at that."

"Why are you saying all these things?" I try to get up but my legs buckle beneath me again. "Of course I would want to be with you."

Would I?

"Just choose me . . ." I push the thought away. "I . . . I love you?" My tone is questioning, asking him if this is the right thing to say, if this is what he wants from me. Does he want me to love him? I can love him if he wants me to.

"No, you don't." Years of chastity-training are blasting sirens in my head, like a broken fire alarm. *Abort, abort.* Why am I even saying this? I don't love him. isabel took any love I might ever have been capable of. She sucked my heart dry of it.

"I need you to choose me," I say, and I am shattered by the way he looks at me. It's the same way that I look at myself in the mirror, the disappointment, the traces of longing, the useless wish that I could be different.

"You know you're not allowed say that, freida. It's forbidden."

"Please, just choose me. I'll do anything you want."

He stares at me in silence for a long time before saying simply, "Who are you?"

Who do you want me to be? I want to ask him. Just tell me who you want me to be. I'm tired, so tired. And I'm running out of time. He is the only one who can save me now. I wrap my arms around his legs like a limpet and he shakes me off, catching the right side of my face with his foot. I fold over, feeling something hot and sticky melting at the corner of my eye. The bell rings, releasing the door latch, and he falls out like a man coming up for air.

"Please don't do this to me, Darwin. I can't be a concubine. I can't."

"I don't know," he says. "If today was anything to go by, I think you could be a natural."

The door closes behind him, cutting the overhead lamps out. I lie face down, something steadily dripping onto the cool glass beneath me.

A chink of light breaks in.

"Well?" chastity-ruth's impervious tones.

"She's not there," cara replies. "I told you, I saw her leave with the rest of the eves. You must have missed her."

The chastity grunts before loudly shooing any stragglers out of the classroom. The door closes. I listen to my heart beating relentlessly, wishing that it would just stop. A crack of light splits the darkness again.

"She's in there. I didn't know who else to get. If chastity-ruth finds her . . ." cara doesn't finish the sentence. She doesn't need to.

"What's wrong with her?"

Everything.

"I didn't ask. I went straight to get you."

There is a heavy silence before cara speaks again. "I'm doing the best I can, isabel."

"I know." isabel sounds more animated than she has in weeks. "Let's bring her back to the dorms."

"What if we meet a chastity?"

"The chastities won't be a problem if I'm there."

"But . . ."

"*Fine*, cara," isabel sighs. "Get chastity-magdalena. She'll help us."

isabel creeps in and darkness covers us again. Her hand is on my hair, peeling it off my sticky face. She's whispering, soothing words that sound of nothing. A few minutes or a few hours later I hear the door opening again, flooding the cupboard with light, turning the inside of my eyelids red.

"She's bleeding," isabel gasps. "It's all over my hands."

I want to apologize but I have no words.

"What happened?" chastity-magdalena must have arrived.

"I don't know," cara answers, her voice thick with relief now that a chastity is here. "She and Darwin had a Heavenly Seventy session and she never came out after." She pauses for emphasis. "I wonder what happened. You know he chose megan last—"

"She's exhausted," isabel cuts across cara. "I'm sorry to involve you, but cara insisted on getting a chastity."

"You did the right thing. You two grab her under each arm and lift her. I'll walk ahead of you."

I feel a pinch under my left armpit, then the right. They groan as they haul me up. *Am I too heavy?* My arms are wrapped around two sets of shoulders, their collarbones stabbing into me. They carry me, my feet skimming the floor. My eyes flutter open and I see flashes of the chessboard tiles and painted toenails. Whiskers of hair brush against my skin, tickling my nose. Then they let go and I have the sensation of falling into something soft.

"You can go now, chastity-magdalena," isabel says.

"But I—"

"I said, you can go."

A swish of robes, and then silence. I curl on my side, forcing myself to look. I am in my room, isabel and cara standing in a line by my bed. cara is scratching at her scalp, scabs scraping off in little clouds of dry skin. I watch as they land on her shoulders, dusting the inky silk of her cap-sleeved dress.

"CanIgonow?" the words collide together.

"What?"

"Er . . . can I go now?"

"Fine," isabel says curtly. A clatter of heels, running away.

isabel sits at the end of the bed, taking one of my feet into her hands, then the other. She loosens the laces and removes my shoes. They fall to the ground with a bang, my feet throbbing.

"There's something on your dress," isabel says, moving closer and rubbing the material between her fingers. I look down. My perfect dress, fit for a princess, is crumpled like a used tissue, a stiff stain in the middle turning the gold a dark gray color. isabel's hands are stained with my blood, her nails crusted with it.

"Do you want to talk?" She looks at me with clear eyes, the medication fog lifted. I pull the pillow from under my head and hug it to me, hiding my body from her, afraid she'll be able to tell what I've done. What I've lost.

"You wouldn't understand."

"You'd be surprised at what I would understand."

"Darwin isn't going to choose me, is he?"

I'm hoping that she'll deny it, but she doesn't reply, and her silence rips through me.

She rifles through the top drawer of my bedside locker and takes out a packet of wet wipes. She swabs at my face, her touch so gentle that grief swells up inside me again. I can feel everything fall apart, twelve years of tears gushing out of me.

"Stop that," she says automatically.

"Just leave me alone," I sob. "You're good at that."

I roll onto my stomach. What did megan say? "This is who we are. This is who we were designed to be." It's my fault for allowing myself to become vulnerable. It is all my own fault.

"I'm sorry," she says, resting her hand between my shoulder blades. "I thought it would be easier this way."

I shrug her hand off me and sit up cross-legged on the bed. The head rush leaves me dizzy, and she reaches out to steady me and again I shrug her off.

"I'm not sure why you're pretending like you care about me, but I'm fine. Your good deed for the day is done."

"I just thought—"

"Yes, yes," I interject. "You thought it would be *easier*. I get it. Can you please go?"

She pulls down the delicate fabric of her chiffon dress so it reaches her knees and stands before the mirrored wall, staring at herself. She reaches into the pocket of her dress and takes out a small test tube, clicking a tablet into the palm of her hand and swallowing it down.

"You had better go," I say, fighting the temptation to ask her to share, "in case chastity-ruth finds you in here."

"She won't say anything to me."

"How can you be so sure?"

"Because I'm special. Don't you know that, freida? Didn't you ever realize just how special I am?"

I ignore her, grabbing the packet of wet wipes from where she left them on the bedside locker, and kneel on my bed to face the front wall. I lose my breath when I see myself up close. Blood is bubbling out of my temple, dripping down one side of my face. My eye makeup is smeared around bloodshot eyes. There are tears tracking down my cheeks, dissolving my foundation in patches. I flip my hair quickly to cover my face from isabel, knowing that it's too late, that she's already seen how ugly I really am. Hands trembling, I pry my locket open until three tablets tumble out.

"freida, I don't know if that's such a good idea."

"You're one to talk."

"You need to get cleaned up."

"The laser machine won't turn on until bedtime," I remind her as I pull out a few more of the wipes to clean myself. "Just go, isabel," I tell her as I scrub at my face, watching in the mirrors as it melts into smudges of colors, wishing I could scour the feelings away as easily. "I don't need you here."

Chapter 29

My body shakes my brain awake like a toy rattle and darkness presses into my eyes. Where am I?

My memory is a jigsaw puzzle made of identical black pieces, until there is a flare of colors, words. An image flashes. Then another.

"It didn't mean anything . . . I didn't force you . . ."

The memories explode like hand grenades.

"If today was anything to go by, I think you could be a natural."

I focus on my breathing. I visualize taking all these Unacceptable Emotions and locking them up in a box, throwing away the key, never to be found again.

What time is it? I'm deliberately not thinking about that thing I said I wasn't going to think about.

12:00 flashes on my ePad.

Why are the lamps still off if it's noon? Did I miss wake-up call? Why didn't freja wake me? I grope my way blindly across the room, feeling the smooth glass of the walls turn to a ribbed metal beneath my hands. It's the corrugated steel of the door. But my door is never closed.

I fumble until I find the steel handle at the base of the door and I try my best to pull it up, my arms feeling as if they will be wrenched out of their sockets with the effort. I give up with a scream of frustration. Feeling my way back to my bed, I pat the covers until I find my eFone.

"The service has been cut."

I can't think straight. Why did I take all that Sleep-Sound? I can taste the scum left behind, my mouth crusted over with its caustic icing sugar. I gag with thirst and stick my tongue out, searching for moisture.

There's water in my changing room.

Using my eFone as a flashlight, I press my hand into the pink outline of a handprint etched into the mirror wall opposite my bed.

"Mismatch," says a robotic voice.

I force myself to slow down, pressing my hand into the glass with more care this time.

"Mismatch."

I try once more, lining my hand up with the plastic handprint as precisely as I can.

"Mismatch. That is the third mismatch today. This room shall be secured for the next twelve hours."

I turn to the exit and start banging my fist against the steel. The beat sounds too solid, as if the outside of the door has been overlaid with slabs of stone. When I stop, the air feels thinly quiet.

An overwhelming urge to urinate hits, my bladder swelling like a tumor within me. I cross my legs tightly, the stiff material of my dress rubbing against my skin as I fold myself onto the bed. I realize I've sat on the hard edge of my ePad and I fumble for it, opening it to cast the room in its dim glow.

"MyFace," I say.

"Access denied."

"VideoChat . . . Your Face or Mine . . ."

"Access denied."

"Stream TV," I try, calming a little when this VoiceCommand works. I peer closer, frowning. "Change channel."

Nothing happens. I tap the screen repeatedly but it's frozen on the Chit-Chat network, spitting out commercial after commercial. *I need a toilet. I need a toilet right now.*

I jump up, hopping from one leg to the other, squeezing my upper thighs together as hard as I can. I don't know how much longer I can last.

"Need to inject sensuality into your life?" a warm voice comes from the ePad. "Ylang Ylang and Patchouli Shower Gel has nourishing plant extracts that will tighten your skin, reducing any pesky fat cells while reversing the aging process."

A concubine removes her orange kimono, piles her tight curls into a bun on the top of her head and steps into the open shower. She turns the tap on, the pressure of the running water hissing.

I need to switch it off, but the off button won't work, *it won't.* Drizzling the shower gel into her hands, she lathers up and soaps every inch of her perfect body.

"PLEASE HELP ME. I NEED TO GO TO THE BATHROOM."

I'm screaming, the words tearing my throat like sandpaper. I thump the door as hard as I can until finally I have to stop, my fist aching.

I hear a scraping noise and there is a tunnel of light from the base of the door. I fall quickly to my knees to talk to whoever is at the other side of the open square, but a bucket is pushed into my face and the shutter slots back in immediately, so neatly that the joins are invisible. I pick it up, full to the brim with bottles of water.

Surely they can't expect me to . . . I can't . . . What if this is a test? Have some control, freida. Control yourself . . . I can't . . . oh shit.

I tip the bucket over, the plastic bottles tumbling out, and fall back on it, the steel rim cutting into me. And I let go, feeling everything fall away until all that is left is an awful, corrupted relief. I grab the half-empty packet of wet wipes strewn by the bed to clean myself up, throwing the cloth away and watching as it swims in the yellow liquid like a ghostly jellyfish. I gingerly pick the bucket up and place it at the base of the bed, wincing at the stench. What is happening to me?

I kick the door in frustration. My bare toes crack against the metal and I fall onto the bed, screaming again. I rock back and forth, losing all sense of time or place, falling endlessly into a chasm of fear.

"Previously, on *The Chit-Chat*," the volume on the ePad spikes, "the ladies have been talking about . . ."

"Well, I hate to judge, you know," a sunny-sweet voice says, "but I think breastfeeding is so important. As long as it's done in private of course. And you know me, tyra, I hate to say anything bad about anyone, but when I see a mother who bottle-feeds her son, I do wonder."

"Wonder what?" a third voice says, bored, and I squint at the screen, my eyes swollen from tears.

"Well, about her level of commitment, I guess," grace, the blond host simpers, hands clutching at a string of pearls around her neck.

"grace, girl, let's face it. These 'women' who can't be bothered to breastfeed are bad mothers," the stunning black girl shrieks, huge emerald-and-diamond earrings flashing as she shakes her head vehemently.

A tiny smile curls on grace's lips, hand pressed against her chest. "Oh, tyra, you shouldn't say such things," she says before looking at the audience, her eyes downcast. "But, I must admit, it's the sons I feel sorry for."

A smattering of enthusiastic applause breaks out, grace blushing at the attention.

"Yuck," georgia, the third host, says in disgust as she cups her vast breasts and winks at the camera. "These bad boys are for fun times only."

"And now, for today's live show! Welcome to *The Chit-Chat!*"

I stare at the ePad, a merciful distraction from my panic. The set has been designed to look like an old-fashioned country kitchen. The walls are a gray stone facade, grille windows with white lace curtains pulled down to disguise the fact that there's nothing behind them. Framed water-color paintings of babies in blue onesies, boats, and flowers are dotted around, and there's an old pine dresser filled with mismatched vintage teacups and plates. The pièce de résistance is a stove cooker in a faded hunter green. It's obsolete, of course, but rare, and worth a fortune.

"And here are your hosts! grace!"

There is frenzied clapping as she appears, white-gloved hands resting at her heart in gratitude. She looks so lady-like in a white sleeveless collared shirt tucked into a full pistachio-green skirt that comes to midcalf, a white belt accentuating her tiny waist. The ubiquitous pearl necklace is hanging around her neck, pistachio-colored kitten heels on her feet. Her blond hair is set in pin curls and tied in a bouncy ponytail with a white-and-pistachio striped rib-bon, her blue saucer eyes huge in waxy skin. She's been a companion to a prominent Zone official for about twelve years now but thanks to frequent skin peels and injections she doesn't look a day over twenty-one.

"Aaaaaand tyra!"

tyra emerges from backstage. She's lightened her hair and it falls around her face in relaxed waves. Her cobalt-blue dress is one-shouldered and knee-length, clinging to every curve. The camera zooms in on her doll-like face, the wide green eyes with oversize lashes, the arched eye-brows, the high cheekbones under that flawless skin.

"And, lastly, georgia!"

georgia struts onto the set wearing a navy playsuit dot-ted with white anchors, slashed to her navel. It's far too

small for her, but georgia won "Best Body" when she gradu-
ated two years ago and likes to remind people why. Impossibly slim, with the biggest breasts I've ever seen, she is
constantly voted #1 in those hottest concubines lists. She
waves at the audience, tossing her waist-length espresso-
colored hair away from her tanned face, full lips painted
red, her dark brown eyes outlined with liquid liner. She
beams at the muted response she's receiving. georgia has
never been popular. Before she started appearing on *The
Chit-Chat* it was unheard of for concubines and companions
to mix, but the controversy drove viewing figures up so
they kept her. She settles into a wicker armchair at the
round pine table.

grace ignores her and points at the baby-blue tea cozy
covering the teapot in the middle of the table. "I knitted
that myself!" she says proudly, and I giggle despite my
misery, wiping my runny nose with the back of my hand.
There is no way grace made that thing. I can see from the
skeptical look georgia is throwing her that she agrees with
me. tyra smiles as grace pours tea into a floral china cup
for her, delicately crossing her feet at the ankles as she
takes a seat. Neither offers georgia any tea.

"Welcome, ladies!" grace says, and I roll my eyes as
the audience cheers excitedly. I can't listen to an entire
program of this garbage. I tap the screen forcefully, but it
still won't switch channels. I have an overpowering urge
to throw the thing against the wall and see it shatter into
a million pieces.

"... **freida** ..."

My head jerks up, hoping someone might have come to rescue me, but the door is closed. I get up to inspect my wardrobe, but it's still shut down.

". . . **freida** . . ."

I check under the bed, using my eFone as a flashlight like I'm in 5th year and searching for bogeymen, but there's nothing there but those snakeskin ankle boots isabel gave me last year. I was afraid to wear them in case megan asked to "borrow" them and never gave them back, so I hid them under my bed. I can't believe I forgot.

"They're incredible, isabel," I said, touching the boots reverently. "Where on earth did you get them?"

"They're yours," she said. "I don't want them."

"But . . ." I stuttered, confused. "They're real snakeskin. You must love them."

"I hate them," she turned away from me. "I hate them."

". . . **freida** . . ."

Where is it coming from? There is no one else here. It's only me and my infinite reflections, flickering in the weak light.

". . . **freida** . . ."

It's coming from the ePad. Is my VideoChat working again? I grab it, desperate to find out why I've been imprisoned in my room. But the screen is still frozen on *The Chit-Chat*.

"Hello?" I tap it again. "Can you hear me?"

"She needs to be sent Underground right away. There is no room for this sort of behavior in the Euro-Zone." tyra sniffs.

"Oh, tyra, you know that's not for us to say," grace says as she takes a sip of tea. "It's up the men to make those decisions."

"But this freida girl sounds dangerous," tyra says, touching grace's hand to stress her point.

This freida girl sounds dangerous. This freida girl sounds dangerous. This freida girl sounds dangerous. This freida girl sounds dangerous.

There must be someone else called freida in the Euro-Zone. An older eve.

"I hate to judge . . ." grace says, georgia barely suppressing a smirk, "but apparently she's been spreading rumors about . . ." She swallows before saying in a stage whisper, ". . . female aberrants."

There is a gasp from the audience, and tyra and georgia look suitably stunned. But it can't be. Why would they be talking about me on one of the highest-rated shows in the Euro-Zone? Fotos begin to flash on-screen. I can hear someone saying, "Oh no, oh no, oh no . . ." over and over and over again. I look at the wall and I realize it's me, mouthing the words frantically. The fotos are of me. They're all of me.

"Thank goodness she's being confined at present," grace says, a blond tendril escaping her ponytail. Confined. She's being confined. I'm being *confined*. "According to my darling Winston." She breaks off as the audience gives a communal *awwww*. "I know, I know. I've been so blessed."

"We both have," tyra says smoothly.

"We really have, haven't we, dear? They've been so generous, allowing us to take the time to record this show. We're so lucky."

"Winston can be very *generous*, can't he?" georgia says with a wicked glint in her eye.

"Let's focus on the matter in hand," tyra says quickly as grace bristles. "What does Winston say?"

"According to *my* darling Winston," grace says, her pale pink lips pursed sulkily, "this freida is in quarantine at the moment. You know me, ladies—I would hate for anything bad to happen to anyone, but it does seem as if it might be safer for her to be sent Underground, out of harm's way."

"And that's not all," tyra adds, "apparently she tried to coerce one of the Inheritants into choosing her as his companion."

"No!" grace says, as the audience shifts in their seats with barely suppressed excitement. Why isn't this censored? Darwin said anything like this would be censored in the School.

"Did you not watch the *Daily Tale* today? Their sources say she *begged* him. They're launching one of their Tale Campaigns to shame her. And it wasn't just any Inheritant." She pauses for dramatic effect. "It was Darwin."

"Who's Darwin?" georgia asks, bored, adjusting her cleavage.

"He's only the son of Judge Goldsmith," tyra says slowly, every word coated in sarcasm.

"Judge Goldsmith!" georgia shudders slightly as tyra says, "This girl declared her love for him . . ."

"*Before* the Ceremony?" grace interrupts, her eyes widening in shock.

"Her best friend reported her to the chastities and gave an interview to the *Tale*. She told them she couldn't allow the School's reputation to be damaged." I mentally bash megan's face in. "Apparently she had sex with him in an attempt to persuade him. When that didn't work, she resorted to pleading with him to choose her."

grace sits back in her armchair, waving her hand in front of her face like a fan. "Why would she think *that* . . ." she wrinkles her nose—"would make him choose her to be his companion? That's for the concubines."

The injustice of not being able to explain or defend myself renders me paralyzed. I sit there, staring at the screen, watching as my life is dissected for the entertainment of the Euro-Zone.

"Having sex isn't the issue. Who cares?" georgia ignores grace as she clucks loudly. "And love isn't that big a deal either."

"Love before marriage is forbidden." grace frowns. "How dare this eve assume that an Inheritant would love her before he had formally chosen her? It's the height of presumptuousness."

"Yeah, but come on," georgia says. "It's not like it hasn't happened before. Every few years or so, some eve always gets a bit soppy and forgets her place."

"It's still unacceptable. The eves have extensive training in the correct behavioral procedures."

"It's still not that big an issue," georgia insists. "Not to my generation. I know I'm a lot younger than you . . ." the look grace gives her could shred skin—"but young people won't care that she had sex with him, or even that she fell in love before marriage. The real problem is that she tried to coerce him into choosing her." She shakes her head in disbelief, in agreement with the two companions for once.

"She should have had more control," tyra says, looking straight to camera. For a moment I feel as if she can see me and I duck out of view. A loud ringing in my ears is drowning them out, only a shrill *should have* breaking through the white noise. *She should have . . . She should have . . . She should have . . .*

megan couldn't have told them about me begging him to choose me; she didn't know about it. My mind is racing, following every possible trail through the maze, but it always comes back to the same person. Darwin. It had to have been Darwin.

"Will they put her on trial?" grace asks.

"Out of respect for Judge Goldsmith, they will have a private one in the School. Just this freida, Darwin, the Judge himself and the principal chastity," tyra answers, thrilled to be the one with the inside information.

"Will she offer a defense?" georgia asks, examining her nail polish for chips.

"What defense?" grace exclaims. "She is an eve. She was designed to meet a purpose and she has been trained for the last sixteen years to perform in a way that meets that purpose." I'm nodding in agreement until I remember it's me they're talking about. "Any deviation from that is unacceptable. This freida has failed in her duty. She has no defense."

There is a huge cheer, the camera moving slowly across the audience, their fervent faces. All of them agree with grace. The screen freezes on them chanting, baying for my blood.

"Thank you for watching! Tune in tomorrow at 1:00 p.m. for a brand-new episode of *The Chit-Chat*."

The room is filled with commercial jingles. They seep in through my ears, swilling around the emptiness in my head before leaking out again.

The Chit-Chat theme music blasts out again. I can't remember how to move my limbs; each one feels like a separate entity from the rest of my body, disconnected and unbearably weighted. Throw it at the walls, I'm screaming silently to myself, staring at the ePad cradled in my hands, but I can't move.

"And now for the viewers' comments. Thanks to all of you who called in today in such unprecedented numbers!"

The screen crackles and a face appears and another face and then another. There are hundreds of them. Concubines and companions. Youthful faces, faces stretched young. Blondes, brunettes, redheads. They are all women, of course. And every one of them hates me.

"Disgusting . . . Has she no self-control?"

"I couldn't believe it when I saw the report on the *Daily Tale*. They said this girl is threatening the very foundations of our society."

"The *Daily Tale* said that she's not even that good-looking. I mean, she was designed perfectly, of course, but I heard reports she was over target weight at the start of the year."

"Oh, I thought the *Daily Tale* said she was too skinny."

"We all went through the School system and we obeyed the rules. Who does this girl think she is?"

"Poor Darwin. He must have felt so manipulated. The eves are supposed to be trained properly and behave themselves."

"Of course he was going to take it if it was offered to him. He's a man—it's only natural for him to want to have sex."

"Her skin is wrecked-looking, isn't it?"

"The *Daily Tale* says that she has an addiction to sleep medication. They had a report by a physician from the Americas-Zone. He's never treated her, but he's seen fotos and said she definitely looks like an addict."

"I can't believe she's only sixteen. She looks thirty at least."

"I agree with the last viewer. Her skin is aged. I could see crow's feet in some of those fotos."

"She should have known better. It's the Inheritant I feel sorry for."

"What does she think is so special about her?"

I can't turn it off. I'm shaking the ePad, pressing the off switch as hard as I can and muting the volume, but the comments keep coming. Every doubt I've ever had about myself, every whisper of self-hatred that I buried deep inside, it's all there, pouring from the mouths of strangers. I'm ugly. I'm stupid. I look old. I'm repulsive.

My stomach heaves and I can't stop that either. Vomit fills my mouth, sputtering through my lips, and I rush to the bucket at the foot of my bed, hunching over until it's finished. The smell corkscrews up my nostrils, twisting inside my head. It's spreading through the small room, painting the walls in its stench.

3:00 p.m. "Welcome to *The Chit-Chat*! And here are your hosts . . ."

4:00 p.m. "Welcome to *The Chit-Chat*! And here are your hosts . . ."

5:00 p.m. "Welcome to *The Chit-Chat*! And here are your hosts . . ."

Every hour a repeat of the show is shown and *I can't turn it off*. It's the same, again and again and again, but each time I pick up a nuance, a new slur that I missed the first time. I've buried the ePad underneath my bed and I'm cowering at the opposite side of the room, hands thrust into my ears to drown it out. But it's getting louder, the words bouncing off the glass surfaces, hunting me down.

6:00 p.m. "Welcome to *The Chit-Chat*! And here are your hosts . . ."

A red glaze descends over my eyeballs and I grab the ePad from underneath the bed and open it, throwing it as hard as I can at the wall. It bounces off the glass, falling to the ground with a reassuring thud. An electric spark jumps, like a match being struck. The computer screen is shattered, tiny shards of glass glittering on the floor. For a blissful moment, all I can hear is my jagged breath.

Then the walls turn black, an ear-splitting crack whipping through the room. Crackling lines of static appear on the walls as the mirrors melt away, shaping into pictures, into people, moving and talking.

"I knitted that myself girls!" grace is saying proudly, not a blond hair out of place. And she's in the walls and she's on the ceiling and they're all there and they're talking about me, about me, about me, about me.

7:00 p.m. "Welcome to *The Chit-Chat!* **And here are your hosts . . ."**

8:00 p.m. "Welcome to *The Chit-Chat!* **And here are your hosts . . ."**

I'm clawing at the glass wall hiding my dressing room, trying to open it with my ruined nails and the heels of my shoes, blood splitting through my skin. My SleepSound is in there. If I can get to it, I can stop this. I can drown it out.

9:00 p.m. "Welcome to *The Chit-Chat!* **And here are your hosts . . ."**

10:00 p.m. "Welcome to *The Chit-Chat!* **And here are your hosts . . ."**

I'm electrified. My skin is crawling with a million fleas eating into my flesh. The smell of the urine and bile is billowing through the room. I'm breathing it into my lungs, deep into my body. The walls flash with faces, all listing my failings.

11:00 p.m. "Welcome to *The Chit-Chat!* **And here are your hosts . . ."**

Midnight. "Welcome to *The Chit-Chat*! **And here are your hosts . . ."**

I'm banging my head against the steel door, blood clots popping in my head like bubble wrap, and *I don't care, I don't care, I don't care.*

4:00 a.m. "Welcome to *The Chit-Chat*! **And here are your hosts . . ."**

tyra, grace, and georgia dance across the glass; they are everywhere and everywhere. I cover my ears and close my eyes but they are inside my head.

They are inside my head.

8:00 a.m. "Welcome to *The Chit-Chat*! **And here are your hosts . . ."**

My bones are growing and my skin is shrinking. I am too much, too big for this body. I want to break every bone inside me. I want to scrape off all this flesh, clean out the shit that makes me what I am, start anew. Maybe then they'll stop.

I watch grace sip her tea in the ceiling.

"She is an eve. She was designed to meet a purpose and she has been trained for the last sixteen years to perform in a way that meets that purpose."

I'm mouthing the words along with her. I know it all by heart now.

"I can't believe she's only sixteen. She looks thirty at least," jordan, twenty-seven, a companion with three beautiful boys who are the light of her life, says, and I agree with her, I agree with her. "What do you think, jordan?" I ask her in a friendly voice. "Tell me what you think.

Because I can't believe this freida girl is only sixteen. She looks thirty at least." Fotos of me flash on the walls, on the ceiling, red circles looping around my tired eyes and gray skin and what looks to be the beginning of a frown line. jordan and I chorus together, "I can't believe she's only sixteen. She looks thirty at least," again and again and again.

I am eating myself. I am an identity cannibal.

10:00 a.m. "Welcome to *The Chit-Chat*! And here are your hosts . . ."

grace is pouring the cup of tea for tyra again (is it my imagination or does hurt briefly flicker on georgia's face when she isn't offered any? I hadn't noticed before) when the power suddenly cuts, folding the room in darkness. The door inches open and the room explodes with light, particles of dust shimmering in its steamy haze. I fall back in the corner of the bed, pressing my spine against the crook where the base and side wall meet. I hold my hand in front of my face, blinking furiously. A black blob comes toward me, and for a moment I think the door has come to life in an effort to grant me my freedom. The edges harden as the blob morphs into chastity-anne. Her eyes, like two navy buttons sewn into her face, dart around the room, taking in the empty plastic bottles, the disheveled bedding furrowed around me, the streaks of blood smeared on the steel casing of my changing room. The stink hits her and she gags, her face concertinaing in on itself. She stares at the overflowing bucket, clumps of vomit floating in it. There is a puddle pooling around the base of the bucket, staining the edges of the snow-white valance sheet.

"What?" I ask.

She points at the wall behind me. The gold lace dress clings to my grimy body, soiled with dark patches under my arms and around the skirt. My skin is dreary with sleeplessness. *(I can't believe I'm only sixteen. I look thirty at least. Don't you agree, jordan? Don't you agree?)* My hair is matted with dried blood and vomit, clumped into knots, and there is a shadowy ring forming around my forehead, creeping into my eye, like a crown of bruises. I touch it, gasping as the pain pulsates.

"Come with me, freida."

"Where's chastity-magdalena?" She's the only one who might be able to help me. "I need to talk to her."

"magdalena has been assigned a different duty at this time," chastity-anne says, her voice sounding rehearsed. "Now let's go."

"Out of respect for Judge Goldsmith, they will have a private one in the School. Just this eve, Darwin, the Judge himself and the principal chastity," tyra had said, barely concealed glee in her voice.

"Where are we going? Are we going to see Darwin?" I ask again, my voice rising anxiously. "Can I get changed first?"

He can't see me like this. He'll think I'm ugly. The open corridor beyond my room beckons, the black-and-white tiles forming a road map to freedom. I shuffle to the edge of the bed, pressing the soles of my feet against the ground. Gritting my teeth, I propel myself forward, aiming for the now deserted dormitory.

"Oh, freida." chastity-anne steps neatly in front of me, shaking her head. "Where would you run to?"

We are sealed in.

"Do I have to go?"

"Do you have a choice?" she replies, hands folded within the shroud of her cloak so it looks as if her head is floating on top of a black cloud.

"Do you have any meds you can give me?" I come as close as I can to her without touching and she takes a step back, gagging at my ripeness.

"I'll be calmer." I'll promise her anything. "I'll give a better impression of the School that way."

"Fine," she sighs, pale hands peeping out of the sleeves of her cloak and reaching into a pocket at her waist. She pulls out a test tube, clicks a small lever twice and dispenses two capsules, which she drops into the palm of my hand. They are chalk-white and round without any distinguishing markings.

"What are these?" I gulp them down before she has a chance to answer. "I've never seen them before."

"Does it matter?"

The halls are empty. In the few minutes it takes to get to the chastity quarters, the meds start blowing bubbles of serenity through my bloodstream. I stumble, grazing off chastity-anne, and she flinches.

"Ssssorry," I whisper.

She curls her body around the small golden box to input the access code without my seeing it. The gates spring open and she hurries along the candle-lit passageway, urging me to keep up with her. The brass peephole in the huge oak door slides open.

"You're late," chastity-ruth says in reproach, a frown line burrowed between her flint-gray eyes. She shudders when I come into the light, but it doesn't bother me. A luscious dullness seeps into my brain. She raises an eyebrow at chastity-anne.

"Somnolin. I thought it would make her more manageable."

"True." chastity-ruth waves me in. "Perhaps we should start grinding it into their food. You may go now, anne."

I follow her into the chastity office. It has exploded with light since I was last here; it's shining from every wall. There is a man sitting in chastity-ruth's chair, one with snow-white hair, deep lines scored into his forehead. His navy suit and navy-and-yellow polka-dot tie do little to disguise his bulk, rolls of fat spilling from his shirt like a ruff collar. His features are scrunched into the middle of his moon-shaped face, sparse white eyebrows over deep-set eyes, thin lips pulled back disdainfully.

"So this is the girl who has been causing so much trouble," he growls. "Really, ruth, has the benchmark for beauty at the School fallen so low?"

"She's been unwell, Judge Goldsmith. Ordinarily she would be of a higher standard."

That's the nicest thing chastity-ruth has ever said about me.

He clutches the sides of the chair and heaves himself up, the armrests quivering in protest. Within two strides he is in front of me. His mud-brown eyes are cold. "You reek," he says, and backs away, sinking into the wooden seat. "Let's get this over with."

"Yes, Judge Goldsmith." chastity-ruth grabs two chairs from the side of the room and drags them around the desk. She sits on the edge of a seat, an eager student. Why is she staring at me like that?

"#630." Her voice sounds as if it is drowning within a wall of water. "Sit down."

She points at me, then to the seat beside her. I collapse limply, the chair so low that my face is level with the edge of the desk.

"Obviously we don't want the eves to be too intelligent, ruth, but the ability to follow simple directions would be helpful."

"I'm sorry, Judge Goldsmith."

"Just one more thing we will address in our investigation," he replies, cracking his hairy knuckles one by one. "But that's a matter for another day. Today we are here to consider the claims that eve #630 attempted to manipulate an Inheritant, Mr. Darwin Goldsmith, into choosing her as his companion, despite knowing that such behavior is prohibited. She also declared love before marriage, despite knowing that this too is prohibited." He taps his ePad and gives a VoiceCommand to start recording. "Do you have anything that you want to say for yourself, eve #630?"

I have no words.

He pushes the sleeves of his suit back, creasing them up to his elbows. His arms are covered in hundreds of white hairs. "We shall introduce the main witness." He shouts at the door. "Darwin, you can come in now."

Deep beneath the clouds of the drugs, something moves in my heart. I let it go.

"Thank you," Darwin says politely as chastity-ruth dashes to hold the door open. He walks toward the desk, taking his place at his father's right-hand side. They're wearing identical suits. Darwin has slicked back his dark curls with gel and his tanned face is closely shaven.

"freida!" he cries out when he sees me. "What happened? Are you okay?"

"Control yourself," his father says, and grabs his broken wrist. Darwin's mouth forms a soundless gasp, his face blanching in pain. Judge Goldsmith lets go and Darwin falls back into place, staring at a spot on the wall behind me.

"Darwin," Judge Goldsmith begins, reaching into a pocket on the inside of his suit jacket and retrieving a pair of spectacles. He takes an eggshell-colored handkerchief from his breast pocket and sets about cleaning the lenses meticulously. "Please tell us exactly what happened between you and eve #630. Speak slowly and clearly."

"freida . . ." Darwin begins before the Judge coughs pointedly.

I don't want to hear this.

"I mean, #630 and I got to know each other through the eve/Inheritant Interactions. I chose her a number of times for Heavenly Seventy . . ."

This is a play, like they used to have in the time before us, I decide, and I make myself float out of the top of my head and hover on the ceiling, looking down at the bodies in the room below. *This is a performance. This has nothing to do with me.*

"Please explain to the court what Heavenly Seventy is," the fat man interjects, putting his glasses on. The younger boy looks around at the office and the few people in it.

"Um, sure." He continues. "It's a task where the Inheritants choose an eve that they want to spend time with in private."

"And whom did you choose?" the man asks.

"You know who I chose. I've told you this already." The Judge swivels slowly in his chair, his eyes glacial. "I mean," the young man adds quickly, "I chose #630."

"And why did you choose #630?"

"What do you mean?"

"Was she the only person you could have chosen? Were all the other eves taken when you made your selection?"

"No," he answers. "I always got to choose first."

"And why was that?"

"Because I'm the #1 Inheritant."

"Any why is that?"

"Because I'm a Judge's son."

"So, as a Judge's son, you were entitled to certain privileges."

"Yes," the son says in a low voice.

"How fortunate you are. You may continue."

"I chose her a few times and I guess she got the wrong idea, because the last time we were together she was hysterical and started begging me to make her my companion."

A look trembles between the two men. Did one of them forget his lines? The older man trains his brutal stare on the young girl. She's slumped in a chair, her legs and arms falling at strange angles, like a broken doll.

"#630, an eve may only love a man that has chosen her to be his companion. This is because men have the necessary experience and intelligence to choose better for you than you could choose for yourself." He looks at the hollowed-out shell of a girl, openly sneering. "And how you thought that the son of a Judge would choose *you* . . ." The boy beside him winces. "The standards are slipping, ruth," the man says, pressing his fingertips against the wooden desk. "She should be thrown on the pyre."

The girl's head lolls on her shoulders, as silent as if they had cut out her tongue.

"What?" the boy cries out. "You can't do that."

"Be quiet." The older man turns to look at him, anger crackling off him like hot oil spitting from a pan.

"No." The boy is rash. "You can't do that. You're making too big a deal out of this." He stares at the younger girl. "freida, I'm——" he begins before his dad cuts across him.

"Too big a deal?" he says, hefting his bulk back into the chair. The wood moans in protest. "Well, that's where you're wrong. We have rules. You do realize we have rules, don't you, *boy*?" The younger boy nods, his face coloring with embarrassment.

"I don't know if you do. Because if you did, I don't think you would say that we were making 'too big a deal' out of this at all."

"I'm sorry, Dad."

"You're right to be sorry. Because you, of all people, need to believe that it's imperative to stick to the rules. Rules that you, the future Judge of the Euro-Zone, will one day enforce. How can you do so if you are prepared to encourage illicit behavior?"

"I didn't—"

"Maybe some of those rules seem outdated to you. Maybe they seem overly stringent or exacting. But they are there to protect us. To ensure our survival. If we begin flaunting those rules, what will we have?"

None of the other characters meets his eyes; all are staring at the floor. I don't think I like this play very much.

"Anarchy," the Judge announces. "Chaos. Destruction. Is that what you want?"

"No," the boy mutters.

"Of course not. Take a look around you. This world is not what it used to be. We are the final bastion of a faltering people."

"Yes, Dad."

"But only faltering. Not dying, as our forefathers feared. We have survived because we created a system that works. If we break one rule and then another and another, our system might warp. It might disintegrate. And what would happen then? How can we risk that? How can we jeopardize our survival?"

"I understand, Father." The boy hesitates, doubt written on his face. "But why the pyre?" He holds his breath.

"Why? Because she broke the rules? Because she must be taught a lesson?" The Judge shrugs. "Because we can, I suppose."

"It's not because of me, is it?" the boy says in a very small voice.

"Darwin, you are the only son of the Euro-Zone's Judge." He pats his hair. "These little sluts need to know their place." He takes off his suit jacket, his flesh straining against his white cotton shirt. "But don't worry, this one won't be thrown on the pyre. She isn't even going Underground, although we should be making a proper example of her, show the rest of them what happens if they get ideas above their station."

The bald woman cowers. "I'm afraid that is outside of my control now."

"Yes, I know," the Judge harrumphs. "She's a lucky one, isn't she? Aren't you lucky, freida?"

freida. That's me. They're talking about me.

I melt back through my bones and I stretch out inside myself, filling my body once more. But it doesn't feel right. It feels as if I'm wrapping myself in an old coat, familiar and warm, but suddenly ill-fitting. It constricts at the neck, pulls at the arms. I must need more meds. The room is losing its hazy quality; colors are bleeding back in.

"Lucky?" I croak, as if it's a word I've never heard before.

"But . . ." he dismisses me with a wave of his hand— "you have been disqualified from the Ceremony at least. You are to become a chastity. In a nonteaching role of course. We can't have you infecting the younger eves with your *abnormalities*."

A chastity. I will never leave this School. I will never see beyond these walls. I wait for sorrow to sweep through me but I feel nothing. I am wasted with nothingness.

"I want to say again, on behalf of all the chastities and myself, how truly sorry I am for this regrettable incident, Judge Goldsmith." chastity-ruth leans forward in her seat, her chin almost resting on the table. "I will ensure nothing like this happens again."

"It had better not," Judge Goldsmith says. "I'm only glad that it happened with Darwin. He knew the correct protocol to follow at least." He swivels in his chair to look at his son. "I must say, this almost makes up for your previous indiscretion. I'm proud of you, Darwin."

Darwin merely nods, but when his dad turns away to tuck his ePad away in a real leather briefcase, he bites his lower lip to hold in his smile, almost glistening with bliss, and I know how much this means to him. I understand.

"Darwin," his dad adds. "This is confidential."

"Sure." Darwin nods, undoing the top button of his shirt and loosening his tie, relaxing now that the trial is over. Judge Goldsmith gets to his feet again, his belly bulging through gaping buttons. He picks up his briefcase, folds his jacket over his arm and dabs his damp face with a handkerchief. Darwin meets my eyes briefly as he walks out. I understand, I try to tell him silently. I understand. And it seems to me that everything we had, everything we ever meant to each other or could have meant, shimmers between us.

We both look away. We are strangers now.

"Darwin." I hear the Judge's voice behind me. "That includes your mother. I don't want cecily knowing about this. It's not her place."

"But who will I talk . . ." Darwin halts midsentence.

"Who will you talk to?" Judge Goldsmith's voice rings out. "Don't be such a pussy, Darwin." His voice continues: "And as for you . . . you're lucky we're being so lenient. This is your own fault, isn't it?"

He's addressing me. I twist my upper body around, holding onto the back of the chair. The Judge is standing in the doorway, so large I can barely see Darwin behind him.

"Isn't it?" he repeats when I just stare blankly at him.

"Yes," I whisper. The word tastes gray.

"Yes, what? I want to hear you say it."

"Yes. This is my own fault."

"I can't believe you thought you would corrupt my son. I have him well trained. Don't I, boy?"

He grabs Darwin and puts him in a headlock under his armpit, rubbing his hair roughly. Darwin's head is pressed up against the huge sweat stain on his dad's shirt, the leather briefcase coming precariously close to hitting him in the face.

"What is this shit?" Judge Goldsmith says, shoving him aside and wiping his hands on the lapels of Darwin's suit. "Hair gel? You can be such a *girl* at times, Darwin."

Darwin straightens up, his face flushed, his hair sticking up in untidy spikes, a greasy smear on his jacket. His hand jerks up to fix his hair but he stops, smiling weakly.

And they leave, chastity-ruth escorting them to the train that will take them back to the Euro-Zone, out of my life forever. *I will never see you again.*

I'm staring at the poster of the Father in front of me as someone enters the room and lays cool hands on my shoulders.

"I tried, freida. I couldn't do anything," chastity-magdalena says, her voice wrought with emotion. "Are you okay? Say something," she tries again, squeezing my shoulders tighter.

But there is nothing left to say.

"The Ceremony marks the day when the eves can finally be divided into their thirds for easier categorization. Whether they become a companion, a concubine or a chastity, all eves must play the role that has been assigned to them."[5]

---

[5] *Audio Guide to the Rules for Proper female Behavior*, the Original Father

Chapter 30

July
The day of the Ceremony

Dawn is slowly pouring out of the light-lamps, chasing the shadows away.

I get out of bed, tossing my hair back to scan myself in the walls as I do every morning. The bruising has turned purple, blackberries blossoming from my scalp to my temples. My eyes look old in my scrubbed face.

"Happy design date," I mouth at my reflection. I am seventeen today.

My room has been cleaned. New bed sheets, the surfaces are sparkling, any signs of my time here removed. It won't be vacant for long. A new tribe of 4th years will move in tomorrow, eves at the beginning of their journey. Some other girl will call this room her own for the next twelve years until, at last, it is her turn to await her fate in the Ceremony. I wish her better luck.

Inside my wardrobe I peel off my nightgown and throw it into the trapdoor set in the wall underneath the vanity table. The steel trap of the changing room opens, beeping loudly. I step in, the door closing like a greedy mouth around me. Sensor beams emit from the ceiling and the walls, measuring and evaluating my naked body.

"You are at target weight. Close your eyes and remain still."

After dressing in the chaste black dress that has been selected for me, I stand in my cubicle, staring at my reflection. My hair, slicked into a low bun, looks so beautiful. Why did I never appreciate how beautiful it was?

"The Ceremony is today. I repeat, the Ceremony is today," the intercom shrieks. "Please leave all your belongings in your cubicle. These are the property of the School. You will receive appropriate replacements once you join your designated third."

A rustle of clothes, of nervous laughter. Muttered curses, furious commands to hurry.

"What happened to your eye makeup?"

"I m-m-moved my head too soon. Is it awful?"

"Well . . ."

"It IS awful. I should just KILL MYSELF right now."

I slip into place between freja and daria. We walk in single file, stopping at the checkpoint set up at the main dormitory door.

"I'm not hungry." angelina puts her hands on her hips, an open-weave knitted dress clinging to her body like a crimson cobweb.

"I'm sorry, angelina," chastity-anne says, standing behind a display case. There are dozens of bottles lining the glass counter, and individual test tubes under this, each one full of brightly colored capsules. She reaches into the desk, pulls out the vial with angelina's foto on it and hands it to her with one of the bottles. angelina scowls but unscrews the top and gulps down her meds with the thick beige liquid.

"Good girl," chastity-anne says. "It's a high-protein drink. It will keep you full until after the Ceremony."

"I told you, I'm too excited to be hungry," angelina says. "Not that other people seem to be having that problem," she mumbles under her breath as cara swallows the drink down eagerly.

"I'm not hungry either . . ." cara rushes to catch up with angelina, her face reddening with guilt—"but chastity-anne said we had to. I'm too nervous to be hungry."

The others start to protest as well, claiming stomach pains and cramps, competing to see who is the most anxious. If anyone asked me, I would tell them the truth. I am unaffected by nerves. But no one will ask me.

"You next." chastity-anne points at me, handing me my meds and a glass bottle. I hold the bottle up to her in salute. It slides in chunks down my throat.

I follow the others through the cloisters and up the long nave, counting the tiles beneath my feet.

"Careful!" daria snarls when I bump into her. She smooths down the brocaded satin of her clinging cheongsam.

"Sorry."

She doesn't acknowledge my apology. We're waiting at the entrance to the Hall, chastity-bernadette flapping her hands in worry.

"Oh, for goodness' sake, girls, do you ever walk in sequence properly?" she asks, splitting the twins up and raising her voice to be heard over their complaints.

"The twins don't, but the rest of us do," agyness pipes up cheerfully, and jessie and liz narrow their eyes at her.

"Thank you, agyness," chastity-bernadette says. "Ordinarily it's not that important, but today—"

"chastity-ruth said the rules are always important," megan says, pulling at the emerald gemstone necklace tucked neatly underneath the buttoned-up collar of her sleeveless shirt dress. "Especially after recent *events*."

"Of course," chastity-bernadette splutters. "Excellent point."

"And now, freida." She's calling us out alphabetically. "Between daria and freja."

"Unfortunately," daria stage-whispers, smirking as the other eves giggle.

"Isn't isabel next?" heidi asks jessie. "Where is she?"

"How am I supposed to know?" jessie answers petulantly, tousling her hair over the left side of her face to cover up her botched eye makeup. "Can you still see it?" she bleats to liz, a few places back.

"chastity-bernadette?" heidi can't let it go. "Isn't isabel supposed to be before jessie?"

"Oh," chastity-bernadette says, her cheeks tingeing with pink. "isabel won't be here today."

"Why not?" megan says gleefully. "Is she going to be a chastity, like freida?"

"eves!" chastity-bernadette's entire face is flushing with heat now. "Enough of this. Get in sequence."

Is isabel going to be a chastity too? I catch my breath but I will not hope. I have learned my lesson about hope.

We take our seats in the Hall and I lean back to look at the soaring ceiling, the murals etched in gold paint, the colors sparkling in the crystal chandeliers. How much did it cost to build this room? It's a relic, the vestiges of a lost fortune. They could have used the money for the Engineers' research, to make the eves prettier and prettier and prettier. There's always room for Improvement.

I drop inside myself, urging the Somnolin to weave its magic spell, to blow like fairy dust into my brain.

The lamps sink, the chandelier light dappling around us as if we're moving through water. A few of the girls laugh, coiling their hands in the air to watch the lights rippling against their skin.

The national anthem curls beneath us, the triquetra blazing onto the huge screen, each triangle of the thirds sliced into the other. The chastities sweep past us, marching silently up the marble steps. They line the stage, six on each side of an opulent jewel-encrusted gold throne. Gazing at the triquetra, they fall to one knee, their heads bowed low. The music reaches a crescendo, drum rolls booming throughout the Hall as the screen draws apart like curtains.

"Is it?"

"oh my . . . it is . . . it is . . ."

"IT'S THE FATHER!"

Girls are screaming, clutching at each other wildly as they jump to their feet. I am the only one who is unmoved. It doesn't matter anyway. No one turns to grab my hand, to hug me with excitement.

The Father stands in the spotlight, one hand raised in salute. He's wearing a plush gold-colored cloak, an oversized gold medallion around His neck. He slicks back His gray hair as the screen closes behind Him again and the triquetra divides into separate triangles with a swishing sound.

"Thank you. You are too kind," He says as the Hall rings with applause. He settles into the throne, His bejeweled fingers resting on the velvet-covered armrests. His black shoes are poking out under the cloak, not quite touching the ground.

"Thank you," He says again. "You may be seated."

The chastities get to their feet and form a single line behind him. freja claims our shared armrest as her own. She, like all the others, is on the very edge of her seat, feet tapping restlessly against the floor. They are excited, I tell myself. I try to remember what excitement tasted like.

"I am delighted to be here today to welcome you into your thirds. I know how eager you are to finally make a

contribution to the society that has done so much for you."
He licks his lips, His tongue flickering briefly out of His
mouth. "I must admit, I'm looking forward to testing that
contribution very soon." miranda and karlie nudge each
other at this. "I know there have been issues this year,"
He says, peering into the spotlight. He is looking for me.
I should feel embarrassed. I can feel the fury radiating off the
other eves. *I should feel guilty.* I have ruined everything. *I
should feel worried.*

"But let's not allow one girl's selfishness to ruin the
day." This provokes another round of applause. He waits
until it settles before continuing. "We will begin with the
third of the companions, the eves who shall bear the future
sons of the Euro-Zone. In tenth place, Socrates has chosen
heidi."

Rumor has it he had to choose heidi because of my dis-
qualification. megan was wrong. A girl who had sex before
marriage *has* been chosen for the companion third.

heidi doesn't look very happy as she shuffles onstage to
accept her ivory cloak from the Father, taking her place
beneath the white triangle of the companions. She throws
longing glances at her former friends, glances that are duly
ignored.

"Inheritant #9, Abraham, has chosen cara."

cara gets to her feet a little unsteadily. I know she
expected to rank higher than that.

"Better be prepared," rosie yells from the row behind
me, her voice crystal clear. "Abraham likes to use the back
entrance!"

Confusion colors cara's face as she accepts her cloak and stands next to heidi, a determinedly composed expression on her face. There is no room for hurt feelings in the thirds.

A name and a name and another name. One girl walks up the steps to receive her cloak, then the next. I can't remember which Inheritant each eve has been paired with and I doubt the other girls do either. What does it matter? We may be interchangeable, but so are the Inheritants, in their own way.

"And now, our last Inheritant. Darwin Goldsmith," the Father announces. I look around at the thinning group of girls. It's only megan and me left from this year's original top ten.

"He has chosen . . ." The Father stops to mouth His thanks to chastity-anne, who has broken the rank of the chastities lined up behind his throne to place a bottle of EuroCola at His feet. He slowly removes the cap from the bottle, sniffs the drink and wipes the bottle neck carefully. He looks at each of us in turn. Maybe Darwin chose christy. Maybe he chose naomi. ". . . megan."

megan's hands curl into fists of victory and she takes her place onstage, wrapping the cloak around herself, her hair almost blue-black against the material. *I should feel resentment.*

"All of you have been chosen to join the noble third of the companions. Do you swear to devote your lives to fulfilling your purpose as women? To be the best companions and mothers that you can be?" the Father solemnly asks.

They swear to honor and obey their future husbands and to bear as many sons as their wombs will hold. I repeat, *That should have been me,* to myself over and over, as if I'm worrying a broken tooth with the tip of my tongue, waiting for the pain to come.

"And now, for the third of the concubines, we have rosie . . ." She jumps up, clapping in delight, "and angelina . . ." The two girls embrace each other onstage, ecstatic smiles on their faces.

More names. Increasingly lethargic applause. Stifled yawns becoming louder the further down the list He goes.

". . . and lucy . . ."

"It's liu, sorry," she murmurs, her dark eyes downcast. He hands the cloak to her without further comment. He has no need to learn the name of a lesser concubine.

". . . and finally, as concubine #17, we have christy."

The stilted clapping jolts me out of my stupor as christy joins the large group of girls standing beneath the red triangle, her jaw clenched.

"This year's Inheritants have recommended that you all join the third of the concubines. Do you swear to devote your lives to the physical gratification of the good men of the Euro-Zone?"

"We do," the girls chorus. The original Heavenly Seventy girls are crowded toward the front, the leftover eves lurking behind, tugging anxiously at their scarlet Ceremony cloaks at the thought of what is in store.

"And for the first time in years . . ." the Father gestures at the chastities, "actually, I believe it's the first time since your inauguration, magdalena. Am I correct?"

"You're *always* correct," chastity-ruth says as chastity-magdalena nods.

". . . we have an eve with the vocation to become a chastity. Can you join me onstage, agyness?"

My name has not been called, but I follow agyness anyway. We move as one. There is no individuality in the third of the chastities.

"So this is the girl that caused all the fuss," the Father says, His eyes narrowing as He hands me my raven cloak. agyness and I stand beneath the black triangle, wrapping the robes around ourselves. I bury my hands in the deep pockets, feeling the coarse material against my skin. I am one of them now. "You're lucky you have such good friends in high places, girl." He turns to chastity-ruth. "I will make the announcement now," he says, and she nods in automatic agreement.

"Your attention, eves." He hops onto His throne, sweeping His golden cloak back over His shoulders. All the eves stare up at him in rapture. "My current wife, after providing Me with two sons, has sadly become *inefficient* a little earlier than expected. She has graciously decided to bow out with honor . . ."

"Step on the pyre, he means," daria mutters to freja.

"Well, she's like thirty-four," freja replies.

". . . so I have chosen a new companion from this batch of eves."

megan's face pales. A Judge is one thing, but to be a companion to the Father himself? She looks around wildly. Who is the eve with the audacity to beat her?

"The lucky lady is isabel." He waits for the clapping to begin, a bemused look settling on his features when none is forthcoming. "Did you hear Me? isabel is to be My new companion."

isabel.

Even if Darwin had chosen me, I still would have lost.

"What?" gisele croaks, her queasy expression replicated on the face of each eve onstage as they realize the girl that they have spent the last School year tormenting is going to be the most powerful woman in the Euro-Zone.

"isabel and I have always had a very, er, special relationship." He rubs His hands together, the metal rings scraping against each other. I meet megan's eyes across the stage and I see in them the same realization that is dawning on me. All year isabel left a trail of breadcrumbs for us to follow, but we were blind to them. And it's too late now. It's too late. "I suspected from the moment of her design she would become My companion when she came into her prime, but I made My final decision known to her before your School break last year."

So that's why she has been distancing herself from me all year. She knew I wasn't good enough to socialize with the Father's future companion, and that I never would be good enough. But she still saved me in the end. I failed, once again, and she had to step in and fix my mess. *I should feel grateful to her.*

"When will my new bride be joining me?" The Father twists around to face chastity-ruth.

"She'll be ready for you the day after tomorrow, Father," she says, approaching the throne timidly. "I didn't feel it would be appropriate for her to share a train with the ordinary companions." I see megan flinch at the word "ordinary."

"Quite right," the Father says, jumping down from the throne. The cloak is too long for Him, trailing on the floor. "She must be treated with due respect. Anyway, I've waited seventeen years for her. What's another few days?"

megan's face is colorless against the ivory robe. She takes a step back, crunching gisele's toes under her heels, ignoring her cry of pain.

"anne and mary, take care of them," chastity-ruth orders as the Father walks toward the marble steps and she dashes to catch up with Him. The other chastities follow her. None of them says goodbye or wishes us good luck, not even chastity-magdalena.

"What now?" the twins ask as the Hall doors slam behind the Father and the chastities. "megs? What happens now?"

"I don't know," megan snaps. "Why do you two always expect me to know the answer to everything?"

"Now, now. Less of that, please," chastity-mary says, beaming. "I want the concubines and the companions to follow me. I will escort you to the trains where you will be transferred to the main Euro-Zone."

"In different carriages, I hope," megan mutters. She picks at her nails, the mint-green nail polish flaking off and drifting onto her cloak. Her triumph has been spectacularly short-lived.

"The concubines will go to their new lodgings," chastity-mary continues. "And the companions will be presented to their respective husbands."

"Whose Inheritant am I again?" liz whispers to jessie. "Leonardo's?"

"I think I'm his. Aren't you William's?"

"That's enough," chastity-anne interrupts. "You're not getting any younger. Please form two separate lines and follow chastity-mary."

megan goes first on the right-hand side, rosie on the left. All the others divide effortlessly into their new formation. They march down the steps, through the Hall and out the doors. They do not look back.

And then they are gone.

"Another year over," chastity-anne says to agyness and me. "Done and dusted."

How can this be the end of School? How can this be the great Ceremony that we have spent all these years preparing for? After everything, after all our worrying and waiting, all today amounted to was a tedious roll-call of names. I feel hollow with anticlimax, an emptiness mushrooming inside me.

I look at agyness, and my disillusionment is echoed on her ordinarily cheerful face. She turns to look over her shoulder at the Hall entrance as if she's hoping one of the eves will reappear and say it was all a joke.

chastity-anne sighs. "It's always the same, every year. I'm not sure what you girls were expecting."

More than this, I think. A lot more.

"You'll get used to it. I promise."

agyness and I still don't move, and her voice becomes stern. "That's enough, chastities. Follow me. It is time for your training to begin."

Day One

As a chastity, I must be silent.
As a chastity, I must be humble.
As a chastity, I must be selfless.
As a chastity, I must be modest.
As a chastity, I must be obedient.
As a chastity, I must be pure.
As a chastity, I must be dutiful.
As a chastity, I must be constant.
As a chastity, I must be devoted.
As a chastity, I must be ordinary.
As a chastity, I must be faultless.
As a chastity, I must integrate.
As a chastity, I must sacrifice.
As a chastity, I must surrender.

Day Two

Dawn recitation for all chastities

I give myself up for the good of the Euro-Zone. I give myself up for the good of the Father. I give myself up for the good of my fellow chastities. I give myself up for the good of the School.

What little I am, I give myself up. What little I am, I give myself up. What little I am, I give myself up.

Midmorning recitation for all chastities

I give myself up for the good of the Euro-Zone. I give myself up for the good of the Father. I give myself up for the good of my fellow chastities. I give myself up for the good of the School.

What little I am, I give myself up. What little I am, I give myself up. What little I am, I give myself up.

Prelunchtime recitation for all chastities

I give myself up for the good of the Euro-Zone. I give myself up for the good of the Father. I give myself up for the good of my fellow chastities. I give myself up for the good of the School.

What little I am, I give myself up. What little I am, I give myself up. What little I am, I give myself up.

Afternoon recitation for all chastities

I give myself up for the good of the Euro-Zone. I give myself up for the good of the Father. I give myself up for the good of my fellow chastities. I give myself up for the good of the School.

What little I am, I give myself up. What little I am, I give myself up. What little I am, I give myself up.

Predinner recitation for all chastities

I give myself up for the good of the Euro-Zone. I give myself up for the good of the Father. I give myself up for the good of my fellow chastities. I give myself up for the good of the School.

What little I am, I give myself up. What little I am, I give myself up. What little I am, I give myself up.

Bedtime recitation for all chastities

I give myself up for the good of the Euro-Zone. I give myself up for the good of the Father. I give myself up for the good of my fellow chastities. I give myself up for the good of the School.

What little I am, I give myself up. What little I am, I give myself up. What little I am, I give myself up.

Day Three

I do nothing but by the good grace of the Father.
I say nothing but by the good grace of the Father.
I have nothing but by the good grace of the Father.
I am nothing but by the good grace of the Father.

Thank you, Father, for your good grace.
I promise to use my life as a chastity attempting to be
    worthy of it.

Day Four

I can't sleep. I am finding it difficult to adjust to the eerie quiet of the chastities' quarters, any sleepy sighs muffled behind the closed doors of our individual rooms. Here there are neither the nighttime Messages to distract me nor any SleepSound to push me into dreaming. chastities are not allowed to waste the School's medication supplies, chastity-ruth told me.

ruth. I keep forgetting that I must call her ruth now.

Day one, day two, day three, day four.

How many days are there in a lifetime?

I've been assigned a room, a concrete square with a large oak door on one side. There is a single mattress dressed in black bed sheets, a wooden chest of drawers, painted black, and a matching rocking chair at the foot of the bed. A strip of wood is nailed into the wall opposite, seven identical black cloaks hanging from seven brass hooks, seven pairs of rubber-soled shoes lined up neatly beneath. There is a sink in the corner of the room, a narrow concrete ledge above it holding a plastic jug and a rotting rag with which to wash myself. The only light comes from a thick white candle enclosed in a glass lantern hanging from the ceiling. There are no mirrors here and I am glad of that. I do not want to see how depreciated I have become in a mere matter of days.

I am lying on my stomach on the bed, my ePad propped up on the pillow as I scan through hundreds of fotos of the new megan Goldsmith. The restrictions on School to Zone internet access have been lifted now that I am a chastity, and although I know I shouldn't look, I can't help myself. I have been staring at one foto for at least an hour. It is from their wedding. In it, he is slipping his ring onto her finger. I search his face for a hint of regret, of wistfulness. I find none.

There are other fotos too, of cara and the twins and daria and the rest of them, their faces radiant as they are given away to their husbands by the Father. Do any of them ever think of me? It seems impossible that they could forget me in such a short time.

There is no mention of isabel on MyFace. I wanted to see fotos of her wedding dress. She was probably adorned in silk, pearl beading, real vintage lace, no expense spared; no plain ivory cloak for the bride of the Father. But her home page has been shut down. I suppose it would be unseemly for someone in her position to be so easily contactable. I should shut my page down too. I doubt isabel would want to get in touch with someone like me, not now anyway. And who else would be interested in the details of the chastity training program? Today they shaved my head. Today they ripped my useless womb out and I am empty, so empty.

As a chastity, I must sacrifice.

"felicity."

I am chastity-felicity now. They have even taken my name from me.

"Why is your door open, felicity?" chastity-ruth says, pulling her black bathrobe firmly around her waist.

I turn my ePad over so she can't see what I've been looking at and sit up straight, using the pillow to protect my back against the cold concrete wall.

"I said, why is your door open?"

"Sorry, ruth." My voice is hoarse from lack of use. "I always sleep with the door open."

I feel trapped otherwise.

"Yes. Lots of changes," she says, and sits on the wooden rocking chair at the end of my bed. She runs her hands along the armrests, clucking as she rubs dust between her fingertips.

"How is agyness?" I ask. Because my role is as a non-teaching chastity, her training takes place separately to mine.

"agyness?" She frowns at me. "I assume you are referring to chastity-agatha. You saw her at dinner, did you not?"

agyness always sits at the other end of the table to me, her head turned away from me. Not that it matters. We chastities are forbidden to speak during mealtimes.

"It tends to take new chastities some time to become accustomed to our way of life. Not me though. I took to it like the proverbial duck to water." Something in my face must have registered my surprise and she smiles slowly at me. "You're not the only one who watches the Nature Channel."

She leans back in the chair, never taking her eyes off me, and begins to rock back and forth, the sound of creaking wood filling the dead room.

"I knew you would be awake, #630."

"SleepSound withdrawal."

"I knew you would be awake," she says again, as if I haven't spoken. "And do you know why?" She peers at me across the dimly lit room. "Do you?"

"No, ruth."

"Because I know *you*. I always have." I wait, unsure of how I am supposed to react. "I know your exact eye color and the texture of your hair. I know what weight you are. Obviously, I know about your difficulty sleeping. I know you pretend to dislike chocco but secretly it's your favorite food. I know how much you resented isabel at times and how hard you tried to hide it. I know you hate #767. And I know how prone to flights of fancy you are. I've been trying to crush it out of you for years, haven't I?" I nod, as she seems to expect me to. "But even I was astonished at your conviction that Darwin Goldsmith could somehow save you from your fate. Foolish little girl. Did you believe he was going to choose *you*? Did you? It has been amusing watching you scurry about the place, all fret and bother, scrambling to improve your ratings, desperately trying to cling onto Darwin. Honestly, #630, I'm sure he thought you were good for a bit of fun, but it's unlikely he ever considered you companion material, my dear. Not you. He'll probably find some . . ." she pauses, looking me up and down, "*exotic* companion to quench any physical urges. Maybe, from time to time, he'll even close his eyes and pretend it's some girl he used to know, some girl whose name he can't quite remember." I force my face to remain very still. "No, Judge Goldsmith made the right decision with #767. She will follow the rules. Don't you agree?"

"Yes, chastity-ruth," I say on reflex, and her lip curls.

"You see, I knew you would agree. You really are utterly predictable. Always so eager to please other people, so willing to do whatever it takes to make people like you. It's just so, so . . ." she stares at me as she searches for the word that best describes me—"*repellent*. That's what you are. #767 never acted like that, did she? She didn't snivel and beg for scraps of approval like you did. And look at her now—the companion of a Judge." The chair keeps rocking back and forth, back and forth. I don't understand. I thought we eves were supposed to be willing to please.

"I've been doing this a long time, you know," she continues, gripping the armrests tightly. "I was made the principal chastity almost twenty years ago, the youngest principal in the history of the School. Twenty years, and every year a new batch of eves, countless girls, as you can imagine." She half smiles. "Yet I still remember the day when you and your sisters were hatched. And that's because of you, #630."

"Me?" I repeat, my voice barely a whisper. I grab the black blanket on my bed and hug it close for warmth.

"Yes," she says. "I walked from cot to cot, looking at each new-design in turn. And there you were, your face screwed up, making so much noise and commotion, drawing all that attention to yourself." She shudders at the memory. "If my instincts were right, and they were *always* right, you were the runt of the litter, the one who wouldn't withstand the race. There's always one, every year, an eve that has a little 'accident,' then another, then too many accidents to ignore and the eve has to be taken Underground, to help the Engineers with their studies. Waste not, want not." I swallow hard. "But not you, #630. Because isabel—wonderful, darling, *special* isabel—took a shine to you, didn't she? And that changed everything. She loved you."

"Really?" My voice is small, like a child's.

"Why of course she did." chastity-ruth says the words plainly and, hearing them, I know deep within my bones that she's telling the truth.

"And with her love came her protection. It was all so *inappropriate*. I could hardly bear to look at you, as with each passing year you continued to undermine the natural order of things with your very existence. And then you broke the rules so flagrantly with Darwin. It really was deliciously stupid of you, #630." Her lips tighten. "But, once again, isabel fought for you. It was she who pleaded with the Father to grant you immunity, and He agreed, provided isabel promised to maintain her target weight.

Judge Goldsmith was most displeased, but what could he do? The Father had spoken. My goodness, He did spoil isabel. There was always a present for his 'special girl' on her design date, lockets and jewelry boxes and other such nonsense." She rolls her eyes to heaven. "He even gave her a pair of snakeskin boots in exchange for her maidenhood last year. As if He wasn't taking something that didn't belong to Him already."

My stomach goes into free fall. "What are you talking about?"

"You didn't know? And I thought you two were such good friends. The Father and isabel celebrated her design date together every year, of course, but on her sixteenth He took her for a 'test drive,' as it were." She chuckles at her own wit.

"How . . . how . . . how do you know that?"

"Unfortunately, I had to clean her up afterward. He did make a bit of a mess."

isabel never told me. She never told anyone.

"It has been a strange year, I must say," she muses, folding her hands across her stomach. "If the Father hadn't chosen isabel, she would have been the perfect companion for Darwin; he would never even have noticed you if isabel had been in her full health. It would have been more natural than some second-tier eve leapfrogging over more suitable girls. For a few weeks there I was almost concerned. Darwin kept choosing you; he seemed as blind to your many failings as isabel had been. But I told myself to trust my instincts and to wait. If I just waited, you would ruin it all by yourself." She starts to slow-clap. "And you did, #630. Spectacularly so. Well, *well* done."

"Why are you telling me all this?" I say, feeling as if the question is being torn from my throat.

"Why?" She raises an eyebrow at me. "Hmm. Yes, I must admit you're correct. I am talking more freely than I ordinarily would, even with a fellow chastity. It's all irrelevant now though, isn't it? You won't be able to tell tales where you're going."

"Oh, did I not say?" She smiles at my confused expression. "I do apologize, #630. It has been hectic this evening, fone calls back and forth with the Euro-Zone, frantically trying to arrange a replacement. Quite selfish of isabel to leave the Father *hanging*, if you'll excuse the pun." She shrugs. "But she always was impetuous, that one. She clearly didn't consider the possibility that your immunity could be revoked after her death."

Her words seem to float between us, and somehow it's as if all the air in the room has been completely sucked away, and I can't breathe. My ribs feel as if they are withering in my chest, squeezing my lungs together, breaking my breath down into shallow gasps.

"Oh, silly me. I didn't mean to just blurt it out like that. But yes, isabel has decided to decline the honor of being the Father's companion, rather permanently. Do you want to know how she did it? Do you, #630?" She waits expectantly for my answer, but the inside of my mouth is dry, painted in drought. "Fine," she says. "I'll give you a few hints. A bathrobe belt. A sturdy hook. An open door. You get the picture. It puts me in mind of that ridiculous rhyme magdalena insists on teaching the eves to help you tie your shoelaces. What is it again? Come on, #630. I know you remember."

"Here's a little rabbit, and here's a great big tree," I say quietly, the words coming to me effortlessly. "Watch the little rabbit run around the tree. Out pops his head, to see what he can see. Look how neat a knot he made around his . . ."

I can't finish.

"I wish these eves would choose a more aesthetically pleasing manner to bid us farewell. I keep asking the Father if we can change the door frames, but there never seems to be enough money to fund it," chastity-ruth says. I turn my face away from her. "Oh dear. You're not going to cry, are you, #630?"

Her gray eyes are flickering with excitement as she leans forward in her seat, coming closer and closer to me, as if she wants to lick the very first teardrop, taste its saltiness on her lips. I close my eyes.

isabel. isabel. isabel.

I choose a memory of isabel and me as children and I hold it close to my heart, like a naked flame, waiting to feel it burn, but I feel nothing, numbness spreading through me like frostbite.

There are no tears in me. There is nothing left.

"Good girl," she says, when I remain dry-eyed. "At least you learned how to do *one* thing right."

She pushes herself out of the chair and glides past me until she reaches the doorway, beckoning for me to follow.

As a chastity, I must surrender.

Time stretches out before me, the possibility of infinite hours with this grief gouging itself into my heart. How many hours are there in a lifetime?

"Come, #630. We haven't got all day," she says, and I nod mutely.

As a chastity, I must be obedient.

I follow her out of the chastity quarters, past the garden gate and through the cloisters. She stays very close to me, but she need not be concerned. I will not try to run. Where could I go? Darwin does not want me. megan would build my pyre with her own hands. And isabel . . . my isabel, my isabel, my isabel, my isabel.

We have reached our old classroom. I avoid looking at the mirror-board.

"It's time, #630," chastity-ruth tells me, pointing at the glass coffin on the right-hand side of the chastity's desk. She takes her eFone from the pocket of her bathrobe and presses a button, the box lighting up immediately.

"Time for what?" I ask, but I step in anyway. I don't really care what will happen to me now. The doors close and we stare at one another through the panes of glass.

"Time for you to finally be of use," she says as the elevator descends into the bowels of the earth, maintaining eye contact until she disappears behind a wall of steel.

The elevator keeps going down, further into the ground than I have ever been outside of my most feverish nightmares. The doors open into a room I've never seen before, a waiting room of sorts. Wrought-iron chairs, gray concrete floors, steel-plated walls. A loud buzzer sounds and a red light above the heavy steel door before me flashes.

The buzzer sounds again. I move toward it, almost involuntarily. The door handle is icy to the touch. I walk into a corridor. It's dark, muted-yellow bulbs melting into the walls. The path drops, the darkness deepening, swarming in to blind me, and I have to hold onto the frosted wall for guidance until I see a crack of light before me. It's seeping out from underneath a door and I fumble toward it, patting the wall until I find the handle.

Inside, I blink in the dazzling white room, the edges cut with steel. When my eyes adjust to the glare, I can see that it's a vast laboratory, about the same size as the Hall. One wall is made up of steel shelves lined with clear glass jars. In each of them what looks like a tiny chick-chick carcass is floating in fluid, wrinkled and red-raw. Lining the other wall is a row of clear boxes, each containing a naked sleeping woman. They're bald too, held in a standing position by white belts secured around their feet, waist and head. The left arm of each one is strapped into a machine, red wires wrapped around their bodies like bulging veins.

"I've been expecting you." A man approaches me. He's wearing the white cloak of the Engineers, a white mask covering his face. Thick furry eyebrows are knitted together over pale brown eyes. "#630, isn't it?"

I can't move.

"Now, stop wasting time, girl. This is important." I stare at him blankly. "You want to help me with my research, don't you? Don't you want to be of some use?" He walks toward me, snapping white gloves on. Snap. Snap.

I look at the naked bodies marinating in the clear containers. Some of them look so familiar, evoking memories of high jinks and raucous misbehavior, dropped trays in the Nutrition Center, raised voices screaming at the chastities.

"You know what we do with girls who break the rules, don't you? We send them Underground. Do you want to go Underground, #630? Do you?"

I should be afraid, but all I can feel is the loss of her.

"I heard about your friend." He inches closer to me. I do not want to think about her. I am tired now. I am so very tired. "This won't hurt, I promise. You won't feel a thing."

"Nothing?"

"That's right," he says. "You could say that it will feel like nothing."

Is this how isabel felt before she jumped? Did she feel ready, so very ready, for it all to be over?

I hold out my arm, offering myself to him. The needle sinks into my skin, the liquid whispering, *forget, forget*, to my blood. I can feel it burning through me, licking at my veins with thousands of tongues.

I am ready now too.

I am ready to feel nothing, forever.

Acknowledgments

None of this would have been possible without my parents, my two favorite people in this world. I love you both more than words can say.

I want to thank my sister, Michelle, for being as excited about my novel as I was, if not more. I hope you know how much your support has meant to me.

I've been blessed with incredible family and friends, far too many to list here. I must, however, mention Katie Grant, who read the first three chapters and encouraged me to keep writing, and who gave me a place to stay in London whenever I needed it. I'm equally indebted to Jonathan Self for his generosity, kindness, and advice.

I'm so grateful to the team at Quercus for all of their hard work. I was lucky enough to have a great editor, Niamh Mulvey, and *Only Ever Yours* is immeasurably better as a result of her insightful notes.

Thanks also to George, Milly, Philippa, and all at the Capel & Land agency, but especially to the lovely Rachel Conway. Thank you, Rach, for understanding what I was trying to achieve with this book from the very beginning.

About the Type

Text set in Perpetua Regular at 12/14.25pt.

Perpetua is a book typeface designed by Eric Gill, released by Monotype in 1929, and modeled in the style of transitional serif fonts of the late eighteenth and early nineteenth century.

Typeset by Scribe Inc., Philadelphia, Pennsylvania